Alfred F Robbins

The Early Public Life of William Ewart Gladstone

Four Times Prime Minister

Alfred F Robbins

The Early Public Life of William Ewart Gladstone
Four Times Prime Minister

ISBN/EAN: 9783337415648

Printed in Europe, USA, Canada, Australia, Japan

Cover: Foto ©Raphael Reischuk / pixelio.de

More available books at **www.hansebooks.com**

THE

EARLY PUBLIC LIFE

OF

WILLIAM EWART GLADSTONE

FOUR TIMES PRIME MINISTER

BY

ALFRED F. ROBBINS

WITH THREE PORTRAITS

DODD, MEAD & COMPANY

NEW YORK

1894

In youth a student and in eld a sage—
   Lover of freedom, of mankind the friend,
   Noble in aim from childhood to the end—
Great is thy mark upon historic page.

TO

MY WIFE

WHOSE CONSTANT AID

AND CORDIAL ENCOURAGEMENT

HAVE LIGHTENED MY TASK

THIS WORK

IS DEDICATED.

PREFACE

'I CONCEIVE that the facts of my Parliamentary
history during the nineteenth century are such as
will obtain conspicuous notice on the page of history.'
Thus, with the addition of some characteristic qualifications, wrote Mr. Gladstone in the summer of 1894,
in accepting the address of farewell presented by
the National Liberal Federation; and the truth of
the remark is so obvious that no blame will attach
to any who attempt to make those facts at once
available and clear. Not for many a year will it be
possible for the full story of Mr. Gladstone's public
life to be told. By that time, the last of the generations which have been swayed by his leadership,
and influenced by his presence, will have passed
away; and, although no such other commanding
personality may have arisen to obscure his memory,
the detailed relation will come too late to be
appreciated by the majority of those to whom he
has acted as an inspiration, and by whom he has
been accepted as a guide.

It has not been attempted in the following pages
to deal, even from an external point of view, with
the whole sixty years' span of Mr. Gladstone's public
career. Apart from the impossibility of intelligibly
bringing within brief compass a story which covers
the period from the Premiership of Lord Grey to
that of Lord Rosebery, from the Conservative leadership of the Duke of Wellington to that of the
Marquis of Salisbury, from the Ireland of the prime
of O'Connell to that of the fall of Parnell, the time
has not arrived for contemporaries to thoroughly
analyse and apportion Mr. Gladstone's later work.
In the present endeavour, it has been sought simply
to set forth the influences which shaped his earlier
years, and the manner in which his career opened
and evolved. The period during which, with but a
brief interruption, he stood outside the official circle,
and acted with marked independence upon both
political and ecclesiastical affairs, is presented with
an amount of detail which has not before been
attempted ; and it has thus been dealt with because
of the conviction that the later developments of so
long and striking a career cannot be appreciated,
cannot even be understood, without a close study of
those opening years.

Wherever it has proved possible, it has been
sought to show, step by step in the progress of Mr.
Gladstone, the impression he created upon his contemporaries, and to give that impression in the

words of the contemporaries themselves. Those who examine his career with the eyes of 1894, possessed of the knowledge which the progress of the years has accumulated, cannot see with the vision of 1834, when he, whom the whole world knows to-day as the veteran hero of a hundred fights, and as the only man in our history who has been four times Prime Minister, was merely a promising and aspiring student, who had been but a short time in Parliament, and of whose future high anticipations were entertained by his friends. The political and theological atmosphere of the closing years of the century is so markedly different from that of its fourth decade that it has seemed to be not only of interest but to be just that, as far as possible, the early words and actions of Mr. Gladstone should be shown as they affected those to whom they were addressed, or for whom they were performed.

The task was undertaken with sympathy, and all that is claimed is that it has been attempted to be executed with fairness. Every fact which could be obtained by an independent investigator, and for which authority could be found, has been set forth. While nothing has been set down in malice, naught has been extenuated ; and the conviction has been deepened, after minute inspection of Mr. Gladstone's career during a decade which has had scarcely a parallel in recent history for the malevolence of party feeling and the consequent malignity of partisan accusation, that

> Whatever record leap to light
> He never shall be shamed.

Happily, Mr. Gladstone has reached that point in his life when even those who were his political antagonists can own to being his personal admirers. The staunchest Conservative can echo concerning the parliamentary appearance of the greatest of Liberal leaders what the Puritan poet could say of the beheaded king in his supreme hour,

> He nothing common did, or mean.

And the writer has felt it as the keenest of incentives that he was endeavouring to make clearer and more widely known the opening incidents in so striking a career.

September, 1894.

CONTENTS

xi

IV.—AT OXFORD.

V.—THE CONTEST AT NEWARK.

VI.—THE YOUNG PARLIAMENTARY HAND.

VII.—HIS RELATION TO SLAVERY.

VIII.—HIS ECCLESIASTICAL DEVELOPMENT.

Wm. Bradley, Pinxt.

THE RIGHT HON. W. E. GLADSTONE, M.P.
1845

THE
EARLY PUBLIC LIFE

OF

WILLIAM EWART GLADSTONE.

———◆———

I.—HIS FATHER AS MERCHANT.

THE year 1809 deserves a more memorable place in the history of this country than, as far as can yet be judged, any other the nineteenth century has seen, for within its compass were born the leading scientist, the chief poet, and the greatest statesman of the Victorian era. The final verdict upon the work of such men as Darwin, Tennyson, and William Ewart Gladstone is not to be passed by contemporaries. These can admire; they cannot appraise. But to aid an approach to true appreciation is a task worthy the undertaking though difficult to execute; and, in the case of Mr. Gladstone, that task, as far as the earlier portion of his public career is concerned, will be attempted here. It is only by a full knowledge of that period, and a close study of the formative influences which then affected him, that the developments of his later life can be

1809, Darwin, Tennyson, and W. E. Gladstone born.

A

understood; and it would not be possible to comprehend his intellectual growth and political expansion without a more elaborate investigation of his youthful environment than has yet been essayed.

'I am not slow to claim the name of Scotchman,' said Mr. Gladstone in one of his latest speeches north of the Tweed; 'and, even if I were, there is the fact staring me in the face that not a drop of blood runs in my veins except what is derived from a Scottish ancestry.'[1]   Almost simultaneously he wrote, 'I am a man of *Scotch* blood only, half Highland and half Lowland, near the Border;'[2] and the claim is completely justified by genealogy. On his father's side, the Glaidstanes, Gledestans, Gledstanes, Gladstaines, Gladstanes, Gladstones, or Gladstone family is to be traced in southern Scotland, under its varying names, for at least six centuries; and the earliest of its members would be indicated to have been of Scandinavian connection, if not of Scandinavian extraction.[3]   Its

Mr. Gladstone's Scotch descent.

The earliest Gladstones.

[1] Speech at Dundee, Oct. 29, 1890.

[2] Feb., 1890 : Letter of Mr. Gladstone to M. Paul du Chaillu, given in ' Ivar, the Viking.'

[3] As regards the Scandinavian connection, Mr. Gladstone himself, in his letter to M. du Chaillu, observed that one branch of his family had established itself in Scandinavia in the first half, as he supposed, of the seventeenth century ; and Mr. André Lütken, writing from Copenhagen to the *Daily News* of March 8, 1894, corroborated this with the statement that one Herbert Gladstone, who is supposed to have gone to Sweden with the Scottish soldiers engaged by Gustavus Adolphus, was naturalised, on March 15, 1647, as a Swedish nobleman, under the name of Herbert Gladsten, the last Swedish Gladsten dying in 1729.   Lovers of the curious in coincidence will note Herbert de Gledestan of 1296, Herbert Gladsten of 1647, and Herbert John Gladstone, First Commissioner of Works and Buildings in 1894, as a striking sequence in the history of the family.

recorded history commences with 1296, when one Herbert de Gledestan 'del counte de Lanark' signed, with other leading Scotsmen, the 'Ragman's Roll,' acknowledging the sovereignty of Edward I. of England ; while David II. of Scotland, some seventy years later, granted by charter certain lands to William Gledestanes, heir of a dead knight of similar name; and this William's son, John Gledstanes, was allowed by the Scottish Robert III. to receive, by her own will, his mother's lands during her life.[1] As the centuries pass, one representative of the family is found assisting, in time of feud, Walter Scott of Buccleuch, ancestor of the Dukes of the latter name, while another fought and fell on the Covenanting side during the troubled days of Charles I. But from lairds the branch of the family from which the statesman sprang became traders. Speaking in his own birth city, when Premier for the first time, Mr. Gladstone observed, 'I know not why commerce in England should not have its old families rejoicing to be connected with commerce from generation to generation. It has been so in other countries : I trust it will be so in this country. I think it a subject of sorrow, and almost of scandal, when those families who have either acquired or recovered station and wealth through commerce turn their backs upon it, and seem to be ashamed of it.'

From a trading family in its later generations, therefore, William Ewart Gladstone came. Towards the close of the reign of Charles II., John Gladstones, the last of the lairds, sold his estate of Arthurshiel in Clydesdale ; and his son William commenced trade as a maltster in Biggar,

---

[1] Mrs. Florence M. Gladstone, in an article upon 'The Gledstanes of Gledstanes and Coklaw, 1295-1741,' in the *Genealogist* for January, 1893 (N.S., vol. ix., part 3, pp. 153-7), gives some interesting particulars of the earlier known members of the Gladstone family.

a picturesque Lanarkshire village, lying on the banks of a tributary of the Tweed, and at that time mainly inhabited by weavers. This was close to the very cradle of the family, for Gledstanes, the site of the ancient property, which had passed out of its keeping over a century before, is only a few miles to the north. Of William's sons, the third, John, who carried on the business, made himself locally a man of mark, for he was not only an elder of the kirk and a burgess of the town, but 'the keeper of the baron's girnal'; and, dying just as the rule of George II. was coming to an end, he was the first of the family to be interred, a portioner of Biggar, in a burial-ground there, which has since received many of his descendants. Of these, it is Thomas Gladstones, his fourth son, with whom we have most concern. He was just twenty-five at his father's death, but before that event he had crossed Scotland and settled at Leith, where, as corn and flour merchant and ultimately as shipowner, he so succeeded in all his undertakings as to revive the family fortunes; and he passed away in 1809, only seven months before the birth of that one of his grandsons who was destined to make the name immortal.

W. E. Gladstone's Grandfather.

The eldest son of Thomas Gladstones, of Leith, was John Gladstone, for, although it was not until 1835 that the final letter was formally abandoned, the present spelling had been adopted by the latter at an early stage of his business life. Born on December 11th, 1764, John Gladstone was one of sixteen children, of whom the seven sons were so long-lived that, when William Ewart Gladstone was first returned to Parliament in 1832, his father and five of his six paternal uncles still survived, the sixth having died little over two months previously; while his uncle David, Thomas Gladstones' youngest son, expired at the age of eighty in 1863,

John Gladstone.

over 131 years after his father's birth, and when the nephew was within measurable distance of becoming Prime Minister. And, as an indication of the source from which Mr. Gladstone's own remarkable vitality was derived, it may be noted that his grandfather lived to be seventy-seven and his father eighty-seven, and that the average age of his paternal uncles was over sixty-six; while of his brothers, Thomas, the eldest, was eighty-four at the time of his death, Robertson, the second, was seventy, and John Neilson, the third, may be considered in such a family to have died young at fifty-six.

Although John Gladstone (whose mother was Helen, daughter of Walter Neilson, of Springfield,) was no more minded to settle at Leith than his father had been to remain at Biggar, his education and his first instruction in business were acquired in the former town. As to the education, the frequent taunts levelled at him in later days by personal and political opponents would indicate that it was not of a thorough character. Thomas Gladstones had too many children for any to be long at school; and, at an early age, John was introduced into the business, in the management of which he took an active part. He made voyages to the Baltic in connection with the corn trade, and to America with very large commissions on behalf of Claude Scott, a London banker who in later years was created a baronet; and in these he showed that great capacity for commerce which afterwards raised him to fortune. In 1786, when about twenty-two, he went from Leith to Liverpool as partner in the firm of Corrie, Bradshaw, & Co., a large house dealing, as his father did, in corn; and the story has in various ways been told of how, within two years of his entering into partnership, John Gladstone,   His business by a courageous operation in corn in the   abilities. United States, saved his firm from threatened ruin, and

established for himself a commercial reputation which was
destined never to fade.

The firm of Corrie, Gladstone, & Bradshaw, thus
strengthened, was successful throughout ; it received the
appointment of Government agents at Liverpool when the
Pitt Administration in the earlier days of the long French
War determined to hold stores of grain at the greater ports ;
and, after an existence of some fourteen years, upon the
partnership terminating by effluxion of time, Corrie retired
wealthy, Bradshaw returned to his native Wigan, and John
Gladstone was joined in a new firm by his brother Robert.
The other brothers later walked the same returnless road
from Leith to Liverpool ; and it is related how, when John
Gladstone took Henry Brougham, then a rising barrister,
as his guest to a local theatre, early in the nineteenth
century, and Macduff asked 'Stands Scotland where it
did ?' the unexpected answer came from the gallery, 'Na,
na, sirs ; there's pairt o' Scotland in England noo—there's
John Gladstone and his clan."

Having successfully established himself in business, John
Gladstone, at the age of twenty-eight, took unto himself a wife

His marriages.   from the town in which he had cast his lot.
This lady—Jane, daughter of Joseph Hall—
died, without issue, in 1798 ; and on April 29th, 1800, he
was again married, and now to Ann, daughter of Andrew

Ann Gladstone's   Robertson, of Dingwall.   Highland with
ancestry.   Lowland blood was thus joined ; and, noteworthy as had been the Gladstone ancestry, the family of
Robertson claimed a higher distinction.   The Clan Donnachaidh, its Gaelic name, sprang from Duncan, King of
Scotland, eldest son of the third Malcolm ; and the branch
to which Ann Robertson belonged had for its immediate
ancestor Conan, second son of the last of the Celtic Earls

of Atholl. She was of kindred with the Munros of Foulis, the Mackenzies of Coul, and the Mackenzies of Seaforth, High Chiefs of Kintail, all Highland families of fame ; and she was thus descended not only from the older line of Scottish monarchs, and from such Celtic princes as the Lords of Kintail and Eilean Donan, but from Henry III. of England, and King Robert the Bruce and James I. of Scotland. In the seventeenth century, Colin Robertson, of Kindeace, had married the eldest daughter of Sir Robert Munro of Foulis, the third baronet of his line ; and George Robertson, the second son of this union, became Sheriff-Depute and Commissary of Ross. Andrew Robertson, a son of this last, followed, as his father had done, the legal profession. He was a solicitor, was three times Provost of Dingwall—being provost, indeed, from 1776 to 1796, and taking a leading part in all the improvements of the time— and served as Sheriff-Substitute of Ross; and on April 12th, 1760, he took as his wife Annie Mackenzie, with whom he was already connected by a slight family tie. Sir John Munro of Foulis, fourth baronet, brother of Colin Robertson's wife, and who won the striking name of the 'Presby-terian Mortar Piece,' had married a daughter of Sir Kenneth Mackenzie of Coul; and that lady's brother became grandfather of Mary Mackenzie, wife of Colin Mackenzie who kept a hostelry at Dingwall, of which place he became provost, as did his son-in-law, Andrew Robertson, after him.[1]

Ann, second daughter of Andrew and Annie Robertson, was born on August 4th, 1772 ; and she W. E. Gladstone's was, therefore, nearly eight years younger mother,

[1] The *North Star* (Dingwall) of November 30, 1893, contained a full genealogical account of the maternal descent of Mr. Gladstone, who is an honorary member of the Clan Donnachaidh Society, established in 1892.

than John Gladstone, to whom, as has been said, she was wedded in 1800. Of her, various memories remain to testify to her benevolence and accomplishments. She was the dearest friend of Sir Roderick Murchison's mother; and concerning her that great scientist noted in one of his journals that his father, when he married, proposed that the bride's nearest companion, who had acted as her bridesmaid, should stay with them ; and, finding she was very delicate, he attended to all her ailments for a year or more with beneficial results, for which she was always grateful. 'The first young lady's lap on which I was dandled,' wrote Murchison, 'was that of the mother of the present [Lord Palmerston's] Chancellor of the Exchequer.'[1] And when Murchison was laid to rest at Brompton in 1871, the most conspicuous among those who walked bareheaded behind the bier was Mr. Gladstone, then First Minister of the Crown.[2]

John Gladstone's second union was fruitful, but in the midst of family cares his wife was modestly conspicuous in

John Gladstone's children.

more than one good cause in Liverpool, the place of her adoption, while she founded a charitable institution at her native Dingwall, which town she used often to visit with her offspring, and her affection for which she always retained. Five of the six children with whom John and Ann Gladstone were blessed lived to long age, and were known in various ways to the outside world. The eldest son, Thomas, born on July 25th, 1804, and the third, John Neilson, born on January 18th, 1807, were in after years returned to the House of Commons ; the second son, Robertson, born on November 15th, 1805, became President of the

[1] Geikie's 'Life of Sir Roderick Murchison,' vol. i., pp. 10, 11n.
[2] *Ibid.*, vol. ii., p. 344.

Financial Reform Association; while a daughter, Helen Jane, was converted to the Roman Catholic faith early in the days of the great movement towards Rome which marked 'the Forties,' and she ultimately died in a convent.[1] The fourth son and youngest child was born at 62 Rodney Street, Liverpool, on December 29th, 1809; W. E. Gladstone and on the ensuing February 7th, as the born. register shows, there was christened at the parish church of St. Peter, in Liverpool, and, therefore, when the infant was some six weeks old, 'William Ewart son of John Gladstone merchant Rodney Street and Ann (Robertson) his wife.' The child was so named after one of his father's personal and political friends, the son of a Scotch Presbyterian minister, who had come to Liverpool in early life and, like John Gladstone himself, had there succeeded; and who was father of the William Ewart, afterwards Liberal member for his native place, to whose exertions, as having passed the Public Libraries Act, William Ewart Gladstone later paid eloquent testimony.

While the family of John Gladstone was thus increasing, he was steadily strengthening both his commercial and his public position.   It was as a Presbyterian John Gladstone's and a Whig that, in a popular capacity, religion Liverpool first knew him.   As Presbyterian he was numbered in 1793 among those Scottish residents who, having previously worshipped in the Nonconformist chapels of the town, subscribed to build a kirk of their own; while as Whig, for a full sixteen years after the commencement, in 1792, of the long struggle with and politics. France, he condemned the policy of the war.   But he was

[1] Thomas (Sir) died March 20, 1889; Robertson, Sept. 23, 1875; John Neilson, Feb. 7, 1863; and Helen Jane at Cologne, Jan. 16, 1880.

so little a partisan at that period that, although he professed
Whig sympathies, his name is not to be found among those
who voted at the general election of November, 1806, when
William Roscoe, the Whig candidate—remembered now as
the author of biographies of Lorenzo de' Medici and Leo X.
—headed the poll, General Tarleton, one of the retiring
members, being at the bottom.

When, however, the Short Parliament of 1806 was suddenly dissolved the next April by George III., John Gladstone took distinct action in support of Roscoe, though,
to the observation of all men, that candidate was fighting
1807.
Supports the Whig
candidate. a losing battle. His popularity, indeed,
had been virtually destroyed in the borough,
every stone of which, according to the old taunt, was
cemented with the blood of a slave, by the support he
gave to the 'Ministry of all the Talents' upon its measure
for the abolition of the slave trade—to be discriminated, of
course, from the abolition of slavery itself, not to be
effected for another quarter of a century—and upon that
and a 'No Popery' cry he was decisively beaten. In the
versified 'squibs' which accompanied the contest, 'Lang
Johnny' and his 'Scotch fiddle' were in evidence, while in
the list of a mock auction, 'Lot 4' was 'Sawney, out of
Highland Fling, out of Snap, by Whiskey,' the humourist
being careful to label this, 'J. G—ds—e.' John Gladstone,
therefore, though, as he afterwards declared, never a keen
Whig, obviously acted with the party; and in 1808,
he and his younger brother Robert, with whom he
was now, for one portion of his business, in partnership,
were among the firms of merchants trading with America
1808.
Opposes the Orders
in Council. which signed a requisition calling a public
meeting to petition Parliament against the
Orders in Council issued by the British
Government as a retaliation upon Buonaparte's Berlin Decree,

and the irritation created by which was one of the causes of a subsequent war between England and the United States.

Anything which interfered with trading in the Atlantic was a direct injury to such merchants as John Gladstone. By this time, in addition to having commercial concern with the United States, he had large dealings with the West Indies; and, as a fruit of this latter connection, he became, in 1809, chairman of the Liverpool West India Association, and found the opportunity for making himself better known to the outer world. But it was the year 1812 which may be regarded as the turning-point in his career, for, from a local politician, he then developed into a national one. The Commons had decided in the spring to consider, in committee of the whole House, the petitions which had been presented relating to the Orders in Council; and, a month after it had commenced taking evidence, there was called John Gladstone. Still President of the Liverpool West India Association, he *May, 1812.* had been for some months in London, as *His evidence before the Commons on the* representing, in conjunction with the Mayor, *Orders in Council.* the United Committee of the Common Council and Merchants and Shipowners of Liverpool, opposed to the renewal of the trade monopoly created by the old charter of the East India Company. He told how the employment of shipping had fallen off at Liverpool since the abolition of 'the African trade' five years before, because the ships had not been suited to commerce with North America, and how the Orders in Council, the repeal of which would have a very destructive effect upon the West India interest, had done good rather than harm, and ought to *Conditionally* be maintained as long as Buonaparte's *opposes their repeal.* Berlin and Milan Decrees were attempted to be enforced.[1]

[1] 'Parliamentary Papers,' 1812, vol. iii., pp. 481-511.

John Gladstone, in fact, like many of his mercantile com-
patriots, had gradually drifted from among the Whigs, who

He leans to the Tories, opposed the Orders in Council and mildly
deprecated the war, towards the Tories, who
supported a continuance of the struggle until Buonaparte's
power should be destroyed ; and the general election was
approaching when first he gave proof of the change.

The two old members for Liverpool — General Gascoyne, of whom much was subsequently heard, and General
Tarleton, returned over Roscoe in 1807—were willing to
stand again at the dissolution of 1812 ; but John Gladstone
and other seceding Whigs, of the same political stamp and
commercial position, desired that one of their representatives should be a statesman worthy of so important a constituency; and they accordingly turned to George Canning,

*and proposes Can-
ning as candidate for
Liverpool.* who, though one of the most brilliant
Tories in Parliament, was at the moment
out of office, and, because of personal
considerations, seemed likely to remain so. John Gladstone himself was so eager in the matter that, when he
had persuaded his friends to choose Canning as their candidate, he offered with his customary resolution to become
personally responsible for the amount of the election expenses, whatever they might be ; and not only this, but, as
his youngest son long afterwards told a Liverpool audience,
he issued a second appeal to Canning's friends, when the
polling was drawing out to unusual length, and secured so
liberal a response that, at the close of the contest, he was
able to return them a full half of their subscriptions.

The Whig candidates were Henry Brougham, afterwards
Lord Chancellor, and Thomas Creevey, later returned for
more than one constituency, whose battle-cry was ' A free
trade to America and the East Indies,' Gascoyne remaining in

the field as a Tory, but Tarleton, though not retiring, being abandoned by his old friends. The fight   Oct. 1812.
The Canning con-
was keen, and, as it proceeded, the Can-   test.
ningite Tories offered to support Brougham with their second vote, if Creevey as well as Gascoyne would withdraw ; but, as Roscoe thought both Whigs would succeed, the compromise was rejected, the Canningites supported Gascoyne, and the two Tories won. Every evening after the close of the poll, which lasted eight days, a crowd flocked to John Gladstone's house, where Canning resided during the contest, to hear an address from the candidate and his chief supporters ; and the vigorous attitude of Canning's host provoked reprisals from the party he had left. It was not merely in versified   John Gladstone
Canning's host.
squibs—in calling him ' Merrystone,' or even 'Sir Pertinax McSycophant,'—that the anger of the Whigs found fullest vent, for a savage attack was made upon his personal honour, arising out of one of the war-risks to which, at that time, the British merchant was subject.

In the summer of 1807, John Gladstone had been owner of an American ship laden with sugar, which, though sailing with United States' papers, was seized   Is severely
criticised.
at Amsterdam and confiscated, the Dutch authorities declaring that the sugar was of British origin, and that the vessel had come from this country. As a fact, she had, Liverpool having been her port of departure ; and the licence she had received from the British Government, under the regulations then existing, did not cover her case. John Gladstone, when before the Commons' Committee on the Orders in Council earlier in the year of the Canning contest, had been bluntly asked —and not improbably by Brougham, against whom he was accused during the fight of harbouring a personal

grudge because of the manner in which that Whig lawyer
had questioned him—whether the ship was condemned
on the ground of the papers proving fictitious ; and this
he virtually admitted, for, as she pretended to have come
from America, she made a fictitious entry into Holland.[1]
This was a subject of charge against him during the contest ;
but in his speeches he contended that, as no oaths were required, no perjury had been committed, and that it was all
part of a plot to deceive ' our arch enemy, and the enemy
of the world,' Buonaparte—a contention that laid him
open to obvious rejoinders, which, with counter-rejoinders,
occupied the columns of the rival Liverpool journals for
some weeks.

The night after the contest closed, the successful candidates, in accordance with the custom then prevailing,
were 'chaired ;' and, having been carried in procession
through the principal streets, were halted at John Gladstone's house, from the balcony of which the leading
personages spoke, while at the window was held a three-
year-old child, who gazed wonderingly at the cheering
crowd below, and who, like the chief orator of the occasion,
was destined to be Prime Minister. Two days later, John
Gladstone presided over a dinner in celebration of the
victory ; and, responding to the toast of his health, he defended himself from the charge of political inconsistency,
averring that, while he had remained the firm friend of
peace as long as he thought it was practicable for peace to
be obtained with safety and honour, he had always utterly
opposed the French idea of universal dominion, and had
Desires peace with taken no share in the general politics of the
honour.   Whigs. And it is of more than common
interest now to note that, by not far from seventy years,

[1] *Ibid.*, pp. 494-9.

he twice anticipated in this speech Lord Beaconsfield's most famous single phrase, ' Peace with honour.'

A more pronounced step into the outer world of politics was taken in the following spring, by the publication in pamphlet form of 'Letters addressed to the Right Honourable the Earl of Clancarty, President of the Board of Trade, &c., &c., &c., on the Inexpediency of Permitting the Importation of Cotton-Wool from the United States during the Present War.' In this 'John Gladstone of Liverpool,' as he called himself on the title-page, submitted that the direct import from the United States in neutral vessels for neutral account, or by ˙British subjects under licence, ˙upon payment of the existing duties only, assisted the United States to raise funds for carrying on the war then waging with this country, while causing great loss and inconvenience to the West Indian colonies.   He was equally against the same mode of importation, but subject to increased duties and a restriction of import to British vessels from neutral ports; and he argued strongly in favour of a total prohibition of import during the war, some of his reasonings, in their frank application of commercial pressure to the promotion of peace, being a remarkable anticipation of a leading doctrine of 'the Manchester School.'

March, 1813. Publishes a pamphlet on trade.

But, while the war with the United States continued and the American trade of John Gladstone was, in consequence, considerably lessened, an outlet was found for his commercial enterprise in another direction.   The monopoly of the East India Company, despite its own protests and the objections of Indian administrators of the experience of Warren Hastings and Sir John Malcolm, was much modified in the early spring of 1814.   Malcolm had declared that the general population of India were not likely to become customers for European articles, because they did not possess the means to purchase them; but that was not the view of the English mercantile class in general, or of John Gladstone in particular. 'John Gladstone and George Grant, of Liverpool, Merchants,' were, indeed, the earliest in the kingdom to endeavour to share the advantages of the new concession. They applied for a licence for their ship, the *Kingsmill*, on March 28th, eight days before any other firm; it was the first of the three granted on April 12th, previous to which date none were issued;[1] and on May 27th, the vessel was despatched from the Mersey with a full cargo for

May, 1814. Bengal. Those were the days when com-
First to send a full
ship to India. merce needed active protection; the long war with France was not yet formally concluded; the inglorious struggle with the United States was to smoulder for nearly another year; and this precursor of the great Liverpool trade with our Indian Empire had to be sent to join the naval convoy at Spithead.

The *Kingsmill* returned to Liverpool laden with Indian goods in September, 1815, after a prosperous voyage, and she was the first vessel to enter the Mersey from India. In the early days of May of the next year, the local Whig organ could congratulate the public upon the arrival of the second, 'a large valuable East India built ship from Bombay, called the *Hannah*, and consigned, as we believe, to John Gladstone, Esq.,' and within a further week a third came into the port with a full consignment from Calcutta for the firm of John and Robert Gladstone,[2] from which time such arrivals were

---

[1] *Ibid.*, 1813-14, pp. 142, 143.

[2] *Liverpool Mercury*, May 10, 1816. In Baines' 'Liverpool' (p. 573), the credit of the second arrival from India is given to a ship of another firm, but that did not come in until May 30 : see *Liverpool Mercury*, May 31, 1816.

so frequent as not to demand attention, even from the
Liverpool newspapers, outside the usual 'Shipping List.'

While the commercial prosperity of John Gladstone was
thus advancing, his political activities were increasing, and
his ambition to obtain a seat in Parliament   His political
was becoming marked.   But the path which   ambition.
leads to St. Stephen's was beset for him as for many another
with annoyances and difficulties.   The dislike he had aroused
among the Liverpool Whigs by what they considered his
desertion of their cause laid him open to their constant and
critical scrutiny of his every public act; and, as his keen desire to take part in national affairs was not always accompanied by the clearness of expression and candour of conduct
which are necessary to the securing of entire confidence, he
was more than once exposed to suspicions of disingenuous-
ness, which may have been undeserved but were certainly
not unnatural.

When he had severed himself from the Whigs, the insults
to which he was subjected seemed only to strengthen his
connection with the Tories; but he remained so free from
party obligations that in the summer of 1814, at a town's
meeting to consider the propriety of peti-   May, 1814.
tioning against a Corn Bill, introduced Opposes a Corn Law.
by the Cabinet of Lord Liverpool, and proposing to
raise the average price at which foreign wheat might
be imported free of duty from 65s. 6d. to 87s. per
quarter, and other grain in similar proportions, he moved
a series of resolutions, adopted by the assembly, declaring 'that it is at present unnecessary, and would be
unwise and hazardous, to alter the existing laws which
regulate the importation of foreign grain;' and, in so doing,
he pointed out that the landholder and the farmer, when
secured from the just competition of the importer, would,

B

as they had always done, successfully exert themselves to raise the price. The ability of the speech was recognised even by the local Whig organ, and its author claimed it afterwards as proving his political independence; but the occasion upon which he so claimed it was for him unfortunate, it being one which, in the opinion of those who were watching his public career, was fatal to the ambition he was understood to harbour of becoming member for Liverpool.

The story, which is somewhat curious, created much interest among politicians at the time, not only in Liverpool but in the metropolis. Its origin was the belief, current towards the end of 1814, that the Tory Ministers intended to continue imposing the Property Tax, an idea intensely distasteful to the commercial classes, who considered that, with what appeared the close of the long continental struggle, that which had been avowedly a war impost ought to be dropped. Lord Liverpool, foreseeing a storm, attempted to sound various representatives of the mercantile community on the point.

Dec., 1814.
Consulted by the Premier.

One to whom he applied was Hart Davis, the Tory member for Bristol, and another was John Gladstone; and, although he had intended the communications as confidential, both speedily became known. It was on December 28th that John Gladstone received a first letter from the Premier, who, in reply to one from his correspondent, assured him in a second communication, of January 2nd, that it was not the Government's intention to propose that the obnoxious tax should continue beyond the end of the ensuing financial year, or even that it should be resorted to except war were renewed.

When John Gladstone received these, the Liverpool

opponents of the impost were organising a requisition to the Mayor, asking the convention of a town's meeting of protest; and, not content with instigating the preparation of a counter requisition and talking over the matter with his friends, he wrote to the chief magistrate on January 5th, enclosing the essential extract from the Prime Minister's letter.   His   communication   was   marked   'Private,' but the contents leaked out; and the *Liverpool Mercury* of the following day mentioned the correspondence as an   incredible   rumour,   and   expressed   its   disbelief that any individual citizen would have taken the liberty to answer for the town at large that it would submit to the tax for another year.   The name   Accused by the of John Gladstone was carefully excluded   Whigs. from this paragraph, but the *Morning Chronicle*, the leading Whig organ of the metropolis, was less reticent; and on the 7th it published an editorial note asserting that the Premier's letter, 'addressed to Mr. Gladstone of Liverpool (the friend of Mr. Canning), was shown about by that gentleman with great self-importance;' and the recipient was referred to without reserve as one of the devoted and expectant friends of the Treasury, against whose insidious artifices the country would do well to guard.

This was published on a Saturday, and on the Monday John Gladstone wrote from Liverpool to the *Morning Chronicle* that its assertion as to the letter was without foundation; and   he   added   in   words   of   His reply. remarkable precision—' I have not received such a letter, nor has his lordship put any question to me on the subject.   I therefore desire that you will, as an act of common justice, insert this in your next Paper, and I also trust that in future you will be more

cautious how you lend yourself for the purpose of giving
circulation to statements, not less false than evidently
founded in motives of the most malignant nature.   The
other assertions contained in the paragraph I hold beneath
my notice.'   The *Chronicle*, naturally staggered at this
prompt and apparently complete denial, called upon its informant to substantiate his statement ; and 'A Liverpool
Merchant' immediately wrote to hint that the contradiction
extended no further than to John Gladstone having received
precisely 'such a letter' as had been described, and to having had 'questions' put to him by the Premier, and challenging him to disavow the receipt of any instructions or communications whatever from the Minister concerning the
Property Tax.

This challenge was not taken up by John Gladstone ; but
the *Globe*, another Whig organ, having repeated the story,
Charge and Counter- he wrote to it on the 15th—'I have no
charge.   hesitation in stating that I have not
received such a communication or letter as you have
described from any person on the part of Ministers,
neither am I acquainted or have ever corresponded, with
any of his Secretaries or Clerks.'   But the London Tory
journals did not need this added disclaimer; almost with
one accord they accepted the earlier; and the *Sun*, a
specially violent newspaper, which scarcely allowed a day
to pass without bitterly attacking the *Chronicle*, excelled
itself by writing—'The story was so evidently false and
nonsensical that we did not notice it ; we were persuaded
that the common sense of every man who read the paragraph
would detect the absurdity of so doltish an imposition.'

But not every Tory journal was so easily and ecstatically
satisfied, for the *Courier*, which had not inserted the original
statement but had published the disclaimers, accepting them

in full, demurred to the accusation of malignity against its rival, the *Chronicle*, and asked how it could be justified.   In reply, John Gladstone somewhat shifted his ground, saying he considered the original paragraph malignant because of its false description of him as a devoted and expectant friend of the Treasury.   'I value my independence,' he wrote, 'as much as any man can do; with the Government I have no connection : when I consider their measures calculated to promote the good of the country, I give them my humble support; when I think them otherwise, I do not hesitate to express my opinions.'

Meantime, the suggested town's meeting at Liverpool had been called, and had resulted in an explosion, for John Gladstone, while repeating that his charge of malignity was confined to the *Chronicle* paragraph, admitted the receipt of the Premier's communication and the use he had made of it.   This avowal exposed him to a running fire of insult from successive speakers, according to one of whom—an Irishman who owed him a personal grudge—he was an abject Ministerial flatterer, low and uneducated, vain, pragmatical, impertinent, wicked, and insolent; and, when he rose to defend Canning from a charge of neglecting the town's interests, the hooting was of such violence that he could not readily obtain a hearing.   His explanation, indeed, had satisfied no one, for, while his enemies openly rejoiced with epigram and sneer, his friends deprecated his use of 'a very slip-shod phrase,' and could only urge that he had not intended to mislead, and that the misunderstanding had arisen from his 'slovenliness of style,' which in turn was due to his 'deficiency of authorship.'   But of far more importance was the comment of the *Times* upon the

*Jan., 1815.
Attacked at a Town's Meeting.*

His explanation generally condemned.

incident and the explanation. 'It seems tolerably evident,'
it wrote after the meeting, 'that Mr. Gladstone did in fact
receive from Lord Liverpool a letter, which in substance at
least resembled that which he was said to have received.
Mr. Gladstone, however, in the first instance denied, in the
most unqualified terms, the receipt of such a communication; though at the Liverpool meeting he acknowledged that
the Minister had written to him on the subject of the
property-tax. We profess ourselves quite unable to reconcile these apparent contradictions.'

There can be little doubt that it was this untoward incident—the more inexplicable because the original equivoca-
tion was so certain of discovery—which for some time kept
Is politically quiet John Gladstone silent in Liverpool politics;
and he apparently took no share in a bye-
contest in 1816, caused by Canning's acceptance of office,
and it was with another merchant that the statesman then
stayed. Throughout the period, however, he in various
ways was displaying all the activity of one who was not
but locally active. merely a merchant but a public-spirited
citizen. In the summer of 1811, he had
had conferred upon him the unusual honour of the freedom of Liverpool, one which was given to his most illustrious
son in the winter of 1892, when for the fourth time Prime
Minister; in 1814, he became President of the Liverpool
Infirmary, and received thanks for his attention and liberality; in the next year, having ceased to be a Presbyterian,
he erected at his own cost the church of St. Thomas at
Seaforth, where he was now residing, and that of St.
Andrew at Liverpool, the advowson of which latter continues the property of his descendants; in the winter of
1816, William Ewart and himself contributed £500 each
towards a fund for employing, at the Liverpool Docks,

some of the great number of men then out of work ; and in 1817, he was to be found giving plants to the local Botanic Garden, and presenting to the Dispensary upon two occasions his share of an arbitration fee.

But by the spring of 1818, he was once more embarked upon the full stream of local and imperial politics ; and it would have been almost impossible, indeed, for him to have been otherwise. Having mentioned, for instance, when presiding over a Bible Society meeting, that Canning was a zealous supporter of such bodies, the local Whigs pounced upon the statement as an electioneering device, denounced it in almost hysterical terms, and exhorted its utterer, when he assumed the saint, to sink the politician. The politician, however, was destined just then not to be sunk for long. In an interval between proposing to Canning's friends that the statesman should be asked to seek re-election at the impending dissolution and the contest itself, he seconded, at a town's meeting, a petition to Parliament against the continuance of the death penalty for forging bank-notes ; while, a few days later, he presided over a meeting of local merchants engaged in the cotton trade, to protest against the imposition of an additional duty upon raw cotton.

April, 1818.
Opposes the Death Penalty for Forgery.

II.—His Father as Politician.

It has been seen how John Gladstone was gradually working his way into public life; and, although the merchant was never completely absorbed in the politician, it is henceforward as politician rather than as merchant that he has to be considered.   The dissolution of 1818 afforded

June, 1818.
John Gladstone con-
tests Lancaster,

him the first opportunity for seeking to enter Parliament; and the constituency he wooed was Lancaster, which long had been and which long remained one of the most corrupt boroughs in the kingdom.   He stood, as an independent candidate, against the two old members, Gabriel Doveton, a Whig, and John Fenton Cawthorne, who had once passed as of the same party, but who had come to be regarded as a Tory.   It seems certain that the friends of John Gladstone and Doveton worked to some extent together against Cawthorne, whose personal record was far from bright; and there was nothing in the colourless published address of the first-named to prevent such a coalition. The poll occupied nine days, but the relative positions on the first—Gladstone, Doveton, Cawthorne—was maintained to the end, John Glad-

and is returned.

stone increasing his lead until he closed with 1870 votes, or more than 700 above Doveton and 800 above Cawthorne. His address of thanks was little more explicit than his earlier election document; but he was decidedly more open at a dinner given in honour of his return, when he is recorded to have delivered two great and eight lesser speeches, in one of which he distinctly opposed anything like a thorough reform of Parliament. For this he was told by the Liverpool Opposes Parliamentary Reform, Whig organ that he had apostatized from his former principles of patriotism; and, as a merely political hit in those days never seemed to suffice, it was added that his oratory, though copious, was ungrammatical. Those were editorial opinions; and the correspondence column furnished even stronger criticisms. 'It may be too late to reform an apostate, it is always seasonable to expose him,' exclaimed one indignant Whig; but a more serious criticism even than being labelled as apostate and dishonest was that of Peter Crompton, the defeated Whig candidate for Preston, and and is attacked by the Whigs in letters himself a Liverpudlian, who resented some of John Gladstone's remarks concerning the contest in which he had been engaged. Yet, even Crompton could not resist the temptation to sneer at the new member for Lancaster as 'a builder of churches,' a name he was later more to deserve.

Absence from Liverpool during the contest in that constituency had not saved John Gladstone from personal attack. Among the lampoons circulated by the Whigs and lampoons. was a supposed poetical epistle to him from his old friend, William Ewart, indicating that both swam with the stream most likely to lead to success, and that Canning was their choice because he could help them to pension or place. Another thus parodied a favourite song:

> John Gladstone, now, my jo, John,
>   Ere we were first acquent,
> We baith were Whigs, ye know, John,
>   To power we had not bent;
> But now how things are changed, John,
>   Since we have changed our sides,
> And all we ance thought just and true
>   Now each of thus [*sic ?* us] derides,

While a third, in imitation of Burns' 'Jolly Beggars,'
summarised the customary accusation in the stanzas:

> John Gladstone was as fine a man
>   As ever graced commercial story
> Till all at once he changed his plan
>   And from a Whig became a Tory.
> And now he meets his friends with pride,
>   Yet tells them but a wretched story,
> He says not *why* he changed his side,
>   He *was* a Whig—he's now a Tory.

But, if the Liverpool Whigs were virulent, the Liverpool
Tories were generous, for they subscribed £6,000 to
pay John Gladstone's election expenses. It was a large
amount for a small borough, but Lancaster, down to the
day of its disfranchisement by Disraeli, was never a cheap
place to fight.

Even when, as in this case was proved, the voters for the
successful candidates were unbought, the loser was loth to
believe in the existence of such abnormal electoral virtue;
and the new Parliament, summoned to assemble early in
August, had not met many days before a petition was presented against the Lancaster return, both
the members being accused of having, by
themselves, their agents, and their friends, committed
bribery and treating. But, before the case could come
on for hearing, John Gladstone was called upon to give
his opinion at Westminster on a subject of pressing
interest. Each House of Parliament had resolved at the
opening of the session to appoint a secret committee to
consider the state of the Bank of England; and over that
of the Commons Robert Peel, still a young
man, who had withdrawn from the Chief
Secretaryship for Ireland not long before
and who was at the moment out of office, was chosen to

His election petitioned against.

1819.
Gives evidence concerning resumption of cash payments,

preside. John Gladstone, as one of the witnesses, attributed the very considerable pressure then felt to over-production and the scarcity of money; but he suggested that the period for a resumption of cash payments ought not to be an early one, eighteen months being the shortest time to be adopted with safety. In its report the Committee so far acted upon this idea that it *which the Committee accepts,* expressed the decided opinion that it was expedient to continue the then existing restriction beyond the following 5th of July, quoting John Gladstone's evidence in support of this view.[1] And when Peel moved his famous resolutions in favour of the resumption of cash payments based upon that report, he instanced as proof of the distress which in 1816 and 1817 had followed upon the over-strained hopes and exertions of the former year, the testimony John Gladstone had given, showing *and Peel quotes.* that the over-trading had been productive of no advantage, but, as respected the labouring classes, had been attended with incalculable mischief.[2]

Meantime, the Lancaster petition had been disposed of. When it was, by order, taken into consideration by the House of Commons, the sitting members claimed to appear as separate parties on distinct interests; and so well did they defend themselves that not only were they declared duly elected, but the petition was found to be *April. The election petition dismissed.* frivolous and vexatious, the most absolute condemnation that such could receive.[3]

Six weeks later the only record of John Gladstone's action

---

[1] 'Second Report from Secret Committee on the Expediency of the Bank resuming Cash Payments,' 1819, p. 11; John Gladstone's evidence is on pp. 104-114.

[2] 'Hansard's Parliamentary Debates,' 1st series, vol. xl., f. 682.

[3] *Commons' Journals*, vol. lxxiv., pp. 75, 298.

in the House of Commons itself during this Parliament can be traced, he then appearing among an overwhelming Ministerial majority against a motion by Tierney, the leader of the Opposition, for a committee on the state of the

Votes with the Tories. nation. There was, however, at that time no official issue of division lists, and the informal catalogues then given by 'Hansard' are in nearly every instance those of the minority alone.

John Gladstone had been a silent member for Lancaster, and, therefore, could have offended none of his supporters by excessive speech; but, despite the overwhelming majority

Feb., 1820. Withdraws from Lancaster, he had secured in June, 1818, he did not seek re-election after the dissolution of February, 1820, consequent upon the death of George III.; and Cawthorne took the vacant seat unopposed. John Gladstone, meanwhile, had sought the suffrages of Woodstock. Both the previous members had retired—Sir Henry Dashwood, great-grandfather of the present baronet, who had sat continuously for the borough from 1784, and Lord Robert Spencer, one of the ducal house of Marlborough which had long influenced the constituency, and continued to do so until its disfranchisement in 1885, with Lord Randolph Churchill as its last and

and is elected for Woodstock. most famous member; and John Gladstone was returned without opposition, in company with a Whig, James Haughton Langston, after an election concerning which no details of moment appear to have survived. One, however, has come down to us regarding his next public appearance, that being in January, 1821, when, presumably because of his father-in-law's long connection with the burgh, Dingwall did him special honour; and its Treasurer's account embalmed for the biographer the bald yet significant record, 'To Tavern

Bill, in giving the freedom of the Burgh to Mr. Gladstone, £1 7s.' His youngest son was present on the occasion, and he later appeared to have believed that the function conferred the freedom by paternity upon himself, though, in point of fact, it was not formally accorded to him for over another thirty years, and when he was Chancellor of the Exchequer under Lord Aberdeen.

It has been observed that John Gladstone had been silent in the Parliament of 1818, but that of 1820 had not long assembled before he showed that this was not always to be his character. February 2nd, 1821, is Feb. 2, 1821. the date which can be marked as the oc- His maiden speech. casion of the delivery not merely of one but, if the expression be allowed, of two maiden speeches, and each, though on widely differing subjects, was characteristic. Lord Sefton (then an Irish peer), who had been defeated at Liverpool when he stood in the Whig interest at the election of 1818, was now member for Droitwich; and, on the February day named, he presented a petition, signed by ten thousand inhabitants of the former town, praying that the question of Queen Caroline should be agitated no longer, that she might be restored to all her rights and dignities, that inquiry should be made into the outrages at Manchester—better known both then and now as the Peterloo Massacre—that the taxes should be diminished, and that the people should be admitted to a larger share in the legislature than they at the moment enjoyed. There was a comprehensiveness about this series of demands which in any case would scarcely have appealed to a cautious mercantile man ; but it was not to that phase of the document that John Gladstone addressed himself.

Sefton had observed that he could vouch for the

respectability of many of the names appended to the petition;
but John Gladstone, after an incidental defence of the
Liverpool Corporation and freemen—who were at that
period a frequent and deserved target for parliamentary
attack, and in. extenuation of whom, as will afterwards be
noted, two of his sons made, like himself, their maiden
parliamentary speech—remarked that, while he was not
personally acquainted with many of the signatories, and was
not inclined to dispute the character and respectability of
Defends the Liver- some, he had had opportunities of knowing
pool Corporation, the sentiments entertained by many gentlemen and merchants of Liverpool of great wealth and character, who did not approve of this petition but did of the
measures of the Government.[1]   And he sufficiently showed
the side he himself was on by being one of the majority
four days later against a vote of censure, proposed by
                    Lord Tavistock, eldest brother of Lord John
and votes Tory.   Russell, upon Ministers for their proceedings against the Queen.

On the evening of his maiden speech, John Gladstone
offered, in discussion of the Navy Estimates, a second
series of remarks, declaring his opinion, as a shipowner,
that there was no scarcity of seamen, his test being that no
rise had taken place in the rate of wages.[2]   But a week
later he touched a far wider subject, and delivered his
longest House of Commons utterance.   It was in Committee of Ways and Means that he combatted an assertion
made in debate, that the friends of many Members of
Parliament lived upon the taxes.   It had been particularly
mentioned that this was the case at Liverpool; and,
while denying this accusation, which ten years later was

[1] 'Hansard,' 2nd series, vol. iv., f. 327.
[2] *Ibid.*, f. 347.

specifically levelled against himself by O'Connell, he declared that he could see no impropriety in the relatives of Members being appointed to situations of trust. It was very natural, he held, that as such places were to be filled, Ministers should attend to the recommendations of those in whom they placed confidence; but he averred, for his own part, that his support to the Government arose from his conviction that the system by which it had guided the counsels of the King was the best and safest for the country.[1] That support, however, did not extend to the point of opposing Roman Catholic Emancipation, this, in the strictest sense, not being a party question, though the overwhelming proportion of those in its favour were Whig, of those against it Tory, for when, early in this session of 1821, a division was taken upon a motion by Plunket for a committee upon the Catholic claims, it was carried by a majority of six, of whom John Gladstone was one.

Supports Catholic Emancipation.

In the same year, the House of Lords reappointed a Select Committee to inquire into the means of extending and securing the foreign trade of the country, and a message was sent to the Commons requesting leave for John Gladstone to be examined as a witness. Just a month previously, the latter House had placed him upon one of its own Select Committees 'to consider of the means of maintaining and improving the foreign trade of the country;' and, on consideration of the Lords' message, 'Mr Gladstone being present, stood up in his place, and declared that he was willing, with the leave of the House, to go to the House of Lords, as is desired by their Lordships in the said Message,' it thereupon being resolved 'That John Gladstone, Esquire, have leave to go to the Lords, as is desired by their

[1] *Ibid.*, ff. 572, 573.

Lordships in their said Message, if he thinks fit.'[1]   Five days later he appeared before the Lords' Committee, over which Lord Lansdowne presided; and in his evidence he stated that the opening of the Indian trade to the country at large

Gives evidence on the Indian trade.

had considerably increased the volume of our commerce to the East, and suggested the abolition of certain minor restrictions which still remained, as likely to lead not only to an extension of commerce with our Indian possessions but to a more general employment for British shipping.   But, when he was asked if he had any means of knowing whether British ships were, on the whole, navigated as cheaply as those of European nations, he answered with characteristic caution, 'That question embraces a very wide field,' and he gave a carefully discriminating reply.   The tone of his evidence, in brief, was in favour of free trade by means of reciprocity, and generally in praise of the British seaman.[2]

Later in 1821, when Sir James Mackintosh sought to move into committee his Forgery Punishment Mitigation Bill, and the Solicitor-General (Sir John Copley, afterwards

Opposes capital punishment for forgery.

Lord Lyndhurst) proposed to postpone that stage for six months, and thus strangle the measure, John Gladstone, in accordance with the action he had years before taken at Liverpool, voted in the majority in favour of proceeding.   A fortnight after, he was once more in a majority in its support, and this time on the third reading; but Lord Londonderry (then Tory leader of the House of Commons, and better remembered as Castlereagh) took advantage of a technical stage, now abolished in the Commons; and, by what Mackintosh declared to be the most unworthy manœuvre

---

[1] *Commons' Journals*, vol. lxxvi., p. 153.
[2] *Lords' Journals*, vol. liv., pp. 296-301.

he had known in Parliament, secured the rejection of the measure.[1] But eleven years later, when John Gladstone had left the House of Commons for ever, the reform he had so long supported was carried into effect.

From this point John Gladstone's parliamentary career was uneventful. He took no discoverable part in debate, but steadily voted with the Tories, varying only upon the admittedly open question of Catholic Re- *Ceases to be active* lief. The fact was by this time patent to *at Westminster.* him, as it was to his friends, that he had entered the House of Commons too late in life to become a figure there. He was consulted by Ministers upon commercial questions; he sat on many a select committee; but his voice was heard no more at St. Stephen's. In Liverpool, however, his influence was re-established; and it was at his residence at Seaforth House that Canning was staying when the statesman, having gone thither to take farewell of his constituents upon accepting the Governor-Generalship of India, received the news of Londonderry's suicide, news which determined him to remain in England but no longer as member for Liverpool. In his place, with John Gladstone's aid, was chosen his tried political friend, William Huskisson, then sitting for Chichester, who years before, while Canning was at Lisbon, had done what he could for Canning's constituents; and what was Huskisson's opinion of John Gladstone may be illustrated by the story of how that politician, as President of the Board of Trade, was once standing under the gallery of the House of Commons with a Liverpool supporter, when a sugar question was under discussion. Goulburn, another member of the *Huskisson's opinion* Tory Ministry, was labouring with a number *of him.*

[1] 'Hansard,' 2nd series, vol. v., ff. 971·3 and 1112·14.

C

of details which, as obviously not grasped by himself,
failed to impress the House. 'Goulburn,' quietly observed Huskisson with a smile, 'has got his facts and
figures and statistics from Mr. Gladstone, and they are all
as correct and right as possible, but he does not understand
them, and will make a regular hash of it.' [1]

The politics of John Gladstone long remained as clearly
those of Canning as when that statesman represented
Liverpool. He had never been a virulent partisan, and in
Continues to support 1823 he seconded the nomination of the
Canning.   first Whig mayor the town had had for
many years; while, in the beginning of the next year, he
bore testimony to the valuable public services of Egerton
Smith, the founder of the Whig organ, the *Liverpool Mercury*, though that journal had never lacked frankness in
dealing with opponents. But he made a purely political
effort, and that in plain sympathy with Canning, on February 14th, 1824, when at a town's meeting, the mayor
presiding, 'for the purpose of considering the best means of
assisting the Greeks in their present important struggle for
independence,' he proved himself one of the few sympathetic
Tories at what was largely a Whig gathering. The re-
approach towards the Whigs thus indicated was repelled,
however, by local causes, as well as by his share in a fierce
controversy which just at this moment was aroused concerning the vital question of colonial slavery.

John Gladstone as merchant and John Gladstone as politician had much to do with moulding certain phases of the
character of his illustrious son ; but, at the outset of that
son's public career, it was the influence of John Gladstone
His ownership of as slave-holder that might have proved malign.
slaves.   It has been frequent matter for taunt against

---

[1] 'Liverpool, a Few Years Since,' p. 89.

William Gladstone that his earliest parliamentary effort was a defence of the West India planters; but it has never been attempted to estimate how far he was affected on this subject by his environment. And yet, when he was at the impressionable age of fourteen, there occurred that which could not but leave its stamp upon him, and concerning which it was inevitable that he should hear the planters' case most favourably put. For the autumn of 1823 was marked by an event which was not alone of special interest to John Gladstone as planter and politician but to all of us to-day, for it was owing to the discreditable incidents attending upon an abortive rising of the negroes in Demerara, which commenced upon John Gladstone's property, that English public opinion was so concentrated upon the iniquity of colonial slavery that the tide of abolitionist feeling never ceased rising until it had swept the infamy away.

Parliament, which sixteen years before had destroyed the African slave trade, had felt constrained during the session of 1823 to make a distinct movement towards ameliorating the condition of the slaves held by the planters in our various colonies. Thomas Fowell Buxton moved a resolution declaring that the state of slavery was repugnant to the principles of the British constitution and the Christian religion, and that it ought to be gradually abolished throughout our colonies, with as much expedition as might be found consistent with a due regard to the well-being of the parties concerned. Canning, as representing the Ministry, proposed in substitution a modified series of resolutions, affirming the expediency of adopting effectual and decisive measures for ameliorating the condition of the slaves, so as to prepare them for freedom at the earliest

1823.
The Commons and
Colonial slavery.

period that should be compatible with the well-being of the slaves themselves, with the safety of the colonies, and with a fair and equitable consideration of the rights of private property.

Canning's proposals did not go far, but, being as much as could be hoped for at the moment, they were unanimously adopted, and were attended with instant and most important results.   The Colonial Minister (Lord Bathurst) forwarded them without delay to the governors of the colonies concerned ; and the West India interest in England protested with impotent rage, while the West Indian planters echoed the protests with insolent fury.   But the worst effect was witnessed in Demerara, where the Governor (General Murray), though he received the despatch on July 7th, communicated its contents only to the planters, kept them jealously guarded from the slaves, and thus contrived to set about whispers which aroused in the excited minds of the negroes the belief that they had been freed, and that the news was deliberately being held from them by their masters.

Negro discontent in
Demerara.

Seven years before, there had arrived in Demerara, as a representative of the London Missionary Society, a minister named John Smith, who had settled upon a plantation known as Le Resouvenir, and this adjoined the estate of Success, the property of John Gladstone.   Smith had been instructed by the Society not to do anything which could render the slaves dissatisfied with their condition—an instruction which of itself was eloquent testimony to the general feeling upon slavery at that day—and this he sedulously endeavoured to carry out.   But the surrounding sights and sounds, the hard labour of the fields and the frequent use of the whip impressed upon him, as they would have done upon any but a planter, the horrors of slavery ;

and, fatally for him, some of these impressions were committed to a diary.

He had not long been settled in Demerara before he entered in this book : 'The negroes of Success have complained to me lately of excessive labour, and very severe treatment. I told one of their overseers that I thought they would work their people to death;' and this is of special significance as it was from that plantation, when owned by John Gladstone, that the ringleaders of the outbreak came. Originally devoted to the cultivation of coffee, it was put in sugar, and from that time the negroes complained of hard and late work—complaints which, as Success adjoined Le Resouvenir and could be seen from Smith's house, did not fail to reach the missionary. This was the more certain because one of John Gladstone's negroes, named Quamina—'Quamina Gladstone' as he is called in some official records, 'Quamina of Success' in others—was a deacon at the chapel, and had grievances of his own, small in themselves but great as touching his religion. In May, 1823, just when England was awaking to the necessity for treating the slaves with more lenity, and the planters were resenting interference by construing the laws to the greater disadvantage of the negroes, Governor Murray, who was to prove a fitting tool in the slaveholders' hands, issued an order that no negro should go to worship without a pass from his master. Such passes were difficult to obtain, and were often refused ; and the Sunday fortnight after the instruction was issued, Smith, noting a striking diminution in his congregation, incidentally wrote in his diary, 'Quamina and the rest of Success people were sent to the sea-side to wait the arrival of a schooner, and remained there all day for nothing.'

'Missionary Smith' and John Gladstone's slaves.

Petty tyranny of this kind on the part of the managers, added to the criminal silence of the Governor regarding the receipt of the ameliorating circular from home, paved the way for insurrection. The house-servants of some of the planters had overheard talk at the tables of a 'new law,' which would be for the advantage of the slaves; and the

August, 1823.
Insurrection in the
air.

whisper went around that the King of England had given them a freedom which was being withheld by the masters. Matters thus ripened for revolt; and, after the service on the morning of Sunday, August 17th, Smith overheard Quamina of Success and another negro talking of the 'new law' in a manner which he considered to demand rebuke. 'Oh, it's nothing particular, sir,' replied Quamina, 'we were only saying it would be good to send our managers to town [Georgetown, the capital] to fetch up the new law.' Smith warned them that such talk was foolish and improper, as it might provoke the Governor in the colony and the Government in England; and Quamina rejoined, 'Very well, sir, we will say nothing about it, for we should be very sorry to vex the King and the people at home.'

The next evening the outbreak took place. Smith, while preparing for a walk, received a note from a slave, named Jackey Reed, which, referring to Quamina's son, a cooper upon Success and a somewhat irregular character, said: 'Jack Gladstone has sent me a letter, which appears as if I

'Jack Gladstone' as
a rebel.

had made an agreement upon some action, which I never did; neither did I promise him anything; and I hope that you will see to it, and inquire of the members whatever it is they may have in view, which I am ignorant of; and to inquire after and know what it is: the time is determined on for seven o'clock to-night.' 'This letter,' partially ran the enclosure, 'is written by Jack Gladstone and the rest of the brethren of Bethel Chapel, and all the rest of the brothers are ready, and put their trust in you.' Smith at once endeavoured to stay the movement, but without success ; and, though he was able to prevent violence being done that night towards the manager of Le Resouvenir, the negroes refused to listen to his entreaties to desist from proceeding with the revolt.

Two nights later, Quamina, who had saved John Stewart (John Gladstone's manager at Success) from being hurt by the rest, hurriedly entered Smith's house ; but, upon being remonstrated with and asked to explain where he had been, he as suddenly departed, only—after a heavy price had been placed upon his head—to be caught unarmed in the bush, to be shot as a runaway, and to be hanged in chains between two cabbage-trees in front of Success. His son, Jack Gladstone, for whose capture an official reward also was offered, was so much the more fortunate or unfortunate that, suborned to false testimony against the missionary, he escaped death ; but some of his Success companions were *Outbreak suppressed on the Gladstone plantation.* hanged and several flogged, various of these latter receiv- ing the appalling number of a thousand lashes, with the added penalty of working in chains for life.

Governor Murray and the Demerara planters were, in fact, in that mood of malicious cruelty which customarily follows abject terror. The revolt commenced on August 18th ; on the next day, Murray issued a pro- *Punishment by the planters.* clamation threatening the slaves with, as he phrased it, all the horrors of martial law ; on the following, the movement was at an end ; but the proclamation was not revoked for over five months. While it was in opera- tion some fifty negroes were hanged, others were shot in the bush, more were nearly torn to pieces by the lash; but all these iniquities might, at that time, have passed with little heed in England if it had not been for what came to be known as the 'martyrdom of Missionary Smith.'

The missionary, arrested on August 21st, was incarcerated until October 13th, when he was brought to trial before a court-martial, which ended on November 24th with his sentence to death, on the ground of having been concerned in the conspiracy. In order to secure such a sentence, hearsay evidence was admitted, suborned testimony was welcomed, all the rules which guide our courts of justice were ignored; and when, after a recommendation to mercy, which under the circumstances was the most hollow of shams, the sentence was sent to England for confirmation, it was at once commuted to banishment from British Guiana. But before this news could reach Demerara, Smith, confined in a loathsome dungeon and suffering from an incurable complaint, had died under his accumulation of miseries; and so fierce was the persecution by the planters that his widow was not allowed to follow his body to the grave, and, when some of his humble admirers endeavoured to mark his resting-place, their work was immediately scattered to the winds. Not since the mean revenge which the first Charles took upon the remains of his noblest opponent, Sir John Eliot, after death in the Tower, had such an atrocity been committed by governing Englishmen.

Upon receiving the first news from Demerara, John Gladstone communicated with Huskisson, sending him the letters he had had from his principal attorney in the colony. The reply, though not intended for publication, became common property, and, while damaging Huskisson's reputation for candour and John Gladstone's for caution, had the more important effect of exciting much suspicion among the abolitionists as to the good faith of Ministers.   Writing from Eastham on November 2nd, Huskisson expressed his *Huskisson's opinion.* sorrow that the forebodings of those who vainly deprecated the agitation of the slave question in the House of Commons had so soon been realised ; and he assured his correspondent that the Government, and Canning in particular, did everything possible to prevent Buxton's motion coming forward.   'I perfectly agree with you,' he continued, 'that, in a matter of this portentous difficulty, it is only by gradual amelioration—by moral and religious improvement—by humanity and kindness—by imperceptibly creating better domestic habits and feelings among the slaves — by countenancing and encouraging all that can have that tendency in the conduct of the owners and white people— by repressing with the strong arm of the law, and stigmatising with the moral power of opprobrium and disgrace, whatever leads to an opposite result, that we have a chance of ultimately, and even then remotely, providing for the termination of so great an evil, moral and political, as the existence of a large population in a state of chattel possession and personal slavery.   In principle, this is the end which every good man ought to wish for, perhaps to look to ; but it is an end, which, so far from publishing or proclaiming at the outset, he ought almost to conceal even from himself.'

Huskisson proceeded to condemn Wilberforce and his associates for not pursuing such quietist methods as he approved, and uttered the hope, rather than the expectation, that the Demerara outbreak would teach them more discretion.   Measures of improvement, such as a greater encouragement and provision for ministers of the Established Church, either of England or Scotland, ought, he considered, to be persevered in by the Government ; and he added, in words afterwards used against him as showing he had prejudged the case, 'I think the example of Smith, of whom it is difficult to presume he was altogether innocent of the late conspiracy, proves that the colonies and the Government must look for the religious instruction of the negroes to men whose situation and tenure will afford a better security that they will not overstep the views and intentions of their employers, than can be found in the voluntary zeal, even if always honest and sincere, of the missionaries, for the interests of religion.'   And the letter thus concluded : 'I am sorry that the vicinity of Smith to your estate, and his connexion with some of your slaves, has involved you in some loss of property ; but, looking to the immense stake you have in this colony, you may console yourself if the result of this formidable conspiracy should be, that its premature explosion affords the chance of a better insurance against the repetition of a similar danger.'

With this comforting letter in his pocket, John Gladstone sat down with a light heart to enter upon a newspaper controversy with a prominent local abolitionist, named James Cropper, who happened to have published, in the *Liverpool Mercury* of October 31st, a contribution upon the impolicy of slavery. 'Mercator' at once stepped into the breach, and on November 5th he wrote to the *Liverpool Courier*, attacking Cropper's position.   In the nine letters which he then penned (of which this was the first, and which, with the main portion of the correspondence, were reprinted by the West India Association of Liverpool), he defended the cause of

John Gladstone's controversy on slavery.

the planters with vigour. Disclaiming any intention to advocate slavery in the abstract, he protested against unjust and indiscriminate abuse being levelled at those who, under the guarantee and safeguard of the law, had vested their property in the labour of slaves ; and his main contention was that negroes were better-behaved and more willing labourers in slavery than they would be free, and that their condition compared favourably with that of the English peasantry. If, however, there was to be abolition, he held that the title of the West India planters to property in their slaves was as strong as the law could make it ; and that if, for any purpose whatever, the public interfered with, injured, or took that property, they were bound to make full compensation—a view ten years later adopted by the Reformed Parliament itself.

Smarting under his own recent losses, Demerara loomed largely throughout John Gladstone's contributions to the controversy. He described the Canning Resolutions as having been strong and precipitate measures, pregnant with extreme danger, but which, in a great degree, had been forced upon Ministers ; he traced the outbreak to the abolitionist agitation in England ; he expressed the hope that not only would 'that well-meaning but mistaken man, Mr. Wilberforce,' perceive this, but that 'the more intemperate, credulous, designing, or interested individuals who have placed themselves in his train,' would be induced to pause ; and he took the guilt of Smith for granted, repeating, with almost touching credulity, the wild tales of appalling negro atrocities which had reached him from Demerara, and which were speedily shown to be false. He added, with a pain which could not at that moment have been appreciated by the public, that the ringleaders almost wholly belonged to the estates most distinguished for kind and

indulgent treatment ; and, having denounced the missionaries as hired emissaries, whose objects seemed to have
been to revolutionise the colonies in place of promoting
their professed object of diffusing religion among the people,
he exclaimed : ' I would have the negroes to receive the
benefits of religious instruction, but from pure sources,' and
these he defined as ' Clergymen of the Established Churches,
and not the Missionary Societies.'

For the time, his opponents were content to answer John
Gladstone with the successive batches of news from
Demerara, and which steadily aroused the public, first to
attention and then to heat.   The earliest impression had
been that the planters' allegations against Smith were
certain to be well-founded ; and some of the supporters of
the London Missionary Society withdrew their subscriptions
because of the conviction that it was his meddling that had
made the mischief.   But, as the details became known, as
the progress of the court-martial was watched, as the capital
sentence was pronounced, and as the intelligence of his
prison death was received, there was a keen revulsion of
feeling ; and when, in the spring of 1824, Sir James
Mackintosh presented to the House of Commons a petition
from the Society setting forth the facts, not a murmur was
raised, even by the planters' assured advocates, against its
reception.[1]

Public opinion was stimulated ten days later, and in an
unexpected fashion, for, upon the arrival of a batch of
newspapers from the West Indies, there was re-published in
the London press from the *Jamaica Journal* the private
letter from Huskisson to John Gladstone, already described,
which had not previously been seen in England.   Both the
matter of the epistle and the manner in which it had been

[1] April 13, 1824 : ' Hansard,' 2nd series, vol. xi., ff. 400-8.

made known were criticised. While an advanced Whig organ declared that the letter would not raise Huskisson in the opinion of the country, and a Tory journal considered that it reflected every possible credit upon its writer, the *Times* cautiously observed that it could not detect in the communication, 'although written manifestly under the strictest confidence to a friend, and that friend an extensive proprietor of land and slaves at Demerara, any expression of opinion upon the general subject of slavery which can be considered, if fairly construed, as discreditable to Mr. Huskisson's reputation.'

But even those who were inclined to praise the under-lying sentiment of the letter, or to excuse Huskisson's apparent pre-judgment of the case of Smith, were emphatic in condemning its publication. Journals of all shades asked for an explanation of this private communication having been made public; and John Gladstone, who at once took up the challenge, was again shown to have acted, as on the occasion of the Liverpool letter of nine years before, with an incaution singular in so business-like a man when dealing with a confidential document. It appeared that because his brother-in-law, Colin Robertson, held property in Jamaica, John Gladstone sent him a copy 'most confidentially,' but with permission to mention its contents to some of his friends. In such circumstances, the added injunction not to permit any copy or extract to be taken proved as ineffective as a keen-witted man ought to have foreseen ; for the letter, having been sent for perusal to one of Robertson's fellow Jamaica proprietors, was transcribed and forwarded to a friend of the latter in the colony, and from that further friend it, of course, proceeded to the *Jamaica Journal.* The fashion, indeed, in which each individual in the long chain thought to keep a secret by

telling it to someone else, would have had more fitting
place in a comedy than in a concern of business and
political life.

When, on June 1st, after many petitions had been presented to the House of Commons, praying for an inquiry
into the proceedings attending the trial of Smith, Brougham
formally brought the matter before Parliament, the planters
felt they had a poor case.   The great lawyer moved an address to the Crown declaring that the Com-
mons contemplated with serious alarm and
deep sorrow the violation of law and justice
which had been manifested, and 'most earnestly praying that
his majesty will be graciously pleased to adopt such measures
as to his royal wisdom may seem meet for securing such
a just and humane administration of law in that colony as
may protect the voluntary instructors of the negroes as well
as the negroes themselves, and the rest of his majesty's
subjects, from oppression.'   The weight of evidence upon
the side of Smith was as strong as the body of eloquence
called forth in his extenuation was emphatic; and, after
a two nights' debate, in which Ministers could do no more
than propose the previous question, the motion was defeated by only 193 votes to 146.   'Hansard,' which devotes
many a page to the discussion, gives the list of the
minority alone, but there is extant one of the majority, and
in that, singular to say, John Gladstone is to be found.[1]
With remarkable scruple, his political opponents had kept
his name out of the debate; it is so possible to read it
from end to end without suspecting that it was his property
which was primarily concerned, that the most painstaking
of our historians of that period has missed it, and has even,

June, 1824.
*An address to the
Crown,*

[1] 'Report of the Committee of the Anti-Slavery Society for 1824,'
p.   11

in an admirable summary of the events, placed Quamina upon the adjacent estate of Le Resouvenir;[1] and the return John Gladstone made for the forbearance of his old antagonist, Brougham, was to form one of the narrow majority which sought to evade condemning, *which John Gladstone opposes.* without daring to exonerate, the guilty court-martial. But the discussion had done its work. It was not merely the one in which Wilberforce last prominently figured as the veteran abolitionist, or that which gave Macaulay the text for his first great public speech ; it was that which shook the system of colonial slavery to its foundations; and the martyrdom of Smith in Demerara, like that of John Brown in Virginia at a later day, marked a prodigious stride in the history of human freedom.

John Gladstone, whatever losses he might be encountering in the West Indies or annoyances in journalistic and parliamentary debate, was having some compensation at this moment in the testimony that was being given him of the esteem of his Liverpool neighbours. In the earliest days of 1824, a meeting of his local admirers declared that he had rendered most important *1824.* services to the town, by his great zeal and *Presented with a* ability in promoting and increasing its trade, *testimonial.* and by his support of all establishments having for their object the advancement of its prosperity and refinement ; and added that, as philanthropist and politician, he had likewise done much to deserve a testimonial. A subscription for the giving to him of a service of plate was

---

[1] Spencer Walpole's ' History of England,' vol. iii., p. 399. A striking account of Smith, his labours, and his sufferings, is given in Edwin Angel Wallbridge's ' Demerara Martyr,' a book so little read that its leaves remained uncut in the British Museum Library for over forty years after its publication.

accordingly opened; most of the commercial firms in the
port subscribed; nearly £1400 was raised; and in the
autumn the gift was presented.

As a citizen, indeed, he was always ready to work hard
for the town of his adoption. When the Liverpool and
Manchester Railway—the opening of which was to cost
Huskisson his life—was first projected in 1824, John
Gladstone was among those who promised the scheme his
most cordial support, and his brother and partner, Robert,

Supports the Liver-   became one of the deputy-chairmen of the
pool and Manchester   committee formed to promote it.   The
Railway.
necessary Bill was introduced in the session
of 1825, and John Gladstone, who had been placed upon
the select committee appointed to consider it, gave evidence in its favour.   On the thirty-seventh day of the inquiry, and after sixty-seven witnesses had been examined,
the committee decided by a single vote on a division in
which over seventy took part, that the preamble of the Bill
had been proved; but at the next sitting, owing to the
opposition of the Corporation of Liverpool to compulsory
powers being given for taking land, the measure was lost
for the session.   It was only for a year, however; Huskisson
and John Gladstone as Members of Parliament, Robert
Gladstone as one of the promoters, worked specially hard,
and the next year the Bill was passed and the line
begun.

Meanwhile, the member for Woodstock was meditating
yet another change of constituency; and, in the autumn of
1825, he intimated to the electors of Berwick-on-Tweed that
he should be a candidate, at the next dissolution, as an
independent supporter of Lord Liverpool's Administration.
But after he had organised a preliminary canvass, the old
awkward question of slavery had again to be faced. Early in

1826, the citizens of Berwick, at a Guild, unanimously petitioned the Houses of Parliament, asking that the Canning Resolutions of three years before should be carried into full effect.

*1826.
Stands for Berwick.*

John Gladstone at once wrote to a local supporter, expressing his hearty concurrence in the prayer of the petition ; and adding that he had joined most conscientiously in the original vote, and that he had uniformly used his best endeavours to improve the condition, increase the comforts, and pro-mote the instruction of his slaves in every way consistent with their situation.

Slavery once more.

As to Demerara, the ameliorative measures adopted by the Government had been by anticipation acted upon by himself; and, indeed, such had so generally been the case in that colony that little more had remained for the Administration to do than to confirm them by legal authority ; while, as to those colonial legis-lators who had obstructed such measures, he suggested the adoption of fiscal regulations calculated to compel their assent.

His next utterance on the subject was at the nomination in June, and only a few days after he had once more been ineffectually suggested as a candidate for Liverpool. He reiterated the opinion that the resolutions of 1823 had been admirably adapted to ameliorate the state of the slaves, to afford them religious and other instruction which would fit them for emancipation, and to secure to the merchants a fair compensation for any loss incurred by abolition. These resolutions, he went on, had appeared to him just and reasonable ; they had received his sincere ap-probation ; and he would support every measure of a similar tendency the Government might introduce.

Elected for Berwick.

But speedily after his return as the second member, six votes ahead of the third candidate, a

D

correspondent of the *Berwick Advertiser*, signing himself
'Anti-Jesuit,' took advantage of a wrangle between John
Gladstone and the editor as to whether the former's hustings
address had been correctly reported, to exhume the new representative's original opinion upon the Canning Resolutions, as already quoted from his letters of the winter of 1823,
and to challenge him to reconcile that with the one he now
professed. ' I quarrel not with Mr. Gladstone,' said the
writer, ' for any opinions he may entertain on the subject of
slavery; but I condemn him for maintaining one class of
opinions at Liverpool and their opposite at Berwick—I denounce the impudence with which the man whom the
West India Association of Liverpool has assumed, and
distinguished, and rewarded as the most able champion and
advocate of the existing system of slavery, dared, in writing
and in print, in private conversations and in public
speeches at Berwick, to profess and declare himself a friend
to its abolition.'

Through the customary and convenient medium of a
Berwick supporter, John Gladstone retorted that the letter
was not less coarse and vulgar in expression than unfair in
statement and incorrect in inference; and he endeavoured
to harmonise the apparent inconsistencies by stating that
as, against the wish of Ministers who thought the matter
would better be dealt with by the Colonial Department,
Buxton had brought on his motion, they were compelled to
move amendments, for which, as they were considered by
the whole House to be highly preferable, he most conscientiously voted, ' but the measure was not the less *forced* upon
both the Government and Parliament, and, from its unavoidable publicity, caused much excitement and dissatis-
faction among the slaves in the West Indies. This, I am
persuaded would not have been the case, and that, in all

probability, the insurrection in Demerara would not have taken place, had the untractable abolitionists left the Government at liberty to following their own course.' The reply of 'Anti-Jesuit' was that this reasoning proved John Gladstone's duplicity, and that what had been asked was not a detail of the sophistical process by which he reconciled his own mind to the original Berwick declaration, but what he expected and intended the burgesses to believe. As no answer was given to this further question, it must be supplied by each who studies the circumstances attending it.

But John Gladstone's annoyances at Berwick were only beginning. The defeated candidate had ineffectually demanded a scrutiny immediately the poll closed, and during the autumn a petition was prepared against the junior member's return. The supporters *But petitioned against,* of John Gladstone in meeting assembled denounced this proceeding 'with disgust and indignation,' as it might even hazard the disfranchisement of the borough ; and they were so satisfied with the effort that several of them adjourned to an inn, 'where they spent the evening in a most harmonious manner.' But the promoters persevered and the petition was presented, this charging John Gladstone, both by himself and his agents, with bribery, treating, and other illegal transactions. John Gladstone had, accordingly, to turn his attention from the promotion of the new line of road from Liverpool to London, on which he was just then engaged, to the sordid details of an investigation before an election committee ; and, after this body had inquired into the matter in the spring of 1827, his return *and unseated.* was declared to have been void, not only upon technical grounds as to the rights of certain voters, but because he had been guilty of treating.[1]

[1] *Commons' Journals*, vol. lxxxii., pp. 38, 334.

A few months later, there seemed the momentary gleam
of a chance for John Gladstone to receive a marked
compensation for this disappointment. Canning, his
political hero, who had at length attained the Premiership, encountered much trouble with the House of Lords,
where Wellington carried the majority against the new Administration ; and it was rumoured among the more extreme
Tories that the Minister would endeavour to overbear this untoward opposition by the creation of a batch of peers. ' Mr.
Canning's object at the present moment,' *John Bull* declared,
' seems to be to degrade the ancient Nobility of England,
and to establish a separate personal influence in the House
of Peers by the advancement of his own creatures and
dependents ;' and it averred that John Gladstone was one
of those who had been mentioned in confidence for
elevation to the peerage. Whatever foundation there may have been for the idea, it
was never carried out, for, within a few weeks of the publication of the rumour, the great statesman was dead, and the
alleged chief of ' the Canning cycle ' at Liverpool—who had
remained faithful to the last, for, upon the formation of the
Ministry, he had procured a town's meeting to address the
Crown in its support—passed unrewarded. Nineteen years
indeed, were to elapse before John Gladstone received a
title. In 1827, he was too liberal for Peel ; in 1846, Peel
was too advanced for him ; but, though a peerage failed to be
given by Canning, it was from Canning's leading rival that
there came a baronetcy.

1827.
Rumoured elevation
to the peerage.

III.—His Eton Education.

WHILE John Gladstone was thus tasting the bitter as well as the sweet of public life, his youngest son was growing through childhood into studentship. Of his earliest days, he has recalled some incidents which have historic interest. His first distinct remembrance was that of standing by the side of his nurse, and looking from the William Gladstone's window of his father's house in Rodney earliest recollections. Street upon the crowd which cheered Canning on his original election for Liverpool in 1812 ; and his next that of being taken, when four years old, by his mother to visit Hannah More, then a venerated author, and once the flatterer of Johnson and Garrick, the associate of Reynolds and Burke, who gave the child one of her little books, because, as she told him, he had just come into the world, and she was just going out, and yet she lived to see him enter Parliament. It was about the same period, and in the autumn of 1813, that his father's residence was one of the most conspicuously illuminated in all Liverpool in celebration of the victory of the Allies at the battle of Leipsic ; in the next year the boy was to be impressed, upon his first visit to Edinburgh, with the roar of the Castle guns as they announced what at the moment was thought to be the crowning triumph of Europe over Buonaparte ; and the susceptible mind of the child was soon to be further suffused with the echoes of the great war, as a result of the *naïve* patriotism of a Welsh housemaid, who, ignoring Wellington and unknowing of Blücher, attributed to the then Sir Watkin Williams Wynn the unique glory of having sent millions of men to face the foe.

But, even before the child emerged from the usual period of nursery teaching, John Gladstone had removed his home from the centre of Liverpool to an adjacent hamlet at the mouth of the Mersey.   Here, in a district then little inhabited but now populous, he built a house which he called Seaforth, after Lord Seaforth, Baron Mackenzie of Kintail, who was head of the family of Mackenzie, to which his wife belonged.   A little later, he erected a church

His first school

there ; and it was at the residence of its incumbent, William Rawson, that, in company with a few other boys, William Gladstone first received classical instruction, and displayed such a distaste for figures as made his tutor despair of teaching arithmetic to him who was to become the greatest Chancellor of the Exchequer of modern times.

Among those who very speedily afterwards had similar tuition, it is of interest to note, were Arthur Stanley, one time

and schoolfellows.

Dean of Westminster, and Richard, first Viscount Cross, thrice a Secretary of State, and once a successful rival of Mr. Gladstone at the polls.   The young Stanley was not yet nine, and William Gladstone had been some years at Eton, when the former went to Seaforth for school ; and he had not been there two months before he could write to his mother that he had been asked to John Gladstone's, where he was much impressed with the stuffed animals of Seaforth House.   John Gladstone, indeed, showed continued interest in the lads under William Rawson's care.   On the Guy Fawkes' Day of 1825, he gave them the wood for a bonfire, in which they consumed 'a very tall Pope;'[1] and it was owing to this continuous acquaintanceship between Seaforth House and the parsonage that one of the earliest external glimpses of William Gladstone, yet to be recorded, is due.

'From my father's windows at Seaforth,' Mr. Gladstone told his fellow-citizens of Liverpool when he himself was over eighty years of age, 'I used, as a small boy, to look southward along the shore to this town, even then becoming a large town in the country. I remember well that it was crowned by not so much cloud as a film of silver grey smoke, such as you may now see surmounting the fabrics of some town of ten or twenty thousand people where the steam-engine has as yet scarcely found a place. . . . Four miles of the most beautiful sand that I ever knew offered to the aspirations of the youthful rider the most delightful method of finding access to Liverpool.' Perhaps the youthful rider enjoyed the exercise too much, for he made but little scholastic progress at the vicarage at Seaforth; and, just before he was twelve, and after he had participated in his first public function—that of being present at Dingwall in 1821 to see his father made a burgess of the head burgh of the county of Ross—he passed to the ancient collegiate foundation of Eton, where his eldest brothers, Thomas and Robertson, for some time had been; and, although the entry of Oppidans during the first half of this century has not been preserved, the September, 1821. September of 1821 can be given as the Enters Eton. date of his admission.

Boarding in a house which was subsequently to receive another embryo Prime Minister, known to us as Lord Salisbury, he escaped a probationary stage in the

<hr />

[1] Rowland E. Prothero's 'Life and Correspondence of Arthur Penrhyn Stanley,' vol. i., pp. 11, 12.

Lower School, and was placed in the middle remove of the fourth form, under the tutorship of a somewhat eccentric clergyman, Henry Hartopp Knapp. While he was taught no mathematics and scarcely any arithmetic, he received no special religious instruction—indeed, as he himself long afterwards said, religious instruction when he was at Eton was nearly, if not absolutely, reduced to zero; and, as regards English literature, it was only by hearsay from a schoolfellow that he later knew that Milton had written prose. But, despite his having since recorded of himself that, though sometimes thoughtful and always impressible, he was at first averse from school work, such learning as Eton demanded he readily acquired. It may be that in his day—and the statement is made upon his authority—an idle, stupid boy was rather preferred to a stupid boy who was diligent; but he himself was a Lower Boy for no more than eighteen months, and his diligence was as marked as his brightness was observable.

An idea of his schoolfellows at this period may be gathered from the lists at the 'election' or Midsummer of 1823. In the sixth form were Spencer Walpole, afterwards Home Secretary, and John Mitford, subsequently Lord Redesdale, and for many years Chairman of Committees of the House of Lords. In the upper division of the fifth were Sir Stephen Glynne, the young baronet of Hawarden, later to become the youngest Gladstone's brother-in-law; George Cornewall Lewis, in after years the same youngest Gladstone's successor as Chancellor of the Exchequer; and the Duke of Buccleuch, destined, in the hour of William Gladstone's greatest electoral triumph, to be his real opponent in Midlothian; while in the lower division of the fifth were placed, with the youngest Gladstone, Walter Kerr Hamilton, afterwards Bishop of Salisbury;

His schoolmates.

George Augustus Selwyn, to be bishop in succession of New Zealand and Lichfield; Arthur Henry Hallam, son of the historian, and immortalised by 'In Memoriam'; Frederic Rogers, first Lord Blachford; and (Sir) John Young, afterwards Lord Lisgar, all subsequently associated in friendship or political life. And among younger scholars were Alexander William Kinglake, the historian of the Crimean War; Robert Gray, Colenso's opponent as Bishop of Cape Town; and (Sir) Francis Hastings Doyle, later the groomsman at Mr. Gladstone's marriage.

Of all these, the Selwyns were his earliest friends. There were four brothers, all boarding in the same house with William Gladstone, and each brilliant. William, the eldest, died Lady Margaret Professor of Divinity; George Augustus, the second, became, as has been said, in succession Bishop of New Zealand and Lichfield; Thomas Kynaston, the third, took at Eton the scholarship founded by Mr. Gladstone's earliest political 'patron,' the Duke of Newcastle, but died young; while Charles Jasper, the fourth, was a Lord Justice of Appeal. Neither Gladstone nor Hallam, Gaskell nor Doyle, shone so much in the scholarship of that day as the Selwyns, afterwards observed one of William Gladstone's fags; but although, as will later be seen, George Selwyn became his coadjutor in an important scholastic enterprise, the youngest Gladstone soon attached himself more particularly to Hallam. For this last, to the end he entertained the warmest regard; and of Hallam, when himself advanced in age, he wrote that one special and highly prized advantage he had at Eton was in forming a very close friendship with the youth whom he considered then to have been the foremost among his contemporaries in the school. They had gone to Eton in the same year; and soon after both had reached the fifth

His friends.

form, although they boarded at different houses, they began
to mess together. To their friendship was admitted Doyle,
who took long walks in their company, and who recorded of
Hallam that they all felt, while conversing with him, in the
presence of a larger, profounder, and more thoughtful mind
than any of them could claim.[1] One other school
acquaintance, James Bruce (afterwards created Lord Elgin,
and first of that title to be Viceroy of India), Mr. Gladstone
placed, as to the natural gift of eloquence, at the head of
all he knew either at Eton or Oxford.[2] This is high praise,
but Bruce had deserved a compliment, if only for the
service he rendered in first teaching William Gladstone
that Milton had written prose.[3] But of all the brilliant
band of Eton boys then assembled, one alone of eminence
remained in public life when Mr. Gladstone, in the early
spring of 1894, went into retirement; and that was Lord
Arthur Hervey, who, senior of the statesman in point of
years, was nominated by him to the see of Bath and Wells,
and, after maintaining a constant friendly intercourse, remained a Bishop after his colleague of the far past had
ceased to be a Minister.

What Mr. Gladstone was like as a schoolboy may almost
be guessed from his temperament and home surroundings.
He was little known as a cricketer, he was no oarsman,
but he loved long walks with Hallam and Doyle and
friends of like tastes, thereon to discuss problems new and
His schoolboy tastes old. His political bent, though not very
and pursuits. marked at this period, was shown at the
Debating Society by a declaration, with all the assumption
of age that comes natural to youth, that his prejudices and

[1] Sir Francis Hastings Doyle's 'Reminiscences and Opinions,' p. 41.
[2] Theodore Walrond's 'Letters and Journals of Lord Elgin,' p. 3n.
[3] Ibid., p. 6.

predilections had long been enlisted on the Tory side ; and
it was equally indicated by his appearing at the Montem of
1826 in Greek costume, to show his sympathy with a people
rightly struggling to be free, and with a cause ardently
supported by Canning, but little to the taste of the
Duke of York, then the heir-presumptive to the throne,
who, accompanied by Wellington, was at this very festival.
He was unconsciously engaged, in fact, even as a boy in
endeavouring to harmonise the old with the new, the Toryism of Eldon with that of Canning, repression at home with
liberty abroad.   The struggle, thus early commenced,
proceeded for many years ; it may be doubted whether
it ever truly ceased.   Doyle, indeed, has told with all
seriousness of how, one day at Eton, when he was com-
puting the odds for the Derby as they appeared in a
morning paper, the young Gladstone leant over his shoulder
to look at the list of horses.   It happened, according to the
story, to include a colt called Hampden, and William
Gladstone exclaimed, ' Hampden, at any rate, is in his
proper place—between Zeal and Lunacy.' [1]   One is sorry
to spoil so smart a tale, but no horses with these names are
to be found in the chronicles of the great Epsom race
from the year that Doyle entered Eton to that in which his
friend quitted that foundation. [2]

But it hardly needs the repetition of a schoolboy jest, even
if it were well-founded, to show that Mr. Gladstone in his
earliest days was Tory of persuasion, and, on one other
side of his youthful character, there is as little doubt.   The
time had not come when, as the statesman long afterwards

[1] Doyle's ' Reminiscences,' p. 47.

[2] No horses with these names, according to John Frost's ' Turf
Guide for 1825,' were entered for any engagements whatever in that
year, and the story appears to be purely imaginary.

recorded, it was to George Selwyn, who acted as tutor at
Eton for the ten years from 1831, that no small share of the
movement in the direction of religious earnestness which
marked the school of that period, was due.[1]   But Mr.
Gladstone's mind was always of the religious bent which
at one time led him to contemplate the Church as a possible
profession ; and that his schoolboy influence made for good
is attested by the remark of Walter Hamilton, subsequently
Bishop of Salisbury (who was at Eton for four years from
January, 1822), that, although he was a thoroughly idle boy
at the school, he was saved from some worse things by
getting to know William Gladstone.[2]   And it was not
Hamilton alone who thought highly of his schoolmate, for
so promising a student as Hallam, so clever a boy as
Gaskell, alike foretold the greatness of their friend ; and
schoolboy prophecies, often as sanguine, are rarely as safe.

It was not only even in moral and intellectual force that the
future Prime Minister honestly won the favour of his fellows.
His own period of fagging had sat lightly upon him, for he
had served his eldest brother, then in the fifth form ; and he
made the burden equally light to those who, in turn, served
under himself.   One of these, John Smith Mansfield, in
later days a metropolitan magistrate, afterwards declared
that William Gladstone was not exacting, and that his
fag had an easy time ; and recalled him as a good-looking,
but rather delicate youth, with a pale face and brown curling
hair, always tidy and well-dressed.   And not alone did he
show kindness to his fags : he took an active part in protest-
ing against a cruel practice then annually indulged in towards
the lower animals by some of the Eton boys at a fair ; and,
if it be thought that this was no more than any high-spirited

---

[1] Mr. Gladstone in the *Times*, April 17, 1878.
[2] H. P. Liddon's ' Walter Kerr Hamilton,' p. 2.

and generous-hearted lad would have done in the early 'twenties,' it may be recalled that not until 1823 was the first law placed upon the statute-book for preventing cruelty to horses and cattle; that, even then, its author could not persuade Parliament to prohibit bull-baiting and dog-fighting; and that it was not for another ten years, despite constant effort, that the baiting of bulls, bears, and badgers was, with cock-fighting and other cruel sports, put down by law. And that the young scholar would have fulfilled the threat traditionally attributed to him to use his fists, if that were necessary, against the wantonly cruel, may be considered certain from the fact that, when the now defunct *Morning Chronicle* was proposed to be discontinued by the Eton Debating Society on the ground of its frequent prize-fight reports, the motion was lost by the casting-vote [1] of the future colleague of Palmerston, who is understood to have been the last English Premier to patronise 'the ring.'

Eton, at the period of William Gladstone's entrance, contained some 540 scholars, and Keate, of flogging memory, was head-master. Various tales are told of the encounters between them, and it is certain that, at least once, the future Premier was flogged. The story, as related by the historian of Eton, runs to the effect that the youth, when acting as præpostor, left out of the bill the name of a friend who had omitted a lesson. This Keate discovered, and, before commanding him to kneel, charged him with a breach of trust, to which the lad replied, ' I beg your Threatened with a pardon, sir; it would have been a breach flogging. of trust if I had undertaken the office of præpostor by my own wish, but it was forced upon me.' [2]   Another

[1] Sir Henry Cunningham's ' Earl Canning,' p. 28.

[2] H. C. Maxwell Lyte's ' History of Eton College,' 2nd edit., p. 365n.

version of the answer, given in the most elaborate account yet written of Mr. Gladstone's Eton career, is, 'If you please, sir, my præpostorship would have been an office of trust if I had sought it of my own accord, but it was forced upon me;'[1] and both tales agree that Keate considered the reply so clever that he let the offender off. But that was not Keate's way; and Mr. Gladstone, while later declaring that he did not remember pleading the excuse attributed to him, felt certain he was flogged. It is pleasanter, however, to recall another anecdote, which tells of how, in the earliest full year of his school-life, William Gladstone, Arthur Hallam, and (Sir) James Colville, afterwards a distinguished judge, were singled out by Keate to be called up before him weekly, because the three young friends seemed to take an interest in their lessons.

But some of the elaborately told stories concerning Mr. Gladstone's schooldays have to be dismissed as fiction. The most interesting of all is that which has narrated how, on a visit to his old school on the Fourth of June, 1824, Canning, then Secretary of State for Foreign Affairs, not merely walked and talked with the youngest son of his leading supporter while sitting for Liverpool, but gave the lad advice concerning his verses, and discussed with him the position of affairs in South America; but it was of the eldest brother, and not of William Gladstone, that the statesman took marked notice. His one clear association with the greatest of all 'political adventurers,' for whom, as he has said, his father had a profound and almost semi-idolatrous veneration, was in July, 1821, two months be-

His acquaintance with Canning.

fore he first went to Eton, and then at the opening of the Prince's Dock at Liverpool, a ceremony which Canning performed, and at which

---

[1] James Brinsley Richards' 'Mr. Gladstone's Schooldays,' *Temple Bar*, vol. lxvii.

William Gladstone, 'not as a very distinguished or conspicuous personage,' assisted.

Canning was, indeed, the lad's political hero, for his first literary effort in English now to be discovered—though some of the Greek verses he composed at Eton are preserved at Hawarden in an old copy-book—is a poetic fragment in the statesman's praise, written in January, 1825, when its author was little more than fifteen. As published in the *Eton Miscellany*, nearly three years later, and after Canning's death, it ran thus :

> Yet while I mourn with low and feeble strain,
>   The dearth of children of the lofty lyre,
> And while I weep for that Parnassian plain,
>   Where wont to gleam the Poet's noble fire ;
> Where old Mæonides sublimer sings,
> Than e'er on earth, of heroes, sages, kings ;
> Where Virgil quaffs the waters of the blest—
> The sacred bands in seats of gladness rest—
> Yet let my Muse her humble tribute pay
> To Canning's Eloquence, to Canning's lay.
> Say not the flow'rs of poesy are dead,
> While the Nine wreathe with laurels Canning's head :
> Say not the fount of eloquence is dry,
> It springs from Canning's lip, and sparkles in his eye !
> Yet, ah ! the bright but evanescent fire
> Burn'd but to die, and gleam'd but to expire !
> The buds of Poesy the Muses gave,
> Neglected lie, and wither in the grave.
> Far other tasks his patriot care demand,
>   Far other thoughts his ardent soul employ ;
> The helm of England needs his guiding hand,
>   A nation's wonder, and a nation's joy.
> He is the pilot that our God hath sent
> To guide the vessel that was tost and rent !
> Exalt thine head, Etona, and rejoice,
> Glad in a nation's loud acclaiming voice ;
> And 'mid the tumult and the clamour wild,
> Exult in Canning—say, he was thy child.

At the 'election' of 1826, William Gladstone is found in the upper division of the fifth form, together with Arthur Hallam, John (afterwards Lord) Hanmer, Frederic Rogers, Alexander Kinglake, Henry Glynne (younger brother of Sir Stephen) and Hastings Doyle; with Milnes Gaskell, Charles Kean, (Sir) Edward Creasy, Lord Lincoln (afterwards Duke of Newcastle), James Bruce, Algernon Percy (sixth Duke of Northumberland), James Hope (better known as Hope-Scott), Charles Canning (son of the statesman, first Earl Canning and 'Clemency' Canning by a very different creation), and Colin Blackburn (subsequently a judge of the Queen's Bench) among the younger scholars.[1]

Several of these lads were members of the Eton Debating Society—'Pop,' as it was commonly called—which Member of the Eton William Gladstone joined in the autumn of Debating Society. 1825. Doyle, who, though two 'removes' below him, had been previously a member, heard his maiden speech made a fortnight after his election, and which happened to be upon education, of which all he appears to have remembered was the sonorous opening phrase: 'Sir, in this age of increased and still increasing civilisation.' But he noted that, after his friend's arrival, the institution doubled and even trebled its numbers, and the discussions became much fuller of interest and animation.[2] At the meetings, held over the shop of a pastry cook, William Gladstone for the two more years he remained at Eton was a frequent debater; and William Cowper, afterwards Lord Mount-Temple, in his diary recorded of his schoolfellow's last address, made in the month he left, and upon the not specially exhilarating question, 'Whether the Peerage Bill

[1] H. E. C. Stapylton's 'Eton School Lists,' pp. 122-33.
[2] Doyle's 'Reminiscences,' pp. 33-35.

of 1719 was calculated to be beneficial or not?' that he 'spoke very well: will be a great loss to the Society.'

The Society, which voted thanks to its brilliant member for the speech referred to, owed, indeed, much to his energy in more than one direction. In a contribution to the *Eton Miscellany*, he ardently supported that body. 'It may amuse the gay to laugh,' he exclaimed, 'it may gratify the narrow-minded to rail at such an institution. . . *Scarcely any one* of the great orators of this country has risen to so proud a distinction without previously trying his strength, maturing his faculties, and remedying his defects in a *private Debating Society*. But I may here be met by a triumphant assertion, that they were not societies of boys which have thus contributed to form our orators and statesmen. I am happy to have to adduce what, I believe, is a strikingly powerful and conclusive answer. Of the very few distinguished young speakers in the House of Commons, as it exists at present, (altogether, perhaps, not more than four or five,) three, and those perhaps the first—I mean Lord Morpeth,[1] the Hon. E. G. Stanley,[2] and Lord Castlereagh,[3] have been members of the ETON DEBATING SOCIETY!' After pressing its claims still further upon his readers, whom he evidently considered to care little for the subject, the young Gladstone concluded with this outburst: 'If there is to a humble and unknown writer like myself any truly just and legitimate object of ambition, it is that of being known as one who

[1] Later 7th Earl of Carlisle, and a member of various Whig Administrations.

[2] Afterwards 14th Earl of Derby and Prime Minister. Portraits of this statesman and Mr. Gladstone now hang in the room of the Debating Society they did so much to make illustrious.

[3] Nephew of the historic Castlereagh.

E

feared not the tide of popular prejudice, or the gale of popular displeasure; whose wish it was, to do service even to the unwilling, and to have his name connected with that of an institution which will ever be applauded by Candour and Justice, as it has ever been calumniated by Folly and Misrepresentation.'

Even the frequent meetings of ' Pop ' did not suffice to fill the youthful orator's desire for speaking; and with Gaskell, Charles Canning, and one or two others, he established a more select society, which assembled on summer afternoons in a garden.   Concerning one of such meetings when, under the tuition of Gaskell, the lads were learning the noisy art of parliamentary interruption, Doyle tells how his tutor, overhearing, thought them to be under the influence of liquor, and after having William Gladstone's explanation, only reluctantly refrained from handing him over, with his subordinate orators, to be flogged for drunkenness.[1]   This readiness to suspect intoxication is curious evidence of the then prevailing customs at the school; and an equally instructive picture of the pastimes of the Eton boys of the period is given in a letter of December, 1827, of Charles Canning to Gaskell, in which he mentioned William Gladstone as, with himself, belonging to a club, the members of which, upon convenient occasions, 'went up to Salt Hill to bully the fat waiter, eat toasted cheese, and drink egg wine'; and he added, 'in our meetings, as well as at almost every time, Gladstone went by the name of Mr. Tipple.'[2]   But 'Mr. Tipple's dissipation must have been of a mild order, for the year in which this letter was written had witnessed the development of his talents in a new direction, and one which demanded much

His Eton nickname.

---

[1] Doyle's ' Reminiscences,' pp. 37, 38.
[2] Cunningham's ' Earl Canning,' p. 29.

energy and attention. Recollections of the *Microcosm*, the Eton magazine for which Canning, over forty years before, had written and the *Etonian*, which Praed had edited in 1820—and some of the contributors to which the youngest Gladstone had met during his earliest years at Eton, when they breakfasted with his eldest brother—may be believed to have implanted in him the idea of starting a similar serial.

The *Eton Miscellany*, 'by Bartholomew Bouverie, now of Eton College,' was, accordingly, commenced on June 4th, 1827; and it ran to ten parts, of which *Edits the Eton* were made two volumes, the first being *Miscellany.* dated on the title-page, 'June—July, 1827,' and the second, 'October—November, 1827.' George Selwyn and William Gladstone acted as joint-editors, carrying their division of labour to such a point, indeed, that the opening address, 'To the Many-Headed Monster! An Epistle, Dedicatory, Explanatory, and Conciliatory,' was written in halves. Selwyn contributed the first portion, this conclud-ing with the striking passage usually, though wrongfully, attri-buted to his colleague: 'But in my present undertaking there is one gulph in which I fear to sink; and that gulph is Lethe. There is one stream which I dread my inability to stem—it is the tide of Popular Opinion. . . . Still, there is something within me that bids me hope that I may be able to glide prosperously down the stream of public estimation, or, in the words of Virgil:

"—Celerare viam rumore secundo." '

It was at this point that William Gladstone commenced his part thus: 'With hopes like these, however founded, I, being minded to secure for myself eternal fame, do hereby declare to the world my determination to take up the trade

of authorship.'   And in the same vein of burlesque bombast
he proceeded to the close.

The contributors to the *Miscellany* included Doyle, Gaskell,
Hallam, and Rogers; but the two editors were the most pro-
lific, though, for the second volume Selwyn,
Its contributors. who had now gone to Cambridge, could do
little in comparison with his coadjutor.   That coadjutor for
the first number of all furnished a rhymed epilogue to his
colleague's opening address; but of more interest was his
own introduction to the second part, wherein he wrote with
unconscious prophecy: 'I shall now proceed to bring
before the public some New Members of the Cabinet.
Though my superscription is alarmingly political, I can
assure my readers that the contagion has extended no
further.   I love, like some other people, to give to my proceedings an air of importance: and those whom I shall
now mention are simply companions whom I have admitted
into my Cabinet to aid me in conducting those weighty
affairs in which I have been, am, and hope to continue,
engaged.'   And among his new companions was one who
'would rather keep company with a hyena than with a
Radical.'

Of the other Gladstonian writings in the first volume
beyond those which fell to the task of co-editor, a transla-
The Gladstone contributions. tion of a chorus from the ' Hecuba' of Euri-
pides is an early specimen of work which
later he accomplished with greater ease, while a poem on
Richard Cœur de Lion exhibited the facility with which a
clever schoolboy could frame some 250 lines of sounding
verse.   A paper on 'Lethe,' modelled upon Swift's 'Battle of
the Books,' related how rapidly all printed things descend into
the Lake of Oblivion.   ' In the falling column I perceived
a great number of foolscap sheets of paper, some single,

some double, some in blue covers. These, I was told, came down only for about three or four months in the year, usually from February to June, and were Parliamentary Reports and Proceedings, and other papers procured by divers persons of motion-making notoriety in the upper regions. . . With these were an immense number of political pamphlets, of " Substances of Speeches," etc., which, after making an amazing flutter and hubbub in the upper regions for a brief space of time, all hastened to their common destination.'

The Gladstone contributions to the first volume numbered thirteen, while Selwyn's were ten; but for the second, while the latter's were no more than five, the former were twenty-two. In the introduction to the opening number of that second volume, the future Liberal leader drew a sketch of a supposititious 'Oliver Quincy,' in whose eyes 'incendiaries of Rebellion are the best friends of Freedom; and the haranguers of mobs the regenerators of mankind. No martyrs can occupy a more distinguished place in his calendar than those assigned to the men who have felt the severity of laws making treason a crime and obedience a merit.' And it was over the signature of 'Oliver Quincy,' whose Utopia was 'in the land of—" Freedom, Equality, Higgledum-piggledum,"' that William Gladstone published a burlesque 'Ode to the Shade of Wat Tyler,' which thus commenced :—

> Shade of him, whose valiant tongue
> On high the song of freedom sung ;
> Shade of him, whose mighty soul
> Would pay no taxes on his poll ;
> Though, swift as lightning, civic sword
> Descended on thy fated head,
> The blood of England's boldest pour'd,
> And number'd Tyler with the dead !

Still may thy spirit flap its wings,
At midnight, o'er the couch of kings ;
And peer and prelate tremble, too,
In dread of nightly interview !
With patriot gesture of command,
    With eyes, that like thy forges gleam,
Lest Tyler's voice and Tyler's hand,
    Be heard and seen in nightly dream.

Of the remaining ten verses, the most striking are the concluding :

I hymn the gallant and the good,
From Tyler down to Thistlewood ;
My muse the trophies grateful sings,
The deeds of Miller and of Ings ;[1]
She sings of all, who, soon or late
    Have burst subjection's iron chain,
Have seal'd the bloody despot's fate,
    Or cleft a peer or priest in twain.

Shades, that soft Sedition woo,
Around the haunts of Peterloo ![2]
That hover o'er the meeting halls,
Where many a voice Stentorian bawls !
Still flit the sacred choir around,
    With ' Freedom ' let the garrets ring,
And vengeance soon in thunder sound,
    On church, and constable, and king.

And still the weaving race regale,
On patriotic beer and ale !

[1] Thistlewood and Ings were hanged for their share in the Cato Street Conspiracy, which was a plot for murdering the members of Lord Liverpool's Cabinet in February, 1820.

[2] So-called from the fatal attack by the yeomanry upon a Radical gathering in St. Peter's Fields, Manchester, in August, 1819.

Or let them quaff the dingy stream
To ' Tyler, Liberty, and Steam ! '
And, weaving, let them dream they form
  A banner for the bold and free,
To ride amidst the raging storm
  In brightness and in majesty.

And whether you to spy it please
A cotton-spun Demosthenes ;
Or whether, from the shuttle's throw,
Come forth a weaving Cicero ;
Or whether, midst of smoke and steam,
  Some youthful Tyler's buds expand,
His race from thraldom to redeem,
  And level, yet exalt, the land ;

Still 'mid the cotton and the flax
Warm let the glow of Freedom wax :
Still 'mid the shuttles and the steam,
Bright let the flame of Freedom gleam !
So men of taxes, men of law,
  In alley dun, and murky lane,
Shall find a Tyler or a Straw
  To cleave the despot's slaves in twain !

' These extravagances,' the young editor wrote of the
imaginary contributor over whose name the ' Ode ' appeared, ' are the weeds which a generous soil alone can
produce : which, while by their native rankness they show
its exuberance, by their verdure and their vigour, they bear
equally sure testimony to its fertility. Hence it is to be
trusted, that the hand of experience may remove them, and
plant in their stead shoots of a more worthy origin, and a
more benignant growth.'

In another of his contributions to the second volume,
the now sole editor—for he had then lost not only the active
aid of Selwyn but the occasional help of Hallam, both having

gone to Cambridge—went out of his path, in an essay giving
preference to modern over ancient genius, to pay a high
tribute to Canning, who had just passed away.

Tribute to Canning. 'It is,' he wrote, 'for those who revered
him in the plenitude of his meridian glory, to mourn over
him in the darkness of his premature extinction : to mourn
over the hopes that are buried in his grave, and the evils
that arise from his withdrawal from the scene of life.
Surely if eloquence never excelled and seldom equalled—if
an expanded mind, and a judgment whose vigour was
paralleled only by its soundness—if a brilliant wit—if a glowing imagination—if a warm heart and an unbending firmness
—could have strengthened the frail tenure, and prolonged
the momentary duration of human existence, that man had
been immortal!   But nature could endure no longer.
Thus has Providence ordained that, inasmuch as the intellect of man is more brilliant, it shall be more short-lived ;
as its sphere is more expanded, more swiftly is it summoned
away. . . . Assailed by the pitiless abuse of some, who
forgot the period of his splendid services to their cause,
that they might indulge in unlimited condemnation of one
who, during by far the greater part of his political career,
had fought the same battles with themselves—torn in mind
and harassed in body—he fell, like his great master, Pitt,
a victim to his proud and exalted station.   Distant from all
extremes—firm in principle and conciliatory in action—the
friend of Improvement and the enemy of Innovation,
England fondly looked to him for her peace and glory ;
who, *from first to last*, had been her faithful servant and her
true friend.   The decrees of inscrutable Wisdom are unknown to us : but if ever there was a man for whose sake
it was meet to indulge the kindly, though frail, feelings of
our nature—for whom the tear of sorrow was, to us, both

prompted by affection and dictated by duty—that man was
GEORGE CANNING.'

The young student's devotion to that statesman was further
shown in the same number of the *Miscellany* by some seventy
lines of 'Reflections in Westminster Abbey, Poem on Canning's
October, 1827,' with the motto, 'How are grave.
the mighty fallen!' In this he bade the stranger to believe

> That Pitt was mortal, and that Canning died!
> Death aim'd the stroke at him, at him alone,
> Claim'd him, the first, the noblest, for his own;
> Knew that, in Him, by one unerring dart,
> He gain'd the fated goal, and pierc'd proud Britain's heart!
> In more than eagle's flight he soar'd on high,
> Yet soar'd to fall, and dazzled but to die!
> 'Mid the high Heavens dropp'd his mounting plume,
> And fell, yet struggling, to the yawning tomb.
> And was there none to aid, and none to save
> His beaming radiance from the murky grave?
> Ten thousand voices, that arise in woe—
> Ten thousand streams of Grief and Pity flow—
> Ten thousand sighs are heav'd, and tears are shed,
> Yet HE lies number'd with the silent dead.
>
> .   .   .   .
>
> O Britain, weeping o'er his ashes, prove
> How true thy faith, how fond thy ceaseless love;
> Yes, all combine: the tears of friend and foe
> Mingle their streams in one, in one unceasing flow.
>
> .   .   .   .
>
> But he hath rais'd his monumental stone
> In Mem'ry's soft and hallow'd shrine alone
> Hath writ, in characters of living flame,
> On Britain's weal, on Britain's heart, his name.
> Oft in the sculptur'd aisle and swelling dome,
> The yawning grave hath giv'n the proud a home;
> Yet never welcom'd from his bright career
> A mightier victim than it welcom'd here!

Again the tomb may yawn—again may Death
Claim the last forfeit of departing breath :
Yet ne'er enshrine, in slumber dark and deep,
A nobler, loftier, prey than where thine ashes sleep ! [1]

Of scarcely less interest, as an indication of the bent of
the Gladstone mind, was an essay 'On Eloquence,' in which
it was claimed that 'the ambition of the most ardent and
aspiring minds is usually directed towards St. Stephen's.
The Tò καλòν of most of those who are at all disposed towards oratorical pursuits is situated within the walls of the
House of Commons.   Visions of joy and honour open on

His theory of   their enraptured sight.   A successful debût
eloquence.   —an offer from the minister—a Secretaryship of State—and even the Premiership itself—are the
objects which form the vista along which a young visionary
loves to look.   But there is a barrier to pass, and an ordeal
to endure : there are such articles as maiden speeches,
sometimes calculated to act more generally and more
forcibly on the lungs of such an audience than the most
violent or the most cutting of all the breezes which Æolus
can boast.   There are such things as roars of coughing, as
well as roars of cheering: and the man ought to be endowed with a considerable share of fortitude and presence
of mind, in addition to natural and acquired powers of
eloquence, who allows his hopes of the one to overcome
his fears of the other.'   Yet what the young Gladstone

---

[1] In 'Musæ Etonenses (*Series Nova*,)' published in 1869, are two Latin
poems by Mr. Gladstone, written while at Eton, and dated 1827 : the
second of these (divided from the other by a poem of Hallam) is an
obvious lament for the death of Canning (vol. ii., pp. xcii., xciii., xcvi.,
xcvii. ; and in the *Contemporary Review* for June, 1893 (No. 330, pp.
782-9), are 'Some Eton Translations,' signed 'W. E. Gladstone, Eton,
1827,' these being two choruses in English from the 'Hecuba'of Eu-
ripides.

wished chiefly to do was not to preach political ambition, but to impress upon his readers the existence, the importance, and the condition of the Eton Debating Society ; and this he did in some passages which have already been given.

Poems—'The Shipwreck,' 'The Ladder of the Law,' 'Guatimozin's Death Song,' all of a sombre cast—formed the bulk of the remaining Gladstonian contributions ; but one, a 'Sonnet to a Rejected Sonnet,' deserves quotation as showing him in his lighter vein : His poems.

> Poor child of Sorrow ! who did'st boldly spring,
>   Like sapient Pallas, from thy parent's brain,
>   All arm'd in mail of proof ! and thou would'st fain
> Leap further yet and, on exulting wing,
> Rise to the summit of the Printer's Press !
>   But cruel hand hath nipp'd thy buds amain,
>   Hath fix'd on thee the darkling inky stain,
> Hath soil'd thy splendour, and defil'd thy dress !
> Where are thy 'full-orb'd moon,' and 'sky serene '?
>   And where thy 'waving foam,' and 'foaming wave '?
> All, all are blotted by the murd'rous pen,
>   And lie unhonour'd in their pap'ry grave !
> Weep, gentle Sonnets ! Sonneteers, deplore !
> And vow—and keep the vow—you'll write no more !

This appeared in the last number of the *Miscellany*, which closed with a valedictory Gladstonian article, entitled 'Metempsychosis and Conclusion.' In this the editor whimsically told of how, knowing 'Bartholomew Bouverie' was leaving Eton, his contributors had assailed him with a demand for rewards. 'I thought to soothe them with fair words, and hoped, betwen giving a little and promising a great deal, to get fairly out of their fangs.' But the plan failed, and they His editorial farewell.

threatened to tear him limb from limb, until each had obtained his legal share. 'GEORGE AUGUSTUS SELWYN led the van, and conducted this formidable array of duns to the attack;' and he was assisted by Doyle, Gaskell, Rogers, and Hallam. 'When each had carried off his limb, or his portion of the trunk, nothing positively remained, save the fingers of the right hand, which have contrived to write this Conclusion, and a small portion of the brain—perhaps my readers may incline to think, none at all. These three fingers, however, whether accompanied or not so, by any portion of the spirit, taste, genius, or industry, of the great Bartholomew, are the property of WILLIAM EWART GLADSTONE. It may be said that he is an unworthy representative of the editor of the Eton Miscellany; and I am confident he will not attempt to deny it. He awaits, with those around him, the sentence of his judges; yet humbly advances this plea, if not a title to acquittal, at least a claim to mitigated punishment—the plea, that his own will did not bring him before the world, or urge him to expose to the scrutinising eye of all beholders efforts, which, like the mean and lowly plants of the impenetrable thicket, may indeed sustain their obscure existence, and bud forth their humble vegetation, beneath the shade and protection of darkness and oblivion, but which wither, droop, and die, when they feel themselves exposed to the penetrating rays of a noon-day sun.' And, with the same anticipatory note of a remarkable future frequently to be heard in his boyish writings, he ended with a tribute to his headmaster Keate, 'knowing, that if it [his own literary work] be doomed to the darkness of oblivion, his approbation may, if any can, avert the miserable destiny; that if, on the contrary, to use the glowing expression of one of the greatest orators of the day, my "name have buoyancy enough to float upon the sea of time," it may there be associated with that of one, whose rebukes we have often merited, but whose approbation it will be our pride and our pleasure to receive.' And with that compliment he repaid Keate for two which the headmaster had accorded to him, for that grim functionary is said not only to have observed upon one occasion that he wished he could hear his pupil at the Debating Society without the latter being aware of his presence; but on another, when the youth told how his father had at first thought of sending him to the Charter-house, Keate rejoined, 'That would have been a pity for both of us, Gladstone—for you and for me.'

Doyle has described how, especially in regard to the *Miscellany's* second volume, the young editor with untiring energy supported the whole burden upon his shoulders; and this zeal secured for him a remarkable prophecy from the former's father. 'It is not,' remarked the elder Doyle to his son, 'that I think Gladstone's papers better than yours or Hallam's, but the force of character he has shown in managing his subordinates, and the combination of ability and power that he has made evident, convince me that such a young man cannot fail to distinguish himself hereafter.'[1] And it has elsewhere been told that, while editing the magazine, he used to stupefy his fags by his prodigious capacity for work, and that, although his table would be littered with 'copy' and proofs, he always found time to do his school-work well.

But of both the *Miscellany* and the Debating Society, the two Eton institutions with which he was most closely associated, another pleasant record has been left. In 'The Poetaster's Plea, a Familiar Epistle to W. E. Gladstone, Esq., M.P.,' first published in 1840, Doyle appealed neither

[1] Doyle's ' Reminiscences,' pp. 45, 46.

to 'the warrior of the state,' nor 'to the man or statesman,'[1] but to

> One of a joyous company, who hied
> Through the green fields along the riverside,
> Those laughing fields which wear for you and me
> A garment of perpetual youth and glee
> Where voices call us, that are heard no more,
> And our 'lost Pleiad' brightens as before.
> To one I turn—the monarch of debate,
> President Minos of our little state,
> Who, when we met to give the world the law
> About Confucius, Cæsar, or Jack Straw,
> Saw with grave face the unremitting flow
> Of puffs and jellies from the shop below ;
> At the right moment, called us to forsake
> Intrusive fruit, and unattending cake ;
> And if unheeded, on the stroke of four,
> With rigid hand closed the still-opening door,
> Denouncing ever after in a trice
> That heinous breach of privilege—'an ice'—
> To one, who in his editorial den
> Clenched grimly an eradicating pen,
> Confronting frantic poets with calm eye,
> And dooming hardened metaphors to die.
> Who, if he found his young adherents fail,
> The ode unfinished, uncommenced the tale,
> With the next number bawling to be fed,
> And its false feeders latitant or fled,
> Sat down unflinchingly to write it all,
> And kept the staggering project from a fall.

In strong contrast to the educational and social influences with which William Gladstone was penetrated while
at Eton, a political influence, by apparent accident, was
exerted upon him at this period which proved as the acorn
to the oak. It was not much vacation-time that he spent

[1] Doyle's 'Miscellaneous Verses,' edition of 1843, pp. 25-27.

at Seaforth. The health of some members of the family necessitated frequent removal to more salubrious air; and various of the Eton vacations were passed at Gloucester, whither his father—anxious for the health of the eldest daughter with an anxiety which, unhappily, proved well-founded—was attracted by a specialist's reputation, and where he became a partner in a local bank. The youngest son could long afterwards claim that he well *His recollections of* knew the ins-and-outs of the place; and his *Gloucester* remembrances included 'a dry but learned or able clergyman named Maitland, the rolling thunder of the Bishop's voice in the Cathedral, and an execution.'[1] But *and Macclesfield.* Macclesfield may claim a more striking place in the earlier biography of Mr. Gladstone, for he has related that it was upon a visit to a silk factory in that place, when he was about eighteen, that there dawned upon his mind the first ray of Free Trade light. Huskisson, *His first leaning to* as President of the Board of Trade under *Free Trade.* Lord Liverpool, had just secured the repeal of the prohibition against the import of French manufactured goods, though levying upon them a duty of 30 per cent.; 'and it is in my recollection,' said Mr. Gladstone, long afterwards, 'that there was a keener detestation of Mr. Huskisson, and a more violent passion roused against him, in consequence of that mild, initial measure, than ever was associated in the Protectionists' camp with the career of Cobden and Bright. I was taken to this manufactory, and they produced the English silk handkerchief which they were in the habit of making, and which they thought it so cruel to be competed with by the silk handkerchiefs of France . . . . and what I thought when they showed me those

[1] Letter of Mr. Gladstone to the *Gloucestershire Standard*, dated Hawarden, Jan. 9, 1880.

handkerchiefs was, How detestable they really are, and what
in the world can be the object of the policy of coaxing,
nursing, coddling up manufactures to produce goods such as
those, which you ought to be ashamed of exhibiting?'[1]

Not very long after this experience, and at the Christmas
of 1827, he left Eton. He had been in the sixth form a

Dec., 1827.
Leaves Eton. year, but had missed becoming Captain
of Oppidans, a position attained only by
seniority, because a boy who had entered the school before
him had remained longer than was customary. He had
secured all the learning Eton could give ; he had imperish-
ably associated his name with the school; and what he
afterwards observed of George Selwyn—that he was linked

His love for the
school. to Eton with a love surpassing even the love
of Etonians [2]—was but a foreshadowing of
what, when nearing three score years and ten, he told the
collegians themselves : that his attachment to what he considered the queen of all schools increased with the lapse of
years.[3]   And, while he was proud of his connection with
Eton, the pride was reciprocal. After his school-time, he
revisited her as spectator, as examiner, and as orator.
Within a few days of his first promotion to Cabinet rank,
Etonians of all shades of opinion, in annual festival assembled, acclaimed him as their own ; more than once
in his latest days he lectured to his schoolfellows, far removed; and with Eton his name will be associated for
his honour and her glory as long as the name of either is
spoken by human tongue.

[1] Speech at Dundee, Oct. 29, 1890.

[2] Mr. Gladstone in the *Times*, April 17, 1878.

[3] Lecture at Eton, July 6, 1878.

IV.—AT OXFORD.

IT was in December, 1827, that the Eton education was ended; and on January 13th, 1828, according to the Dean's Book of Entries, 'Guilhelmus Ewart Glad-   January, 1828. stone' was admitted as a commoner of   Admitted at Oxford. Christ Church, Oxford.   But for some months he read with Dr. Turner, at Wilmslow, Cheshire; and it was after that divine had been appointed Bishop of Calcutta that he proceeded in the autumn to the University.   The Oxford of that day was far removed in details, though not in essentials, from the Oxford of this: in religion it was the home of a respectable Churchmanship, and in politics of a decided Toryism; while in learning, though much of its product was sound, it was as yet untouched with that mystic entity, the spirit of the age.   The ecclesiastical upheaval, known as the Oxford Movement, was still to make the dry bones of its traditional High Churchmanship live; but there was already in the University air a feeling of unrest, and Mr. Gladstone was a freshman when Peel astounded the nation by submitting that measure of Catholic Emancipation he had so long opposed, and convulsed Oxford by resigning the seat which Canning had never been able to secure, of which Canning's greatest rival was now to be deprived, and which the ablest disciple of both was in his turn to win by brilliancy and lose by breadth.

A pleasant glimpse of William Gladstone, at the period after his leaving Eton and when he was preparing for

F

Oxford, is to be found in a home-letter of Arthur Stanley, whose early tuition at Seaforth has been described. Writing in the summer of 1828, and just before going to Rugby, the younger lad said : 'William Gladstone is at home now, and last Tuesday, I and one of the other boys were invited to breakfast with him ; so we went, had breakfast in grand style, went into the garden and devoured strawberries, which were there in great abundance, unchained the great Newfoundland, and swam him in the pond; we walked about the garden, went into the house and saw beautiful pictures of Shakespeare's plays, and came away at twelve o'clock. It was very good fun, and I don't think I was very shy, for I talked to William Gladstone almost all the time about all sorts of things. He is so very good-natured, and I like him very much. He talked a great deal about Eton, and said that it was a very good place for those that liked boating and Latin verses. I think, from what he said, I might get to like it. . . . He was very good-natured to us all the time, and lent me books to read when we went away.'[1] One of those books was 'The Etonian ;' and there is something very pleasant in this picture of the elder youth, fresh from his triumphs at a public school, doing his best to cheer the younger, just about to enter upon that phase of life.

As an undergraduate of Christ Church—the College which has given seven other Prime Ministers to the nineteenth century, including Mr. Gladstone's own successor, Lord Rosebery[2]—William Gladstone had no part in the electoral turmoil which marked Oxford in the February of 1829.

June, 1828.
Arthur Stanley and William Gladstone.

Undergraduate of Christ Church.

[1] Prothero's ' Stanley,' vol i., p. 22.

[2] The list is : Grenville, Liverpool, Canning, Peel, Derby, Gladstone, Salisbury, and Rosebery.

The son of his father might have been expected to sympathise with Peel when that statesman startled the nation by proposing Catholic Emancipation ; but the line adopted by Newman, then a tutor of Oriel—who, though supporting Catholic relief in principle, considered that Peel, by his sudden change, had not used the University well— may have been his.　For, although at the Union Debating Society two years later, Mr. Gladstone defended the results of the Roman Catholic Relief Act, he had *His opinion of* in the meantime moved and carried a *Catholic Emancipation.* declaration that the Wellington Adminis- tration, of which Peel was a chief member, was undeserving of the country's confidence.　And ten years later, he under- took to present to the House of Commons a petition for that measure's repeal from the Moderator of the Presbytery of Tain, an ancient royal burgh in his mother's native county of Ross.[1]

Oxford at first must have seemed strange to Mr. Gladstone, for, as has been said, Hallam and George Selwyn, his chief Eton friends, had gone to Cambridge ; but Doyle and Charles Canning, as well as Stephen and Henry Denison, all from Eton, were with him at Christ Church, and Rogers and Bruce were at Oriel, while Lincoln, James Hope, and Charles Wordsworth were likewise at *His University* Oxford, and it was there acquaintance was *friends.* first made with Sidney Herbert, Archibald Tait, and Henry Manning.　Mr. Gladstone had come to the University well prepared by nature and training to take part in the progress of so brilliant a band.　Eton had led him almost imper- ceptibly to be a student ; Oxford taught him, as he himself has said, to value truth and to follow it at all hazard ; and, entering the University with a reputation for high aim and

[1] May 15, 1839 : ' Mirror of Parliament ' (1839), p. 2446.

great achievement, he strengthened that reputation with his years.

In his second term, Mr. Gladstone was elected to the Oxford Union, the debating society which remains fam-

November, 1829.
Joins the Union. ous; and, as a probationary member, he was present at an often-described discussion in November, 1829, between representatives of the two ancient English Universities, as to whether Shelley or Byron was the superior poet. Doyle, when in after life he recalled the circumstances of this debate, was disposed to speak slightingly of Mr. Gladstone in connection with it, observing that the latter 'had really very little to do with the business, except that he came afterwards to supper—a feat that might have been accomplished with equal success by a man of much inferior genius.'[1]   But the record of Monck-

Meets
Monckton Milnes. ton Milnes (the first Lord Houghton), one of the Cambridge visitors, is most to be trusted, for that was contemporary.   'The man that *took* me most,' Milnes wrote to his mother, 'was the youngest Gladstone of Liverpool—I am sure, a very superior person.'[2]

A month after this debate—on December 24th, 1829, according to the records of Christ Church—he was made Student of the House; and he set himself with vigour to the task of learning.   His general bearing at the University was what might have been anticipated from his conduct at

His bearing at the
University. Eton.   He was hospitable but averse from excess; he spoke his mind freely in condemnation of any conduct which appeared to him unseemly; he subscribed to the Society for the Promotion of Christian Knowledge; and he was noted for his regular attendance at

---

[1] Doyle's 'Reminiscences,' p. 110.

[2] T. Wemyss Reid's 'Life of Lord Houghton,' vol. i., p. 78.

chapel. His religious experiences were varied, and his spirit of inquiry led him to brave punishment for listening to the words of those outside the pale of his own Church. 'The most adventurous thing I ever did at Oxford in Mr. Gladstone's company,' afterwards said Doyle, 'if it really were adventurous, as I find he still asserts it to have been, was when I allowed myself to be taken to dissenting chapels. We were rewarded by hearing Chalmers preach on two occasions, and Rowland Hill at another time. . . . Mr. Gladstone thought, and still thinks, I believe, that we should have been rusticated had we been found out. I didn't and don't.'[1] So much for Doyle's version: Mr. Gladstone's is different, for he gives Hope as his companion upon these excursions in search of religious experience. Writing after that friend's death, he recorded their 'partnership on two occasions in a proceeding which in Oxford was at that time, and perhaps would have been at any time, singular enough. At the hazard of severe notice, and perhaps punishment, we went together to the Baptist chapel of the place, once to hear Dr. Chalmers and the other time to hear Mr. Rowland Hill.'[2] It will be seen how the former of these great preachers, a very few years afterwards, influenced an important portion of Mr. Gladstone's political life.

Among his acquaintances at the University, in addition to those with whom he became publicly or privately linked, was Martin Farquhar Tupper, later to earn a curious and transient fame as author of ' Proverbial Philosophy.' Tupper has told how this connection commenced after their taking the Communion together, and how it was cemented when both were members of an Aristotle class

[1] Doyle's ' Reminiscences,' p. 101.
[2] ' Memoirs of J. R. Hope-Scott,' vol. ii., p. 274.

under the tutorship of Robert Biscoe of Christ Church, and of which, among a number destined to be famous, 'the central figure was *Gladstone*—ever from youth up the beloved and admired of many personal intimates (although some may be politically his opponents) : always the foremost man, warm-hearted, earnest, hard-working, and religious, he had a following even in his teens.'[1] Not far from thirty years later, Tupper gave expression to his old admiration in the lines—

Tupper as a fellow-collegian.

> Gladstone, through youth and manhood many a year,
> 　My constant heart hath followed thee with praise
> 　As 'good and faithful ;' in thy words and ways
> Pure-minded, just, and simple, and sincere ;
> 　And as, with early, half-prophetic ken,
> I hailed thy greatness in my college days,
> 　The coming man to guide and govern men,
> 　How gladly that instinctive prescience then
> Now do I see fulfilled—because, thou art
> 　Our England's eloquent tongue, her wise free hand,
> To pour, wherever is her world-wide mart,
> 　The horn of plenty over every land ;
> Because, by all the powers of mind and lip
> Thou art the crown of Christian statesmanship.[2]

But, with a fine impartiality, Tupper included in the same volume what he himself called 'a well-known palinode,' commencing :

> Beware of mere delusive eloquence,

and a still more caustic lyric, beginning with

> Glozing tongue whom none can trust,

and so forth, as a 'caution against a great man's special

[1] M. F. Tupper's ' My Life as an Author,' pp. 54, 55.
[2] ' Three Hundred Sonnets,' No. 53 : *ibid.*, p. 364.

gift, so proverbially dangerous ; ' but even for this—and after Mr. Gladstone had invited him to his residence to meet Garibaldi—there was some compensation in that, during the statesman's last Oxford contest, Tupper published a copy of verses, ending with

> Orator, statesman, scholar, wit, and sage,
> The Crichton—more, the Gladstone of the age.

In other ways, Tupper must have proved a trying acquaintance ; and he unconsciously furnished a strong testimony to Mr. Gladstone's patience and good-temper when he wrote that ' multitudes of letters through many years have passed between us, wherein, if I have sometimes ventured to praise or to blame, I have always been answered both gratefully and modestly.' [1]

The Aristotle class by no means exhausted Mr. Gladstone's outer mental energies. He attended Burton's lectures on Divinity and Pusey's on Hebrew ; but it was at the Union that he made his most noteworthy mark. On February 11th, 1830, he was elected on the committee, and delivered his maiden speech. Later in the year, he became Secretary and subsequently President (in succession to Manning, afterwards Cardinal Archbishop of Westminster) ; and in the former capacity his minutes, which still exist, are remarked as having been neat in form though occasionally exuberant in expression.[2] As soon as he dawned upon the Union, he took the first place ; [3] and that was the verdict not only of Doyle but of all his contemporaries. Yet, not content with

1830.
Office-bearer of the Union.

[1] *Ibid.,* p. 54.

[2] E. W. B. Nicholson's ' The Oxford Union,' *Macmillan's Magazine,* vol. xxviii., p. 569.

[3] Doyle's ' Reminiscences,' p. 113.

even the glories of the Union, Mr. Gladstone established a select debating club, consisting mainly of Christ Church men. This was familiarly called 'The Weg,' after its founder's initials ; but Mr. Gladstone himself has named it ' The Oxford Essay Club,'[1] and it has also been known as ' The Twelve Friends of Charles Wordsworth.' [2] Frederick Denison Maurice having recorded, in an autobiographical letter written in 1870, that ' the circumstance of belonging to a small society at Cambridge brought me into a similar one at Oxford, founded by Mr. Gladstone, to which, otherwise, I should never have been admitted,' Mr. Gladstone has explained that he may have established it on the model of 'The Apostles' at Cambridge, though he believed that that was a more general society. The members of ' The Weg ' assembled in each other's rooms in turn to hear an essay from its occupant ; and it is owing to this circumstance that so excellent an idea has been preserved of what Mr. Gladstone was like when at the University, for this may be gathered from Maurice's remarks to his son more than thirty-five years after he had left Oxford. ' I am glad you have seen Gladstone, and have been able to judge a little of what his face indicates. It is a very expressive one ; hard-worked as you say, and not perhaps specially happy ; more indicative of struggle than of victory, though not without promise of that. I admire him for his patient attention to details, and for the pains which he takes to secure himself from being absorbed in them by entering into large and generous studies. He has preserved the type which I can remember that he bore at the University thirty-six years ago, though it has undergone various developments.' [3]

[1] Hope-Scott's ' Memoirs,' vol. ii., p. 274.
[2] *Ibid.*, vol. i., p. 25.
[3] ' Life of F. D. Maurice,' vol. ii., p. 557.

References to his powers, made contemporaneously, are, of course, more to be trusted as indicating the high expectations he aroused at Oxford than any reminiscences compiled in later life. Among the former such an opinion as that already quoted from Milnes is in its degree no more emphatic than the casual reference, in a letter to Charles Wordsworth by Lord Lincoln, to 'some of the select studious men,' among whom was Mr. Gladstone,[1] or Doyle's remark to the same correspondent, with the half-laugh which embodied a whole truth, that 'the illustrious Gladstone has been bachelorised.'[2]   There is, indeed, one fellow-student who has not joined in the general chorus of praise. 'Gladstone,' wrote Ashton Oxenden, once Bishop of Montreal, 'was a hard-reading, quiet, and well-conducted man, but by no means accounted so great a luminary as he has since become.'[3]   But that was said after a lapse of sixty years, and when Mr. Gladstone had done much to arouse antagonism in the clerical mind.

After the long vacation of 1830, Mr. Gladstone became one of the private pupils of Charles Wordsworth, nephew of the poet, and subsequently Bishop of St. An-   Pupil of Charles drews; and he had as companions Hope,   Wordsworth. Manning, Doyle, and Hamilton, these being added to a few months later by Lincoln, (Sir) Thomas Dyke Acland, and Charles Canning. Wordsworth was one of the finest of the younger Latinists of the day, and the effect of his teaching was seen in the success of Mr. Gladstone, concerning whom the tutor later mentioned for the encouragement of others that at first his compositions, though

1 August, 1831 : Charles Wordsworth's 'Annals of My Early Life,' p. 100.

2 January, 1832 : *Ibid.*

3 Bishop Oxenden's 'History of My Life,' p. 20.

generally correct, were scarcely such as might have been
expected from a distinguished Eton scholar, being decidedly
stiff and wanting in grace ; but that eventually he became
an elegant composer.[1]   In English, however, his fault was
a vague diffuseness ; and it is said that Hussey, afterwards
Professor of Ecclesiastical History, who was tutor of both
William Gladstone and Christopher Wordsworth (subsequently Bishop of Lincoln), observed that, while the latter's
compositions were exquisite in workmanship, without much
substance, the former's were full of grandeur, if one could
only understand their meaning.[2]

Long after the Oxford days, Charles Wordsworth bore
testimony not only to his pupil's 'elegant Latinity,' but to
'the irreproachable excellence of Mr. Gladstone's character
as a young man ; the steady, unremitting perseverance of
his studious habits; of the thoroughness of his studious
work ; the high reputation which he brought with him from
Eton ; the friendships he had formed there, and maintained
at Christ Church ; the early proofs which he gave of his
remarkable powers as a speaker at the Union ; and the
combination of gifts and qualities shown by him in that and
in other ways, which made me (and, I doubt not, others
also) feel no less sure than of my own existence that Gladstone, our then Christ Church undergraduate, would one
day rise to be Prime Minister of England.'   To this high
praise he added 'one other trait not unimportant, and due,
I believe, to his staunch Presbyterian upbringing—I doubt
whether any man of his standing in the University habitually
read the Bible more, or knew it better, than Gladstone did.
Whether it was owing to this, or the natural sobriety of his

---

[1] Charles Wordsworth's ' A Chapter of Autobiography,' *Fortnightly
Review*, New Series, vol. xxxiv., p. 50*n*.

Speaker, Nov. 14, 1891, p. 594.

temperament, or to both combined, it is certain, moreover, that notwithstanding the high esteem with which he was regarded, and notwithstanding all his capacity for future distinction, of which he could not but be conscious, he showed no signs of pride, or vanity, or affectation; on the contrary, I should say he was uniformly modest and unassuming. No doubt, he was ambitious, but no more so than he ought to have been.'[1]

His University ambition was destined, however, to receive a check, and Charles Wordsworth was the confidant of his regret. This first keen disappointment was failure to secure the Ireland Scholarship, awarded for classical composition. To win this he had laboured hard. Three days after the Christmas of 1830, he wrote from Leamington to his private tutor—' for fear that you should infer from the non-reception of my threatened packet, that I have been keeping Christmas in the accustomed manner, and altogether unmindful of severer engage-ments'—that, while he could not pretend to much diligence, he had been working at his Latin in order to unite the objects of the schools with the winning of the Ireland. But, obviously to his own surprise, he failed; and, writing from Christ Church, he supplied Charles Wordsworth with particulars of 'the strange result.' ' The successful candidate,' he said, ' is Brancker of Wadham. Perhaps you do not know who Brancker is? he is a Shrewsbury boy, *i.e.*, has not yet left school, and sent up here to stand by way of practising himself, and to return probably by to-night's mail. This is all very funny. I now proceed to give you details. In the rear of Brancker are Scott[2] and your hopeful pupil placed *æquales*. Next

March, 1831.
Tries for the Ireland Scholarship,

but fails.

---

[1] Charles Wordsworth's ' Chapter of Autobiography,' pp. 50, 51.

[2] Afterwards Dean of Rochester, on the recommendation of Mr. Gladstone in 1870.

Allies,[1] then Herbert of Balliol,[2] and then Grove,[3] these are all the worthies whose names have transpired. Shortly after the grand event was known, Short[4] sent for Scott and me, and he told us plainly the following news: that he was very sorry he could not congratulate either of us, and that it had been an extremely near thing, and that in consequence the trustees had determined to present us both with books; that "taste," which, he said, was a word difficult to define, had gained Brancker his victory, and then he said, "Indeed, I do not know what the result might have been if you two had not written such long answers!" Scott then asked him to furnish some particulars. He told him his Alcaics were good, but his Iambics he seemed to consider, if anything, inferior to mine! He abused him for *free* translation, me for my essay, on which he said his memorandum was "desultory beyond belief," and for throwing dust in the examiner's eyes, *i.e.*, when asked, "Who wrote 'God Save the King?'" answering, "Thomson wrote 'Rule Britannia.'" But indeed, he said that he had as many bad marks against Brancker as against us! Scott says Brancker is not near so good a scholar as he was himself when he came up; but I hear in a roundabout way a report that Butler[5] thinks him the best he has had since Kennedy.[6] The oddest thing, however, of all Short said

[1] Thomas William Allies, subsequently better known as a convert to Rome.

[2] Sidney Herbert, Mr. Gladstone's colleague under Peel, and later to become Lord Herbert of Lea.

[3] William Robert Grove, afterwards a judge of the Queen's Bench.

[4] Then Senior Censor of Christ Church, and afterwards Bishop of Sodor and Man, and, by translation, of St. Asaph.

[5] Samuel Butler, Head Master of Shrewsbury School, and subsequently Bishop of Lichfield.

[6] Benjamin Hall Kennedy, afterwards Butler's successor as Head Master of Shrewsbury, and Regius Professor of Greek at Cambridge.

was his exposition of Brancker's merits: "he answered *all* the questions *short*, and *most* of them right." The old Growler[1] was very kind, and said he had no doubt we should find the disappointment all for the best, to which one of us somewhat demurred; when he asseverated vehemently that it was so, the other assented. Upon this he exclaimed: "Aye, but you don't believe it, I know." He shook hands with us most heartily, and though he moralised rough-shod, certainly behaved in a very friendly way. For myself, this is no cause of complaint in any way, for it has been the best possible combination of circumstances for me except one, namely, that they should have given me some papers in those classes wherein, as I told you long ago, my only hope of gaining ground consisted. But I begin to fear Scott will never get it now.[2] I think it will probably have the effect of keeping us here till after the vacation, as after losing this scholarship I should scarcely feel that I had done my duty towards the college if I did not resume my mathematics. I trust you do not think that on account of this ludicrous defeat, I do now or ever shall appreciate the less the great and undeserved kindness and zeal with which you have guided and assisted my reading, especially as I am conscious that my manner and temper are not the best qualified of all for a tutor to manage or even to bear with. But you have my heartiest and warmest thanks.'[3] And not the least curious touch about the whole description of the incident is that Mr. Gladstone was obviously unaware that Brancker was a Liverpool boy, and son of a merchant who had just been mayor of his own native town.[4]

[1] Short's nickname.   [2] He won it in 1833.
[3] Charles Wordsworth's 'Early Annals,' pp. 88-91.
[4] Thomas Brancker became Rector of Limington, Somerset, and Prebendary of Wells, and died in 1871.

So full was he of his scholastic defeat that, in this letter, he had not a word to say upon the great question which was agitating the land from end to end, and in the discussion of which he himself, within a very few weeks, was to claim a somewhat prominent share. On March 1st, Lord John

The Reform agita-tion. Russell had introduced the first of the three Reform Bills, the last of which became the Reform Act of 1832. Eight days later, it had been read a first time without a division, and on March 21st, five days after Mr. Gladstone had written to his tutor, it secured its second reading by a majority of one. In that majority was Thomas Gladstone, a fact which could have been little to the taste of either the father or the youngest brother of the then member for Queenborough, a Kentish constituency which was customarily regarded as under the control of the Treasury, and for which Thomas Gladstone had been returned at the general election of the previous year, but seated only upon petition. What John Gladstone thought of the Reform Bill may be imagined : what William Gladstone thought was soon to be publicly said : it may have been pressure from both which caused Thomas Gladstone to change sides, and in a very few weeks to vote for the amendment of Gascoyne, still a Liverpool representative, which, carried by eight, strangled the Bill and forced a general election, whereat the member for Queenborough was not re-chosen.

In the various local capitals of England, county meetings were called to strengthen the hands of the Grey Administration. The majority of one on the second reading foretold defeat in committee, and the demand of the Reformers the country through was for an early dissolution. Mr. Gladstone had left his mathematics at Oxford to spend his leisure as before at Leamington, where ' people do nothing but sing and that incessantly;' and while there, and be cause of one of these county meetings, he made his earliest contribution to the daily press, and took his first political step outside Oxford. 'If you refer to the *Standard* of last Thursday,' he told Charles Wordsworth on April 9th, 'you will find an anti-reform letter there which I wrote; it is merely an account of the Warwickshire county meeting, to which I went expecting to be disgusted, and was not disappointed in my expectations. They inserted the letter civilly enough as I did not send my name, but *extrapolated* or *metabolised* a part where I had mentioned Canning.'[1] The gathering referred to was officially described as 'a public meeting of the nobility, gentry, clergy, freeholders, and inhabitant householders of the county of Warwick, convened by the High Sheriff, pursuant to public advertisement, and held at Warwick, on the 4th day of April, 1831; George Lucy, Esq., High Sheriff, in the chair.' A peer, the son of a peer, four baronets, and five ministers of religion, as well as Thomas Attwood and Joshua Scholefield, the leaders of the Birmingham Reformers, took part in the proceedings, the main result of which was to adopt an address to the Crown endorsing the Ministerial measure and praying for a dissolution in case of defeat, and a petition to the House of Commons declaring that 'the present disproportional and corrupt state of the representation of the people is a most alarming grievance, demanding immediate and effectual redress.' And the *Times*, in copying from a local journal a full account of the proceedings, seven days after date, recommended attention to 'this important addition to the weight of evidence already before the eyes of all men; proving incontestably the pitch of determination which the

April.
Describes a Reform meeting.

[1] Charles Wordsworth's 'Early Annals,' p. 91.

people of England have arrived at in support of His Majesty's Government.'

Mr. Gladstone, as 'Spectator,' conveyed a very different impression of the meeting to the readers of the *Standard*. His letter, which was written at Leamington the day after the gathering, and was published on April 7th, opened by declaring that 'the advocates of the Reform Bill have, as I think will be generally admitted, been much more assiduous in establishing cases of anomaly than of grievance, and more ready to appeal to the manifestation of popular will, than to abide the contest of argument and the decision of truth.' He, therefore, set himself to analyse the character of the Warwick meeting, at which he roundly averred, 'the gentry present were few, the nobility none; the clergy one only,' while 'the mob beneath the grand stand was Athenian in its levity, in its recklessness, in its gaping expectancy, in its self-love and self-conceit—in everything but its acuteness.' As to the speakers, 'they seemed to think the necessity of reform demonstrated when an anomaly had been proved. Now,' he asked, 'what do anomalies signify? Who would not gladly purchase one single substantial advantage at the price of ten thousand verbal absurdities?' His conclusion was that 'these meetings are instruments of power, though not of good, and are to be met with other and sterner arms than those of ridicule, since they are as effectual for the purposes of intimidation as inimical to the empire of truth.' And it was with this outburst that Mr. Gladstone ended: 'If, sir, the nobility, the gentry, the clergy, if the sterling sense and stable principle of the country generally, are to be alarmed, overawed, or smothered, by the expression of popular opinion from meetings such as this—and if no great statesman be raised up in our hour of need to undeceive this unhappy multitude, now eagerly rushing or heedlessly sauntering along the pathway of revolution "as an ox goeth to the slaughter, or a fool to the correction of the stocks," what is it but a symptom, as infallible as it is appalling, that the day of our greatness and stability is no more, and that the chill and damps of death are already creeping over England's glory. May God avert the omen!'

There is no mention of Canning throughout the letter, and, if the deleted allusion were in praise, as it was practically certain to have been, the *Standard* was the last journal likely to publish it, for Canning was the object of its special detestation ; and a full eighteen months later, and when the statesman had been five years in his grave, it was still denouncing 'such acts of treachery as Mr. Canning's usurpation in 1827.' It seems probable that the omitted reference had been suggested by the fact that a Robert Canning was one of the speakers, though of what he said not a word was caught by the reporters ; but he proposed a resolution in favour of the Reform Bill, 'whole and entire,' and of a dissolution if it were at all altered. And it may well have furnished material for reflection to Mr. Gladstone that one bearing the cognomen of his political idol should have taken a prominent part in a meeting at which, according to his version, 'those who were really in earnest were not the disciples of the Whigs or the Ministers, but of the French and Belgian revolutions, who are now making by stealth their first step towards the ballot, universal suffrage, and a National Guard.' It was not they alone who were 'making by stealth their first step' towards those ends: before their young censor concluded his political career he had been at the head of an Administration which adopted the ballot ; he had endorsed the principle of ' One Man, One Vote '; and he had acceded to the establishment of a force of civilian soldiers, numbering over two hundred thousand men.

G

But this was only the beginning of Mr. Gladstone's manifestation of anti-Reform zeal; and in it he had the cordial
support of most of his cherished friends.   There was much
ferment, indeed, at both the universities on the question.
On April 21st, the day before the sudden dissolution on
Reform, it was agreed in a Convocation at Oxford by 79
votes to 36 to affix the university seal to a petition against
the Bill; and this majority would have been larger had
not several decided opponents of the measure declined,
for no obvious reason, to vote, while others, in truly academic and unpractical fashion, opposed the petition because
its sentiments were not expressed with sufficient strength.
What the heads did at Oxford, the students desired to do at
Cambridge.   A notice was issued calling a meeting for April
28th of the bachelors of arts and undergraduates to petition
against the Bill; but, on the previous day, the authorities
circulated a document declaring that 'We, the Vice-Chancellor and Heads whose names are subscribed, think it
necessary to admonish all persons *in statu pupillari*, that
every one who attends this, or any similar meeting, will be
proceeded against as a violator of the discipline of the
University.'

On the day upon which the Cambridge undergraduates
had thus sought an opportunity for opposing Reform, Charles
Wordsworth was writing to his brother Christopher, ' Gladstone is quite furious in the cause;' Arthur Hallam was recording in the same month the receipt from
him of a long letter which showed his
bitterness against the Bill; and an opportunity soon came for
him to publicly show what he felt concerning
the measure.   On May 16th, it was moved
at the Union, ' That the present Ministry is
incompetent to conduct the government of the country,' to

His Anti-Reform
zeal.

May.
The Union and
Reform.

which Mr. Gladstone proposed as a rider, ' That, moreover, they have unwisely introduced, and most unscrupulously forwarded, a measure, which threatens not only to change the form of our Government, but ultimately to break up the very foundations of social order in the country, as well as materially to forward the designs of those who are engaged in the same project throughout the civilised world.' And the rider, after a three nights' debate, the most celebrated in the history of the Union, was carried by 94 votes to 38.

Charles Wordsworth, writing to Christopher on the 24th, thus described the occasion : ' Our Debating Society has been distinguishing itself most gloriously. Last week we had a debate on the present Ministry, which was kept up with the greatest spirit for three nights. The motion " that the present Ministry is incompetent to manage the affairs of the country" was introduced by a son of Sir E. Knatchbull : who was followed on the same side by, among others, Roundell Palmer,[1] Sidney Herbert, Lincoln, Doyle, Bruce, and lastly GLADSTONE (a certain double *His speech against* first), who, after the most splendid speech, *the Bill.* out and out, that was ever heard in our Society,' moved the amendment already given. ' Does this prove nothing ? ' Charles Wordsworth asked, and he finished and italicised his own reply : ' I say it proves that the *Oxford Union Society will yet save the country.*' ' I assure you,' he added, ' that I cannot even conceive speeches more eloquent, or more powerful in argument, than both Bruce's and Gladstone's. . . . On the other side . . . they possess no aristocracy either of rank or talent . . . while our ranks were crammed with prize and first-class men. So that, however

---

[1] Afterwards Lord Chancellor in two of Mr. Gladstone's Administrations, and first Earl of Selborne.

the talent may be nearly balanced with you [at Cambridge], thank heavens it is not so with us." ' [1]

The impression of that debate was never lost by those who were present, and Mr. Gladstone's speech was specially singled out for remembrance. It was told how the son of Rowland Alston (afterwards Liberal member for Hertfordshire, and a fellow slaveowner with John Gladstone in Jamaica) was so moved by it that, immediately upon its conclusion, he crossed amid loud acclamations from the Whig to the Tory side of the House; [2] but, as against this, may be set an alleged remark the next day of George Anthony Denison, later the combative Archdeacon of Taunton, that the speaker would end in becoming a Radical, because he had supported his Tory position upon Radical grounds. [3] Concerning the manner, rather than the matter, of the speech, however, there was no difference of criticism. 'The great oratorical event of my time' was the record of Doyle: 'most of the speakers rose more or less above their ordinary level, but when Mr. Gladstone sat down, we all of us felt that an epoch in our lives had occurred.' [4] And the echoes of that debate rumbled down the wind, for long afterwards, and when in 1866, Mr. Gladstone was introducing a Reform Bill of his own, Disraeli in the House of Commons revived the memory

---

[1] Charles Wordsworth's ' Early Annals,' pp. 85, 86.

[2] Wilfrid Ward's ' William George Ward and the Oxford Movement,' p. 23.

[3] G. A. Denison's ' Supplement to Notes of My Life ' (1893), pp. 41, 42. The Archdeacon himself, however, does not vouch for the remark, observing, ' I thought I must have said so, because I had been asked before whether I had said it, and that there was in my mind a shadowy remembrance of my having said it.'

Doyle's ' Reminiscences,' p. 116.

of the famous rider—which he appears to have somewhat misquoted—and, with a compliment to the Oxford Union, said he should be quite prepared to adopt at that day, and in existing circumstances, the proposal it had then passed.[1] But Mr. Gladstone, in immediate reply, observed that he had long and bitterly repented of the opinions thus announced when just emerged from boyhood, though he claimed that, while he had expressed this early ungovernable alarm clearly, plainly, forcibly, and in downright English, Disraeli did not care to tell the nation what he really thought, but was content to skulk under the shelter of a meaningless amendment to the new Bill.[2]

Mr. Gladstone's contemporary account of the debate was written the day after it concluded, and it appeared in the *Standard* of May 21st, as a letter signed 'Alumnus.' 'Amidst the defection of so large a proportion of those who were once deemed friends of the constitution,' he said, 'it has been matter of hearty congratulation to your readers, that the Universities have not renounced their allegiance to her principles. His account of the They will, perhaps, be pleased, though not debate. surprised, to learn that, in so far at least as Oxford is concerned, the rising generation promise in no degree to fall short of their seniors.' After giving the result, and remarking that 'the proportion of persons distinguished in the university was even greater' in favour of the motion than the mere figures indicated, Mr. Gladstone proceeded : 'Every one knows that this was a fair expression of the opinion of the society, the meeting being a particularly full one ; and the society, taken collectively, is certainly not

[1] April 27, 1866 : 'Hansard,' 3rd series, vol. clxxxiii., ff. 94, 95.

[2] *Ibid.*, ff. 129, 130.

more "illiberal" than the rest of the university. Now, it is doubtless true that there are many in the present day who conceive, and assume as an indisputable truth, that the members of our Universities are neither competent to form, nor entitled to pronounce, any opinion on any political question. Still there are others who conceive the circumstances under which our youth are educated here, by no means such as to impose this total disqualification. If on the one hand, they are denounced as expectant and reversionary corruptionists, on the other hand it may [be] observed that their period of life, warmth of feeling, and want of experience, render them peculiarly liable to be led away by those seductive and fascinating phantoms which have lately been presented with such fatal effect to the view of the English populace. The very spirit of opposition to authority might perhaps be deemed, by an impartial person, a consideration proving them rather liable to err against than for existing institutions. As far as their studies, and the effect produced by them on their mind are concerned, I know not whether the stimulating food of the daily press, which forms the ordinary diet of reformers, be more sound or more wholesome aliment, than that study of philosophic history, and that rigorous adherence and attention to principles, for which Oxford has long been, and is at this moment, so peculiarly and so honourably distinguished. Long may their studies flourish and these results continue to issue from them.'

Yet, in the same number of the *Standard* appeared the report of a speech made three nights before by Peel at Tamworth, which should have brought home, even to an ardent young Oxonian, the impossibility of maintaining a purely negative position. The Conservative leader—for 'Conservative' was just then coming into use as a party name—after noting the fact that the two ancient Universities had shown themselves adverse to the Reform Bill, declared that he had never been the decided supporter of any band of political partisans, but had Peel's caution. always thought it much better to look steadily at the political circumstances of the times in which they lived; and, if necessities were so pressing as to demand it, there could be no dishonour or discredit in relinquishing opinions or measures, and adopting others more suited to the altered circumstances of the country. For this course of proceeding he had been censured by opposite parties—by those who, upon all occasions, thought no changes were required, as well as by those who, in his opinion, were the advocates of too violent and sudden innovations. But that middle course, he averred, he would continue to pursue, for he held it to be impossible for any statesman to adopt one fixed line of policy under all circumstances; and the only question with him when he departed from that line should be—' Am I actuated by any interested or sinister motive, or do I consider the measures I contemplate called for by the circumstances and necessities of the country?' This utterance, which appears to have escaped the notice of Peel's biographers, was an exact anticipation of the course adopted by the statesman after the Reform Bill had passed, as well as of what came to be known in history as 'The Tamworth Manifesto,' after reading which no one can be surprised at his subsequent resolve to repeal the Corn Laws.

But Mr. Gladstone, who was not yet a 'Peelite,' was to do one thing more while at Oxford to oppose the Reform Bill. The story has been variously told of how he assisted Char es Wordsworth and Lincoln to form an Anti-Reform League among the undergraduates, and

of how he, with them, drew up a manifesto on the subject which appeared in the *Times;* but what
really happened was that, after the debate
at the Union, the three Oxonians named

June.
Mr. Gladstone drafts
an Anti-Reform
petition.

resolved to take a more definite step to show what the
youth of the university thought of Reform, and that, meeting in Lincoln's rooms, Mr. Gladstone had the chief
hand in drafting a petition to the House of Commons, intended to be signed by resident bachelors and undergraduates of the University.   It is a document which has
often been referred to but never re-published; and yet, as
being in a sense Mr. Gladstone's first State-paper and as
containing in most explicit form his earliest views upon
constitutional subjects, the giving of its text is sufficiently
justified.   It ran thus :—

'That the Bill of Reform lately submitted to Parliament
seems to your Petitioners far more than commensurate with
any existing amount of grievances, which, however, appears
to be the legitimate test of the necessity of change, and the
measure of its extent.   That the balance of powers is the
vital principle of the British Constitution, but that this
balance is necessarily destroyed if of the old Elective Body
the Aristocratic portion be disfranchised at once, the popular only in reversion, so that the entire weight is removed
from one scale, while it is permitted to remain in the other.
That anomalies are only defensible when found by experience to be beneficial in their effects, but that this measure
introduces a system of untried anomalies, and moreover
thus affords to the ill-affected a specious plea for continued
innovations.   That it promises to admit an alarming proportion of Roman Catholic influence into Parliament, and
thereby falsifies the implied pledge of conservation of existing establishments, under which many were induced to vote

in favour of the Roman Catholic Claims. That, notwith-standing experience has shown that an Aristocratical Order cannot co-exist with a popular assembly, except by an in-fluence to be exerted in that assembly, the measure aims at leaving the Three Estates of the Realm to act independently of all mutual communication and controul, so that, should collision arise, it will be unmitigated by any reciprocal sympathies in the different members of the Legislative Body, and tend to disorganize the whole mechanism of the Government. That the popular clamour recently excited has been urged as the strongest argument in favour of this particular measure of Reform, which ought never to carry any weight except in cases where its sentence is found, on independent grounds, to be reasonable. And, further, that as this cry indicates in its tone and character, not a deliber-ate desire for the remedy of evils, but a rash and intem-perate spirit, looking to ulterior measures rather than prac-tical relief, any concession granted specifically to such a demand, will inevitably increase whatever of evil there might be in a refusal. That your Petitioners, however alien to their condition the expression of any opinion on political questions might appear under ordinary circum-stances, and however reluctant to intrude on the attention of the Legislature, are nevertheless unwilling to contem-plate such results in silence, and therefore most humbly and earnestly pray your Honourable House that the said Bill may not pass into a Law.'[1]

The heads of Oxford were as little inclined in the June as those of Cambridge in the April to allow the undergradu-ates a voice in political affairs. Through Estcourt, their senior representative, the Oxford dons were at the moment

[1] *Commons' Journals*, vol. lxxxvi., p. 600 : *Votes and Proceedings of the House of Commons* (1831), Appendix, p: 51.

praying the Commons to exercise due caution in the contemplated changes ; and, if Mr. Gladstone and his young
co-zealots in the Tory cause had been as tamely submissive
to authority as their Cambridge colleagues, the petition just
given would have been dropped, for a similar document,
which had been extensively signed by bachelors and undergraduates on the Cam, was considered unnecessary of presentation because the Heads had already spoken, and it was
withdrawn from the hands of a member to whom it had
been entrusted.   Mr. Gladstone and his Oxford colleagues
were not so easily put aside. The Proctors intervened,
but with the only effect that the document was despatched
to London without so many signatures as it would otherwise have received, though still with 770 names attached
out of the little over a thousand resident bachelors and
undergraduates of Oxford.

The task of presentation was entrusted to Mahon
(afterwards the historian and fifth Earl Stanhope), who
had been returned the year before for the soon-to-be-dis-
franchised Wiltshire borough of Wootton Bassett, and who,
in discharging this duty on July 1st, remarked that, although,
compared with the one to the same effect, submitted a few
days before from the masters and graduates,
this might be inferior in weight, it was important as showing that the earlier did not
proceed merely, as had been stated, from timid old age or
long-rooted prepossessions, but that attachment to the
Constitution, as it then existed, was as strong among the
younger as the elder members of the University.   He recalled that one of the arguments two years before, in favour
of Catholic Emancipation, had been the inclination to that
measure of nearly all the young men of promise, and that
the vote of two to one in its favour by the Oxford Union—

July 1.
The petition pre-
sented.

' comprising nearly all the rising talent and knowledge of the University '—had been quoted in its favour. And, he concluded, ' with this precedent before me, I shall take the liberty of stating that the same institution still exists—that it comprises, as formerly, the most able and aspiring young men at Oxford ; and that the Ministerial Bill for Reform being there debated, was rejected by a majority of not two to one but three to one. I shall make no comment on these facts, but leave them to the impartial consideration of the House, and shall only express my great satisfaction that a declaration of attachment to our ancient institutions should be the first step in a career which may, I trust, to all and each of the petitioners prove a career of private work and public usefulness '—a hope which, as regarded the three chief promoters of the petition, was well fulfilled. Morpeth (subsequently seventh Earl of Carlisle, and, long afterwards, as Viceroy of Ireland, a colleague of Mr. Gladstone under Lord Palmerston), who had been returned for York-shire in 1830, was the only other to speak upon this mani-festation from 'a body from whom I have so lately emerged, and with whom throughout my life I shall feel myself con-nected by so many recollections, I can hardly say of profit, but of pleasure.' And, while urging that ' a very respectable minority ' existed in the University on this question, he was equally happy in the expression of his prophetic trust : ' I mean to pass no censure upon those who have petitioned. Still, I entertain a strong hope that, when those who have subscribed this petition shall have an opportunity, in ad-vanced life, of mixing with large masses of their country-men, even they will see reason to entertain sentiments more in unison with the wishes of the people, of whom I hope that they are destined to be one day the support and ornament.[1]

[1] 'Mirror of Parliament' (1831), pp. 254, 255.

The Tory papers were much pleased with the petition.
The *Morning Post* declared, on the day after its presentation,
The Tory Press that the feeling shown by the undergradu-
upon it. ates at both universities proved how decidedly the rising talent of the country was opposed to the
Bill, and added : ' Such an opposition is not less honourable
to the young men themselves — unswayed by Utopian
theory at the very age when it is most likely to dazzle and
bewilder—than it is gratifying to the country of which they
will hereafter prove the pride and the protection.' The
Standard the same evening characterised the signatories as
' the *élite* of the youth of England,' and the petition as ' a
serious warning to the revolutionists to make the most
of their opportunity, as the rising as well as the matured
talent of the country is so clearly against them.' And
John Bull of the day later, while agreeing that the
Proctors' interference had not been improper and that
it would be regrettable if the undergraduates took
too conspicuous a part in politics, averred that ' they
must, however, have more philosophy or more patriotism than we give them credit for, if they can view
with indifference the necessary consequences of the Reform
Bill ; and we do think that any fault which is to be found
with their expression of opinion on it, must be referred to
those, who, by their inconsiderate and unpardonable folly,
have brought the country to a crisis which no man of
common foresight and common feeling can bear to look
upon with indifference.' But, after all, the most effective
comment was that of the House of Commons itself. The
petition was presented on July 1st, and five days later the
Reform Bill, which had secured a majority of one in the
preceding March, was read a second time in the new
Chamber by a majority of 136. At no time before or since

had university opinion, both young and old, been more emphatically shown to be out of touch with that of the country; and although Mr. Gladstone (who had already made acquaintance with the interior of the Palace of Westminster by hearing some of Canning's greatest speeches in the Commons) was to feel himself strengthened in his antagonism to the Bill while present in the Lords during the final night's debate three months later, and when, despite Brougham's theatrical appeal upon his knees, the Peers rejected the measure, it was the country which won in the end.

Mr. Gladstone's last appearance at the Union had by this time been made, he having on June 2nd moved an amendment, which will demand subsequent consideration, to a motion for immediate emancipation in the West Indies. But he was still to win his chief university glory, that 'double first class' in classics and mathematics which Charles Wordsworth had prophesied for him, which has been so often recalled, and the importance of which has been so much exaggerated.   There are certain of his achievements for which his friends may claim that he has not had sufficient praise, but for this one, brilliant as it was, he has received something more than its due.   It was on November 24th, 1831, that the list of successes in *Literis Humanioribus* was placarded, and of the five in the first class, 'Gladstone, Gulielmus E., ex Æde Christi,' was one; and this was followed on December 14th by the list of those victorious in mathematics and physics, in The double first-which, and again among five, Mr. Gladstone class. once more figured in the first class. But it has not previously been noted that he was one of two 'double firsts' of that year, Henry Denison (also a Student of Christ Church, and afterwards a Fellow of All Souls) having secured a like place in both lists; and, therefore, although

Charles Wood, first Viscount Halifax, is traditionally reported to have observed that his own double first must have been better than Peel's and Mr. Gladstone's better than both, the fact stands, despite the possible increase of difficulty in the examinations between 1808 and 1831, that Peel was the earliest Oxonian ever to achieve the honour, and that not merely had he no rival in his year but he alone was placed in the first class in classics. With one more incident, Mr. Gladstone's university career now closed, for on January 26th, 1832, in company with (Sir) Robert Phillimore, like himself a Student of Christ Church, who had taken a second class in classics, and

Bachelor of Arts.

Martin Tupper, from the same college, he received the degree of Bachelor of Arts, becoming a Master of Arts rather over two years later.[1]

In triumph, therefore, Mr. Gladstone left Oxford, but it was a triumph dimmed with regret at severance from a place he loved so well. How deep was his affection for

Leaves Oxford.

the University was often proved in after years. It was not alone indicated in the terms in which his earliest works were dedicated to his *Alma Mater;* it was not merely shown while he was her representative in Parliament; it was continued throughout his life. No praise was too high to be awarded her. To call a man a characteristically Oxford man remained, in his opinion, the highest compliment that could be paid to human being. Her education, while tending in his day to indicate that liberty should be regarded with jealousy and fear, taught a love of truth, provided men with principles of honour, and inculcated a reverence for what was ancient and free and great. In the hour when Oxford rejected his services as its member, he declared that he had loved her with a

[1] May 21, 1834.

deep and passionate love and should so love her to the end. When he revisited her in the days of his age—when, as in 1890, he addressed the Union concerning Homer, and when, as two years later, he delivered the first Romanes Lecture upon mediæval universities—he was received with a warmth of welcome which testified that Oxford honoured him as he had honoured her. And formal proof of this was afforded in the sonorous Latin of the Senior Proctor's oration on resigning office in the spring of 1893, with this testimony to the latest visit :—'Est et Georgius Iohannes Romanes laudandus, a quo institutam quae annua foret oratio primam habuit Gulielmus Ewart Gladstone, alumnus omnium nostrorum clarissimus, summus orator, regendae civitatis dux et princeps. Horresco referens turbam juniorum in arctiore vestibulo et scalis confertorum, confligentium, exanimatorum. Verum ubi tandem ipse ingreditur, quo clamore ac quo plausu spissi theatri excipitur! Adstat in conspectu omnium, augusto ore, erecto corpore, acerrimo lumine, tanquam vi et robore ingenii senectutis suae domi-nator et victor, qui onus trium et octoginta annorum prope ludibundus sustineat, nec imperii Britannici Atlanteo pondere incurvetur. Quanta autem in illa oratione ubertas, quanta majestas ! Qui nervi, qui aculei ! Quam clarissima et suavissima voce ita recitabat ut nemo in tanta corona non exaudiret, nemo non quasi carmine captus miraretur. Nun-quam de eorum qui aderant memoria exciderit illud specta-culum et vox viri vere digni heroicis aetatibus.'[1]

[1] "Praise must be accorded to George John Romanes, who founded the annual oration, given the first year by William Ewart Gladstone, the most distinguished of our *alumni*, a supreme orator, a leader and master in the art of statecraft. I shrink from the task of describing the crowd of young men,who filled the narrow vestibule and staircases, a thronging, struggling, breathless mass. But when he for whom they waited at last came, what shouts and what applause fill the crowded

Having left the University, Mr. Gladstone, for whom no seat had yet been selected, but whose early return to Parliament was regarded by all his friends as certain, took a six months holiday in Italy.   Towards that land, for the liberty and unity of which he was to do so much, his eyes had long been turned; and the earliest in date of the translations he thirty years later published, in company with his brother-in-law, Lord Lyttelton, had been executed in 1831, and was a Latin rendering of the lines in 'Paradise Regained,' commencing—

1832.
Visits Italy.

> The city, which Thou seest, no other deem
> Than great and glorious Rome, queen of the earth,
> So far renown'd, and with the spoils enrich'd
> Of nations.

It was a visit to be often repeated, but the first impression left by Rome of a population of men anxious for freedom but condemned to servitude in the supposed interests of a Church was never eradicated.   That was seen even before the statesman who, by constant sympathy, assisted so greatly to secure the unification of Italy, perceived that unity was necessary

theatre.   He stands up in the sight of them all, of venerable aspect, with erect figure and flashing eye, as though by the strength and vigour of his spirit he overcomes and conquers his old age—the man who bears his three and eighty years as though they were nothing, and who is not bowed down by the Atlantean weight which he bears of the British Empire.   What eloquence too in his oration, and what majestic language !   What force, what point !   With such perfect clearness and mellifluousness did he speak that no one in the whole circle of listeners but heard, none but admired, spell-bound by the music-like charm of the speech.   Never from the minds of those who were there will fade the sight, and voice of this man, worthy indeed of the Heroic Ages." Twelve months later, the Senior Proctor was able to congratulate the University that to Mr. Gladstone as Premier, Christ Church had supplied a successor in the person of Lord Rosebery.

or even desirable; and the thoughts it suggested to Mr. Gladstone concerning the worth of the temporal power and the righteousness, from the earthly point of view, of the Papal system were of utmost importance in aiding his political development.

But, while the days of his pupilage were in this fashion drawing to a close, great events were being shaped at home. The cry of Browning in after years—

'Oh, to be in England now that April's there,'

might well have been that of the young student, eager for public life, as mail after mail brought to Italy news of the closing throes of the long battle over Reform. The carrying of the third Bill through the Commons, the struggle with the Lords, the resignation of Grey, the refusal of Peel to join Wellington in a hopeless fight, the return of the Whigs to office, and the final triumph of the measure—who that knows the history of that thrilling spring can doubt the excited interest such a succession of events created in Mr. Gladstone? His old comrades at the Union were solemnly discussing, and almost adopting, a motion declaring that an absolute monarchy was a more desirable form of Government than the constitution proposed by the Reform Bill; and Lincoln, who remained at the University for a term after Mr. Gladstone had left, was not only continuing to rally his friends to further denunciation of the Whig Ministry, but was persuading his father, the Duke of Newcastle, to a step which assisted to make history. For there came to Mr. Gladstone at Milan in the summer not alone the general call from home to take *Invited to contest Newark.* action in what he deemed to be the cause of right, but a special invitation to contest, at the first election under the new system, the ancient borough of Newark-upon-Trent.

H

V.—THE CONTEST AT NEWARK.

THE Seventh of June, 1832, the day on which the Reform Bill became law, must always be a memorable date in our constitutional history.   When the Commons were summoned to the other Chamber, to hear the royal assent given by commission, it was noted that every member present accompanied the Speaker save one, and that one Sir Robert Harry Inglis, Peel's successful opponent at Oxford three years before, who had been brought into Parliament by the influence of the same Duke of Newcastle who was soon to exercise it on behalf of Mr. Gladstone.   It was further observed that when the Speaker, on his return, made the customary announcement of the royal assent, no sign of joyful animation was evinced by any member.   The Bill's supporters were too wearied with the continuous exertions of fifteen months to cheer; its opponents were moodily awaiting their electoral doom : but the apathy of the Commons was not reflected outside.   Rejoicings took place in every town and almost in every village.   Bells were rung and dinners eaten, flags waved and processions marched; even almshouses were erected in celebration of the people's victory. With many, this was an expression of hate for the past; with most, it was an outburst of hope for the future.   The old system, which restricted the power of government to a few, was swept away; the new was speedily to be at work.

An early dissolution was obviously to be anticipated; and every constituency was quickly filled with the bustle of preparation for the general election.   Newark, even at that moment, had a special claim upon public attention, for the names of Russell and Grey were not more closely linked with the Reform struggle than were those of the Duke of Newcastle and his pocket-borough of Newark-upon-Trent. Henry Pelham, fourth Duke of Newcastle, was the type and exemplar of that aristocratic Toryism which, never bending to the public will, had ever sternly opposed Mr. Gladstone's first any extension of the people's power.   Per- political patron. sonally well-disposed to those of a lesser social station, and kind in dealing with any who depended upon him, as long as they obeyed the master-will, he was resolute to suppress all manifestation of free opinion.   Succeeding to the dukedom when only ten years of age, he entered the House of Lords just as the Whigs had their one transient tenure of office for half-a-century and when, that brief hour of triumph passed, they were about to be doomed to what for long looked like perpetual exclusion from power.   A boy when the horrors of the Reign of Terror were being daily told as news, a man when the great struggle with Buonaparte was being fiercely waged, the Duke of Newcastle, steeped in Toryism from his birth and hardened in Toryism by all that surrounded him, never showed even a glimmer of sympathy with any but the straitest sect of the party to which he belonged.   The first political patron of Mr. Gladstone was, indeed, one of the most consistent, one of the most honourable, and one of the most bigoted Tories whom the political conditions of England ever produced.

During the prolonged but quietly-maintained rivalry of Canning and Peel for the leadership of the Commons, Newcastle was decidedly for Peel.   In the spring of 1822, when the former proposed and the latter opposed a measure for allowing Roman Catholic peers to sit and vote in the

House of Lords, the duke felt that he could not 'go to
bed and expect quiet rest' until he had written to thank
Peel for his 'unanswerable and triumphant answer to Mr.
Canning's ill-judged speech.'[1]   Peel replied that the communication was on every account very gratifying to his
feelings; but a few months later, when Newcastle sought to
influence him against assenting to the re-admission of
Canning to the Cabinet, Peel promptly but effectively resented the interference.[2]   The snub did not prevent Newcastle either from intriguing against the one statesman or
supporting the other.   When Canning was awaiting, in 1827,
the call to form a Ministry, Newcastle was busy with George
IV., endeavouring to secure that Catholic Emancipation
should not be granted; when Canning had succeeded in
the task which killed him, Newcastle joined the pack
that hounded the statesman to death, and publicly described him as 'a profligate Minister and an unprincipled
man;[3] and even when Canning had passed away, the
duke carried on the opposition to his principles by seeking
to exclude from the Wellington Cabinet, Huskisson, the
dead Premier's chief lieutenant.

These exhibitions of the extreme of Tory feeling were,
however, marked only by the few: the time was rapidly
approaching when the opinions of the Duke of Newcastle
should be known to the many, and should powerfully
assist to wreck the cause to which their exponent was so
deeply attached.   The borough of Newark, situated at no
great distance from Clumber, the chief residence of the
Newcastles, returned two members to Parliament, and one
of the seats the Whigs had long and vainly striven to win.   It

---

[1] C. S. Parker's 'Sir Robert Peel,' p. 314.

[2] *Ibid.*, p. 331.

[3] Lord Colchester's 'Diary,' vol. iii., p. 499.

happened that, at a bye-election in 1829, caused by the retirement of a kinsman of the duke owing to a difference upon
Catholic Emancipation, Serjeant Wilde, the Whig candidate and an active and eloquent lawyer, polled an
unexpectedly heavy vote against Newcastle's nominee,
Michael Thomas Sadler, a strict Tory who deserves lasting
honour for his action on behalf of the then miserably-treated
factory children.   This display of independence was considered by the duke to be so reprehensible that prompt
measures were taken on his behalf to check its spread.
His influence in the borough was mainly derived from the
possession of lands held under lease from the Crown ; and
an idea which had been prevalent during the contest that
any sub-tenants who supported Wilde would be ejected,
was confirmed immediately after its close by forty of such
receiving notices to quit.   One of these, having assured
the ducal agent that his vote had been given by mistake,
was told, 'Then the notice to quit is a mistake ; ' but for
the rest, though only seven were actually evicted, there was
no similar consolation.   A public meeting was called to
petition Parliament against this interference ; and the duke,
upon being made acquainted with the fact, declined to give
any explanation beyond a note in which he said that 'he had
a right to do as he liked with his own.'   He was speedily
undeceived ; the land was not 'his own,' and, even if it had
been, he had no right to do what he pleased with it.   The
discussion within the borough spread to Parliament ; from
Parliament it permeated the nation ; and the indignation
aroused by the ducal claim so reacted upon Newark itself
that the great wave of feeling in favour of Reform in the
spring of 1831 swept Wilde to the head of the poll.

Newcastle was thus at length beaten, and beaten badly,
with the added annoyance, which must have proved

especially bitter, that no one man more than himself, by his bluntly-worded claim to coerce his tenants for electoral purposes, had assisted to make Reform possible. But he was not easily baffled; he speedily looked for a candidate to retrieve his fallen political fortune; and it was not long before such a one was found. After Mr. Gladstone's attack upon the Reform Bill at the Union, Lord Lincoln is recorded to have written to his father that a man had uprisen in Israel; and an invitation to spend at Clumber a portion of the ensuing long vacation was given and accepted. The chief result was seen the next summer, when the country was alive with expectation concerning the first general election under the Reform Act; and it was at

July, 1832.
Invited to contest
Newark.

Milan during July that, through his father, Mr. Gladstone received the duke's invitation to stand.[1] He at once returned to England; and, at the beginning of the following month and some weeks before going in person to Newark, he issued his first electoral address, which, like his earliest important political document, appears, though well-deserving it, never to have been reprinted. It was as follows:

'To the
Worthy Electors of the Borough of
Newark upon Trent.

'GENTLEMEN,

August 4.
His first election
address.

'Induced by the most flattering assurances of support, I venture to offer myself as a Candidate for the high honour of representing you in the ensuing Parliament.

'It has been recommended to me to avoid introducing excitement in the town by a personal canvass at this early

[1] Mr. Gladstone's own statement in Cornelius Brown's 'Annals of Newark-upon-Trent,' p. 275.

period, unless the example of any other Candidate should render it necessary. Let me, however, briefly express, as my claims on your confidence and favour, a warm and conscientious attachment to our Government as a limited Monarchy, and to the Union of our Church and State, as having been to us the source of numberless blessings, and as most strictly adapted to a Christian Nation. I consider that this attachment itself involves the strongest obligation, both to secure the removal of real abuses, and to resist the imputation of those which are imaginary.

'I admit facts and abstract principles only in subservience to facts, as the true standard of Agricultural, Commercial, and Financial Legislation, and recognise the sedulous promotion of British interests as its first and most proper object. The alleviation of the public burdens consistently with the strict adherence to our national engagements—the defence, in particular, of our Irish Establishments—the amelioration of the condition of the labouring Classes—the adjustment of our Colonial Interests, with measures for the moral advancement and further legal protection of our fellow-subjects in slavery—and the observance of a dignified and impartial Foreign policy—are objects, for the attainment of which, should it be your pleasure to return me to Parliament, I hope to labour with honesty, diligence, and perseverance—recognising no interests but those which are truly national.

'When the proper time shall be considered to have arrived, it will be alike my duty and pleasure to enter into the most unreserved personal communications, conscious as I am that they form the only satisfactory basis of mutual confidence.

'I have the honour to be, Gentlemen,
'Your obedient and faithful servant,
'W. E. GLADSTONE.
'London, August 4, 1832.'

The *Nottingham Review,* a Whig organ, remarked in its ensuing issue: 'The Red Club, at Newark, after searching the kingdom almost through for a candidate, have at last found one in the person of W. E. Gladstone, Esq.; who he is no one knows there; he has announced his intentions in a hand-bill.' The *Nottingham and Newark Mercury,* another Whig organ, was even less

Local opinion upon the candidate.

complimentary, its comment being: 'The Red Club, at Newark, after ransacking almost every part of the kingdom in search of a candidate, have at last got one in the person of Wm. Gladstone, a Liverpool merchant, whose address was distributed early on Monday morning, which had been got up the day before, being of such precious consequence, as to admit of no delay.[1] A more jumbled collection of words has been seldom sent from the press, professing to proceed from a candidate for parliamentary honour.' The *Nottingham Journal,* a Tory paper, in which alone the address had been advertised, was for all reasons more complimentary. 'It will be seen,' was the complacent observation, 'that Mr. Gladstone, a gentleman of considerable commercial experience and talent, is a candidate for the borough of Newark, on Conservative principles. From the sound political feeling lately manifested in that town, we venture to predict his success.' Thus, while one Whig journal frankly expressed ignorance, the other, with its 'Liverpool merchant,' and the Tory, with its 'considerable commercial experience,' alike showed how little they knew of the young parliamentary aspirant.

The candidature, however, was at once accepted as a reality; and in a list of candidates for the general election, compiled by the *Globe* in the third week in August, 'Mr.

[1] The address had been dated on a Saturday, and it was at once transmitted from London to Newark.

Gladstone' was given as the Anti-Reform champion for Newark, with Wilde as the only other suppliant for its suffrages. On August 24th, a more specific reference was made to the former in the advertisement columns of the *Times*, for the Committee of the Agency Anti-Slavery Society then issued three schedules, the first of which contained 'the names of those gentlemen who are either members of the existing Parliament, or reported to be candidates for the next, and whose past conduct, or present professions, or admitted personal interest in the question, leaves the Agency Anti-Slavery Committee without hope that they will support the reasonable object [of immediate abolition].' This schedule, it was added, 'contains, as a matter of course, all who are known to be slave proprietors,' and among its thirty names was 'W. E. Gladstone, for Newark,' in whose company was 'Joseph Hume, for Middlesex,' while, in the third schedule, 'those whom the Committee recommend with perfect confidence to the support of all electors who concur in desiring immediate abolition,' was Wilde, in company with Buxton, O'Connell, and Macaulay.

For another month there was little to indicate the sharpness of the Newark struggle; but the appearance in the borough of Wilde and Handley, respectively the old Whig and Tory members, to commence their canvass, hastened the movements of Mr. Gladstone, who has thus recorded his earliest *September. Mr. Gladstone visits Newark.* entry into the constituency which will always be linked with his name : 'I arrived at Newark, after a journey of forty hours from Torquay, at midnight, on Monday, 24th September, 1832, an absolute personal stranger, aged twenty-two. Next morning, I set forth on my canvass, with band, flags, and badges of every kind, and perhaps a thousand people.

The constituency was, I think, 1570 in number,[1] and the duke's tenants rather under one-fourth.   But his influence was my sole recommendation.   It was, however, an ardu-

His canvass.

ous contest, extending, with intermissions, over three months.   The canvass was old-fashioned and thorough.   We went into every house, be it what it might.   Even paupers were asked for their influ-ence.   "Oh, sir !" replied one old woman, " my influence is but very shallow."   A clergyman, recently come, entered another old woman's house with a memorandum book, which happened to be red.   "God bless you, sir," she cried ; "I wish you success."[2]   And, in another personal account of the contest, furnished in a letter of December 27th, 1875, to an old Newark supporter, Mr. Gladstone wrote : 'I remember, as if it were yesterday, my first arrival in the place, at midnight, by the Highflyer coach, in August or September, 1832, after a journey of forty hours from Torquay, of which we thought nothing in those days. Next morning at eight o'clock we sallied forth from the Clinton Arms to begin a canvass, on which I now look back as the most exciting period of my life.   I never worked harder or slept so badly, that is to say, so little.'[3] And as to what he was like at this time, Dean Hole, of Rochester, could recall, close upon sixty years later, that as a little boy at a Newark dame's school he saw Mr. Glad-stone in the Middlegate on his first canvass, and when, pale with the cast of thought, the young politician possessed one of the most winsome and intellectual faces that divine ever looked upon.

The contemporary record of the local Tory journal shows

[1] The exact total was 1577.
[2] Brown's 'Newark,' p. 275.
[3] *Daily News*, Nov. 16, 1876.

the pleasing progress Mr. Gladstone's candidature speedily made. 'If candour and ability have any influence,' it exclaimed, 'it is presaged there will be a change of one Representative in the next Parliament;' but, as it quickly waxed more positive in prediction, rumours of intimidation began to be circulated by the Whigs. The reign of persecution, it was declared, had again commenced: one Tory had discharged his Whig butler; another had given a Whig schoolmaster notice to quit; and two workmen had been discharged 'because they would not vote for Mr. Gladstone, the slavery man,' even though one of them had avowed himself willing to give one of his suffrages for that candidate if he were allowed to cast the other for Wilde. But the Tories worked while the Whigs worried, and they did so with the more zeal because at the commencement of the contest the victory of Wilde was confidently expected by his friends to be repeated. The Newark correspondent of the *Times*, indeed, was sufficiently rash to observe at the beginning of October that it was the opinion of many that 'the champion of Toryism, Mr. W. E. Gladstone, will not come to the poll. He appears instinctively to shun all meetings of the people, as if he relied wholly on the duke's influence, and was determined not to expose himself to a cross-examination by the other candidates or the electors.'

This was published on October 4th, and four evenings later, Mr. Gladstone gave effective reply by making what is described as an eloquent, but which was certainly an unreported, address at a meeting of the Red Club; and on the following morning he issued to the constituency from the Tory headquarters his second address, which has been accustomed to be described as his first. A few weeks before, his friend Lincoln had put forth a similar document 'to the gentry, clergy, and

October 8. His first speech,

electors' of South Nottinghamshire—a style significant of much—and now Mr. Gladstone, varying his own original opening, appealed in the following terms 'to the worthy and independent electors of the Borough of Newark':—

'GENTLEMEN,

'Having now completed my canvass, I think it my duty as well to remind you of the principles on *and second election* which I have solicited your votes, as *address.* freely to assure my friends that its result has placed my success beyond a doubt.

'I have not requested your favour on the ground of adherence to the opinions of any man or party, further than such adherence can be fairly understood from the conviction I have not hesitated to avow, that we must watch and resist that unenquiring and undiscriminating desire for change amongst us, which threatens to produce, along with partial good, a melancholy preponderance of mischief; which, I am persuaded, would aggravate beyond computation the deep-seated evils of our social state, and the heavy burthens of our industrious classes; which, by disturbing our peace, destroys confidence, and strikes at the root of prosperity. Thus it *has done already;* and thus, we must therefore believe, it *will do.*

'For the mitigation of those evils, we must, I think, look not only to particular measures, but to the restoration of sounder general principles. I mean especially that principle, on which alone the incorporation of Religion with the State, in our Constitution, can be defended; that the duties of Governors are strictly and peculiarly religious; and that Legislatures, like Individuals, are bound to carry throughout their acts the spirit of the high truths they have acknowledged. Principles are now arrayed against our institutions; and not by truckling nor by temporising—not by oppression nor corruption—but by principles they must be met.

'Among their first results should be, a sedulous and special attention to the interests of the poor, founded upon the rule, that those who are the least able to take care of themselves should be most regarded by others. Particularly it is a duty to endeavour by every means that *labour may receive adequate remuneration;* which, unhappily, among several classes of our fellow-countrymen, is not now the case. Whatever measures, therefore, whether by correction of the Poor Laws, allotment of Cottage Grounds, or otherwise, tend to promote this object, I deem entitled to the warmest support: with all such as are calculated to secure sound moral conduct in any class of society.

'I proceed to the momentous question of Slavery, which I have found entertained among you in that candid and temperate spirit which alone benefits its nature, or promises to remove its difficulties. If I have not recognised the right of an irresponsible society to interpose between me and the Electors, it has not been from any disrespect to its members, nor from unwillingness to answer their or any other questions, on which the Electors may desire to know my views. To the esteemed Secretary of the Society I submitted my reasons for silence; and I made a point of stating those views to him in his character of a Voter.

'As regards the abstract lawfulness of Slavery, I acknowledge it simply as importing the right of one man to the labour of another; and I rest it upon the fact, that Scripture, the paramount authority on such a point, gives directions to persons standing in the relation of master to slave, for their conduct in that relation: whereas, were the matter absolutely and necessarily *sinful*, it would not regulate the manner. Assuming sin as the cause of degradation, it strives, and strives most effectually, to cure the latter by extirpating the former.   We are agreed, that both the physical and the moral bondage of the slave are to be abolished. The question is as to the *order*, and the order only : now Scripture attacks the moral evil *before* the temporal one, and the temporal *through* the moral one, and I am content with the order which Scripture has established.

‘ To this end, I desire to see immediately set on foot, by impartial and sovereign authority, an universal and efficient system of Christian instruction, not intended to resist designs of individual piety and wisdom for the religious improvement of the negroes, but to do thoroughly what they can only do partially.

‘ As regards immediate emancipation, whether with or without compensation, there are several minor reasons against it ; but that which weighs with me is, that it would, I much fear, exchange the evils now affecting the Negro for others which are weightier—for a relapse into deeper debasement, if not for bloodshed and internal war.   Let *fitness* be made a condition of emancipation ; and let us strive to bring him to that fitness by the shortest possible course. Let him enjoy the means of earning his freedom through honest and industrious habits ; thus the same instruments which attain his liberty, shall likewise render him competent to use it : and thus, I earnestly trust, without risk of blood, without violation of property, with unimpaired benefit to the Negro, and with the utmost speed which prudence will admit, we shall arrive at that exceedingly desirable consummation, the utter extinction of Slavery.

‘ And now, Gentlemen, as regards the enthusiasm with which you have rallied round your ancient flag and welcomed the humble representative of those principles, whose emblem it is, I trust, that neither the lapse of time, nor the seductions of prosperity, can ever efface it from my memory. To my opponents, my acknowledgments are due for the good humour and kindness with which they have received me; and while I would thank my Friends for their zealous and unwearied exertions in my favour, I briefly but emphatically assure them, that if promises be an adequate foundation of confidence, or experience a reasonable ground of calculation, our victory is *sure*.

> 'I have the honour to be, Gentlemen,
> 'Your obliged and obedient servant,
> 'W. E. GLADSTONE.

'Clinton Arms, Newark, Tuesday, Oct. 9, 1832.'

Of this 'excellent address,' as the Tory organ considered it, Mr. Gladstone long afterwards wrote to the historian of Newark that it 'certainly justified criticism. It was that of a warm and loyal Tory, who was quite unaware that it contained in it the seeds of change to come. I remember that the Duke [of Newcastle], a singularly kind, honourable and high-minded man, questioned me a little Newcastle's criticism. about the passage on the wages of labour, which seemed somewhat to startle him. But he was far too delicately considerate to interfere.'[1] For one passage in the address—that relating to allotments—Mr. Gladstone himself claimed credit close upon half-a-century later, when addressing a gathering in London of agricul- Mr. Gladstone and tural labourers who were delegates to a con- Allotments. ference on rural reforms;[2] but his continued interest in the question was much earlier proved by his presentation to the House of Commons of a petition from certain

---

[1] Brown's 'Newark,' p. 277.
[2] Dec. 11, 1891.

inhabitants of Stradbroke, 'complaining of distress, and praying for the allotment of small portions of land for the poor.' [1]

Charles Fox (according to his biographer, Sir George Trevelyan) began his public course utterly unprovided with any fixed set of political opinions : of his one successor in the Whig or Liberal leadership who has been a man of genius, the exact reverse is to be said. Mr. Gladstone, indeed, was equipped with a full set of which, though various shifted, some had a binding influence throughout his life. Politically the progeny of the finest orator and the earliest practical Free Trader Britain in the nineteenth century possessed, and having the good fortune to become the pupil of the greatest constructive statesman of modern times, Mr. Gladstone at the very outset of his career indicated the possession of ideas of his own ; and, although his natural abilities were ripened by the memories of Canning and Huskisson and the training of Peel, those ideas were to carry him far. Oxford had not taught, any more than his father was likely to teach him, to set, as he himself has said, a due value on the imperishable and the inestimable principles of human liberty, for the dominant temper in academic circles was suspicion of freedom : but the University had instilled in him a fervent following of the truth, regardless of consequence ; and the germs of his later Liberalism are to be traced beneath the Toryism, partly inherited, partly acquired, and never wholly dispelled, which encrusted his earlier years. That Toryism, in fact, was far more of an ecclesiastical than a political tinge. He had denounced the Reform Bill, yet, when it became law, he was frankly prepared, like his leader, Peel, to make the best of a constitutional experiment he

His earliest views.

[1] Aug. 10, 1835 : 'Mirror of Parliament' (1835), p. 2367.

could not help regarding as dubious ; but the emphasis he laid upon Church matters in each of his election addresses at Newark indicates with precision that he would have made no such compromise with circumstance if any similarly doubtful experiment had been made with the Establishment. In that distinction lay the measure of difference between his political and his ecclesiastical attitude : he could acquiesce in the defeat of the borough-mongers ; he would have resisted to the utmost an attack upon the bishops. And although, by his own confession, he did not in his youngest period understand the value of liberty for its own sake as a principle of human action and a necessary condition of all high political excellence, there is nothing in his earliest political utterances which would rank him as ever having favoured that mere negation of progress, that frank denial of the inherent goodness of freedom, which marked the stern and unbending Tory of 1832.

But for the moment he was, what *Old England*, a local Tory periodical, called him, 'the thorough Conservative candidate' for Newark; and, as the canvass was made complete, his success at the poll became assured. In the belief of his supporters he was already not merely one who had won golden opinions from all sorts of people, but who promised to be an ornament to the House of Commons; and his opponents, even though attacking him as the mere nominee of a tyrannical duke, had nothing to say to his personal discredit. His oratorical faculty stood him in good stead ; and although of his campaigning speeches only one was at all fully reported, that deserves note as a declaration at once of temper and of policy. It was delivered at a special meet- Dec. 4.
ing of the Red Club, held for the purpose of Important
Newark speech.
affording an opportunity to the ladies of
Newark to present that body with an appropriate flag. One

I

of the ladies submitted an address on behalf of the rest,
in which they said, 'We beg sincerely to congratulate you
on the circumstance of your energies being first called into
action to secure the return to Parliament of so estimable a
character as Mr. Gladstone, a gentleman whose high mental
endowments and excellency of heart fully qualify him, in
our estimation, for filling the important and responsible
situation in which you are desirous—and we feel the greatest
confidence in your being able—to place him.'   Mr. Gladstone, in reply, expressed his hearty rejoicing in the extraordinary countenance given to their cause by the gentler
sex, not only because of reaping honour and encouragement from their smiles, or because the ladies graced by
their presence those ruder assemblages, but for a weightier
reason:—the Red Party were stigmatised as the friends of
tyranny and as men determined to grind the faces of the
poor, to trample on the necks of the oppressed, and, in
particular, to perpetuate the thraldom of the negro; but,
though willing to allow their opponents all possible latitude
of thought and expression, he really thought it was a little
presumptuous that they should arrogate to themselves a
monopoly of the feelings of justice and humanity, when
they, the supposed oppressors, numbered among their
friends so preponderating a portion of that sex which was
pre-eminent for acuteness of conscience and gentleness of
feeling.   With this preface, he broke into an enthusiastic
rulogium of the British flag.   They all knew, he declared,
how the red flag of England had ever been the symbol
both of national moderation and national power; how it had
waved during the awful period of revolutionary war as,
quoting from a speech of Canning, a signal of rallying to
the combatant and of shelter to the fallen.   When every
throne of the Continent had crumbled into dust beneath
the tyrannous strength of France, England remained the

last refuge of civilisation and the last hope of mankind. Our countrymen did not dally, or compromise, or concede, but they stood boldly in the breach, firm in their reliance in Almighty Power, and so that refuge became sure and that hope proved triumphant. The blast which tore every other ensign to tatters served only to unfold their own, and display its beauty and its glory. Nor would that meeting, comparatively trivial though it might seem to some, be void of its purpose and its use if it served to combine more strongly in their minds the cause in which they were engaged with those indelible recollections associated with the red flag of England. No man could say whether the civil struggles into which the country was entering might not prove even more arduous than those in which she had been heretofore engaged ; and, in the meantime, they would look forward with confidence to their own struggle, and, conscious of the justice of the end, would be scrupulous in their choice of the means.[1]

Eulogy of the British Flag.

At the public nomination on Monday, December 10th, the chairman of the Red Club put forward Mr. Gladstone as one who, by talents, information, integrity, morals, and character was highly qualified for a seat in the great council of the nation; but, despite the attribution of all these virtues, the young candidate had to endure a severe heckling. Cries of 'He's a lad!' had greeted the introductory encomium, but the 'lad' speedily proved his skill in fence. He turned a question as to whether he was a nominee of Newcastle by requesting a definition of the word, which the querist was not instantly able to give; being asked what he meant by the desire expressed in his second address to return to sounder general principles, he replied that he had in his mind the

December 10. The nomination.

[1] *Nottingham Journal*, Dec. 7, 1832.

manly and God-fearing principles of two hundred years before—'when they burned witches,' the questioner interjected; and, pressed as to why a stamp duty ought to be continued on newspapers when it was not placed upon Bibles, he rejoined that the latter were of certain and the former only of doubtful good.   But all this, with opposition to the ballot, approval of septennial parliaments, and the expression of a pious opinion that the appetite for political controversy ought to be restricted, was child's play compared to the fight over slavery.

It had not been surprising, under the circumstances of the contest, that Wilde, during the canvass, had laid emphasis upon this last question; and that, when asked whether he conceived that anyone could have property in his fellow-man, he had replied with a decided negative.   Mr. Gladstone, therefore, was probably prepared

The slavery question.   for an attack on the hustings concerning this point, and the attack came. His principal questioner, having denounced the Gladstone family as traffickers in human flesh, deprecated the candidate's habit of quoting scripture in his election addresses, and showed his own consistency by asking Mr. Gladstone whether he knew such a passage in the Bible as that in Exodus, which declares that 'he that stealeth a man, and selleth him, or if he be found in his hand, he shall surely be put to death.'[1] The reply was that the candidate was perfectly aware that the crime of man-stealing was condemned; but such an admission did not go far, and, accordingly, the questions put by the Newark Anti-Slavery Association at the beginning of the contest and then unanswered by him, were now again recited, and a long time was occupied in arguing the slavery problem in its details. The net result was

[1] Exodus, c. xxi. v. 16.

that Mr. Gladstone declared his unequivocal desire for
emancipation upon such terms as would preserve both the
negroes and the colonies from destruction, and his belief
that the slaves ought first to be fully prepared for freedom.

Questions being ended, the candidates had to speak in
order of seniority of service; but Wilde, who was second,
talked at inordinate length, carrying on his address even
until the reporters had to cease taking notes because of the
growing darkness, and winding up by criticising in elaborate
detail Mr. Gladstone's arguments concerning slavery.
Whether, as was by some suspected, this was deliberately
done to prevent his young opponent from having a fair
chance is not certain, but it had that effect; for although,
when Mr. Gladstone's turn came, he addressed himself at
once and with much energy to the emancipation question,
the crowd, which by that time had been assembled for
nearly seven hours on a dull December day, was too im-
patient to listen. His fluency was already so well recognised that even his friends thought that if he began he
might speak for three hours; but the groaning, hissing, and
shouting prevented him from continuing; and, upon a
show of hands being called, it was given against him, with
the result that he at once demanded a poll, which was
fixed to be opened the next morning.

There was a two days' poll, in the fashion of those times;
and, at the close of the first, Mr. Gladstone had a distinct
lead, he having secured 690 votes against 618   Dec. 11-12.
given to Handley, and 564 to Wilde. A   The polling.
turbulent scene followed the knowledge of these numbers,
the Blues, who favoured Wilde, being angry at the apparent
proof which had been afforded that there was a coalition
between the Gladstone Reds and the Handley Yellows.
There had been some fighting all round, with destruction of

banners and breaking of heads, when, as Mr. Gladstone has written, ' in pitch dark I spoke to a friendly crowd out of the window of my sitting-room in the Clinton Arms. A man on the outer line of the crowd flung at me a stone nearly the size of an egg, which entered the window within a foot of my head. He was seen and laid hold on. I understood at the time that he arranged the matter by voting for me on the next day.' [1]

The second day more than sustained Mr. Gladstone's lead, but the polling was slow, the great majority of the voters having cast their suffrages on the first, and the remainder of the struggle lying between Handley and Wilde. It happens that in the British Museum is to be found a privately-compiled collection of poll-books for Newark, containing detailed records of the elections between 1826 and 1847; and appended to some of these is a complete reprint of the addresses, hand-bills, and lampoons issued prior to, during, and at the close of the contest. To political biography, it is a distinct loss that there is no such reprint in the case of either of Mr. Gladstone's contests— those of 1832 and 1841—there simply appearing for these a record of the votes polled ; but even this, as regards the first fight, supplies an indication of its severity. 1577 electors were on the register ; of these 1522 came to the booths, of whom four were rejected ; and the close of the Mr. Gladstone heads poll saw Mr. Gladstone at the head with a the poll, total of 887 votes, [2] Handley coming next with 798, and Wilde bringing up the rear with 726. An analysis of the voting shows that the loser had the most

[1] Brown's ' Newark,' p. 283.

[2] The canvass must have been exceedingly well done, for a calculation on the Conservative side some six weeks before the poll, gave Mr. Gladstone ' about ' 890 votes

individual support; but, while 413 electors 'plumped' for
Wilde, 175 for Mr. Gladstone, and only 33 for Handley,
582 split their votes between the two winners, 130 between
Mr. Gladstone and Wilde, and 183 between Wilde and
Handley, the contention of the deeply-disappointed Blues
that there had been a virtual coalition between the Reds
and the Yellows being apparently well-founded.

In any case, Mr. Gladstone was thus an easy winner;
and the coffin, labelled 'Young Gladstone's Ambition,'
which had been carried about the streets, had to be put
away once and for all.   But the supporters of Wilde, who
had shown their temper not only in this fashion but by
frequent stone-throwings, were so infuriated at defeat that
they attacked the polling-places, and broke the windows of
many of their opponents.   Even the quieter Whigs were
much chagrined; their expressions of anguish, a friendly
chronicler observed, were deep and sincere; and they
could extract little comfort from the reflection that, as the
Times phrased it, 'Newark is thus again returned under
the nomination of the Duke of Newcastle, or, to use the
language of the Red Club, the recommendation of his
Grace.'

On the morning after the voting ended, the Mayor made the
formal declaration of the poll then customary; and Mr. Gladstone, in returning fervent thanks, showed
himself so satisfied with the result that he even   *and returns thanks.*
spoke well of the conduct of the Blues.   He stayed in the
town some days longer in order to see the unopposed choice
of his friend Lincoln for South Notts.; and, on the evening
this had taken place, there was a dinner in its celebration,
at which, according to an ecstatic Tory print, he 'delivered
a truly eloquent speech, replete with sound constitutional
sentiments, high moral feeling, and ability of the most

distinguished order.' And even this was not the end of his
oratorical labours, for, when passing through Nottingham
two days later on his way to Leamington, he by invitation
made what the same authority declared to be a most admirable address. It was with an admitted pang that the
editor of the *Nottingham Journal* had to omit a report ;
but there was compensation in adding of the new member
for Newark, that ' he is a young gentleman of amiable
manners and the most extraordinary talent ; and we venture
to predict, without the slightest exaggeration, that he will
one day be classed among the most able statesmen in the
British Senate.'

That kind of prophecy has been often made, and has
seldom been so signally fulfilled ; but, seeing that the
admiration he had won at Eton and at Oxford was now
being even more flatteringly voiced in the Press, it was as
well that, while he was resting at Leamington from his
electoral labours, Mr. Gladstone had a less pleasing account
of himself to peruse. The *Reflector*, a London weekly
paper not long started, wrote of the Newark result :
' Serjeant Wilde, the liberal candidate, opposed a couple of
tories, both of them nominees of the Duke of Newcastle.
One of these tories was a young man of two or three and
twenty, son of Mr. Gladstone, of Liverpool, a person who
(we are speaking of the father) has amassed a large fortune
by West India dealings. In other words, a great part of
his gold has sprung from the blood of the black slaves.
Respecting the youth himself—a person fresh from college,
and whose mind is as much like a sheet of white foolscap
as is possible—he was utterly unknown. He came recommended by no claim in the world, *except the will of the
Duke !* The Duke nodded unto Newark, and Newark sent
back the man, or rather the boy, of his choice . . . The

voters for Gladstone went up to that candidate's booth (the slave driver, as they called him) with Wilde's colours. People who had on former occasions voted for Wilde, and were about to vote against him, said on being asked to give their suffrage, "We cannot, we dare not. We have lost half our business, and we shall lose the rest, if we go against the Duke. We would do anything in our power for Serjeant Wilde, and the cause : but we cannot starve !" Now, what say ye, our merry men, touching the ballot ?' 'Our merry men,' if the writer meant the Whigs, were not in the mood, on that subject, to say much, for it was to be left to the 'sheet of white foolscap' to have impressed upon it the carrying of the Ballot Act. 'Since that time,' wrote Mr. Gladstone, more than forty years later, to an old Newark acquaintance, 'both Newark and I have materially altered our politics. What then ? At that time we were endeavouring to do our duty as best we could see it, and we are making just the same endeavour now.'

VI.—THE YOUNG PARLIAMENTARY HAND.

IN order to appreciate in any degree Mr. Gladstone's progress in political thought and action from that January day in 1833, when first as a senator he crossed the threshold of the House of Commons, it is necessary to realise the condition of the world of thought, the world of manners, and the world of works as the young member for Newark entered upon public life. It was a time when men were still hanged in chains, when slavery existed in our colonies, when soldiers received lashes by the hundred for trivial offences, when the duel was recognised as a method of adjusting political quarrels, when the bread of the people was taxed, and when Useful Knowledge was a vaunted panacea for social ills. In medicine, there was no chloroform ; in art, the sun had not been enlisted in the service of portraiture : the farmer used the flail as his fathers had done from the most distant ages ; and the house-keeper still extracted fire from flint-and-steel by almost as prolonged and painsgiving a process as the stick-rubbing of a savage. Though railways were just struggling into existence, the electric telegraph was unknown ; gas was regarded as an unfashionable light ; postage was dear, newspapers were taxed, and the masses, sunk in pauperism, had no effective means of dispelling their inherited ignorance.

Those were days when the rulers of men spoke much of the Constitution and little of the commonweal ; it was of the Church, and not of religion, that they talked. The

State to them was made up of 'interests,' of which they were themselves part. There was the landed interest, always foremost in the list; there was the manufacturing interest; there was the shipping interest; no one seemed to dream that there was a labour interest. While 'the land' was referred to with bated breath and whispering humbleness, labour was customarily associated with contemptuous epithet. The world has moved fast and has moved far since then. Even the phrases that period applied to the great body of the people—the lower orders, the common herd, the mob, or, when pedantry demanded, the *mobile vulgus*—vanished with the incoming of household suffrage.

In literature, when Mr. Gladstone entered Parliament, Scott, broken with hard work and heavy losses, had just died; Carlyle, disappointed in his earlier visits to London, and eating his heart out at Craigenputtock, was awaiting the publication of his first characteristic book; Tennyson was being recognised by the few as worthy of hope because of his juvenile poems; Macaulay was simply a brilliant young Whig member, who had written some stirring verse and splendid prose; the Brontës were school-girls; Thackeray, dabbling in unsuccessful newspaper enterprises, was dreaming of becoming an artist; Dickens had not written a line of fiction; and Browning and George Eliot, among our greater names, were yet to come. In theology, Newman, upon a voyage from which he thought to never return, was just emerging from Evangelicalism; Pusey was known only as an Oxford tutor; Samuel Wilberforce was a village curate, and Henry Manning a young graduate; Edward Irving was mystifying the multitude with 'the gift of tongues'; and Chalmers was but a party leader in an undivided Kirk. And in science, when geology was yet to be placed upon a sound basis and biology was virtually unknown, Darwin was on the *Beagle*, voyaging in distant seas, and commencing that series of investigations which revolutionised the popular conception of created things.

In this January of 1833, Princess—for nearly sixty years Queen—Victoria was a girl of thirteen; Cobden was a young calico-printer, and Bright a younger cotton-spinner; Palmerston was generally regarded as a man-about-town, who in politics had mistaken his vocation, and Disraeli as a brilliant novelist with eccentric habits and parliamentary ambitions. The future Marquis of Salisbury and Prime Minister of Britain was an infant scarcely out of arms; Lord Rosebery (Mr. Gladstone's successor in the Liberal Premiership), Lord Spencer, Lord Herschell, Mr. John Morley, Mr. Campbell-Bannerman, Mr. Asquith, Mr. Bryce, Mr. Acland, and Mr. Arnold Morley—or more than half the members of his latest Cabinet—remained to be born; as did also the Duke of Devonshire, Mr. Balfour, and Mr. Chamberlain, among those who were his keenest opponents towards the end of his public career. And even the legislative chamber in which the new member sat was completely different from that of to-day. It was the old St. Stephen's Chapel, given by the Sixth Edward to the service of the Commons, wherein Bacon and Raleigh, Eliot and Wentworth, Coke and Selden, Pym and Hampden, Cromwell and Henry Vane, St. John and Walpole, Pulteney and Burke, the elder and the younger Pitt, Fox and Canning had in turn displayed their distinguished abilities; and the tapestry upon the walls of which even yet concealed the sacred symbols of a once holy place. And in that chamber Mr. Gladstone was to sit with men who had witnessed the Gordon Riots, and who could remember the entrance into Parliament of the younger Pitt; with members who had watched the whole course of political events from the Coalition of 1783, throughout the half-century during which the Whigs had been virtually deprived of power; with men who had been in the House before the birth of Peel, and to whom Burke was more than a memory; with those who had assisted in the impeachment of Hastings; and with one who had been thanked by Parliament for his share in suppressing the Mutiny at the Nore. On the opposite benches he saw George Byng, who had been first returned for Middlesex in 1780 as the colleague of Wilkes; on his own was Sir Charles Burrell whose earliest colleague for Shoreham had been the father of Shelley. And among the politicians with whom he talked outside was Thomas Grenville, who, over fifty years before, had arranged the terms of separation between this country and the United States.

But if the past spread its notable men before the gaze of this ardent beginner in politics, the present had many a striking example, and the veil which hid the future only temporarily retarded the recognition of some who were destined to be illustrious. Upon the Treasury Bench sat 'Honest Jack' Althorp as leader, with Palmerston and John Russell, Stanley and Sir James Graham among his lieutenants, while Peel and Goulburn and Herries, soon to have the two last-named as their supporters, were upon the bench opposite. It was an assembly which abounded in practised and promised talent, and the mere record of its remembered names stirs the politician's blood even now. O'Connell and Sheil led the Nationalist representatives of Ireland, one of them a son of Grattan himself; Cobbett and Burdett were acute specimens of that type of Radicalism which has a habit at unexpected moments of strengthening the Tories; Grote and Ricardo were of the philosophical

Radical school, which had little in common with the erratic Roebuck, the literary Bulwer (not yet Lytton, and a Tory), the fantastic Silk Buckingham, or the severely economical Hume. On the Opposition benches were such dogged Tories as Sir Robert Inglis and Sir Richard Vyvyan, both as persuaded as Croker and Sir Charles Wetherell that England's sun had set on the previous Seventh of June, both dimly suspicious that Peel did not share that belief, but both prepared to fight for Throne and Altar to the end. The same side saw representatives of a younger school of Conservatism—Lincoln, Herbert, and Gladstone—destined all to be Liberal in later life, and Lord Ashley, who, as Earl of Shaftesbury, left an enduring mark upon the philanthropic development of the age. And among those who sat in that House, and who still survived when, on March 3rd, 1894, Mr. Gladstone surrendered the seals of office for the last time into the hands of the Queen, were the Lord Howick who became Earl Grey, the Lord Grimston who was afterwards Earl of Verulam, the Lord Stormont who was later Earl of Mansfield, and Lord Charles Russell, in after years Serjeant-at-Arms to the House of Commons.

Into an assembly which calls the politician back to the days when there were giants at Westminster, the young member for Newark was entitled to enter with no uncertain step. His equipment, indeed, was a striking example of scholastic training as applied to plastic genius, for it was not only at Eton and Oxford that this had been in process, his home life having similarly served to prepare him for a public career. The mental atmosphere of the Gladstone family was disputatious or, at the least, argumentative by the express wish of its head. The first Sir Robert Peel had trained his greater son to debate by setting him as a child upon the dining-room table, and there bidding him discourse. John Gladstone His training in —himself, as has been shown, of a comba- argument. tively reasoning turn—varied the example by enjoining his sons to argue. In the case of that one of them who was to become the most illustrious, little paternal pressure was necessary to stimulate a natural bent. Mr. Gladstone's youngest daughter has told that perhaps his earliest authenticated remark was, 'Take it away : how can I do two things at once?' addressed to a nurse who, while he was learning his lessons, was bringing him some physic. The astute question of the child developed into the dialectics by which he is traditionally alleged to have saved himself from a flogging at Eton, and, according to his own acknowledgment, to have attempted to throw dust in the eyes of the examiners for 'the Ireland.' A college friend who visited him in the new Kincardineshire home at Fasque during the summer of 1829, observed that the children and their friends argued upon everything. It was no matter whether the topic was great or small—whether an intrusive wasp should be killed, upon which nail a picture should be hung, if a particular window ought to be shut, whether a trout should be boiled or broiled, and, first and last subject of all in these islands, the probability of the next day's weather : all which arguments were not merely the dialectical differences of children, but were smiled upon by the family's head.

It needed little training, therefore, to cause Mr. Gladstone to love argument for its own sake. As a boy, playing with other lads, he was noted for never being content with a simple answer to a question, and for desiring to probe everything to the bottom ; and, even when apparently beaten for the moment, it was recognised by members of

his own family as well as by those around that his persist-
ence would win in the end. Often, indeed, it was by sheer
force of will rather than strength of reasoning that he succeeded in dominating his companions ; but, whether it was
the one or the other, he was always certain of hearty
approval for his victory from his father. What in John
Gladstone was shrewdness heightened by caution became
in his youngest son keenness tempered to subtlety ; but,
with each, an over-exactitude of phrase caused misunderstanding. More than once, the father's words, to the
majority of those who listened, bore a meaning which their
speaker disclaimed : how often this happened in regard
to the son passes the power to count. Thus it has been
that, while there were critics of John Gladstone who hinted
that his mind was of the type known of all as Jesuitic, the
same taunt was a thousand times levelled at William
Gladstone by those who had no idea that they were condemning an hereditary instinct, and not an acquired power.
But in each case there is a fairer explanation than that
of intention to deceive, of keeping the word of promise to
the ear and breaking it to the hope. The wish to make a
point absolutely clear involves a danger of so marring the
outlines as to puzzle those unpossessed of the same desire
to discriminate. What the mass of men require from a
speaker is the effect of scene-painting : if they are given the
detail of copper-plate, they are of necessity confounded.
Bold in design and distinct in colour must be the picture
which is to impress the mass ; and Balzac's old painter,
whose hidden masterpiece became by long-continued labour
a mere blur of confused tints, crossed by eccentric lines,
was the extreme exemplar of that longing to make clear
the already comprehensible and to improve upon the
perfect, which in politics is apt to darken counsel and

confound the general understanding, and which proved the root defect, inherited in marked degree from his father, of certain of the mental processes of Mr. Gladstone.

But this was not all the inheritance which, even thus early, affected Mr. Gladstone's career. There were always two instincts at work drawing him in diverse directions— the metaphysical which led him to religion, the practical which attracted him to politics; and both he owed to the father, who was born a Scottish Presbyterian and became an English merchant. And why that which, in the father, remained to the end commercialism became in the son a political development, is to be understood from the circumstances surrounding the younger's up-bringing. When William Gladstone was growing into manhood, John Gladstone had passed the more striving stage of his business career into monetary success; and he was, therefore, under no obligation to train his youngest and most brilliant son to the counting-house. For the further reason that the health of certain members of the family suffered by confinement to Liverpool, William Gladstone lived but a small portion of his early days in his native town, and, therefore, was not penetrated with that atmosphere of trade which is inhaled by all who dwell in a great commercial centre. And, by the time he was able to think in the least for himself, he was to find his father spoken of everywhere as 'the friend of Mr. Canning' and 'the confidant of Mr. Huskisson,' and to have in the parental home statesmanship rather than shipping as the staple of conversation. It was thus, at a period when his father was erecting churches and entertaining the more expansive Tory statesmen, that William Gladstone's religious and political instincts were fed in a measure which affected the whole of a prolonged career.

K

'I was bred under the shadow of the great name of Canning,' Mr. Gladstone has declared; 'every influence

Influenced by
Canning connected with that name governed the politics of my childhood and of my youth; with Mr. Canning I rejoiced in the removal of religious disabilities from the Roman Catholic body, and in the free and truly British tone which he gave to our policy abroad; with Mr. Canning I rejoiced in the opening he made towards the establishment of free commercial interchanges between nations; with Mr. Canning and under the shadow of that great name, and under the shadow of the yet more venerable name of Burke, I grant my youthful mind and imagination were impressed.' [1]   And this reference to Burke is of the more significance when read in relation to another autobiographical allusion in a speech delivered not long before—as the one just quoted was delivered not long after —he became the Liberal leader in the House of Commons. The ideas under the influence of which he was brought up, he therein observed, ' were not ideas which belonged to the old current of English history; nor were they in conformity with the liberal sentiments which pervaded, at its best periods, the politics of the country, and which harmonized with the spirit of the old British Constitution.   They were, on the contrary, ideas referable to those lamentable excesses of the first French Revolution, which produced

and Burke, here a terrible reaction, and went far to establish the doctrine that the masses of every community were in permanent antagonism with the laws under which they lived, and were disposed to regard those laws, and the persons by whom the laws were made and administered, as their natural enemies.' [2]

[1] April 27, 1866: ' Hansard,' 3rd series, vol. clxxxiii., f. 129.
[2] May 11, 1864: *Ibid.*, vol. clxxv., f. 322.

Trained, therefore, in an atmosphere of reverential remembrance of Burke and semi-idolatrous veneration for
Canning, and accustomed to hold Huskisson in highest
respect, it was a statesman differing in quality and degree
of genius from all, and on the surface more reactionary
than any one of them, who was destined to be Mr. Gladstone's model and exemplar in public life.   The one man
in the new House of Commons who was to influence the
career of the young member for Newark was, in fact, Peel.
That statesman was then in his forty-fifth year ; and, great
as had been his services to the State, he was
to achieve still greater.   But at the moment, ^{but mainly by Peel.}
he was distinctly under suspicion with his own party.   For a
considerable portion of his public life, he had been the idol of
the straiter sect of the Tories.   Entrusted with office at an
early age, he had won from them golden opinions for his
conduct as Chief Secretary for Ireland, in which capacity,
indeed, he had somewhat unfairly received the nick-name
of ' Orange Peel ' for his supposed excessive devotion to the
section of ascendancy.   Because of his ' Protestantism '—
using the term as it was then employed simply as indicating
sturdy opposition to the Roman Catholic claims—he had
been the chosen candidate of the Eldon faction for the
University of Oxford, in preference to Canning.   He had
adhered to that faction in 1827 on its breaking away, with
Wellington at its head, from Canning when undertaking the
Premiership.   But from that time events began to accumu-
late which ultimately drove him from the leadership of the
Tory party, and split that party itself into fragments.

The adoption of Catholic Emancipation under a Ministry
of which Wellington was the chief and Peel his most influential supporter, fell as a heavy blow upon that portion
of the Tory party on which, more even than upon its

aristocratic connections, it found itself necessitated for the
next forty years largely to lean.   The clergy were not
content with ousting Peel from his cherished seat at Oxford:
they brooded at home over the treachery of which they held
him to have been guilty, and they never wholly forgave
his action in 1829.   But not alone were the clergy distrust-
ful: many Tories believed that Peel had committed a tactical
error of cardinal importance in not rising immediately after
Russell upon the introduction of the first Reform Bill, and
then and there securing—as it was thought he could have
secured—its instant rejection.   And, while his subsequent
attitude towards that measure did not satisfy either the
high-flying Tories or those of the stamp of John Gladstone
(who, indeed, denounced it in emphatic terms at a Liverpool
anti-Reform meeting, just as his son was absorbed in securing the 'double first'), it was considered by some of the
party that he had acted unchivalrously towards Wellington
by withholding his support in the spring of 1832, when the
duke was called upon by the King to form a Ministry after
Grey's temporary retirement.

In addition to all these causes for Tory discontent with
Peel, there was the fact, of overwhelming importance to the
purely partisan mind, that, at the beginning of 1833, he was
at the head of less than a quarter of the House of Commons,
and that the prospect of his securing a majority was so remote that men troubled not to discuss the contingency.   It
is, of course, when a political leader is beaten that his ill
qualities are most easily discovered and most freely discussed; but it is necessary to remember, in at least semi-
justification of the more extreme Tory attitude, that Peel
had yet to show the full extent of his powers, and that,
when the Reformed Parliament first met, he was hampered
by the reactionary traditions which enchained his party, and

by the exaggerated anticipations of political evil in which many even of its leading members indulged. There is no reason to doubt the sincerity of these fears, which, expressed in the gravest terms by the Duke of Wellington, the venerable leader of the Tories, touched the nadir of absurdity in the bemoanings of the youngest of their band, who, as Lincoln confided to Charles Wordsworth, were 'horrified' at the outlook.[1]

But, although there was a compact body of Radicals in the new House, the fears, whether of bigoted Tories or timid Whigs, were soon seen to be baseless. Many of the Reformers who had clamoured the country through for 'the Bill, the whole Bill, and nothing but the Bill,' showed in an unexpected sense at Westminster that, when they had obtained the Bill and the whole Bill, it was nothing but the Bill that they wanted. Satis- *Quietist Reformers.* fied to have turned the stage-coach into a steam-train, they had no desire to travel appreciably faster. The first Reformed Parliament was strongly in favour of removing such grievances as the ten-pound householders felt and the Whig peers did not profit by; and in that direction it did much striking work. But never for a moment after its meeting was there a danger of it becoming revolutionary; the majority of the majority would have resented as the deepest insult even a hint that it might prove Radical; and a House of Commons which was capable of rejecting a motion directed against the continued existence of the press-gang, and a Ministry which opposed, in the person of one of its law officers, the allowance of counsel to prisoners charged with felony, were not lightly to be accused even of being Liberal.

The first session of the earliest Parliament in which Mr.

[1] Charles Wordsworth's 'Early Annals,' p. 101.

Gladstone sat was opened on Monday, January 29th, 1833 ;

Jan. 29, 1833.
Opening of the Re-
formed Parliament.
but four days previously, the young member for Newark had undertaken another than a political duty, thus formally recorded in the archives of Lincoln's Inn: 'William Ewart Gladstone of Christ Church Oxford B.A., aged 23 years, fourth son of John Gladstone Esq., of Fasque, County Kincardine-shire is admitted into the Society of this Inn the 25th day of January 1833. Admitted by the Rt. Hon. Sir Lancelot

Jan. 25.
Mr. Gladstone
admitted a law
student.
Shadwell [1] Treasurer.' It is not to be presumed that Mr. Gladstone intended adopting the bar as his profession : this entrance to the Inn was simply another means of securing every advantage of a liberal education : but he could not have avoided reflecting that George Grenville and Pitt and Canning, all of them afterwards Prime Ministers, had in turn been enrolled upon the list of students of the Honourable Society of Lincoln's Inn : it is for us to note that Benjamin Disraeli, himself like Mr. Gladstone to become Prime Minister, had entered as a student seven years previously, and had left the Society rather more than a twelvemonth before his future rival was admitted. [2]

There had never been a time when a young politician of genius had a better opportunity for making his mark. Many brilliant speakers and practised administrators were already at Westminster, but the revolutionised conditions of parliamentary life and thought were all in favour of a new man being both heard and felt. Before Mr. Gladstone had sat in St. Stephen's Chapel a week, the dashing young novelist and, at the moment, nondescript

[1] Then Vice-Chancellor of England.

[2] Disraeli, who was admitted on November 18, 1824, kept seven terms, and left the Society on November 25, 1831.

politician who was destined to be the member for Newark's greatest rival perceived, and placed upon record, the chance afforded to the aspiring. Disraeli had listened to a debate on the Address in which Bulwer and Stanley, Macaulay and Sheil, Charles Grant and Russell took part; in his opinion it was one of the finest there Disraeli and the new had been for years; 'but,' he wrote the   Parliament. next day to his sister, 'between ourselves, I could floor them all. This *entre nous:* I was never more confident of anything than that I could carry everything before me in that House. The time will come'[1]—an echo in anticipation of the historic prophecy which concluded his maiden speech five years later.

Mr. Gladstone, less boastful but equally confident, had not sat in Parliament a month before his voice was heard in debate. In his later years, he noted that the deference, and even the reverence, with which in his day every man entered what he always considered the noblest deliberative assembly in the world, had undergone a woeful change; and there was no longer the same preparation of mind to defer to the wish of the House as to the mode, time, and degree of laying his opinions before it. No lack of temptation existed to cause him to speak early and to speak often. His friends had such an intense belief in his powers that Arthur Hallam wrote, just as he was elected, 'We want such a man as that. In some things he is likely to be obstinate and prejudiced; but he has a fine fund of high, chivalrous, Tory sentiment, and a tongue, moreover, to let it loose with.' As early, indeed, as February 15th, he was approached by Pusey in regard to the Irish Church Temporalities scheme,[2] explained by Althorp, on behalf of the

---

[1] Disraeli's 'Correspondence with his Sister,' p. 16.
[2] H. P. Liddon's 'Life of E. B. Pusey,' vol. i., p. 273.

Ministry, only three evenings before; but it was not upon a burning question, it was upon a subject concerning which Mr. Gladstone's first parliamentary subject. he had local and personal information, that he first spoke. The discussion was upon a petition, signed by over three thousand inhabitants of Liverpool, complaining of the bribery practised with the freemen there, and of the manner in which was conducted the election of the Corporation's officers—for municipal reform was yet to come as the wholesome and most useful fruit of parliamentary. Prior to the Reform Act, the voting Corruption at Liverpool. power of that borough had been entirely in the hands of the freemen, and among these corruption had been known to extensively prevail. This had come to a head at a bye-election in November, 1830, consequent upon the death of Huskisson. Two candidates, differing only slightly in their politics, and both professing to be favourable to parliamentary reform, were put forward —William Ewart, son of John Gladstone's old friend, who had died seven years before, and John Evelyn Denison, afterwards Speaker of the House of Commons and Viscount Ossington. Ewart won, after a seven days' poll, by no more than 29 on a total of 4401, of whom it was calculated that not a fourth voted without being bribed, the market price of votes rapidly rising from £5 on the first to about £40 on the seventh day.[1]

Mr. Gladstone, who was then at Oxford, and whose family had supported Denison as the least advanced candidate, was speedily made aware of certain of these facts, for, writing on the following December 28th to Charles Wordsworth from Lansdowne House, Leamington, where he was spending the Christmas, he observed: 'Since I

[1] Sir James Picton's 'Memorials of Liverpool,' vol. i., pp. 423, 424.

came here I have heard a good deal of that sorry business, the Liverpool election, from one of my brothers,[1] who resides there and who took part in it.   He declined having anything to do with the expenditure during the contest, and so had not direct access to knowledge of the amount disbursed.   The current rumour is that Ewart's expenses are 36,000*l.* and Denison's 46,000*l.*;[2] but my brother says Ewart's are the greater of the two, and he knows Denison's to be 41,000*l.*   Ewart's party have had no public subscription opened, and are, therefore, at liberty to call their expenses what they choose; but Denison's are necessarily revealed.   About 19,000*l.* has been subscribed for him. The election, they say, is absolutely *certain* to be set aside, and Denison will, probably, come in on the next opening. There is an idea, however, that the writ may be suspended and Liverpool remain with only one member.'[3]

This prognostication would have been precisely realised but for the sudden dissolution of the next April, for a select committee of the Commons reported in the March that Ewart had not been duly elected, and that gross bribery and treating had prevailed.   The writ was temporarily suspended, but, before any further action could be taken, Parliament was dissolved.   According to a story current at the time, Denison had meanwhile written, through Robertson Gladstone, to his Liverpool friends, inquiring whether they would recommend him to stand again, but they made no reply, 'dreading, it was supposed, the necessity of another subscription among themselves'; but, although he accordingly stood for Nottinghamshire, he and Ewart were chosen

[1] Robertson Gladstone.

[2] Sir James Picton says Ewart's expenses were estimated at £65,000, and Denison's at more than £50,000; 'Liverpool,' vol. i., p. 424.

[3] Charles Wordsworth's 'Early Annals,' p. 88, 89.

for Liverpool over Gascoyne : and, when he decided to sit for Notts., Lord Sandon replaced him, and the last-named, with Ewart, was re-elected after the dissolution of 1832. But the Whigs attributed Sandon's return to bribery, and hence the petition of February, 1833.

At that period, it was allowable for the member presenting a petition to raise a discussion upon its merits, a custom abolished, because of its growing inconvenience, during this same session; and Sandon accordingly seized the opportunity to defend himself and his friends.   Rigby Wason, then a well-known Radical member, denounced the corruption for which Liverpool had become too famous ; and Mr. Gladstone came to the rescue of his native town.   He submitted that no corrupt influence had been used either by Sandon or any of his supporters at the latest contest ; he waxed sarcastic over the effects of the Reform Act, 'that cure for all our grievances ; ' and he protested against the injustice that would be inflicted by disfranchising, as prayed in the petition, all who had been admitted to the freedom since the notorious election of November, 1830.[1]   And this, in reality, was Mr. Gladstone's maiden speech.

Feb. 21, 1833.
His first speech.

'Mr. W. Gladstone was understood to protest against the statements made by the petitioners, and to state that he believed there had been no undue practices at the late election for Liverpool, either on the part of the noble lord or of his supporters : ' thus was reported in the *Times* the first of the thousands of addresses from the same speaker it would have to record.   'Mr. Gladstone made a few remarks, which were not audible in the Gallery : ' this was how the *Morning*

---

[1] 'Hansard,' 3rd series, vol. xv., f. 1030 ; 'Mirror of Parliament' (1833), p. 351.   Mr. Gladstone, it is known, prefers the latter authority for his early parliamentary speeches.

Chronicle commenced a five-line summary of the maiden speech. 'Mr. Gladstone, who spoke under the gallery, and who was almost entirely inaudible in the gallery,' was the *Sun's* account; while the *True Sun* and the *Morning Herald* similarly referred to the speaker only as ' Mr. Gladstone '—no attempt at discrimination between Thomas of Portarlington (where, despite the opposition of O'Connell, he had been returned, but by no more than one vote), and William of Newark being made in any journal except the *Times*—as a prelude to their summaries of three and four lines respectively. But reporting in the House of Commons was conducted under extreme difficulties in those days. Not only was there no special gallery set apart for the convenience of the Press; not merely were there so many new representatives that ' an honourable member, whose name we could not learn,' was a frequent speaker; but the noise and confusion in a cramped and overcrowded Chamber, filled with new members all bubbling over with enthusiasm for work, was so great that, on this same evening and shortly after Mr. Gladstone had risen, Althorp could not be heard when he addressed a question to the Speaker, and the reply was equally indistinct. No sensation, therefore, attended upon Mr. Gladstone's earliest speech in the House of Commons. Unlike the brilliant failure of his future rival, which was a portent to keen observers of greatness to come, it was not an excursion into high politics but an utterance upon a local matter, delivered from a dim corner and only imperfectly heard. But, though it was not accompanied by any of the signs which romantic retailers of legend love to attach to such occasions, one omen was furnished which the critic will mark, for this earliest parliamentary address was held by the immediately succeeding speaker to lack clearness, and the young member had to rise and explain precisely what he desired to convey:

A counter-petition from Liverpool, signed by over eight thousand persons, was speedily presented; and this was supported on March 6th by Thomas Gladstone in a speech of some significance. Two years previously, and on the day before the sudden dissolution of 1831, an attack had been made in the House upon 'an association in Liverpool called "The Canning Cycle," which disposed of whatever patronage that right honourable gentleman had with respect to the town, according to the subscriptions paid, the subscribers having a voice in the disposal according to the sums paid by them;' and to this Thomas Gladstone, in his solitary speech during his first Parliament, had at once replied, 'I do not rise to defend the conduct of a great part of the freemen of Liverpool at the last election, for I believe it to have been infamous; but I rise to repel the unwarrantable attack that has been made on Mr. Canning and Mr. Huskisson, whose memories I revere. . . . That neither was guilty of such conduct I need hardly say —but I happen to be the son of one of Mr. Canning's The Gladstones and leading friends; and I do most unhesitat-
Canning. ingly declare, on the authority of those who were conusant of all that took place during his elections, that at no time were bribes given to promote his return.' While admitting that Canning's election expenses were paid —a point which, with regard to both Canning and Huskisson, William Gladstone sixty years later corroborated—he contradicted the 'cycle' story; and the assailant thereupon allowed that he had been 'mistaken in saying that the "Canning Cycle" shared the patronage of Mr. Canning in Liverpool.' [1]

[1] 'Mirror of Parliament' (1831), p. 1616: the 'Canning Cycle' had

But this admission was made grudgingly, and the original allegation was repeated with emphasis outside the House by one of the leading parliamentarians of the day. In the debate of March 6th, 1833, now under consideration, Thomas Gladstone replied to an attack of O'Connell upon 'the bribing cycle of the friends of Mr. Canning'; and observed, 'The honourable and learned member has, how-ever, attempted to turn that body to his own account; for he made an attempt—I am happy to say an ineffectual one—to deprive me of a seat in this House, by denouncing me to those whose suffrages I sought [at Partarlington], as the spawn of a member of this corrupt cycle,' the composition of which the speaker asserted to be independent.[1] It was thus as spawn be-gotten by corruption that O'Connell spoke of the eldest of John Gladstone's sons; a few years later the youngest repaid the insult with interest; but his opinion of O'Connell subsequently changed.

O'Connell and the Gladstones.

Despite a decided protest from Sandon, the House resolved without a division to appoint a select committee to inquire into the matters alleged in the earlier Liverpool petition; and it will be convenient to at once dispose of Mr. Gladstone's connection with this matter during the session of 1833. The committee was chosen after some further wrangling, but it found various difficulties in the way. The aid of the House had to be sought to compel a witness to present himself for examination and to force another, in this case a woman, to answer questions; but by April 1st it could bring up its report. There the matter rested until July 4th, when a Whig proposed the appointment

first been publicly heard of during the discussion of the John Gladstone and Lord Liverpool correspondence of 1814-15.

[1] *Ibid.* (1833), pp. 595, 596.

of another committee to carry on the inquiry, the earlier
one having declared that no systematic bribery had
taken place. Various members of that body objected to
such a slight being placed upon its report; and Gaskell,
Mr. Gladstone's old Eton friend, now sitting for Wenlock,
emphatically protested against a motion which, he held,
would affect the security of the elective franchise in every
town throughout the empire. As he sat down, a few Whigs
ejaculated 'Question! Question!' and Mr. Gladstone rose
with the remark, 'I am happy, sir, at least for one reason,
to hear some honourable members cry " Question!" for I
am bound to conclude that those who call for the question
have at least read the evidence.' As it was his avowed
Mr. Gladstone and
Liverpool once more. fortune to be intimately connected with the
town of Liverpool, he admitted that the
proceedings at the election of 1830 were sufficient to
secure for it an immortality of disgrace; but he assured the
House that that was in a great degree attributable to an
accidental combination of events, which would have produced very nearly the same results in any constituency in
England. He argued that, as bribery was a guilty practice,
the giver of the bribe ought to be punished as well as the
taker: 'Why,' he asked, 'should you let the bribers, and
those who profit most by the guilt, and who, in my mind,
are chargeable with by far the greater share of it, escape
scot-free?' [1] The cases of bribery at the 1832 election
had, however, been so miserably few that he implored the
House ' in the name of principle, in the name of equity, in

---

[1] Wason's reply reads strangely now : ' The honourable gentleman,
the member for Newark, says that you ought to punish the briber ; but
I have never been of that opinion.' The course of subsequent legislation has been all in favour of Mr. Gladstone's contention and against
Wason's

the name of common sense, to refuse the prolongation of
this enquiry; to refuse to immolate, on such insufficient
pretexts, the rights of these poor freemen; not imperceptibly to be led into the decision of a general principle
under cover of a particular case; and not to offer so poor
a tribute to the hunger of the Genius of Reform.'[1]   But
the appeal was unavailing; the motion was adopted by two
to one; and on July 8th, when the question of the precise
quorum of the committee was discussed, Mr. Gladstone
was similarly unsuccessful in endeavouring, with Sandon,
to have it larger than the Whigs desired.

While these prolonged and far from satisfying discussions
were proceeding, Mr. Gladstone was moving in other directions.   On March 6th, he was elected to the
just-established Carlton Club, on the motion
of John Young, an old schoolmate at Eton,

March 6.
Elected to the
Carlton.

then a fellow-student at Lincoln's Inn, afterwards a colleague
in two Administrations, and created a peer by Mr. Gladstone in his first Ministry, he being seconded by Sir
Edmund Hayes; and both mover and seconder were Irish
members, the one representing Cavan and the other Done-
gal.   But Young and his Irish membership were the parent
of an even more interesting connection for Mr. Gladstone,
and that with the greatest Irishman of his day.   O'Connell
was at the moment, and with a view to appearing if he so
desired at the English bar, 'eating his
dinners' at Lincoln's Inn, the chosen legal
home of the member for Newark.   Very

His earliest
acquaintance with
O'Connell.

shortly after the latter entered Parliament, O'Connell,
who was placed upon a select committee with him in this
earliest session, talked to him concerning his fellow-Tory
members, and remarked of Young that he was a very

[1] *Ibid.,* pp. 2755, 2756.

sensible man. But a closer connection was the fruit of a singular parliamentary incident of the next year. Daniel Whittle Harvey, then member for Colchester and afterwards for Southwark, a well-known Radical of that period, had applied years before to be called to the bar, and had been refused because of some curious transactions in which he had been engaged while a solicitor. The matter had been more than once discussed in the House of Commons; and at length, on May 15th, 1834, a select committee was appointed to inquire into all the circumstances attending the rejection of his claim to be 'called.' Peel, O'Connell, Hume, Hardinge, Grote, and Bulwer were among the members at once nominated; and two days later Mr. Gladstone, with Evelyn Denison, was included with those added. Peel, Hardinge, and Denison soon asked to be relieved from serving, but the others worked on; and on June 30th the House empowered the committee, with three as a quorum, to adjourn from place to place, with the result that, on Thursday, July 10th, the committee met, with O'Connell as usual in the chair, at a house at Coggeshall, in Essex, to examine a special witness,[1] who was disabled by age from travelling. The three members of the sub-committee were O'Connell, (Sir) George Sinclair, and Mr. Gladstone, and to reach Coggeshall they had to travel together some fifty miles in an open carriage. The situation was favourable for much and close conversation; and Mr. Gladstone's recollection long afterwards was that O'Connell brought with him a theological work to prove to his young companion and antagonist that all who had been baptised were, in a certain sense, in the Church. O'Connell, to whom such a dialectical encounter must have been a keen delight, himself thought that the argument had fallen on

[1] 'Parliamentary Papers,' 1834, vol. xviii., pp. 327-840.

fruitful ground, for about five years later, when Mr. Gladstone had published his most famous single work, that touching the relations of Church and State, he observed to the member of Newark, when meeting him behind the Speaker's chair in the House of Commons, ' I claim the half of you '—a remark concerning theology which embodied an unconscious prophecy in regard to politics.

Late in the session of 1833, as afterwards and in detail will be told, Mr. Gladstone took an active part in discussing the Ministerial measure for the emancipation of the colonial slaves ; but, as bearing upon his political future, the one truly important speech of the year was upon the question that the Church Reform (Ireland) Bill should pass. This measure, one of a series designed to save a doomed Establishment, was not satisfactory to either thoroughgoing Churchmen or Radical lovers of uncompromise ; and its attempt at harmonising the incompatible may, to some extent, account for the occasionally halting nature of Mr. Gladstone's address. His arguments will more fittingly be considered later ; but the point concerning the speech which deserves note here is that the succeeding speaker was so puzzled by his criticisms that, not having heard the whole, he understood Mr. Gladstone intended voting for the measure on the ground that it would strengthen the Church in Ireland. But Thomas Gladstone, who was sitting by his brother, corrected the impression by at once exclaiming, 'No! no! Against it';[1] and, in point of fact, both brothers were in the minority opposed to the Bill—that minority being composed of such antagonistic elements as Peel and O'Connell, Inglis and Hume, a good many Tories and a few Radicals, the former objecting because the Irish

July 8, 1833. Speaks upon the Irish Church.

---

[1] 'Mirror of Parliament' (1833), pp. 2827-2828.

L

Church would be weakened, the latter because it would be strengthened by the Bill.

Stanley, who had lately been moved from the Irish to the Colonial Office, observed, after Mr. Gladstone had

intervened in this debate, that he had

Stanley (afterwards Derby) and Mr. Gladstone.

heard him with more pleasure on a previous night—referring to his first striking speech, that on slavery—and that he thought the line he had taken was a little singular; and it was not many evenings before the former once more found occasion to criticise his future antagonist. In the slavery discussion on July 25th, yet to be alluded to, the Secretary for the Colonies somewhat sourly, and yet with an accent of unconscious prophecy, retorted upon an argument of Mr. Gladstone : ' Really, if it should ever happen to the honourable gentleman to have a place in his Majesty's Councils, and he should find such a vote of the House of Commons against him as was given last night upon this question, he may depend upon it, it will not require any great skill to ascertain what inference should be drawn from it.' [1]   And Mr. Gladstone concluded a first session in which he had established a claim upon such notice from a Secretary of State, by moving on August 8th for some returns regarding education in Ireland, thus early connecting himself with one further subject upon which he was to attempt much.

Mr. Gladstone had not been in the House a session when he was called to other work than speaking, and

Aug. 5. Placed upon a select committee.

was directed to serve upon a select committee. This was appointed to inquire into certain apparently exaggerated allegations of jobbery made by several London stationers and paper-manufacturers in

[1] *Ibid.*, p. 3328.

connection with the management of the Stationery Office; but the matter is now of no interest, save for the fact that those with whom the young member was summoned to associate included Althorp and Russell, Peel and Hardinge, Shaw-Lefevre[1] and O'Connell.[2]   Of greater significance, as bearing upon the development of his career, are his votes in the course of this first session upon various questions of more than immediate interest.   Speaking generally, such votes of his as remain recorded—for it was to be another four years before the Commons consented to publish official division lists—were those of the average ardent young Tory of the day.   It was as natural for the new member for Newark to oppose O'Connell's endeavour to turn the King's Speech into an occasion for debating the repeal of the Union as to support the most stringent clauses of a drastic Irish Coercion Bill; while to vote alike against abolishing sinecures, establishing the ballot, and shortening the duration of Parliaments, and to resent any attempt to touch the temporalities of the Irish Church may be considered the common form of the Tory of 1833.   But there was a touch of eagerness in the assertion of the Toryism which more plainly marked his youth.   He had no objection to be in minute minorities on occasion, as when he was one of ten, all told, who favoured a motion declaring political unions to be illegal; or when, with a bare couple of dozen, he took part in two divisions obviously called in order to delay the Jews' Disabilities Bill, a measure of relief against which he voted at every stage, and which he had the satisfaction of seeing rejected by the Peers.   As a social reformer, he was in a majority which,

His earliest votes.

---

[1] Afterwards Speaker and Viscount Eversley.

[2] *Commons' Journals*, vol. lxviii., p. 638 : the proceedings and report of the commi ee are in ' Parliamentary Papers,' 1833, vol. xvi.

contrary to the wish of the Whig leader of the House, pressed forward Ashley's Factories Regulation Bill; as a young man of strong religious conviction, he was in a minority in favour of Sir Andrew Agnew's Bill for the Observance of the Sabbath, designed to prevent all manner of Sunday work; but in neither capacity could he bring himself to support a motion of Hume providing that flogging should not be inflicted under the Mutiny Act except for mutiny and drunkenness, in the narrow majority against which his name appeared. But votes and speeches alike indicated that there had entered the House a man who possessed ideas without fear of expressing them. In regard to his votes, a wide gulf sundered those of 1833 from those of his latest years; but no one can read his speeches of that date without perceiving much of the brilliance and certain of the defects which marked his oratory thenceforward throughout his public life.

VII.—His Relation to Slavery.

BEYOND local or legal, social or religious considerations, all of which affected Mr. Gladstone in various degrees during the first year of his parliamentary life, the one subject which most occupied his thoughts in 1833 was colonial slavery. It has been seen how his father—whose earliest political effort-was in support of a candidate who lost his seat mainly because he had voted for abolishing the African slave-trade—was not merely personally interested in the question of colonial slavery, but had written and spoken much upon it. Not only was it, however, in the reprinted newspaper letters of 1823, or in the course of the Berwick contest of three years later, that John Gladstone and slavery. John Gladstone had taken so active a part in the controversy, for, in 1830, he had published a second pamphlet, this being 'A Statement of Facts, connected with the present state of slavery in the British Sugar and Coffee Colonies, and in the United States of America, together with a view of the present situation of the lower classes in the United Kingdom.' In this, which was cast in the shape of a letter to Peel, there was recognised with a clearness not to be seen in his contributions of some years before, that emancipation was loudly though, as he still thought, erroneously called for. He admitted the well-intentioned zeal of the abolitionists ; he no longer talked, as he had done in 1823, of 'that well-meaning, but mistaken man, Mr. Wilberforce, as well as the more intemperate, credulous, designing, or interested individuals who have placed themselves in his train'; but he once more urged the strength of the legal sanction that had been given to the system. The negroes, in his opinion, were happier when forced to work; and, as the colonies could not be cultivated without them, he considered the difficulties in the way of emancipation to be insurmountable, however gradual the process might be made. Instances of cruelty or individual oppression he contended to be comparatively few; and, if it were asked whether slavery was to be interminable in our colonies, he replied, 'I humbly conceive, it is not for me to attempt to say when a system should terminate which Almighty God, in the divine wisdom of his over-ruling providence, has seen fit to permit in certain climates since the origin and formation of society in this world.' He was willing to do all he could to ameliorate the lot of the slave, to improve his condition, and to raise his character; but he could not forbear from calling the attention of Peel 'and that of our warm-hearted abolitionists to the state and circumstances of society among the lower classes in the United Kingdom '—which he did in a sentence forty lines in length—and to 'compare the negro's state with that of the lower classes here, and then determine which calls most loudly for their benevolent efforts in their favour.' And, entertaining no doubt that the result of such a comparison would be favourable to the negro, he claimed that, although he had a considerable vested interest in plantations and in the people who cultivated them, he had written naught but the truth.

This pamphlet brought down upon John Gladstone the wrath of the 'London Society for the Abolition of Slavery throughout the British Dominions,' the organ of which declared that he had employed an unusual share of ingenuity to varnish the crime of keeping men in slavery. His description of it as 'a statement of facts' was ridiculed as a strange misnomer; his theory that the slave cheerfully performed his duty of working in the field was one of 'the delusions by which men of sense, and men too who have some feeling of conscience, try to blind their own eyes and steel their own hearts against the impressions of truth, justice, and humanity;' and he was told that he had written his pamphlet in Liverpool, four thousand miles from his slaves, probably not one of whom had he ever seen. 'He is far removed from the sight of their sufferings, whatever those sufferings may be, and he is evidently wholly without power to control the conduct of his distant agents. Now if he had come forward to give us an authentic detail from the Registry of Demerara, and from his own plantation books, of the changes which have taken place among his Slaves from the time he became possessed of them to the present hour—of their increase and decrease, and of their daily tasks and allowances, and hours of day and night labour, and punishments, etc., etc.,—he would have done more to throw light on the subject than by twenty such pamphlets as this.' The 'memorable period of Missionary Smith,' and the assertions made at and concerning the trial in regard to John Gladstone's estate Success were recalled; and it was added, 'Mr. Gladstone may, doubtless, dispute the truth of these statements; but he was not there himself, and cannot tell that they are false; but true or false, he could have no means of preventing them, or of protecting his Slaves from any treatment to which his stipendiary agent, under whose absolute dominion he had placed them, might subject them.'[1]

John Gladstone, who does not appear to have replied to these searching comments, had indicated in his pamphlet,

[1] *Anti-Slavery Reporter*, Jan., 1831, vol. iv., pp. 19, 20n.

which reached a second edition, the opinion that at the very best emancipation must be an extremely slow process ; but when, in June of the following year, the Oxford Union discussed a motion in favour of immediate

June, 1831.
William Gladstone emancipation in the West Indies, his youngest
and emancipation.
son, though submitting an amendment, went decidedly beyond his father, for William Gladstone's proposal was in these terms—'That Legislative enactments ought to be made, and, if necessary, enforced—(1) For better guarding the personal and civil rights of the Negroes in our West India Colonies. (2) For establishing compulsory Manumission. (3) For securing universally the receiving of a Christian Education, under the Clergy and Teachers, independent of the Planters ; a measure of which total but gradual emancipation will be the natural consequence, as it was of a similar procedure in the first ages of Christianity.' The speech in which the young Gladstone supported that proposal was the first Robert Lowe, afterwards to be opponent as well as colleague, heard him make ; and in the latter's ' Chapter of Autobiography ' it was written : ' As far as mere elocution went, he spoke just as well as he does now in 1876. He had taken just as much pains with the details of his subject as he would have if he had been Secretary of State for the Colonies. He did not launch into commonplaces about the rights of man, but he proposed a well-considered and carefully-prepared scheme of gradual emancipation.' [1]

During the Newark contest, the question of slavery was not unnaturally kept to the front by the local Whigs, and Mr. Gladstone, in reply, advocated once more a gradual emancipation. But, when the Reformed Parliament met,

[1] A. Patchett Martin's ' Life of Lord Sherbrooke,' vol. i., p. 17.

immediate emancipation was seen of all men to be near, though its first session was half gone before Stanley, as Colonial Secretary, introduced to the Commons the Ministerial plan. This *May 14, 1833. Ministers propose emancipation.* proposed that the negroes in our colonies should be apprenticed for twelve years to their then owners; that three-fourths of their time during that period should be given to their masters; that magistrates should be empowered to flog in case of refusal to work; and that fifteen millions should be lent to the planters to tide them over the difficulties the realisation of the scheme might cause. Lord Howick (afterwards Henry, third Earl Grey), the eldest son of the Prime Minister, at once followed Stanley; and from his contribution to the debate much that was of special interest to Mr. Gladstone sprang.

Howick had been an earnest advocate of complete abolition; and, having been appointed Parliamentary Under-Secretary for the Colonies, he prepared, with the assistance of (Sir) James Stephen, then Permanent Under-Secretary, and (Sir) Henry Taylor, who was in the same Department, a plan to that end.   This he submitted to the Colonial Secretary, Lord Goderich—Lord Beaconsfield's 'transient and embarrassed phantom,' afterwards Earl of Ripon, and father of the last of Mr. Gladstone's own Colonial Secretaries—and that vacillating peer, with the assent of the Cabinet, communicated it to the Committee of West India Planters. That body, of which John Gladstone was the moving spirit, rejected the plan, and, on this account, it was refused by the Government.   But some plan was necessary : Goderich was passed into an office where his weakness of will *John Gladstone and Howick's plan.* could do less harm, and Stanley succeeded him at the Colonial Office. The new Secretary speedily drew up a scheme of his own; but, as Howick considered this to be one not for emancipation but merely for substituting a modified system of slavery for that which already existed, he resigned his post. In following Stanley, therefore, he opposed the Ministerial scheme, prophesied that it would prove a failure—which to a large extent it did—and, in illustration of his arguments, specially emphasised the great loss of life upon sugar as compared with cotton estates. The opportunity was to his hand to show how the leader of the West India planters had dealt with his own negroes; and, having referred in passing to Success, a name of un- pleasant recollections, he singled out Vreed-en-Hoop,

Howick (afterwards Grey) and John Gladstone's estate of Vreed-en-Hoop. another of John Gladstone's Demerara estates, and one which then, as in later years, was a mark for abolitionist criticism. The marked decrease in the slave population of Vreed- en-Hoop, Howick directly attributed to over-exaction of labour; and he submitted that a large crop of sugar had been produced, to the great advantage of the owner, but, unhappily, at the price of a dreadful loss of life among the slaves.[1]

Three nights later, having failed to find an opportunity during the sitting the attack was made, Thomas Gladstone

Thomas Gladstone replies. replied in an effort which has customarily been described as William Gladstone's maiden speech,[2] and to which, as such, various fanciful

---

[1] 'Mirror of Parliament' (1833), p. 1788.

[2] This has arisen from the error by which 'Hansard' (3rd series, vol. xvii., f. 1345) attributes it to 'Mr. William C. [sic] Gladstone'; but not merely was the petition, which gave occasion for the speech, from Thomas Gladstone's constituency, but some words of William Gladstone, later to be quoted, prove that he did not take part in a slavery debate until June 3. How difficult, however, it was for the reporters to dis- tinguish between the two brothers may be judged from the fact that

legends have been attached. Under cover of presenting an abolitionist petition from the Wesleyan Methodists of Portarlington, he defended his father and his father's manager; and he contended that, although the slaves at Vreed-en-Hoop had been idle before the latter took them in hand, they had become happy, well-behaved, and industrious, and were thus deserving even greater comforts.[1]

William Gladstone's turn was soon to come. On May 21st, he presented a petition from certain inhabitants of Edinburgh against immediate abolition;[2] and two days later, with his brother, but not accompanied by his father (who, however, was privately hard at work in the matter of negotiation) he was one of the foremost signatories of an invitation to a meeting of 'planters, merchants, shipowners, manufacturers, tradesmen, and all others interested in the preservation of the British West India Colonies,' to consider the situation as developed by Stanley's measure. This gathering was held on the 27th; and, although, owing to confusion of initials, it is not certain which of the brothers was present or whether both were there, it is obvious that neither spoke to resolutions which indicated that the planters were opposed to the Ministerial scheme of emancipation, which, it was predicted, would destroy our colonies while directly encouraging the slave trade and slavery in foreign countries. Even the staunchest supporters of the Cabinet admitted the demonstration to have been a formidable one, and it had had a decided effect even before June 3rd, the day upon which William Gladstone addressed the Commons.

June 3.
William Gladstone's
first great speech.

The House had resolved itself into committee on the

every London morning paper described both the speech of Thomas on May 17 and of William on June 3 simply as delivered by 'Mr. Gladstone.'
    [1] 'Mirror of Parliament' (1833), p. 1843.   [2] *Ibid.* p. 1891.

resolutions of Stanley, who, in the interval, after negotiation with John Gladstone and another Liverpool planter, John Moss, had agreed to turn the proposed loan of fifteen millions into a gift of twenty, though even then the West India interest was not satisfied; and Sandon, at whose house the leading planters had that day met to consider the terms, intimated his intention of proposing amendments to add a loan of ten millions to the gift of twenty, and, in other ways, to soften the blow to the planters.   Howick, who had been absent when Thomas Gladstone addressed the House, was now present ; and William Gladstone, rising from the bench behind Peel, took the opportunity to further defend his father.   His opening remarks showed that this was the first occasion of his addressing Parliament on the subject.   ' I am aware,' he said, ' that I ought to apologise to the Committee for intruding upon them the opinions of an utterly inexperienced person, when they are engaged in the discussion of a question as extensive and as complicated as any that ever came before Parliament.   But having a deep, though indirect, pecuniary interest in it, and, if I may say so much, without exciting suspicion, a still deeper interest in it as a question of justice, of humanity, and of religion, I venture to offer myself for a short time, and I trust it will be but for a very short time, to your notice.'   He then proceeded to traverse in detail Howick's imputations, of no light or ordinary character, upon his father, prefacing the particulars with the remarks : ' I cannot refrain from telling the noble lord—I trust in all good humour—(I will not say, telling the noble lord, because I would rather appeal to the feelings of the House to deter-mine whether I am right or wrong—but I will say that my idea is)—that if I had charges of this grave nature to bring forward, charges materially affecting private character, in a case where the party attacked had two sons sitting in the Assembly where those charges were to be made, I ought to have given them notice of my intention; which, however, the noble lord did not deign to do. For, sir, these charges do affect private character. If I am proprietor of an estate in the West Indies, and continually receive from thence accounts of increasing crops and decreasing population, without enquiry and without endeavouring to prevent the continuance of such a system, no man will tell me that my character does not suffer, and ought not to suffer, for such monstrous inhumanity.'

Mr. Gladstone then adduced a number of facts and figures (which, however, did not convince Howick [1]) to show that his father had not been thus guilty; but he did not for a moment defend slavery as a system. 'Cases of cruelty,' he observed, 'have often been brought forward against the colonists; and I confess, sir—with shame and pain I confess—that cases of wanton cruelty have existed, as well as that they always will exist, particularly under the system of slavery; and unquestionably this is a substantial reason why the British Legislature and public should set themselves in good earnest to provide for its extinction.' He admitted that, as regarded all the colonies, 'we have

[1] Howick published his speech in a pamphlet, a copy of which is not in the British Museum Library, but, according to the *Anti-Slavery Reporter* (vol. vi., p. 130), it contained a note declaring, with regard to his original assertion, 'this is a less unfavourable statement than might have been made of the state of things on Vreed-en-Hoop.' And it is significant that, having also censured in the House the manage-ment of Anna Regina, a neighbouring estate, owned by another Liver-pool man who had just given its care to John Gladstone's Demerara attorney, Howick appended an expression of regret in the reprint that he had created an idea that this other planter was indifferent to the welfare of his slaves,

not fulfilled those Christian obligations which are imposed upon us by the dispensations of Providence, to communicate, wherever our commerce gives us access, in return for the earthly goods which it brings to our shores, the inestimable benefits of our religion.' He contended that 'the notion which prevailed among the early English planters, that if you made a man a Christian you could not keep him a slave . . instead of teaching them to view slavery as a state which ought to terminate, only led them to the monstrous conclusion that they ought not to communicate Christianity to their slaves;' and that the deplorable effects of this could hardly be charged upon the existing generation. But the Ministerial plan for dealing with the whole matter was defective, while the original proposal would have proved impracticable and ruinous; and he was certain that 'if the emancipation of the slaves proceed according to any other law than in an exact harmony with their advancing character, it must be ruinous to the colonies, to this country, and to the slaves themselves. Here I differ entirely with the honourable and benevolent member for Weymouth (Thomas Fowell Buxton), for I would free the slave without assurance of his disposition to industry; I would not redeem him from the hands even of an oppressor and an enemy to place him in a state where he would himself be his own worst enemy; and I believe that, by doing such an act, the honourable and benevolent member for Weymouth and the House, instead of compensating the African race for those heavy injuries which they have sustained from us, would crown and consummate those injuries, and would deprive the negro of his last hope of rising to a higher level in the scale of social existence.'

O'Connell had expressed an opinion during the debate

that the first thing to be done was to free the negro and then to consider the idea of compensation, treating rather lightly the idea that the planters' property was involved. Mr. Gladstone replied : 'I do not view property as an abstract thing; it is the creature of civil society : by the Legislature it is granted, and by the Legislature it is destroyed. The question is not whether slaves are property in the abstract nature of things, but whether this description of possession be not property within the limits of the Constitution. . . . The Legislature has done all that lay within its power to make this property; it had no power over the abstract nature of things ; all the power it had it applied for the purpose I have named ; and by the consequences of its own acts it must abide. . . . You are the British Legislature ; you are identically the same body which established this description of property; and you are bound by their acts, which, though they are not your own personally, are so virtually and in substance.' Mr. Gladstone's next point involved the whole principle of local self-government. He urged very strongly the extreme importance of the cooperation of the colonial legislatures in the proposed work. 'I know well the omnipotence of Parliament ; I am well aware that you could crush these small and puny legislatures into nothing, and, after annihilating them, you can, by a single word, plunge the colonies into bloodshed ; but this, I also know, is not your object. . . . You cannot by power overcome the sullenness, the indifference, the reluctance of the colonists abroad ; you may carry your plan without bloodshed or violent opposition, but, unless the colonists are with you, the continued cultivation of the colonies, I think, is quite hopeless.'

At the close of the speech, Mr. Gladstone once more showed, and in emphatic terms, his detestation of slavery

as a system.   Admitting the existence of a dark side to the
picture, he described the delightful prospect of a favourable
consummation from a safe and gradual emancipation.   But,
if the plan before the House 'shall be satisfactorily arranged, upon a basis which, while it improves the condition,
will also elevate the character of the slave—for certainly any
basis which secures that object must, and any one which
does not secure it cannot, be satisfactory—in case such a
happy result shall flow from patient and cautious delibera-
tion on the part of this Committee, or rather of the British
Parliament—if, under the blessing of Providence, a system
which unquestionably began in crime, in atrocious crime,
and in grievous sin, and which has been continued, not
necessarily in sin, for I do not admit that holding slaves
necessarily involves sin, though it does necessarily involve
the deepest and heaviest responsibility, but at least in much
sorrow and much misfortune and much disquietude to all
parties concerned ;—I say if this system shall be conducted,
by your labours, to a satisfactory termination, and an issue
beneficial to all—delightful, indeed, it will be to all involved, honourable to this nation, honourable to the
Government, if, under their auspices, it shall be effected;
happy for the slave ; but, most of all, delightful to the West
Indian proprietor, who must always feel the burden of that
responsibility which lies peculiarly upon him who holds an
interest in the labour and persons of his fellow men.' [1]   In
the construction of every sentence, in the formulation of
every principle, the Gladstone of 1833 was thus the Gladstone of all his later time ; and what Lowe had observed of
the Oxford Union effort on the same subject just two years
before was true of this : ' It is not too much to say that even

_____

[1] 'Mirror of Parliament' (1833), pp. 2079-82.

then he gave full promise of all which he has since achieved.' [1]

From the point of view of impressing the outside public, the night was not favourable for what was virtually, though not actually, a parliamentary *début*. An important debate, raised by Wellington, was simultaneously progressing in the House of Lords upon the then pressing question of Portugal ; it was with report and criticism of this that the London newspapers were the next day filled ; and the *Morning Post* alone among metropolitan journals alluded to the young member for Newark's appearance, and then merely in the hurried words, ' We can only refer our readers to the able speeches of Lord Sandon and Mr. Gladstone, and to the statesmanlike address of Sir R. Peel, last night in the House of Commons, on the vital subject of the West Indies.' A Radical journal is understood to have declared that it was the best delivered maiden speech within its remembrance ; but the Liverpool papers, though they might have been thought to *Contemporary comments upon the speech.* have a special interest in the matter, were represented by a single comment, and that in the Whig *Journal,* which observed that Mr. Gladstone's logic was defective, and that his statement, while it did credit to his father's humanity, indirectly confirmed Howick's assertion. And this was Howick's own impression, for, writing his remembrance of the occasion within a very few days of sixty years later, he remarked that Mr. Gladstone's argument, though highly ingenious—a description, be it noted, applied in the debate by Stanley himself—seemed to him to be based upon sophistry and to have failed to support the conclusions. [2]

' The speech made a great sensation at the time,' added

[1] Martin's ' Sherbrooke,' vol. i., p. 17.
[2] Letter of Lord Grey to the present author, May 29, 1893.

M

Lord Grey, in the letter just referred to, 'it being thought a
most remarkable one as made by a new speaker. Like others
who heard it, I greatly admired the power as a speaker exhibited by Mr. Gladstone, with the singular charm of voice
and manner which has ever since distinguished him.' Curiously enough, the description penned at the moment of the
parliamentary *début* of Lord Grey's own father might have
been almost literally applied to this earliest marked appearance of Mr. Gladstone :—'A new speaker presented himself
to the House, and went through his first performance with an
éclat which has not been equalled within my recollection.
He is not more than twenty-two years of age; and he took
his seat, only in the present session. I do not go too far in
declaring that in the advantage of figure, voice, elocution, and
manner, he is not surpassed by any member of the House ;
and I grieve to say that he was last night in the ranks of
opposition, from whence there is no prospect of his being
detached.'[1]   This was written by Addington, who was himself to become Prime Minister, about the man who afterwards laid the foundations of our modern Liberalism: it might
have been said of the earliest parliamentary triumph of him
who later raised upon those foundations so splendid an
edifice.

The success of the speech inside the House, indeed,
was pronounced and unmistakable.   Buxton, in replying
the same night, referred to it as very able, eloquent, and
impressive ;[2] and although Peel, who also spoke, gave no
single word of greeting to the young recruit who was destined to do him such distinguished service, there was a
generous recognition of the effort by Mr. Gladstone's
political opponents.   For the effect did not die away with

[1] G. Pellew's ' Life of Lord Sidmouth,' vol. i., pp. 45, 46.
[2] 'Mirror of Parliament' (1833), p. 2084.

the night of delivery ; and, on the resumption of the debate, Silk Buckingham, then a well-known Radical of the philanthropic and idealistic school, *Compliments from opponents.* before taking pains to answer it, declared the impossibility of alluding to it save in terms of eulogy, for the tone temper, manner, and matter by which it was characterised had occasioned it to be listened to with pleasure by all parties in the House.[1]   But the most prized compliment, and one to be referred to more than once with pride by Mr. Gladstone himself in after years, came from Stanley. ' If the honourable gentleman,' said the Colonial Secretary, ' will permit me to make the observation, I beg to say that I never listened with greater pleasure to any speech than I did to the speech of the honourable member for Newark, who then addressed the House I believe for the first time ; and who brought forward his case and argued it with a temper, an ability, and a fairness which may well be cited as a good model to many older members of this House ; and which hold out to this House and to the country grounds of confident expectation that, whatever cause shall have the good fortune of his advocacy, will derive from it great support.'[2]

To this testimony — which, coming from one of the greatest orators in the Commons, must have been grateful indeed—may be added the description by an eye-witness of another of Mr. Gladstone's efforts in this same session, and probably the one of July 25th, yet to be noted.   This, given by George Keppel, then a Whig member for East Norfolk, and best known to later generations as almost the last surviving officer who fought at Waterloo, may be regarded as sufficiently well-founded for quotation.   ' One

[1] June 7 : *Ibid.*, p. 2159.
[2] *Ibid.*, p. 2172.

evening on taking my place, I found "on his legs" a beard-
less youth, with whose appearance and manner I was
greatly struck; he had an earnest, intelligent countenance,
and large, expressive, black eyes.   Young as he was, he had
evidently what is called "the ear of the House"; and yet
the cause he advocated was not one likely to interest a
popular assembly—that of the Planter *versus* the Slave.   I
had placed myself behind the Treasury Bench.   "Who is
he?" I asked one of the ministers.   I was answered, "He
is the member for Newark—a young fellow who will some
day make a great figure in Parliament."   My informant was
Edward Geoffrey Stanley, then Whig Secretary for the
Colonies, and in charge of the Negro Emancipation Bill,
afterwards Earl of Derby; and the young Conservative
orator was William Ewart Gladstone—two statesmen who
each subsequently became Prime Minister—and leader of
the party to which he was at this time diametrically
opposed."[1]

Howick, on the night of June 3rd, had replied to the member for Newark, contending that his main position had not

Howick's reply,

been shaken, but disclaiming any intention of
saying aught of John Gladstone that was in-
jurious: a week later, however, he moved for a series of returns,
showing in detail the condition of the slaves on the Vreed-
en-Hoop estate during the immediately preceding years.
The Government was willing to grant these, but Mr.
Gladstone opposed the motion unless similar returns of

and Mr. Gladstone's
rejoinder.

neighbouring estates were added, as he considered that the proposal was an attempt to
fix upon a single case for the purpose of arguing upon a
general principle.   In deference to this objection, Howick

[1] Lord Albemarle's 'Fifty Years of My Life,' 3rd edition, pp. 368,
369.

withdrew his motion, but took occasion to repeat that there had been a very great mortality of slaves on John Gladstone's estate; and that it appeared to him that the negroes had either done more work than they ought to have been called upon to perform, or that they were infirm originally and ought to have been excused.[1]   The last, however, had even then not been heard of Vreed en-Hoop, an estate of disturbing associations to its owner and his family.   Five years later, as will in its place be told, a series of malpractices towards the coloured labourers upon it once more aroused popular and parliamentary indignation.   And in 1841, during a semi-slavery debate in which Mr. Gladstone had taken part, Howick recurred to this discussion of 1833, and bade the member for Newark remember the proverb concerning the tenure of glass-houses and the throwing of stones.   Mr. Gladstone rejoined with a further defence of his father, 'whom I am bound to love most dearly, and with whom I feel it the highest honour to be connected;' and Howick replied with a renewed disclaimer of having imputed to John Gladstone that he deliberately sacrificed human life for the acquirement of increased wealth.[2]   But the resumed discussion, while throwing little additional light upon the question at issue, plainly showed the abiding stigma which the abolitionists considered to be affixed to the management of Vreed-en-Hoop.

Vreed-en-Hoop once more.

When the Slavery Abolition Bill was being moved into Committee, Buxton secured, on July 24th, by a narrow majority,[3] the adoption of an instruction for reducing the

[1] 'Mirror of Parliament' (1833), pp. 2207, 2208; *Commons' Journals*, vol. lxxxviii., p. 473.

[2] 'Mirror of Parliament' (1841), pp. 1651, 1692, 1717-21.

[3] 158 to 151.

term of apprenticeship 'to the shortest period which may
be necessary to establish, on just principles, the system of
free labour for adequate wages.' On the next evening,
Stanley announced that the Government would accept seven
years as the term instead of the original twelve; but Mr.
Gladstone, while declaring that 'it has been my study and
desire—I know not with what degree of success—to cast
to the winds all ancient feelings and opinions, and simply
and singly to consider this question with a view to settlement,' urged that the suggested com-
promise would throw overboard the West
India planters, and added the opinion that
the previous day's vote had not been taken upon a clear
issue.[1] He was, however, sparing of remark during the
remaining stages of the measure; and, save for a financial
criticism a few days later,[2] he took no further part in the
debates, challenging in after years any insinuation either
that he had opposed the Bill or that, finding resistance
hopeless, he had endeavoured to embarrass its progress.[3]

Mr. Gladstone on
the Apprenticeship
System.

The Emancipation Bill became law in the August; and,
although the questions concerning apprenticeship which afterwards arose will have to be noticed in connection with Mr.
Gladstone's share in their discussion, slavery was from that
time a dead issue for Englishmen. It is not easy for those
who have been born into the freer air of later years to realise
how men of tender conscience and scrupulous honour could
ever have defended its policy or apologised for its incidents;
but, at the beginning of the long struggle with which the
names of Clarkson and Sharp, Wilberforce and Buxton,
will ever be associated, it was only a very small number who

[1] *Ibid.* (1833), p. 3328.
[2] July 29; *Ibid.*, p. 3396.
[3] *Ibid.* (1841), p. 1718.

foretold, or cared to foretell, victory. Mr. Gladstone himself recalled to the Liverpool of 1892 that that great port rose partly to its eminence because of a traffic which, though now looked back upon with shame and sorrow, was then countenanced in the Legislature and advocated in the Church. That is a fact which to-day is not to be forgotten, for, while everyone can see the evil which is condemned by all, it is but few who perceive it as long as it receives the common sanction.

VIII.—His Ecclesiastical Development.

MR. GLADSTONE in his latest days, while disputing the correctness at any portion of his political career of Macaulay's all-too-hackneyed phrase, describing him as the rising hope of the stern and unbending Tories, did not hesitate to admit that he always had been a Tory with respect to ecclesiastical questions; and it happened that, when he entered upon public life, these were to the fore in a strangely marked degree. The extraordinary prominence given to Church affairs at that period affords, indeed, a curious example of one of the varied psychological phenomena of the nineteenth century. It would almost seem as if the mental atmosphere of a nation moved in the mass and passed with periodicity. For, roughly speaking, the intellectual phases of the century were, in England, three, and these occupied an almost equal division of time. In the first, the poetic tendency held sway with enduring results upon our literature; during the second, religion was an absorbing influence that has left its mark upon the nation; in the third, the world saw Britain take the lead in that scientific investigation which has asserted upon thinkers a foremost claim. Mr. Gladstone himself, in his work upon 'Church Principles,' was to observe that, in the revival of poetry which the previous generation had witnessed, there were phenomena somewhat similar to those perceptible in the religious uprising which followed it:[1] it was not given to any man in 1840 to

[1] 'Church Principles considered in their Results,' chap. i., sec. 18.

perceive that the higher imagination, which, in the one phase, added to our mental and, in the other, to our moral possessions, would yield place before the century ended to a chastened materialism that, while doing little to diminish the former, revolutionised the basis upon which the claims of the latter can rest.

But, years before he published anything upon the Church question, Mr. Gladstone was intimately associated with ecclesiastical affairs, into the intricacies of *Mr. Gladstone and* which he plunged with a delight which *ecclesiastical affairs.* never wholly departed. In his case, religion was to some extent a revolt—a revolt against commercialism, against materialism, against the purely utilitarian ideas, the 'diffusion of useful knowledge' spirit, which so largely marked the period of his growing manhood. His early devotion, therefore, was to the Church rather than to the State, and this largely because, while the State was in continual change, the Church in essence was unchangeable. The one was temporal, the other eternal; and the young student, looking out upon a world of confused strugglings after a liberty he had not been taught to understand, found himself forced to the conclusion that only in a religious system, holy in its origin and hallowed by its traditions, could peace be found. The difference, then, between Mr. Gladstone and the bulk of the Tory party, as that party was constituted in 1833, was that he was Churchman and Conservative : they were Conservatives and Churchmen. They drank to 'Throne and Altar,' he to Church and State. And this reversal of the places meant much. If two men ride a horse, says the old saw, one must be behind. That is only the optimistic assurance of the looker-on. In point of comfort, convenience, and even safety, the position matters much to those who ride.

Given these prepossessions, it was little wonder that Mr. Gladstone, when he had once launched into ecclesiastical affairs, attached himself to

His Churchmanship.

that section of the Church which is labelled 'High'; but, in considering the close connection which long existed between the young statesman and the Tractarian party, and which was fraught with much consequence to both, it is essential to remember that what is historical as 'the Oxford Movement' did not begin until he had left the University. No sign of it had appeared in his own period of pupilage as he himself has recorded : 'a steady, clear, but dry Anglican orthodoxy bore sway, and frowned, this way or that, on the first indication of any tendency to diverge from the beaten path. . . . There was nothing, at that time, in the theology, or in the religious life of the University to indicate what was soon to come.'[1]   Newman, afterwards to hold so striking a position in the Movement, was virtually unknown to Mr. Gladstone while the younger man was at the University, and to the end their relation was somewhat casual, and rather by letter

His earliest knowledge of Newman.

than by personal acquaintance. While, indeed, Mr. Gladstone was at Oxford, and when sometimes, as an undergraduate, he heard Newman preach, that divine, though having earned respect for both character and ability, was looked upon with some prejudice as in a degree a Low Churchman. Newman, himself, ever considered and kept the day—Sunday, July 14th, 1833— when Keble preached his famous assize sermon upon 'National Apostasy' from the university pulpit, as the start of the Movement; and the first of the 'Tracts for the Times' was issued anonymously by the future cardinal soon afterwards. It was at first attempted by Newman to link

[1] 'Chapter of Autobiography,' sec. 67.

together in some form of association such clergy and lay-
men as thought with himself; and, writing in the autumn of
the year just named to Frederic Rogers, he   October, 1833.
said: 'We are getting on famously with our   His first connection
                                              with the Oxford
Society, and are so prudent and temperate   Movement.
that [Richard Hurrell] Froude writes up to me we have
made a hash of it, which I account to be praise. As to
Gladstone, perhaps it would be wrong to ask a young man
so to commit himself, but make a fuss we will sooner
or later.' [1]   And he wrote a little later, 'We are
very strong (I hope) in Leicestershire, Cheshire, Hants,
Oxford, and Northamptonshire; but we may miscalculate
our force here and there. Men fall off when they come
to the scratch. The Duke of Newcastle has joined us "in
life and death, so that we are true to ourselves," and . . .
Gladstone.' [2]

This last announcement was somewhat premature, for
Mr. Gladstone, who had been brought up in a Low Church
atmosphere, was not for some years to be definitely ranked
with the Tractarian party. But, from the very outset of
his public career, he was regarded as an assured champion
of the Church, and, as has been noted, he had not
even allowed his first election address or his earliest
session to pass without appearing in that character.
Before he had sat at St. Stephen's a full three weeks,
Pusey, under whom he had studied at Oxford, wrote
to him, with reference to Althorp's Irish Church Temporalities scheme, 'the appearances of things are very formidable, if a Christian might fear.' One of the greatest fights
of the session raged around the Church Reform (Ireland)

[1] Oct. 2, 1833: Anna Mozley's 'Letters and Correspondence of J.
H. Newman,' vol. i., p. 459.
[2] Nov. 13: *Ibid.*, p. 482.

Bill—to which Pusey had objected because the Irish sees, several of which were to be merged, 'might at all events render much aid to Episcopal government'[1]—and, upon the question that it should pass, he declared : 'I am not disposed to shelter myself under the ignoble protection of silence on this occasion, and to have it supposed that I am willing to defend the Church by my vote and not by my voice.' He admitted that the Irish Church had done little for the cause of Protestantism, and that it had slumbered for a long series of years ; but he urged that, since the Union, it had done all for the advancement of 'the true religion' that human agency could effect. 'I think,' he said, 'no one can deny, that in a country situated like Ireland, it must be of immense importance to have scattered over the face of the kingdom a body of men who are gentlemen by education and Christians by profession. I am of opinion that the Irish Church, even as it now stands, is a strong link of connection between Ireland and this country. I do not, however, defend the Irish Church on the ground of these uses alone, for I do not hesitate to say that I consider that Establishment to be essentially sacred in its nature. It will be a desecration of the Church to divert the revenues destined for the advancement of religion to political uses. I, as a Protestant, am bound to recollect that our forefathers had weighty cause for seceding from the Church of Rome ; and I need offer no apology to the Roman Catholic members of this assembly for expressing a desire that the most ample means may be afforded for spreading the Protestant faith— I mean, by the exposition and discussion of its doctrines : and then, let God defend the right. It is because I desire to see the true faith extended for the benefit of those who

Mr. Gladstone and the Irish Church.

---

[1] Feb. 15, 1833 : Liddon's 'Pusey,' vol. i., p. 273.

oppose it, that I object to anything which, in the remotest degree, is calculated to injure the Church Establishment in Ireland. It is because I conceive that the Bill, along with much valuable matter, contains some most objectionable principles, that I feel myself constrained to reject it.' He proceeded to criticise certain details of the measure, which he admitted not to have been conceived in a spoliating spirit, clinging, however, to his leading point : ' I cannot consent to surrender the necessary principle, that the nation may be taxed for the support of a national church.' And Stanley later complained that the line he had taken was ' a little singular,' inasmuch as, although he had stated that there were many parts of the Bill he considered advantageous, there was not one of the principal provisions to which he had not offered some objection.[1]

But it was not only in regard to the Irish Establishment that Mr. Gladstone was active in Church affairs during his first session. Three weeks before it ended, he secured a return showing 'the number of applications to the Board of Education in Dublin, for aid to schools existing, or for new schools, up to the latest period for which such return has been made; and of the number of applications which have been complied with : lists of all books or tracts employed in any schools, whether in the combined moral and literary instruction, or in the separate religious instruction, with the sanction or approbation of the Board ; and copies of the titles of all books or tracts, edited, printed, or supplied for the use of schools, by authority of the same : and a copy of the regulations or conditions on which the Board of Education grants aid, together with any documents explanatory of such conditions, which have been drawn up by the Commissioners, and have received the

and Irish education.

[1] July 8 : ' Mirror of Parliament' (1833), pp. 2827, 2828.

sanction of his Majesty's Government.'[1]   Little came of
this return; little comes from most parliamentary returns;
but the motion was one of the signs that marked the man.

Thus, even in his earliest parliamentary days, Mr. Gladstone was thinking as much of clerical as of political affairs;
and one curious instance of this interest brought him into
unwitting contact with a future Archbishop of Dublin,
whose Church he was himself to disestablish. Arthur
Hallam, writing to Richard Chenevix Trench on March
25th, 1833, observed : ' A friend of mine, Gladstone, the new
Arthur Hallam and member for Newark, has made me a *half
Mr. Gladstone. offer* of a small living in Buckinghamshire.
I don't mean it is in his gift, but in that of a lady whom
he knows.   He will write by to-day's post to mention you,
and *if not already disposed of,* which is possible, but
not likely, he has little doubt it may be yours.'   The living
was that of the Buckinghamshire parish of Mursley, near
Winslow; but the result of the negotiations was disappointing, for Hallam had to inform Trench a few days later that
he had ' no satisfactory tidings . . . Gladstone's friend
has written to say that she wishes to have a clergyman from
her own neighbourhood.'   ' I am much disappointed,' was
added, ' as from what he told me I was led to suppose his
recommendation would have been effectual.'[2]

Within six months of the writing of this latter communication, it may here fitly be noted, Mr. Gladstone's dearest
school-friend, and whose close acquaintance had promised
to continue as a fellow-student at Lincoln's Inn, had passed
away under the saddening circumstances all lovers of
English literature know.   What Mr. Gladstone thought of
his dead friend has been set down in his own words—for

[1] August 8 : *Ibid.*, p. 3632.
[2] ' Letters and Memorials of R. C. Trench,' vol. i., pp. 134-9.

there is no difficulty in identifying him by Henry Hallam's description in 1834 of 'one of Arthur's earliest and most distinguished friends, himself just entering upon a career of public life, which, if in these times there is any field open for high principle and the eloquence of wisdom and virtue, will be as brilliant as it must, on every condition, be honourable.' And this friend wrote : 'It was my happiness to live at Eton in habits of close intimacy with him ; and the sentiments of affection which that intimacy produced were of a kind never to be effaced. Painfully mindful as I am of the privileges, which I then so largely enjoyed, of the elevating effects derived from intercourse with a spirit such as his, of the rapid and continued expansion of all his powers, of his rare and, so far as I have seen, unparalleled endowments, and of his deep enthusiastic affections, both religious and human, I have taken upon me thus to render my feeble testimony to a memory which will ever be dear to my heart. From his and my friend D. [Doyle], I have learned the terrible suddenness of his removal, and see with wonder how it has pleased God, that in his death as well as in his life and nature, he should be marked beyond ordinary men. When much time has elapsed, and when most bereavements would be forgotten, he will still be remembered, and his place, I fear, will be felt to be still vacant, singularly as his mind was calculated by its native tendencies to work powerfully and for good in an age full of import to the nature and destinies of man.'[1] To have earned such testimony would have marked out Arthur Hallam from all his fellows, even if ' In Memoriam ' had not made his early promise immortal.

In the session of 1834, and while this grief was fresh upon him, Mr. Gladstone was again to give proof of his

Mr. Gladstone on Arthur Hallam.

[1] Preface to ' Remains of Arthur Henry Hallam,' pp. xliii., xliv.

earnestness in the cause of the Church.   The English Nonconformists, despite the repeal of the Test and Corporation
Acts a few years before, continued to lie under grievances,
all of which were not removed for another
half-a-century, and some of which, in their
opinion, still remain.   At the beginning of

1834.
Mr. Gladstone
and Nonconformist
grievances.

Mr. Gladstone's second session, they particularly complained
that they had to pay church-rates, that they had no proper
registration of births and deaths in their congregations, that
they could not bury their dead according to their own rules,
that they were obliged in their marriages to conform to
ceremonies at variance with their conscientious opinions,
and that they were debarred the benefit of having their
children educated in the National schools, unless they subscribed to certain Articles which would make them members
of the Established Church.   Early in the session, Russell
introduced a Bill to remedy the marriage grievance, which
was coldly received by both Radicals and Tories.   The
Church party at once put themselves into communication
with Sir Robert Inglis and Mr. Gladstone, and Newman
made himself active against the measure.   But the last-
named—who doubted whether ' a religious M.P. can vote
for a measure which allows of marriage by *any*, and, therefore, if so be, merely civil rites,' and who wished as a ' *quid
pro quo* that no clergyman need marry any but Churchmen,'
—soon perceived that active struggle on the part of his co-
religionists was needless.   ' It is likely,' he wrote to Keble,
' the Dissenters themselves will do our business for us by
their clamouring against the Bill;'[1] and that proved to be the
case.   Russell, when the Bill was read a first time, observed
that he was not very sanguine that it would be acceptable
to the great body of those for whose relief it was intended ;

[1] Anna Mozley's ' Letters, etc., of Newman,' vol. ii., p. 30.

and, as the Nonconformists continued to object to its provisions, it was quietly dropped. But the fact that Mr. Gladstone, thus early, was consulted by its clerical opponents testifies to the position he had already attained.

Towards the end of the same session, the third reading was moved by Hume of a Bill, introduced by G. W. Wood, a Whig member for South Lancashire, allowing the admission, without a religious test, of Nonconformists to the universities. Mr. Gladstone, who had been content to give a silent vote against the second reading, now once more appeared as a defender of the Church, and in a speech which three years later was declared by an admiring journal to have been his first great effort as a debater, and to have 'scattered to the four winds of heaven the flimsy arguments' of the promoter of the measure.[1] The member for Newark declared that the scheme would be inoperative ; he held that the universities had become the preparatory seminaries to the Church Establishment ; he denied that they were national institutions beyond the fact that they were connected with the National Church ; and he expressed the hope that the House would never allow the ⟨Mr. Gladstone and university tests.⟩ admission to them of all sorts of persons, whether they were Christians or not. He was satisfied with the then condition of things, which allowed Dissenters to remain in the universities and participate in their benefits during good pleasure, and which ordained that, whenever there might occur anything in the forms and regulations which the Dissenter did not choose to comply with, he must either comply or leave. He condemned Palmerston for having said, in a previous debate, that it gave him pain to see the students going from wine to prayers and from prayers to wine, declining to believe that even in

[1] *Manchester Chronicle*, July 22, 1837.

N

their most convivial moments they were unfit to enter
the House of Prayer; and he concluded by expressing the
fear that the Commons, in establishing 'their present principle of religious liberty,' would drive from their functions
men who had long done honour and service to their country,
and thus inaugurate their reign of religious peace by an act
of the grossest tyranny.[1]   In the debate which followed,
Mr. Gladstone's arguments—and particularly that one which
indicated the universities as mainly clerical seminaries—
were severely handled by the Whig speakers, while Palmerston specially replied on the wine-and-prayers point, reiterat-
ing the opinion that, when large bodies of young men left
their wine-bibbing assemblies for compulsory attendance on
daily worship, they had not undergone the best preparation
for serious meditation or the proper observance of divine
worship, and that the wisest course had not been adopted
for the promotion of piety and the increase of religion.   The
passing of the Bill was then carried by a majority of over
two to one, the brothers Gladstone voting in the minority;
but, when it came before the Peers, the view prevailed that
the universities, as William Gladstone had claimed, were in
their essence theological seminaries; and, by 187 votes to
85, the Lords threw out a measure which, by 154 votes to
75, the Commons four days previously had passed.

Upon this question an interesting correspondence passed
between Pusey and Mr. Gladstone.   Largely owing to the
former's efforts, a declaration appeared in the spring of 1834,
on the part of members of Oxford University immediately
connected with its instruction and discipline, insisting that
religion, as the foundation of all education, could not be
taught on the principle of admitting persons of every
creed.   A copy was at once forwarded to Mr. Gladstone

[1] 'Hansard,' 3rd series, vol. xxv., ff. 635-9.

by Pusey, who urged strongly the views it contained,[1] and a twelvemonth later the question came up in a new form. It was proposed by the University Liberals that, instead of undergraduates being called upon to subscribe to the Thirty-nine Articles on matriculation, a declaration of general conformity to the Articles should be imposed.   This was strongly objected to by the High Church party, and Pusey drew up a paper of twenty-seven questions in opposition.   A copy of this he sent to Mr. Gladstone, who, writing from Hillingdon, Uxbridge, a few weeks after the fall of the Peel Administration, observed: ‘When I had the pleasure of seeing you, before the expiry of my short tenure at the Colonial Office, I forgot, in the hurry of an interview, to advert to the question referred to in your printed circular which reached me some time back.   What I have to say is little, and I write it with great diffidence; its sum is com·pressed in this, that I should feel inclined to vote against the proposed alteration, but not upon the same grounds as yourself to the full extent, though to a very considerable one. . . . The first *sine quâ non* with me would be, that the University should not be vexed by the interposition of Parliament.   This upon every ground, and not acting peculiarly as a member of the University.   Next to this (in importance however first), and acting in this character, the most essential object seems to be, the maintenance of a Church of England education, and not only its maintenance as at present, but its consummation and perfection in your system.   This being secured—fully and certainly secured, by whatever measures, and whatever degree of exclusiveness may be necessary to give this guarantee—it would give me pleasure to see Dissenters avail themselves, permissively, but to the utmost practicable extent, of our Church education,

[1] Liddon’s ‘ Pusey,’ vol i., pp. 293, 294.

and therefore to see removed, if it be the pleasure of the University and especially of its resident members, any subscription at entrance which is likely to form an absolute and insuperable bar to their becoming students in the University, at a period of life when they are probably little prejudiced in favour of Dissent, and therefore hopeful for the Church, but yet upon the other hand not prepared to make an absolute renunciation of it [Dissent] by a formal subscription. . . . The Declaration now proposed would, it seems to me, be objectionable, as you urge, in sanctioning the principle now operative in a vicious excess, of lowering the tone of institutions to that of society, instead of the reverse process.' He went on to argue that the Declaration would have the effect of rendering entrance into the University more difficult to Dissenters, but this was a line in which Pusey did not care to follow him. The divine wrote that he had pleasure in believing that he agreed in the abstract with the politician, but he averred that he had never thought of the question as with relation to Dissenters, whom he held to be so filled with animus against the Church that they could not be taught, while the Church herself was not yet in a state to receive such pupils with safety. Mr. Gladstone speedily rejoined : 'I do feel most strongly the necessity of putting forward the Articles as a definite basis of teaching and of belief, and of keeping the religious instruction of the University in a fixed form, as the only effectual means of preserving its unity and substance. So far however as regards evil or danger to be apprehended from the contact of the Dissenters, I fear that if we are to wait until the whole body of Churchmen is in such a state that all will be individually as well as collectively secure against labefaction, the prospect of relaxing the entrance will be indefinitely removed. May it not be a question—

whether the study of Church principles, as well as the progress of religion in the great body of individuals professing adherence to the Church, would not be rather quickened by the jealousy for her ensuing upon the apprehended proximity of Dissenters?'[1] The proposed Declaration, it remains only to be noted, was rejected in Convocation a week later by an overwhelming majority.

In the meanwhile, and after, as has been indicated and as later will be explained, Mr. Gladstone had been given office under the Crown, he took an even stronger step in defending the interests of the Established Church. On the second night of the debate upon Russell's proposal to resolve the House into Committee to consider the temporalities of the Church of Ireland, Mr. Gladstone asserted in emphatic terms that there was no proof of the existence of surplus revenue over what was necessary for the due maintenance of that institution. Expressing the belief that Church property was as sacred as private property, he distinguished between the two that the latter was sacred in person and the former to purposes; but he went on to make an admission remarkable in its bearing upon his subsequent political development. He had argued that, at the Reformation, the Legislature, having changed its conscientious belief, made a corresponding change in the conditions upon which Church property was held and administered, but no more ; and he exclaimed, 'Were members of the Church of Rome again to constitute the governing body, I avow my conviction that a return of Church property to its original conditions would be a fair and legitimate consequence : but,' he added, 'till that is the case—till the Union is dissolved— till the representatives of a Catholic population constitute

March 31, 1835. The Irish Church once more.

[1] *Ibid.*, pp. 306-9.

the bulk of the Legislature, I for one shall raise my humble
voice to protest against the doctrine of arbitrary and unlimited alienation now propounded.'

But a far more significant point was to be developed.
Mr. Gladstone argued that, upon the same principles as
were being urged in favour of disestablishing the Irish
Church, the repeal of the Union would have to be granted;
and he asked : ' Will the House be prepared to act on the
same principle with respect to the political government of

Ireland? Because Ireland has been, as

*Mr. Gladstone
argues against re-* has been asserted, neglected, because her
pealing the Union.

resources have remained undeveloped, be-
cause the character of the people, with all its noble capabili-
ties, continues uncultivated, will the House consent to the
dissolution of the Legislative Union? No! The House
would wish to maintain the Union, but would, nevertheless,
give up the Church. What will be the position in which
the House will be placed as regards the question of repeal
of the Union? The advocates of the repeal will hereafter
say, " We came to you with a complaint that the Church of
Ireland was a grievous burden on the Roman Catholic
population, that its revenues are abused, and not applied to
legitimate purposes. By a resolution, you complied with
our demand that the revenues of the Protestant Church of
Ireland should be appropriated by the State. Now, upon
the same principles, and because the great body of the
people of Ireland are dissatisfied with your measures of
government, and plead, as they did before, habitual and
incurable abuse, we call upon you to repeal the Legislative
Union." Surely, this would be a fair parallel argument,
unless, indeed, in respect of the strength which you think
you have to withhold the repeal of the Union, but not to
prevent the demolition of the Church; and, as surely, the

result of this measure would be very greatly to strengthen the argument for repeal, not only in a physical but also in a moral point of view.' And he recurred to this point later in the speech in these words : 'I consider that we have abundant reasons, even of a political complexion, for maintaining the Irish Church : after its destruction we should not be long able to resist the repeal of the Union, partly by loss of strength and more from abandonment of our principles.'

One other department of the argument must be noted as containing the germ of what he was not long afterwards to write concerning the relations of Church and State.   Mr. Gladstone thought there was no principle upon which the Irish Church could be rightly or permanently upheld except that it was the Establishment which taught the truth. ' The Government, as a Government, maintains that form of belief which it conceives to contain the largest portion of the elements of truth with the smallest admixture of error.   It is upon that ground that the Government of this country maintains the Protestant and declines the Catholic religion.   But the noble lord [John Russell] invites us to give up that ground; the noble lord and many of the gentlemen who sit around him tell the House that with the truth of religion the Government has nothing whatever to do.   Their argument is this : no matter what the religion, no matter whether it be true or false, the fact of its existence is sufficient—wherever it exists it is to be recognised ; it is not the business or the duty of a Government to endeavour to influence the belief of its subjects.   But may God forbid that the House should assent to such a doctrine !'

This idea was expanded in a peroration which, as much as any part of the speech, will explain why this young man of twenty-five was regarded by friends and opponents alike

as marked out for high position in the State. 'The science
of Government,' he said, 'involving, as it has done, the
care and direction of the most exalted interests of humanity,
and extending its regards to our destinies for ever, has in
it an aim and intent which attract the highest aspirations
of mankind, and render it worthy to be the occupation and
delight of the most honourable and distinguished among
men ; but if, hereafter, the consideration of religion—the
most vital of all subjects to our permanent happiness and
advancement—be excluded from the attention of Government ; if, on the other hand, they are to be compelled to
view with equal interest or indifference all modes of faith,
to confound together every form of truth and every strange
variety of error, to deal with circumstantial and with
essential differences as being alike matter of no concern, to
refuse their homage to the divine authority of truth ; then,
so far from the science of politics being, as the greatest
philosophers of antiquity fondly proclaimed it, the queen
and mistress of all other arts and discharging the noblest
functions of the mind, it will be an occupation degrading in
its practice and fitted rather for the very helots of society,
for degraded they will be indeed if, being allowed to endeavour to operate for good in all other matters upon the
character and condition of those committed to their charge,
if, striving to amend and advance men in reference to laws
and commerce, to arts and to arms, and to the other varied
interests of life, they be constrained to exclude from their
views and calculations that element which should give
vitality to them all, and which alone can ensure permanent
and substantial improvement.   Such, I for one, conceive to
be the inevitable though, perhaps, indirect result of the
principle contained in this proposition.   Neither am I premature in these remarks, and this discussion has not been

irrelevant, for it has been already announced, in many parts of the country, that the question of union between religion and government is to be solemnly tried and decided. The trial is rapidly approaching, and in this motion is involved, I am convinced, the ultimate fate of that question. I, therefore, have desired, with the utmost anxiety, to protest against the principle that, in reference to those things which are the most important of all, Government is not to seek the amelioration of human nature, but merely to subserve human will—to sanction and follow all its whims and wildest or most mischievous caprices ; and, being deeply convinced that a change so fundamental will immeasurably deteriorate the office of Government, and degrade the character of those by whom it is to be conducted, I earnestly pray that the period of that change may never arrive while we are here to see it.' [1]

The admission of Mr. Gladstone that, although he opposed the motion, he would be ready to bow to it if the time should ever arrive at which the majority of the United Kingdom became Roman Catholic, was fastened upon by Feargus O'Connor, who immediately followed.   But the speech, as a whole, was complimented by Follett, the Tory Solicitor-General, the same evening, and by Praed and Stanley the next night, Stanley defending the 'Church in danger' portion which Spring Rice, as a leading member of the Whig Opposition, had especially criticised.   Outside Parliament, however, the impression made upon the more ardent members of the Church party appears to have been unsatisfactory.   Newman, writing to Rogers a week after its delivery, observed, 'Gladstone's speech raised in my mind your difficulty at once.   It led me to three explanations: (1) That the reporters had not *understood* what was

[1] 'Mirror of Parliament' (1835), pp. 647-9.

above their *captus*. (2) That he was obliged to speak in the language, or according to the calculus, of the Commons. (3) That we floored so miserably at the Reformation that, though the Church ground is defensible and true, yet the edge of truth is so fine that no plain man can see it.'[1]

The fact is that, even up to that time, Mr. Gladstone was not in avowed sympathy or open association with Newman and 'the Movement,' and this despite the hopes entertained by the former concerning him in the autumn of 1833, and the correspondence, already indicated, between Newman and Pusey respectively with himself upon semi-ecclesiastical semi-political topics in the immediately ensuing years. Mr. Gladstone, indeed, has dated his earliest real study of the matter at 'about the year 1836,' when he had his first close talk with Hope—afterwards Hope-Scott, the famous parliamentary lawyer, and a convert to Rome simultaneously with Manning. Hope 'opened a conversation on the controversies which were then agitated in the Church of England, and which had Oxford for their

Mr. Gladstone and James Hope (afterwards Hope-Scott).

centre. I do not think I had paid them much attention; but I was an ardent student of Dante, and likewise of Saint Augustine; both of them had acted powerfully upon my mind. . . . He then told me that he had been seriously studying the controversy, and that in his opinion the Oxford authors were right. He spoke not only with seriousness, but with solemnity, as if this was for him a great epoch; not merely the adoption of a speculative opinion, but the reception of a profound and powerful religious impulse.'[2] The last sentence may now fairly be applied to Mr. Gladstone himself.

Indirect testimony also is forthcoming that Mr. Gladstone

[1] Anna Mozley's 'Letters, etc. of Newman,' vol. ii., p. 97.
[2] Hope-Scott's 'Memoirs,' vol. ii., pp. 274, 275.

was not ardent in the Tractarian controversy previous to the
date he has himself given.   When the question of a Declaration was to come before Convocation at Oxford in the spring
of 1835, as before described, and Pusey invoked the young
politician's vote and aid, it was replied : 'I have mentioned
to my brother [Thomas] the day of your vote in Convocation.   Whether we may be able to go down I do not know,
and I hope you will not attribute it to lukewarmness if, in
the present state of public affairs, and also in the prospect
of your having votes to spare, I do not send you a decisive
answer at the present moment.' [1]   This was not the utterance of an enthusiastic disciple, and it was the same the
next year when the first of the Hampden controversies arose.
Upon the death of Dr. Burton, the Regius
Professor of Divinity, Pusey wrote to Mr.   Mr. Gladstone and
                                              the Hampden con-
Gladstone: 'We are under great anxiety   troversy.
as to our new professor.   Rumour mentions Keble's name.
But this would be too great a blessing for us to dare, in
these days, to hope for, though we may pray for it.' [2]   Keble,
indeed, as well as Newman and Pusey himself, had been
suggested to Melbourne, the Prime Minister, by Howley,
Archbishop of Canterbury; but, upon the advice of Archbishop Whately and Bishop Copleston, there was appointed Dr. Hampden, afterwards Bishop of Hereford,
whom Pusey had keenly attacked in the matter of the
previous year's Declaration, for an alleged departure from
the standard of orthodoxy.   Pusey, like Newman, threw
himself heartily into the fray.   'I have been myself,'
a friend of them both told Mr. Gladstone a few weeks
later, 'hard at work, chiefly on the Bampton Lectures
[delivered by Hampden] making extracts for Pusey, who

[1] Liddon's 'Pusey,' vol. i., p. 309.
[2] *Ibid.*, p. 369.

will publish them with a preface, entering on the main points of Hampden's theological system, if, indeed, one can call such a *farrago a system.*'[1]   But the member for Newark, although thus in obvious touch with the leaders of the anti-Hampden movement, took no part in the storm which convulsed Oxford, and which ended in an attempt by a majority in Convocation to censure the new Professor. This was frustrated by the veto of the Proctors; but a few weeks later Hampden was by vote deprived of the right of sitting at the Board of Inquiry into Heretical Doctrines and at the Board of Nomination of Select Preachers.

During these earlier years of his public life, while holding aloof from purely theological controversy, Mr. Gladstone was active in his political duties, and was steadily progressing in the opinion of Peel.   His votes in his second session were much like those in the first : he was still the strait young Tory with religious tendencies.   In the purely political capacity, he was in a majority of four by which Peel, with the aid of O'Connell and Sheil, defeated the Whigs upon a motion in favour of relieving the agricultural interest, and in the much larger one by which a proposal His early political of Hume for a committee on the Corn votes.   Laws was rejected.   Once more he was in small minorities which sought to hinder the Jewish Relief Bill, and again he opposed the shortening of Parliaments ; and so thoroughly was he at one with the ideas of the past that he voted against the publication of division lists, obviously agreeing with the idea of Peel that it should be left to each member to state to his constituents, if he pleased, what had been his vote on any particular occasion ; and, although no list can be found of a division in the same session upon the question of extending the railway to Eton,

[1] B. Harrison to Mr. Gladstone : *Ibid.*, p. 376.

there is little doubt that he was in the minority which, in accordance with the wish of the heads of his old school, protested against the scheme.   But it was, of course, when anything in connection with the Church was touched that Mr. Gladstone's liveliest sympathies were aroused.   He was in one minority in favour of a Bill which would have made compulsory a payment out of the rates to a Surrey rector that had originally been voted in open vestry as a voluntary sum, and withdrawn when the clergyman became a non-resident; and in another in support of a local Tithes Bill which was roundly denounced by the Radicals as one of the grossest instances of clerical rapacity that had ever come before the House.   And it was of a piece with these votes, and with his general position of supporting any project that might even plausibly be said to be for the benefit of the Church—even when it was obviously only for that of an individual clergyman—that he ineffectually aided a motion for local option in a Sabbatarian direction, thus seeking to enable local authorities to change Saturday and Monday fairs and markets to other days, and as ineffectually opposed the introduction of Wood's Bill to grant Nonconformists the right of admission to the universities.

Such a Church-and-Tory enthusiast was certain of appreciation at his *Alma Mater*, appreciation which even its Whigs shared, for in 'Black Gowns and Red Coats, or Oxford in 1834,' a satirical poem addressed to the Duke of Wellington, then Chancellor of the Univer- Praised by a Whig sity, the author (for the time anonymous, but poet. later known to be George Cox, a Fellow of New College), while severely criticising the moral and intellectual condition of Oxford, made this distinction:

> ' Yet on one form, whose ear can ne'er refuse
> The muses' tribute, for he lov'd the Muse,

> And when the soul the gen'rous virtues raise,
> A friendly Whig may chant a Tory's praise.
> Full many a fond, expectant eye is bent
> Where Newark's towers are mirror'd in the Trent.
> Perchance ere long to shine in senates first,
> If manhood echo what his youth rehears'd,
> Soon Gladstone's brows will bloom with greener bays,
> Than twine the chaplet of a minstrel's lays,
> Nor heed, while poring o'er each graven line,
> The far faint music of a lute like mine.
> His was no head contentedly which press'd
> The downy pillow in obedient rest,
> Where lazy pilots, with their canvass furl'd,
> Set up the Gades of their mental world ;
> His was no tongue which meanly stoop'd to wear
> The guise of virtue while his heart was bare,
> But all he thought through ev'ry action ran ;
> God's noblest work—I've known one honest man.'[1]

And the *Monthly Review*—in praising 'this very lively satire upon the tenacity of the cloistered partizans of old times at the University of Oxford, who see in every little improvement that is proposed, nothing but the overthrow of the institution itself'—particularly noted that 'indiscriminate censure is not passed in Oxford, and amongst the rising youth who promise to become an honour, is Gladstone [to whom] the poet pays warm tribute.'[2]   It was thus no surprise in any quarter when, before the end of the same year and a Peel Administration was formed, room was found in it for Newark's Tory representative.

[1] Part ii., pp. 22, 23.
[2] June, 1834, p. 276.

IX.—IN PEEL'S FIRST MINISTRY.

MR. GLADSTONE's earliest Ministerial appointment was the outcome of the latest royal attempt to directly control the Administration. The King had become tired of the Whigs, and the succession of Althorp, the Commons leader, to the earldom of Spencer gave him a chance, which he eagerly seized, to dismiss the Melbourne Ministry. The immediate consequences of the step are among the best remembered incidents of our modern political history. Peel was in Rome, and Wellington accepted the seals of the leading offices pending his return. William IV. had dismissed Melbourne on November 14th, and given his commission to Wellington on the next day; Peel received the news from the hands of 'the hurried Hudson' on the night of the 25th, and, arriving in London on the morning of December 9th, at once commenced to form a Government. Disraeli has described for all time the lighter side of that intriguing period; the bets which were made upon every political contingency; *December, 1834, Peel's first Ministry formed.* the desires for an under-secretaryship entertained by the 'young Tory, who had contrived to keep his seat in a Parliament where he had done nothing;' the 'brilliant personages who had just scampered up from Melton, thinking it probable that Sir Robert might want some moral lords of the bed-chamber;' and the fact that 'the only grave countenance that was occasionally ushered into the room belonged to some individual whose destiny was not in doubt, and who was already practising the official air that was in future to repress the familiarity of his former fellow-strugglers.'[1]   And of the few whose destiny was not in doubt one was notably Mr. Gladstone.

Reasons abounded, in fact, why he should be chosen. He was one of the small band of young Conservative members who had given good promise of usefulness in the House of Commons; he was already so famed for the most marked of his gifts that the story runs that he had been pointed out by Althorp to the King as a brilliant orator;[2] he sprang from a class and was of a type with which Peel specially and naturally sympathised; and he had the further claim upon the new Premier of high personal character. Disraeli's sneer at the probability of 'some moral lords of the bed-chamber' being required, had, perhaps unknowingly, substantial foundation; for Peel, when pressing a place upon Ashley at this crisis, observed : 'My object is to win the confidence of the country by my appointments; it is to persons of your character that I look.'[3]   A Premier thus actuated was certain at that moment not to pass over his young supporter from Newark, even if all the ordinary stock of Junior Lords and Under-Secretaries had not been swept away in the torrent of Reform.

And this was the case, for one of Peel's earliest acts after his return to England was to write to Mr. Gladstone, inviting him to join the Administration. No moment of a young politician's life can be more fraught with significance for the future than that at which a Prime Minister first asks him to serve; but, at the very threshold of his career, the member

Dec. 26.
Mr. Gladstone
Junior Lord of the
Treasury.

---

[1] 'Coningsby,' book ii., chap. iv.

[2] William Cory's 'Guide to Modern English History,' part ii., p. 309.

[3] Edwin Hodder's 'Life of Lord Shaftesbury,' vol. i., p. 351.

for Newark displayed a scrupulous delicacy in regard to the acceptance of office which was once and again to be repeated, and which the average partisan consistently failed to understand. More than one position was suggested for his selection, and among them the Under-Secretaryship for War and the Colonies, for which, indeed, his special line of political study marked him out; but, owing to his father's connection with the West Indies, he considered that some of his acts might be looked upon as partial and biassed by the interests of his family, and that appointment be declined at once. The post was accordingly given to Lord Wharncliffe's eldest son, John Stuart-Wortley; and Mr. Gladstone, with no past to sustain him and with the future merely an expectation, accepted what in certain respects was an inferior position. On December 26th, a new Commission of the Treasury was issued, in which Peel appeared as First Lord and Chancellor of the Exchequer, with Mr. Gladstone sixth and last on the list, his colleagues including William Yates Peel (the Premier's brother) and his old college friend Lincoln.

Writing to Peel during the Ministerial interregnum, Wellington had observed: 'I think you will find the Tories, Tory Lords in particular, very well disposed to go all reasonable lengths in the way of reform of institutions. . . I have been astonished at their being so docile.' [1] Peel soon put the point to a practical test by issuing an address to his constituents, which has become known to history as ' The Tamworth Manifesto;' and which, because of the moderation of its tone, earned from his own Chancellor, Lyndhurst, the remark that it had evidently been begun at the Constitutional Club and been ended at Brooks's, then a Whig institution. Where Peel had led, the most junior of his

'Memoirs by Sir Robert Peel,' vol. ii., p. 29.

O

Lords of the Treasury followed; and Mr. Gladstone's address, seeking re-election, is a document of much interest as showing his political development.

'To the Electors of Newark.

'GENTLEMEN,

'Having accepted the office of a Lord of the Treasury, I have hereby ceased to be your actual Representative; but I at once announce to you my intention of soliciting a renewal of your confidence when the opportunity of exercising your franchise shall arrive.

He seeks re-election.

'During the two Sessions of the present Parliament my first desire has been to see the Institutions of the Country preserved, whatever the hands in which their custody might be entrusted; and this desire has regulated my votes.

'But the position of parties since the last General Election has in my view essentially changed. We had then a Government, of which it must be allowed that it had been pledged to maintain the existing Constitution of England—to afford fair support to the depressed interests of Agriculture—and, especially, to preserve the property of the Church—property whose application to the purposes of religion, important to all classes, is peculiarly essential to the well being of those not blessed by opulence.

'The late Government assumed, through a series of changes, a very different character; the most respected and most efficient supporters of the Reform Bill, successively separated themselves from it; on one occasion by a refusal to alienate the property of the Church; on another by anxiety to maintain in Ireland personal security and the protection of the law—There remained a body of Ministers, whose preponderating bias tended decisively towards rash, violent, and indefinite innovation; and, it appears, that there were those among the servants of the King, who did not scruple to solicit the suffrages of their constituents, with promises to act on the principles of Radicalism. An intention to invade Church property was avowed; and, I think, few believe that the constitution of the Cabinet, in its closing period, afforded any security against new and extensive changes in our elective system, or for the reasonable protection of the millions dependent on the Land.

'The question has then, as it appears to me, become, whether we are to hurry onwards at intervals, but not long ones, through the medium of the Ballot, short Parliaments, and other questions, called popular, into Republicanism or anarchy; or whether, independently of all party distinctions, the People will support the Crown, in the discharge of its duty to maintain in efficiency, and transmit in safety, those old and valuable Institutions, under which our Country has greatly flourished.

'With the fullest confidence I anticipate that you have embraced the latter, and the better alternative. In no party or sectarian spirit, but upon this elevated principle alone, do I conceive that Sir Robert Peel undertook the formation of a Government, and desired, at the hands of his Countrymen, a fair trial; and we may trust that the same providential care which has raised this country to preeminence, and often saved it from external peril, will, in this time of domestic difficulty, be found its effectual safeguard.

'Let me add shortly, but emphatically, concerning the reform of actual abuses, whether in Church or State, that I regard it as a sacred duty—a duty at all times, and certainly not least at a period like this, when the danger of neglecting it is most clear and imminent—a duty not inimical to true and determined Conservative principle, nor a curtailment or

modification of such principle, but its legitimate consequences, or rather an actual element of its composition.

'I have the honor to be, Gentlemen,

'Your obliged and obedient servant,

'W. E. GLADSTONE.

'London, 24th December, 1834.'

Parliament was dissolved on December 29th, and on the
same night Mr. Gladstone attended a Dispensary Ball at
Newark, in company with the Duke of Newcastle and
Lord Lincoln. His canvass was not to commence until
New Year's Day ; but on December 31st,
Handley, his colleague in the representa-
tion, announced that he would not seek re-election, with
the ultimate result that Newark was freed from a contest
for the first time since 1820, and Mr. Gladstone and
Serjeant Wilde were returned unopposed. Among the
compliments locally paid to the new Lord of the Treasury
was the declaration of the *Nottingham Journal* that he was,
'without exception, one of the most talented young men
who entered the last Parliament. Several of his speeches
manifested research and ability of the highest order, and in
listening to his admirable addresses, we are equally
charmed with the graceful elegance of his manner, and
the polished eloquence of his style.' And, after his re-
election, the same panegyrist exclaimed, 'Of the sound
principles, the splendid talents, and the amiable character
of Mr. Gladstone we have frequently had occasion to speak
in terms of unqualified approbation. His praiseworthy
conduct and his manly exposition of constitutional sentiments at Newark [at the nomination] have, if possible, increased our admiration of his moral and intellectual
qualities ; and we trust that he will long live to exercise his

Jan., 1835.
Is returned unop-
posed.

abilities in support of the best interests of his country, as a Member of the British Parliament.'

At the nomination, Mr. Gladstone, after a passing word of praise to the defunct Whig Government for its attitude on the Poor Law question, and an assertion that he could not himself have concurred in any visionary theory or system that should go to deprive the sick, the infirm, and the aged of relief, denied an allegation that the new Administration was formed upon the principle of denying all reform ; he defended the action of the King in dismissing Melbourne; and he quoted in support of his conten-tion the position of the Tory party upon the Test and Corporation Acts, Catholic Emancipation, *His principles in* and the commercial and fiscal changes *1835.* effected under Lord Liverpool. Change, as change, he held not to be good, but the nature of the change must determine whether it would be a benefit ; and, while the first duty of a statesman was to pre-serve, the next was to improve. Peel and his Ministers, in fact, were the only true Reformers ; and, as no political principles could be more false than those which adopted expedients without regard to justice, he called upon them all to rally round the Throne and the Altar, declaring that it would be more honourable to fall in their defence than to compromise with their enemies. Wilde, though criticis-ing certain of his colleague's ' fine and classical expressions, which would apply either way, for a good change or a bad one,' was in a flattering mood. Mr. *Wilde's compliment.* Gladstone was not merely his honourable but his amiable and talented friend ; he was complimented upon his virtues, and the hope was expressed that he would do even better in the new Parliament. And then, amid the common joy, the 'chairing' took place, and Mr. Gladstone's 'chair was

Beresford,[1] and Pemberton :[2] rather dull, but we had a swan very white and tender, and stuffed with truffles, the best company there.'[3]   It was certainly not a company calculated to be attractive to the brilliant young novelist, who was already one of the best-known men of his time in literature, but whose political experiences up to that period had been disappointing. Only a few days previously, he had met his third defeat at Wycombe; Lyndhurst, with whom he was a great personal favourite, and who was the 'Noble and Learned Lord' to whom he was shortly to dedicate his 'Vindication of the English Constitution,' had a month before unsuccessfully endeavoured to negotiate his return for Lynn, through the influence of Lord George Bentinck ; and the author of the burlesque 'Popanilla' and the bombastic 'Revolutionary Epick' may well have felt out of place amid sober Barons of the Exchequer and preternaturally grave young politicians.   Among such, indeed, the tale might have been believed, which four months later so eminently respectable a Tory as Southey communicated to a friend, that Disraeli had 'once been disordered in his intellect ; how it manifested itself I never heard, but the father was said to have removed from London in order to withdraw him for a time from scenes of excitement.' 'Overweening vanity, with nothing to ballast it, was probably the cause that overset him,' added the then Poet Laureate ;[4] and that was a widespread opinion at the date when Mr. Gladstone and Disraeli first met. And the chief, if not the only impression, which the former

---

[1] Admiral Sir John Poore Beresford, a Junior Lord of the Admiralty.

[2] Thomas Pemberton, then Tory member for Ripon.

[3] Disraeli's 'Correspondence with his Sister,' p. 30.

[4] Southey's 'Correspondence with Caroline Bowles,' p. 323 ; Letter of May 10, 1835.

carried away—as he afterwards told Mr. T. P. O'Connor, Disraeli's best-known biographer—from the dinner which Disraeli considered 'rather dull,' was of the singularity of his future rival's dress.

Not for long did Mr. Gladstone hold the Lordship of the Treasury. John Stuart-Wortley (eldest son of the leader of 'the Waverers' in 1832, who was himself in the Peel Cabinet as Lord President of the Council) had been made Under-Secretary for War and the Colonies, but had failed to find a seat, having been defeated in an attempt to win Forfarshire at the general election. This was on January 19th, and he immediately tendered his resignation, with the consequence that the *Times* of eight days later announced that 'Mr. John Gladstone has been appointed Under Secretary of State for the Colonial Department. Mr. Gladstone had an interview yesterday with the Earl of Aberdeen, and afterwards transacted business at the Colonial-office.' In its next issue, it dexterously but unobtrusively corrected the blunder in name by stating that 'Mr. W. Ewart Gladstone transacted business yesterday at the Colonial-office as one of the Under Secretaries of State for that department.' But the *Nottingham Review*, not perceiving the correction, amplified the original error by inserting the words, 'brother to the members for Leicester [Thomas] and Newark,' after the 'Mr. John Gladstone,' when it copied without acknowledgment the original *Times* statement; and, although Newark was so near as to be interested, it did not ever trouble to set the matter right.

'In consequence of the defeat of my Under-Secretary in the county of Forfar,' wrote Aberdeen, Peel's Colonial Secretary, to his old friend, Hudson Gurney, 'I have been obliged to appoint another. I have chosen a young man

[sidenote] Mr. Gladstone appointed Under-Secretary for War and the Colonies.

whom I did not know, and whom I never saw, but of
Lord Aberdeen's
opinion of him, whose good character and abilities I had
often heard.   He is the young Gladstone,
and I hope he will do well.   He has no easy part to play
in the House of Commons, but it is a fine opening for a
young man of talent and ambition, and places him in the
way to the highest distinction.   He appears to be so
amiable that personally I am sure I shall like him.' [1]   ' The
young Gladstone '— thus distinguished from his eldest
brother, Thomas, who was in the new House of Commons
for Leicester, after a hotly-contested fight—has himself, in a
letter addressed to the son and biographer of Aberdeen [2] after
his old chief's death, and giving his impressions of that
statesman's life and character, described his having been
sent for by Peel on this January evening to receive the offer
of the Colonial Under-Secretaryship.   From the Premier's he
went to the house of Aberdeen, ' who was thus to be, in official
home-talk, my master ; ' and this he did in fear and trembling,
and his of Aberdeen. for he knew that peer only by public rumour,
which, while affirming his high character,
spoke of him as a man of cold manners and even haughty
reserve.   It was dusk when Mr. Gladstone entered his room
—' the room on the first floor, with the bow-window looking
to the Park,' as, with an almost quaint minuteness, he long
afterwards recalled, and this despite the fact that he could
not recollect the conversation, though he could well remember that, before having been with his new chief for three
minutes, his apprehensions had melted away like snow before the sun ; and a friendship was established between the
old and the young statesman which was broken only by

---

[1] Lord Stanmore's ' Earl of Aberdeen,' p. 111.
[2] Lord Stanmore, long known as Sir Arthur Gordon.

Aberdeen's death more than a quarter of a century later.[1]

Although the new appointment did not necessitate the seeking of re-election, Mr. Gladstone issued on February 2nd an address to his constituents at Newark, formally acquainting them with the change. He reminded them that February 2.
Another address to
Newark. he regarded the recent renewal of their trust 'as a mark not only of personal confidence, but of your determination to support the Throne in the exercise of its just prerogative.' A new title to his gratitude had thus been established, which tribute he returned by telling them of his promotion. The conclusion of the address, however, contained something more than compliment, and one of its final phrases was significant of the greater change that was to come. 'I am indebted,' Mr. Gladstone wrote, 'to my intercourse with the various classes of your community for this among other advantages: that it has deeply impressed me with the persuasion that the great mass of the people are truly and warmly attached to the venerable Institutions of their Country, and to the social order established among us, from a solid and experimental conviction of their permanent advantages—a conviction not at all enfeebled by the fact, now sometimes announced with the ostentation, but not the merit of discovery, that like all other human productions, their structure is capable of beneficial change. It has been, and continues to be, my humble, but earnest desire to blend and harmonise the distinct, but not necessarily discordant, principles of preservation and improvement, and to secure their efficacy together with their union, maintaining each in its due relative position, and defending

[1] 'The Correspondence of Lord Aberdeen,' *Edinburgh Review*, October, 1883, p. 573.

each with increased anxiety, according as either of them may be assailed in opposite directions by the alternate political caprices of successive periods. In the support of these principles, until my conscience, if misguided shall have become better informed, I hope by God's blessing to proceed.' And with another word of thanks he ended an address which clearly showed that in spirit he was already passing from the stage of uncompromising because youthful Toryism into that of a 'Peelite.'

When Lord Beaconsfield's unprincipled young politician, Waldershare, was appointed Under-Secretary for Foreign Affairs (in the Peel Administration of 1841, to make the sarcasm more keen), he explained to a lady friend that the holder of such a position, with his chief in the House of Lords, was 'master of the situation,' and he averred that he was going to make a collection of the portraits of such, which would be that of the most eminent statesmen England had ever produced.[1] Had he fulfilled his in-tention, the gallery would have been almost completely un-tenanted, for Canning alone fulfilled the necessary con-ditions; but the description, exaggerated as it would have been in any case, would much more fittingly have applied to the Under-Secretaryship for War and the Colonies than to that for Foreign Affairs. Among the Under-Secretaries of the old days, before Departments were divided, were Matthew Prior and Joseph Addison, Thomas Tickell and David Hume; while among those for Foreign Affairs after 1782, when that Department was created, were Sheridan and Canning. But among those for War and the Colonies had been Goderich and Peel and Stanley, all of them to become Prime Minister and all holding this as their first office, as well as Howick, whose independence of spirit

[1] 'Endymion,' chap. lxxiv.

prevented his attaining the great official position for which his talents qualified him; while Mr. Gladstone's successors in that post included Lord Lyttelton, who held it eleven years later under his brother-in-law himself, when Secretary for War and the Colonies in the closing months of the Administration of Peel.

By a coincidence of circumstance which may not have been undesigned, the first reply Mr. Gladstone had to give in the House of Commons as Under-Secretary for War and the Colonies was to a question from Buxton as to what, if any, provision had been or was likely to be undertaken for the education of the colonial negroes. The answer was admittedly not easy to make. The late Colonial Secretary had February 27. Questioned on Negro education. asked for information immediately before leaving office ; the new holder of the post had to wait for this before committing himself to a plan ; and, although one or two colonies had sent returns and others were arriving daily, it was impossible to form any definitive opinion until the whole had been received. But, if more funds for the purpose were needed than were available, application, Mr. Gladstone promised, would be made to Parliament, under the belief that its pledge to assist in the religious education of the West India apprentices was just as distinct and binding, though it may not have been as determined, as its other to pay twenty millions to the owners of slaves.[1] A fortnight later, Mr. Gladstone secured, in substitution for some returns relating to abolition which had been granted upon a motion by Buxton, that there should be issued a series containing among other papers the correspondence which had passed between the Colonial Office and the West Indian governors as to the state of negro education.[2]

[1] 'Mirror of Parliament' (1835), pp. 140, 141.
[2] March 12 : *Ibid.*, p. 315.

Towards the end of the session, when Mr. Gladstone was no longer a Minister, the question again came forward, and this time upon a proposal by the reconstituted Whig Cabinet that £25,000 should be voted to defray such expenses as might be incurred in aiding the West Indian legislatures to provide for the religious and moral instruction of the emancipated negro population. Mr. Gladstone at once protested, on the ground that, although some provision was necessary, the period of apprenticeship being fraught alike with peculiar opportunities and peculiar necessities for the education of the negroes, the Government had not in this case preserved any regard to the great principle of a church establishment, all sects bearing the Christian name being about to be placed upon an equal footing. Interrupted by cries of 'hear, hear,' from several Whig members, Mr. Gladstone, construing them as satirical, retorted, 'I am alive to the meaning of that cheer; but, though well aware that the principle of a church establish-

Again upholds Church Establishments. ment is not a popular one on that side of the House, I, upon the other hand, believe it to be intimately interwoven with the welfare and greatness of my country : and I am, therefore, of course, incapable of being deterred from the expression of such a sentiment by any taunt or sarcasm, made in whatever shape.' He reminded the House that it had never yet, in educational grants, gone so far as to teach the distinctive peculiarities of all sects alike, in common with those of the Established Church ; but he did not put it to the trouble of a division, the vote, after a very brief debate, being agreed to without dissent.[1]

Among what may be called the routine Parliamentary duties of the Colonial Under-Secretary was the replying to questions concerning trial by jury in Tasmania ; the moving

[1] August 10 : *Ibid.*, p. 2383.

for a select committee, which should include himself, to consider the military establishments and expenditure of the British Empire in the Colonies, in completion of an inquiry which had been commenced in the last session of the previous Parliament; and the rebuking of Roebuck for broaching what to the Colonial Office appeared extraordinary and unwarrantable doctrines in regard to Canada. Of more importance was the introduction of a much-needed Bill to regulate the carriage of passengers between this kingdom and her colonies, this having special reference to the comfort and convenience of emigrants; and, having replied in anticipation to an objection, certain in the days when *laissez-faire* was king, that legislative interference would tend to obstruct emigration by imposing fetters upon what ought to be free, Mr. Gladstone said he could not sacrifice the interests of humanity, when obviously involved, to any speculative principle of commerce, the application of which ought *Introduces a Bill concerning Emigrants.* always to be subject to modification from circumstances. The measure—which, read a second time without a division upon the motion of Mr. Gladstone, was taken up by the Whig Government, piloted through Committee by the succeeding Under-Secretary for the Colonies (Sir George Grey), and passed into law—was welcomed with the complimentary expression of a trust by Patrick Maxwell Stewart, the Whig member for his father's old constituency of Lancaster, that all Mr. Gladstone's Bills would be equal in utility to this, his first step in legislation;[1] and this was probably the more welcome because, only three nights before, Stewart had been somewhat nettled with the young politician. He had been denouncing Roebuck's advice to the disaffected Canadians, when Mr.

[1] March 19 : *Ibid.*, pp. 447, 448.

Gladstone interposed a suggestion that he should abstain from any details likely to excite discussion ; and Stewart retorted, 'My honourable friend has reversed Dr. Johnson's definition of a fashionable patron—who, he says, is one that encumbers you with help, when you have reached the land ; for I was just about landing when my honourable friend thought fit to help me to the encumbrance of his well-meant interruption : I will not trespass long against his wish '—but he doggedly recited his carefully-prepared address with its well-assorted quotations to the end.[1]

Save for the speech in defence of the Irish Church Establishment, previously described, and delivered after a conversation with Pusey, and an attempt to come to the rescue of his eldest brother, whose election for Leicester had been unsuccessfully petitioned against, Mr. Gladstone made no other appearance in the House of Commons as a Minister except to submit a motion for certain emigration returns of no special reason to be remembered now. As far as Parliament was concerned, therefore, he had little chance ; but the impression he created inside the Colonial Office, during this earliest tenure of a position there, is worth noting, and it has been best described by Sir Henry Taylor, long one of its permanent officials : '"I rather like Gladstone," I wrote, Sir Henry Taylor's on making his acquaintance; "but he is opinion of him. said to have more of the devil in him than appears—in a virtuous way, that is—only self-willed. He may be all the more useful here for that." His amiable manner and looks deluded Sir James Stephen, who said that, for success in political life, he wanted pugnacity ! By the time he quitted office, I had, of course, come to know more about him, and what I said then was : " Gladstone left with us a paper on negro education, which confirmed

[1] March 16 : *Ibid.*, p. 356.

me in the impression that he is a very considerable man—
by far the most so of any man I have seen amongst our
rising statesmen.   He has, together with his abilities, great
strength of character and excellent dispositions." [1]   Let it
here be marked that, although Taylor noted the report that
the young politician had ' more of the devil in him—in a
virtuous way—than appears,' the dominant note in his character that impressed both Aberdeen and Stephen was his
amiability ; and in this they but anticipated so keen a critic
as Macaulay, who, four years later, after meeting him in
Rome, and even when preparing his famous onslaught upon
Mr. Gladstone's book on Church and State, wrote to the
editor of the *Edinburgh Review*, ' He is both a clever and
an amiable man.' [2]   And the inside verdict of the chiefs of
the Colonial Office as to his abilities may be taken as having
been confirmed by the outside, for, three years after he had
quitted his post, James Grant, whose personal description
of Mr. Gladstone will in its place be quoted, observed :
' He is a man of good business habits : of this he furnished
abundant proof when Under-Secretary for the Colonies.' [3]

But it was for little more than a couple of months that
Mr. Gladstone had the opportunity for furnishing such
proof.   So evident, indeed, was it from the time Peel's
Administration met Parliament that it would have but a
brief existence, that there was prefaced this significant note
to the opening volume of ' Hansard ' for the session of
1835 : 'It has been thought better to omit the official dignities of Peers, because from the changes of Ministry, the
Lists frequently become useless before the Session or Parliament ends.'   The assault began with the first moment of

[1] ' Autobiography of Henry Taylor,' vol. i., p. 190.
[2] Sir George Trevelyan's 'Life and Letters of Lord Macaulay,' p. 374.
[3] ' The British Senate in 1838,' vol. ii., p. 92.

the session. The Speaker,[1] who had shown himself an active Tory partisan during the Ministerial crisis, was ejected from the chair by a narrow majority and after a fierce fight ; and week after week the Cabinet had to struggle against the

Peel's Ministry falls. continual assaults of the Whigs, who secured victory after victory, until Peel was forced to resign. The net result of this prolonged and painful struggle between a Ministry, specially called to power by an exercise of the royal prerogative, and a majority of the representatives of the people has thrice, in later years, been summarised by Mr. Gladstone. Reviewing, in 1875, the second volume of Sir Theodore Martin's biography of the Prince Consort, he wrote that 'the endeavour of King William IV., in 1834, to assert his personal choice in the appointment of a Ministry without reference to the will of

Mr. Gladstone's opinion upon the King's interference. Parliament, gave to the Conservative party a momentary tenure of office without power. But, in truth, that indiscreet proceeding of an honest and well-meaning man produced a strong reaction in favour of the Liberals; and greatly prolonged the predominance which they were on the point of losing through the play of natural causes. Laying too great a stress on the instrument of Royal will, it tended not to strengthen the Throne but to enfeeble it. Such was the upshot of an injudicious, though undoubtedly conscientious, use of power.'[2] Eighteen months later, commenting on the second volume of the same work, Mr. Gladstone observed that the action of the King was taken 'with no sort of reason and (it is true) without success, but also without any strain to the Constitution, or any penalty other than the

[1] Sir Charles Manners-Sutton, afterwards first Viscount Canterbury.

[2] W. E. Gladstone's 'Gleanings of Past Years,' vol. i., pp. 38, 39.

disagreeable sensation of being defeated, and of having greatly strengthened and reinvigorated by recoil the fortunes of the party on whom it had been meant to inflict an over-throw.'[1]   And, another similar period having elapsed, he returned to the point in his article, ' Kin beyond Sea,' when he said that ' though the act was rash and hard to justify, the doctrine of personal immunity was in no way endangered. . . . Most certainly it was a very real exercise of personal power.   The power did not suffice for its end, which was to overset the Liberal predominance ; but it very nearly suc-ceeded.'[2]   For the time, however, the attempt failed ; and Peel and his political friends had once more to wander in the wilderness.

[1] *Ibid.*, p. 78.   [2] *Ibid.*, p. 231.

X.—Progress In and Out of Parliament.

HAVING found office in the winter and lost it in the spring, Mr. Gladstone was consoled by the congratulations of his constituents in the summer.   It was in June that the Newark Tories gave a dinner in his honour; and his father, with his brother Robertson, accepted an invitation to be present, the latter even bursting into song in the course of the proceedings. 'Gladstone and the Constitutional Cause' was emblazoned on the principal flag; and the company had good reason to rejoice, for, observed a local reporter (who, though with obvious reluctance, had to leave early), 'the dinner was admirably served up, the wines were good, and a pleasant breeze tempered the heat, which else would have been over-powering.'   To add to the general joy, four glee singers had been brought from Lincoln to sing the grace; and, that no element of pleasure might be wanting, a band of music played occasionally during the afternoon.   The chairman, who was the same T. S. Godfrey that had presided over the Red Club three years before, declared that the dinner was not only a tribute of respect to their member, but an endeavour to follow the example of the City of London in showing attachment to the principles and policy of the Peel Administration.   The guest of the day, in responding to the toast of his health, expressed his great satisfaction at having been a member of that Government, and strenuously defended the late Premier from the attacks alike of the Whigs and the extreme Tories.   He proceeded to carry the war into the enemy's camp by declaring

June 11, 1835.
Mr. Gladstone entertained at Newark.

Defends Peel

that the Melbourne Ministry was truckling to the authority of
O'Connell and his party. 'I do not think it expedient,' he
said, 'nor shall I enter into details of the exploits, character,
and political opinions of that gentleman; I   and denounces
would rather say what I think of him in his   O'Connell.
presence than in his absence, because, unfortunately, I can
say nothing of him but what is bad. This being the case,
and the Government having a numerical majority, I say it
possesses that majority only by truckling to the prejudices and
passions of the mob—men of violent revolutionary principles, and to reckless agitators. Under these circumstances,
I will call upon you as men who look deeper than the mere
surface and show of things to say who it is that occupies
the humiliating position, and I am sure you will say that it
is the present Administration and their allies who fill that
dishonourable and degraded position.' Mr. Gladstone then
discussed the questions of Corporation and Church Reform,
the most burning of the moment; and, in regard to the
proposal of the Whig Ministry in the Municipal Corporations Bill to entrust the power of licensing to Town Councils,
exclaimed, 'I cannot understand upon what principles it can
be wise to place the licensing of public-houses in the hands
of a Common Council, elected by a class of men who are
necessarily under the influence of the keepers of the public-
houses.' He emphatically denied that the Conservatives were
opposed to all reform ; he scornfully rebutted the assertion
that they were dead to the existence of abuses or unwilling to
see them removed ; but the question was whether, with the
abuses, their institutions were to be swept away. He took
the Irish Church as an instance, and claimed that it ought
to be upheld, not for self-interested purposes of the Government, but according to the principles of Protestantism.
The separation of the Church of Ireland from the State

would, he held, be a sure step to the repeal of the Union, and, after that, the absolute dismemberment of the Empire; and he, therefore, gave with enthusiasm the toast of 'The Union of Church and State.'

The most interesting portion of the subsequent proceedings was a speech of John Gladstone in response to the drinking of his health. After stating the pleasure which the function of the day had given him, he expressed with much feeling his gratitude to the Almighty for having imbued the mind of his son with those principles which had always governed his conduct, and which, he hoped, would abide with him through life, for they had grown with his growth and ripened with his maturer years. Then the youngest Gladstone had a further oratorical chance, proposing in glowing terms the health of the ladies present, with as many times as many cheers as the enthusiasm of the company should dictate—in the midst of which the ladies, who had stood during the address, retired; and still another speech came later when he gave the toast of the Archbishop of York and the clergy of the diocese. His brother Robertson followed this last effort with a song, and the proceedings became more and more convivial, until even the local reporters had to tear themselves away.[1]

Speedily after Mr. Gladstone's return to London, he presented a petition from the Corporation of Newark against the Municipal Corporations Bill, and offered a few observations in its support, directed to the particular grievances of that body in regard to an adverse report of the Royal Commissioners and not to the measure itself,[2] the second reading

John Gladstone speaks.

June 22.
Criticises Municipal Corporations Bill.

---

[1] *Nottingham and Newark Mercury*, June 13, 1835.
[2] 'Mirror of Parliament' (1835), pp. 1465, 1466.

of which, indeed, he had favoured. But, although he consequently felt bound by its principle, which he understood to be the abrogation of the system of self-election and the substitution of an open and liberal system, he took occasion, on the third reading, after having frequently voted in committee for important amendments, to declare that he could give his honest advocacy to very few of the clauses in the Bill. Without enumerating all his points of objection, he specially expressed disapproval of the frequency of elections which must occur under the operation of the measure; of the restriction which it imposed upon the prerogative of the Crown; and of the extension of the power of licensing public-houses to individuals who were to be subjected to popular election.[1] The House of Lords proved on this last point of the same opinion as Mr. Gladstone; and it remained for that politician himself to invent over thirty years later the term 'local option' to describe the licensing reform he now denounced, and which was at the time defeated.

On one other occasion during this session of 1835 did Mr. Gladstone come prominently forward in debate, and then as a champion of the independence of the House of Lords. The Chancellor of the Exchequer (Spring Rice[2]) had postponed for a week an important stage of the Consolidated Fund Bill in a manner which led Hume and O'Connell to construe the action into a threat to the Lords that no more money would be voted until the leading Ministerial measures were passed. Mr. Gladstone immediately followed O'Connell to declare that he felt bound in honour and conscience to state that, although the

---

[1] July 20 : *Ibid.*, p. 1982.
[2] Afterwards Lord Monteagle.

Commons had the power of carrying into execution the
threat of suspending the grant of public
money for the general emergencies of the
State, there could be nothing more indiscreet or indecent
—the latter epithet being quickly softened to indelicate—
than for a Minister of the Crown to ground his postpone-
ment of a financial Bill on the presumption of the conduct
that another branch of the Legislature would pursue respecting certain measures submitted to their consideration
in their independent capacity, for they were as independent
as the Commons, and as capable of exercising a sound
judgment. Spring Rice retorted that, if he knew anything
of decency or delicacy, both would command him to do
justice to the conduct of a political opponent, and not to
presume to misrepresent his motives. He held that Mr.
Gladstone's charges were as much misapplied as his constitutional doctrines; and he challenged the member for
Newark to justify at once the fairness of his attack and the
tendency of his Tory attempt to draw a distinction between
the obligations Ministers owed to the Crown and those
which they owed to the people. Mr. Gladstone declined
to enter the suggested field, and accepted Spring Rice's
explanation of his course, but transferred his censure to
O'Connell and Hume. The Irish leader was ready with
his reply: ' I accept the transfer, and return it with contempt. I regard the honourable gentleman's doctrine as
exceedingly slavish. It is discreditable
to make a traffic of politics, and specu-
late on the chance of changes.' Hume was equally
emphatic from a different personal standpoint: ' I am
not willing to accept the transfer. I think the honourable member has shown himself to be ignorant of
the powers and duties of this House.' Another Radical

Aug. 21.
Defends the House of Lords.

O'Connell and Hume reply to him.

having expressed his keen delight at the turn the discussion was taking, Mr. Gladstone came back to the charge, and laid it down as a Tory doctrine that each branch of the Legislature was independent, to judge and decide as it might think proper upon every question brought before it, unbiassed by the views of other parties, and, in any event, bowing only to the deliberative opinion of the free people of the Empire. Charles Buller—'the Daphne of Liskeard,' as Disraeli in his historic maiden speech was to call him, and at that time one of the most promising among Liberal members, who was lost to politics by a too early death—followed with advice to Mr. Gladstone, as a young man like himself, that, before he made any other violent attack upon a political adversary, he should attend to and understand what had been said; while Russell grimly remarked that the member for Newark had been indiscreet and unwise to provoke the discussion. But the Radicals generally had been elated with the opportunity for attacking their pet abhorrence, the House of Lords.[1]

Radicals outside were as pleased at the chance as those within. Their principal organ, the *Morning Chronicle*, after lecturing Mr. Gladstone upon his eagerness to assert a Tory doctrine, and approving the rebuke administered to him by Spring Rice, expressed its joy that 'the *fortunate* mistake of the Honourable Gentleman led to some very unequivocal expressions of feeling on the subject of the strange course pursued by the Lords;' and added the opinion that

Press comments on Mr. Gladstone's action.

'the spirited language of Ministers, received with cheers, with which the walls of the Commons' House rang, will bring the Lords to their senses.' It may have been because the Conservatives themselves saw that Mr. Gladstone's

[1] *Ibid.*, pp., 2673-75.

attitude was too uncompromising to be sustained that, while
the *Morning Herald* in its summary of the proceedings gave
another Tory member the credit for raising the discussion, and only mildly commented upon the debate, the
Times and the *Morning Post* alike omitted Mr. Gladstone's
name from the summary, and almost entirely refrained
from criticism. But *John Bull*, always charmed to support
the strongest Tory views, declared that Mr. Gladstone's
attacks upon the Chancellor of the Exchequer had been
powerful and straightforward, denounced O'Connell's reply
as incompatible with his receipt of the famous ' rent,' and
regretted only that no more than eight Conservatives were
present during the discussion.

A heavy bereavement in the death of his mother, which
befell Mr. Gladstone a month later, prevented him from

Sept. 23.
His mother dies.   taking any active part in political controversy during the ensuing autumn and
winter ; and even in the session of 1836 he did not display
all his accustomed energy and fire, and was not merely less
constant in attendance but was little heard in debate.   He

Session of 1836.
He discusses
minor questions   approved, for instance, a motion of Hume
in favour of abolishing the gratuities then
customarily given by members to the doorkeepers and
messengers of the House for bringing them the parliamentary papers ; though he agreed with O'Connell that, as these
gratuities had been considered a portion of the salary, the
recipients ought to be indemnified by the Treasury.[1]   But
beyond this and a criticism upon some decrease in the staff
of the Colonial Office which had taken place since his
tenure of the Under-Secretaryship, and which he deprecated being defended upon the ground of economy—unpopular as it might be, according to the practice of that

[1] *Ibid.*, (1836), p. 73.

day, to find fault with any economical change [1]—he mainly
confined himself at Westminster to work upon two of the
most important select committees of the session, varying
these labours with an excursion into verse, which was not to
see the light of print for many a year. The poem, 'On an
Infant who was Born, was Baptised, and
Died on the same Day' (signed 'W. E. G., *and writes verse.*
July, 1836,' but published as 'by the Right Hon. W. E.
Gladstone"), filled four pages of *Good Words*, and was
in twelve stanzas, three of which may be given :—

> ' How wast thou made to pass,
>   By a short transition, from the womb
>   Unto that other darkness of the tomb,
>   O Babe, O brother to the grass !
>   For like the herb, so thou art born
>   At early morn ;
>   And thy little life has flowed away
>   Before the flowing day ;
>   Thy willing soul hath struggled, and is free ;
>   And all of thee that dieth
>   A white and waxen image lieth
>   Upon the knee.
>
>   .   .   .   .
>
>   One evening thou wert not.
>   The next, thou wert ; and wert in bliss ;
>   And wert in bliss for ever.   And is this
>   So desolate a lot,
>   To be the theme of unconsoled sorrow,
>   Because, thy first to-morrow,
>   Thou wert ordained a vest to wear,
>   Not made like ours of clay,
>   But woven with the beams of clearest day,
>   A cherub fair ?
>
>   .   .   .   .
>
>   Then flow, ye blameless tears, a while,
>   A little while ye may :

[1] *Ibid.*, p. 1591.

The natural craving to beguile,
The task is yours ; with you
Shall peace be born anew,
And sorrow glide away.
Oh happy they, in whose remembered lot
There should appear no darker spot
Than this of holy ground,
This, where, within the short and narrow bound,
From morn to eventide,
In quick successive train,
An infant lived and died
And lived again.'[1]

The session of 1836 had shown the continuance of one phase of Mr. Gladstone's earlier political character as a 'young Tory blood,' which is little remembered by those who knew him only as an 'old Parliamentary hand.' It has been seen how more than once he had been successful in 'drawing' Russell in somewhat the same fashion as in far later years he himself was to be lured into heated conflict by Lord Randolph Churchill ; and he was one of a knot of energetic Tories who

Baits Russell,

acted as thorns in the flesh to the then Whig leader of the House. Russell's chill and somewhat sour manner was employed with small effect upon his daring young antagonist. 'The mode of proceeding adopted by the honourable gentleman is

who sourly replies.

completely at variance from what hitherto has been the usage of this House since I have had the honour of sitting in it,' was a frosty rebuke of 1836, [2] which Mr. Gladstone repaid the next year. Russell had moved, without remark, the reception of the report upon a Ministerial Bill dealing with the qualification of parliamentary

[1] *Good Words* for 1871, pp. 365-8.
[2] June 27 ; ' Mirror of Parliament ' (1836), p. 2109.

electors; and the member for Newark, supporting an un-answered request of Inglis, desired to extract from the leader of the House some statement as to his object in bringing it forward.   He denounced the process as a direct violation of a Ministerial pledge not to press on contentious measures in the thin Houses which almost necessarily followed the accession of a new sovereign and the approach-ing dissolution of Parliament. 'If I am wrong,' he exclaimed, 'I shall be happy to be corrected.   If I am right, I say that the noble lord has forfeited his pledge.'   Benjamin Hawes, the Radical member for Lambeth, sneered at this 'volunteer lecture;' but Russell kept silence until later in the night, when, on the motion for third reading, Herries emphasised Mr. Gladstone's demand, and the leader of the House was forced into the explanation he had denied to his younger assailant.[1]

These were symptoms of a militant temper on the part of Mr. Gladstone which was to be shown outside the House as well. During the autumn of 1836 he paid his first purely political visit to his native town, and that with the object of assisting an old school friend, whose claims upon him were all the stronger as being the son of his then hero in states-manship.   Charles Canning had been marked out from his earliest youth for distinction in Charles Canning. public life.   Upon the appointment of Mr. Gladstone as Under-Secretary for War and the Colonies in January of the previous year, Peel, though the younger Canning was not then in Parliament and had no immediate prospect of being so, offered him the vacant Lordship of the Treasury, and promised his mother (Lady Canning), in words which would partially have applied to the other recruit he had just pro-moted, to give him 'every facility in acquiring that political

[1] July 3, 1837 ; *Ibid.* (1837), pp. 2111, 2113.

knowledge and experience which, combined with his own talents and acquirements, may, I trust, enable him to maintain the lustre of the name he bears.' The offer was declined on the ground that the young man would rather not accept office until he had earned some claim to it by his own exertions;[1] and it was not for a year and a half that he obtained a seat, so as to enable him to qualify himself in the way he desired. In August, 1836, he was returned, after a sharp contest, at a bye-election for Warwick; but it was for Liverpool, his father's greatest constituency, that his friends designed him, and in the October he paid a visit to the town, to be set before the electors as a possible second Tory candidate, in conjunction with Sandon, the sitting Conservative member. On this expedition he was accompanied by two distinguished young Liverpudlians, William Gladstone and Edward Cardwell, both born, it may be noted, in the same house, and both afterwards associated in Cabinet together; and of these the former and Charles Canning were on close terms of friendship, which continued to the end, the future Indian Viceroy being impressed throughout his life with the particularly tender conscientiousness of his old schoolfellow. [2]

The first attempt upon the borough was made at a dinner of the Liverpool Tradesmen's Conservative Association in October. At this festivity, the chairman, a local merchant, proposed the health of Peel and his supporters in the Commons, coupling with the toast the name of Mr. Gladstone, whom he described as a statesman of great ability, well known to them all, and a colleague of Peel, the leading star of Conservatism, upon whom the eyes of the whole country were anxiously fixed. He

[1] Peel's 'Memoirs,' vol. ii., pp. 53-5.
[2] A. J. C. Hare's 'Story of Two Noble Lives,' vol. iii., p. 173.

expressed his happiness in the belief that there was one present who, at no distant period, would prove himself a beacon to the country in a new Administration, who had had the honour of being a member of that never-to-be-forgotten Ministry, when Peel took the reins of government with the intent to save the country from the hands of a faction. And, encouraged by the loud and repeated cheers with which this praise of a fellow-townsman was greeted, the chairman prophesied for that guest still higher destinies than any that had yet been his lot.

Mr. Gladstone excused himself from attempting to fully reply for his leader, observing that he must be a very able or a very weak man who would undertake to delineate a character so richly en- dowed in nature, and so eminently matured by experience. He denied that Peel was actuated by motives of expediency; and he claimed that the cause that statesman had assumed office to uphold was no mere personal or political squabble, and not even a question of civil liberty—it was the integrity of the Established Church, ' which we love as a valuable institution, because it conduces more than any other to the stability of the country, to its peace and to its prosperity, but which also we regard in a more sacred light, as the appointed dispenser and as the most faithful steward of the truth of God.' He defended the Church of Ireland, as embodying the greatest bulwark of the Protestant religion ; he denounced the Government for its various measures, which the Tories had resisted and, by the help of God, would resist again ; and, while expressing a preference for private life over political excitement, urged that in the struggle before them personal convenience would have to be sacrificed to the public welfare.[1]

October 18, 1836.
Mr. Gladstone speaks at Liverpool.

[1] *Liverpool Courier*, Oct. 19, 1836.

At the first anniversary dinner of the Liverpool Operative Conservative Association, three days later, the ' sentiment' was given, ' The genuine rights of the people, may they never be crushed by despotism, nor rent in pieces by democracy.' To this Mr. Gladstone replied, as he observed, with his

October 21.
Again speaks there. whole heart. ' Their opponents represented it as an inconsistency for the Conservatives to speak of the rights of the people. The Conservatives, when they spoke of the rights of the people, did not speak of those wild, theoretical rights which deluged the country with blood; but they supported the more equitable rights of the people from the highest to the lowest, and were anxious that they should receive all the benefits that could be secured to them by the institutions of the country, so that, in fact, the upper classes completely identified themselves with the lower classes of society. The Conservatives contended that, while they adopted the Conservative side of politics, they maintained the general rights of the people against despotism and democracy, and in their conduct there was nothing unnatural.' And he went on to condemn the alliance of Russell and O'Connell, to ridicule the ' popular rights' candidates of the Whigs, and to declare in favour of the Church, the King, and the Constitution.[1]

' Mr. E. W. [sic] Gladstone,' remarked concerning the second dinner the *Liverpool Chronicle*, the Radical organ,

Local Radical
criticism. ' was the crack orator of the night. He made several desperate attempts to be grandiloquent . . . and wound up the whole by a string of commonplace observations respecting the disfranchisement of the Liverpool freemen, which appeared to delight the sage persons in his immediate vicinity.' In its leading article, the journal was a trifle more gracious : ' Mr. William

[1] *Ibid.*, Oct. 26.

Ewart Gladstone spoke tolerably well in the course of the evening. It is rather a pity that the old gentleman at Fasque should have so miscalculated the chances as to launch his sons on the losing side in the political *arena*— we presume he wished them "to run to win," without much solicitude as to which part they should take—at least the world says so.'

'The old gentleman at Fasque,' as this Radical critic so flippantly put it, had some years before ceased to make Liverpool the home of his family. In 1829, he had purchased the estate of Fasque and Balfour, in Kincardine-shire, and thenceforward Liverpool practically knew him but little. Save for occasional visits to Lon-don, he devoted attention to this new home *John Gladstone at Fasque.* and to the concerns immediately around him. During several winters he resided in Edinburgh, where, as one of the directors, he took an active part in the management of the Royal Bank ; and, having been the originator of the Edinburgh, Perth, and Dundee Railway, he showed his accustomed energy at the age of seventy-five by projecting a steam ferry and breakwater pier across the Firth of Forth to Burntisland, and, when the inhabitants of Fife would not take up the project with the warmth he desired, he joined the Duke of Buccleuch to obtain an Act of Parliament, by means of which they did it on their own account. Nor was he idle in a philanthropic direction, for it may here be noted that in 1840 he erected an asylum at his native Leith for women afflicted with incurable diseases, and thenceforward defrayed the entire cost of the establishment. And all these efforts were varied with the building of more churches and the writing of occasional pamphlets in the Tory cause, the while he played the part of country squire by founding the Fasque herd of pure-bred Aberdeen-Angus cattle,

which is said to be still one of the finest in the world, and
to have been always most carefully and liberally maintained.

John Gladstone, in the midst of his many pursuits at
Fasque, had an opportunity presented him, soon after the
Liverpool speeches of his youngest son, of hearing that
rising politician speak in Scotland, in the presence and in
support of Peel himself.   The Conservative leader had been
chosen, after a severe contest, Lord Rector of Glasgow
University, and his appearance at the inauguration was the
signal for an enthusiastic demonstration of Scottish Toryism.
William Gladstone's fame in Lancashire had been so much
increased by his efforts at Liverpool, that he was invited to
attend a Conservative demonstration at Wigan in the
closing days of 1836, but this he was obliged to decline.
In another fortnight, however, he was in the train of Peel
at Glasgow; and at a banquet, at which his father and his
brother Neilson were present and his chief made a
powerful defence of the Constitution and
the conduct of the House of Lords, the representative of Newark was called upon to respond to the toast of 'The Conservative Constituencies of
England and their Representatives in Parliament.'   This was
given by a speaker who declared that Mr. Gladstone, whom
his hearers would find to be an able, eloquent, and uncompromising defender of the principles dear to them all, had
the more particular title to their notice because he had
served in a Ministry of Peel.

*January 13, 1837.
At the Peel banquet
at Glasgow*

Mr. Gladstone claimed, in replying, to speak on behalf of
a majority of the people of England, for the Conservatives formed a majority of the English representatives.
O'Connell—an authority whom he would
willingly trust as his evidence told against
himself, but whom he characterised as a man by whose

*denounces
O'Connell,*

reckless wickedness a great proportion of the Irish people were misled, much to their own and to our debasement—had said that the English nation was determined to refuse justice to Ireland. That he denied, but, amid loud cheering, he affirmed that the English people were resolved at once and irrefragably to withhold their consent from those measures which, under that denomination, were generally understood to mean the dissolution of British connection with that country and the extinction of the Protestant religion. He dwelt upon the steady growth of Conservatism in the constituencies since the Reform Act, but averred that the great struggle in which they were then engaged was not a party but a national contest: their institutions were threatened with destruction, and the assault that was being openly made upon the Constitution which had so long been the boast of Britain, offered to men of all parties—whether called by the forgotten name of Whig or Tory—a neutral ground upon which they might meet to withstand the insidious attacks of their common enemy. Loud applause greeted this appeal, to be renewed when Mr. Gladstone ended with the declaration that he would never believe, with the knowledge he possessed of Scotland, that the people of that country—where the human intellect was, perhaps, more generally cultivated and informed than in any other region of the globe—would consent to abolish institutions under the shadow of which more   and compliments
widely extended and equally diffused free-   Scotland.
dom was enjoyed than in any other quarter of the world. Similarly would he never admit that, in a land where the fear of God pervaded every class of the community, that Church which was dedicated to the dissemination of the principles inculcated by His inspired talents would be destroyed. United in a great and a holy cause, they still bore the name

of a party, but by necessity and not by choice. The establishment of one Minister and the overthrow of another, the
defeat of one party and the victory of another, might be
instruments which they were obliged to employ, but principles and not men were their objects; and he felt convinced that from the walls of that building a voice would
reverberate which had already been sounded to them from
England—the voice of fearless and resolute attachment to
the institutions of this country.[1] Peel might well be proud
at that moment of his follower and John Gladstone of his
youngest son; and the fame of the effort spread soon to
London, where the *Standard* described the member for
Newark as having maintained among the speakers that elevated rank to which his splendid talents entitled him.

Speedily Mr. Gladstone made his way south, and he
reached Newark just in time to participate in a dinner given
by the South Notts Tories in honour of his
friend Lincoln. Entering the room as the
toast of 'The Princess Victoria, the presumptive heiress
to the Crown, and the rest of the Royal Family,' had been
drunk with the old-accustomed 'three times three,' and
immediately before the giving of the sentiment, 'Church and
State, that Protestant Church which has God for its author,
salvation for its end, and truth without any mixture of error
for its matter,' he was welcomed with enthusiastic and long-
continued cheering. This demonstration was renewed when
he rose to respond to the toast of 'Sir Robert Peel and the
Conservative Members of the House of Commons;' and
Mr. Gladstone gave his audience full return for their cheers.
He told them how, at their wish, he had asked Peel to be
present on the occasion, and how his leader regretted, after

Jan. 17.
Speaks at Newark.

[1] James Cleland's 'Description of the Glasgow Banquet, 1837,' pp.
84-6.

having declined invitations to visit Edinburgh, Manchester, Belfast, and other great cities, he could not comply. But Peel had sent to them, and to the people of England, a message of all-importance in his Glasgow speech; and his young lieutenant described himself as having been a proud witness of a scene the most unprecedented that had ever met the eye. Having in the highest terms eulogised Peel and Peel's address, Mr. Gladstone dealt with general politics, and declared that the great distinction of the day was not between Whig and Tory but between Conservative and Destructive, between those who thought our institutions ought to be maintained and those who thought they ought to be abolished. That, he considered, was the cardinal and primary truth of the position, and they might depend upon it that the time had come for a union of men to support, at all hazards and through all dangers, the Church, the Monarchy, and the Peerage.

Vociferous applause warmed Mr. Gladstone to an even higher flight. 'We have,' he averred, 'no under game to play, no party, or paltry, or selfish ends to answer; our great object is to render our institutions productive of happiness and glory to millions of our countrymen, through many ages and future generations. We know the efforts that have been made in Ireland against us, in that land which has been blessed by heaven with abundant means for the enjoyment of freedom and virtue, more than any country on the face of the earth, but which the passions of men have rendered unhappy : and does not that justify us in the course we are taking, in devoting our whole energies to the maintenance of this noble cause? Does it not justify us in disclaiming selfishness and party views, and calling upon all our countrymen to join with us hand and heart, and to unite with us in the common cause of our religion and our country? We are, it is true, a minority in the House of Commons, but we are not inconsiderable in number, and we are led on to battle by the first statesmen of the day; we act with implicit confidence in their steadiness and ability; we are thoroughly at union amongst ourselves, and thoroughly agreed as to the substance and importance of the principles which we are maintaining. Allow me to tell you in conclusion that there is a gracious Power above, who shapes

> All human ends
> Rough hew them as you may ;

and who, by human agency, works out His own magnificent and benevolent designs for the moral government of the world; and that, relying upon that Almighty Power for prosperity and success, especially as we consider our cause to be that which has for its object the preservation of true religion and the promotion of human happiness, we believe that we shall receive assistance and encouragement from extraordinary sources; and we entertain the consolatory reflection that, come what may of danger and difficulty, the cause in which we are engaged is that which must finally be crowned with satisfactory and victorious results.' 'Tremendous applause' is recorded to have endorsed this peroration; and the *Nottingham Journal's* reporter declared the speech to have been delivered in a style of the most graceful and convincing eloquence, and to have been repeatedly cheered by the most enthusiastic plaudits. Twice more had Mr. Gladstone to speak during the evening, once in reply to the toast of his health, and again 'in a suitable address' to propose 'The Ladies of England.' 'It was, indeed, a glorious meeting, and deserving a proud record in the annals of reviving Conservatism,' ejaculated the local chronicler as he ended his report; but when Lincoln, Mr. Gladstone, and their immediate friends quitted the hall seven hours and a half after the dinner had commenced, the hearty hurrahs of those they left must have fallen upon fatigued ears; and the visit paid to the Newark Theatre the next night must have been a source of refreshing to them all.

It may be regarded as a testimony to the abiding nature of certain political ideas which, theoretically sound, have in practice always proved illusory that in both these speeches —at Newark as at Glasgow—Mr. Gladstone declared in favour of a National Party. Macaulay is Mr. Gladstone and a responsible for a widespread belief in the National Party. possibility of this, by his reference to some imaginary and unhistoric period when

> None was for a party
> But all were for the State;

though it is a belief that has been shared by men of such diverse temperament as Lord Beaconsfield and Mr. Chamberlain, as well as Mr. Gladstone, and its expression has customarily been at a period when this country was most sharply divided into hostile political camps. Disraeli in 1834, Mr. Gladstone in 1837, Mr. Chamberlain in 1887 and again in 1894, uttered the opinion that the hour had come for the moderate men of all parties to combine and for the old party distinctions to be destroyed; and partisan spirit was never more bitter—envy, hatred, malice, and all uncharitableness never more thoroughly penetrated the public discussion of politics—than in the years immediately succeeding the respective statements of a beneficent idea.

In Mr. Gladstone's case the expression of it was upon the eve of his coming definitely to the front as what

Macaulay was soon to call the rising hope of the stern and
unbending portion of the Tory party ; for, despite the indica-
tions of promise he had given, he was at first so little
remarked from the reporters' gallery as destined for high
position that James Grant, in his ' Random Recollections
of the House of Commons from the year 1830 to the close
of 1835,' did not once mention him, even incidentally.
And it was not as if the writer confined himself only to the
most distinguished figures or those of longest political
career, for he included a notice of Praed, whom
he described as having been looked upon by the
Tories of the Reform Bill period as 'a youth of great
promise,' but who had failed to fulfil their hopes; and
of Mahon, 'a young nobleman from whom the Tories
expect great things.'   And, though he devoted a chapter to
the 'religious members,' and portrayed Sir Andrew Agnew
and the other leading Sabbatarians with much point, he did
not number Mr. Gladstone among them.   But, as he himself
said, he selected only those whose names were most frequently before the public ; and consequently no mention was made of many members of great weight and value
as legislators, and of even higher talents than several who
were noticed, but who did not take a prominent part in the
proceedings of the House.

The session of 1837 was to change all this for Mr.
Gladstone, though, as far as he was concerned, it opened
quietly enough.   Religious instruction in the colonies
was the first topic which moved his parliamentary
efforts, he securing a return regarding it ; but a much more
serious subject was soon to claim his intervention.   The
rebellion in Canada was a burning question just then ;
and when in March, Russell proposed the first of a
series of resolutions concerning the Dominion which the

Radicals considered coercive, and to which they brought forward amendments, Mr. Gladstone, on the second night of the debate, spoke in support of the Ministerial projects as one who had had the matter under his official consideration. He submitted that, although these were coercive, in that they were intended to set aside for the time, and to a certain extent, the privileges of a free constitution, the necessity for them was incumbent, unless the House was prepared to adopt an organic change in the constitution of Lower Canada with the perfect knowledge and conviction that that would be only the first of a series, and would be entering upon a boundless course of unreasonable concession.

March 8.
Mr. Gladstone on the Canadian Rebellion.

'The case before us,' he declared, 'is not one which involves any party considerations: it is a subject strictly of Imperial interests ; and the question we have to decide is nothing more nor less than this, whether we will consent to the separation of Lower Canada from the mother country. I conceive that, whatever primary aspect the question may assume, this is virtually the amount of it. Now, I am not one of those who would be deterred from any resolution on this subject, at which I might think it on other grounds proper to arrive, by the threat or the apprehension that it was likely to lead to a separation between the colony and the mother country. I do not regard that consummation as one necessarily and at all times undesirable. It is true, indeed, I believe, that the history of modern colonisation supplies few examples of separation effected between them and the mother country without some violent struggle preceding it. But I should freely say, with reference to all colonies, that they are to be regarded, by something more than a mere fanciful analogy, as the children of the parent country ; that there is, therefore, a stage in their existence when they, like children, ought to be emancipated, and that to this emancipation their government ought to be prospectively adapted : I would not, therefore, contend that we ought for ever to maintain the institutions of Canada in their present subordinate position.   But, on the other hand, I hold it to be perfectly vain and fallacious, and, I will add, dishonest, while separation is not proposed as the object in view, to claim for the Houses of Assembly in that country a character of entire equality with the Imperial Parliament in this : so long as Canada continues a colony, it must, from its very nature as such, continue in a certain sense subject to Great Britain.   I had, indeed, hoped that our discussions on the repeal of the Union had set at rest the fallacious supposition that independent legislatures could permanently co-exist and co-operate under the same crown.' [1]

Stanley followed him in the debate, and the always admiring *Standard* the next evening declared that the effect of 'the splendid speeches of Mr. William Gladstone and Lord Stanley . . . was so strongly felt by the separation— we suppose we must not call it the treason party—that they divided the house six or seven times upon frivolous pretences, in order to obviate a decision while the members retained the impression produced by the speeches in question.'   Four times in its leading article, indeed, did the *Standard* link the two speakers, with Mr. Gladstone each time first, and always in highest praise ; but in another week there was more occasion for enthusiasm, for it was then that Mr. Gladstone delivered his first great Parliamentary speech.

As became a young Conservative, the representative of

[1] 'Mirror of Parliament' (1837), pp. 523-7.

Newark was devoted at that time to the two great interests of the Land and the Church. In support of the former, and just after the Canada address, he put in an appearance at a meeting—' of a respectable description,' as the Whig *Morning Chronicle* was pleased to acknowledge—of members of the Central Agricultural Society of His connection with Great Britain and Ireland, of which New- Agriculture. castle was President. This body appears to have been a semi-political organisation, which had then been established somewhat over a year, and which created much feeling by its efforts to reform the currency laws. It is of importance now mainly because the demand which it aroused for a non-political body that would unite all classes of agriculturists led to the establishment in 1838 of the English Agricultural Society, incorporated by royal charter two years later as the Royal Agricultural Society of England. The older body faded away before its young and still-flourishing rival ; and, although an uninfluential section of its members attempted to start another organisation on Protectionist principles, that also collapsed.[1]

A day after Mr. Gladstone had thus been engaged upon agricultural affairs, and when Russell had moved the House of Commons into committee to consider the March 15. question of Church rates, he spoke long in Supports Church support of the existing system. He denied rates. that the motive for the resistance of Dissenters to the payment of this impost was entitled to so sacred a plea as a scruple of conscience ; and he laid it down as a principle that, when the Legislature made a demand upon its subjects for a portion of their property, whatever might be the purpose to which

[1] Mr. Gladstone, it may be noted, has never been a member of the Royal Agricultural Society; but at its Chester meeting of 1858 he made a striking speech on agricultural affairs.

that would be applied, the conscience of the payers was ab-
solved, and that, although they might use every means to
get rid of it, no scruple of conscience could fairly resist it
as long as the payment was law. The Established Church
existed to carry home to the door of every man in the
country who was willing to receive them, the blessings of
religion and the ordinances which its ministers were appointed to dispense; and as, in his opinion, the abolition
of Church rates would conduce to the downfall of that institution, he strongly opposed the course the Ministry was
pursuing.[1]

It was with merely a cold 'hear, hear,' that the report in
the *Times* of the Canada speech had concluded; but 'the
honourable gentleman resumed his seat amidst loud and
continued cheering,' was appended to the Church-rate

Receives hearty praise: address. This testimony, like the further
circumstance that the speaker was once and
again interrupted by the heartiest applause, is to be found
in all the contemporary reports; the fact that Poulett
Thomson, one of the members of the Whig Ministry,
immediately afterwards described the speech as able and
very eloquent, tells for much;[2] and the hearts of the Tory
editors went out to the young upholder of their faith. In
the opinion of the *Times*, the address was not only able
and eloquent, but admirable and unanswerable—an anticipation of the praise awarded by the Conservatives close
upon thirty years later to the 'unanswered and unanswerable' speech of Lord Stanley (afterwards fifteenth
Earl of Derby) on the Russell-Gladstone Reform Bill
against severing the question of franchise extension from
that of redistribution of seats; and with the added likeness

[1] 'Mirror of Parliament' (1837), pp. 678-81.
[2] *Ibid.*, p. 681.

that, just as Mr. Gladstone lived to abolish Church rates, so did Lord Derby to approve in Cabinet a Reform Bill which did precisely what he had contended to be impossible.

The denial that the Nonconformist objection to the impost was truly a matter of conscience was that which most delighted the Tories, and the *Times* did not weary in its praise. It returned to the theme a day later with the observation that 'the combat between giants and pigmies but poorly illustrated the terrible superiority of Peel and Stanley, Follett, Pemberton, and Gladstone over the wretched automata of the Treasury bench;' and on yet a further day it gave prominence to a communication on the debate from 'A Correspondent,' which referred to 'the mauling' Russell's plan had received from, among others, Mr. Gladstone. As usual at that period, the *Standard* waxed enthusiastic over the speech. Baines, one of the advocates of the Nonconformists, had, it declared, 'exposed himself by a dissertation upon church-room and conscientious scruples, to a terrible reply from Mr. W. Gladstone. The speech of the last-named gentleman was a triumph of reasoning and eloquence. The manner in which he disposed of Mr. Baines' superficial measurement of religious wants, doling out the opportunity of hearing the Gospel by the square foot, and of the hypocritical cant of conscience now raised at the end of more than two centuries of perfect acquiescence, left no more to be said on those subjects.' And, satisfied with his triumph, Mr. Gladstone took no further part in the debates on the subject that session, contenting himself later with presenting a petition against the Church Rates Regulation Bill,[1] which the Ministry had by that time introduced.

[1] April 24 : *Ibid.*, p. 1183.

For the remainder of the session, Mr. Gladstone did little
in the House of Commons itself, though much in committee.
What, indeed, with apprenticeship and the aborigines, as
will later be detailed, he had scant time to give even to
select committees on other subjects in this year; and,
although he was appointed a member of one directed to
examine into the system of keeping and
presenting the colonial accounts, and to
suggest a mode for so framing them as to
introduce uniformity, regularity, correctness, and complete-
ness, he attended only one of the ten sittings, and then
put no questions.[1]   He moved occasionally for a return
—once of the imports of West Indian sugar and other
produce,[2] at another time of newspaper stamps and adver-
tisements,[3] with both of which subjects he was in after days
as a Minister to have much to do; while he at first opposed
the grant of a similar document, asked for by Hume, to
show the names of those to whom compensation had been
granted out of the West India fund of twenty millions.   His
objection was that this would expose the private circumstances of individuals, and that the only ground for such a
motion was a suspicion of a dereliction of duty or of mal-
versation on the part of the Commissioners entrusted with
the disposal of the money.[4]

April 28.
On Colonial Accounts Committee.

But though he withdrew his opposition, such a return,
owing to a demur on the part of the Commissioners,[5] was
not issued until the next session, when it
showed that to John Gladstone, for the slaves
on his estates in British Guiana, was awarded on November

John Gladstone's Slave Compensation.

[1] 'Parliamentary Papers,' 1837, vol. vii., pp. 305-544.
[2] March 18: 'Mirror of Parliament,' (1837), p. 757.
[3] April 12: *Ibid.*, p. 978.
[4] July 14: *Ibid.*, p. 2224.   [5] *Ibid.*, p. 2234.

30th, 1835, £22,274 18s. 9d. for 429 slaves; £10,278 5s. 8d. for another 193; £14,721 8s. 11d. for a further 272, and £22,443 19s. 11d. for yet another 415.[1] These were all uncontested, but on a litigated claim,[2] £21,011 2s. 7d. was awarded on the same date to John Gladstone, George Grant, and Robertson Gladstone for 393 slaves, the total award for John Gladstone in British Guiana thus being £69,718 13s. 3d. for the emancipation of 1,309 slaves, and for him and his two partners a further £21,011 2s. 7d. for 393 slaves. But this was not all, though it has been commonly assumed to have been so, for John Gladstone owned some plantations in Jamaica (although these were far from the same in extent as those in British Guiana) and in the greater colony in excellent social company. Among his fellow-proprietors who there received compensation were prelates and priests, the latter in dozens, and the former including Bishop Phillpotts—'Henry of Exeter,' as that combative Churchman was known to his own generation; there were baronets and bankers by the score; and the peerage supplied the names of Breadalbane and Stanhope, Balcarres and Carrington, Airlie and Northesk, St. Vincent and Sinclair, Talbot and Grimston, Thanet and Rivers; and, while the Whigs furnished Lord Holland, the Tories contributed Goulburn. Amid this crowd, and for his slaves in Jamaica, where his estates lay in two counties, John Gladstone was awarded, on February 8th, 1836, on an uncontested claim, £5,624 3s. 1d. for 300 slaves; and, on the same date, £1,037 7s. 5d. for his half-share in another 106 slaves, owned in partnership with Divie Robertson and George Robert Smith, the former having a one-eighth share and the latter a three-eighths in the whole. On a litigated

---

[1] 'Parliamentary Papers,' 1837-38, vol. xlviii., pp. 450-68.
[2] *Ibid.*, p. 652

claim a fortnight later, John Gladstone and Divie Robertson secured £4,295 3s. 3d. for 231 slaves; while, on
November 2nd of the previous year, certain other planters
of the same family name—Thomas Steuart Gladstone,
William Gladstone, and Robert Gladstone—had been
given £9,225 16s. 5d. for 468 slaves.[1] In the two colonies,
therefore, John Gladstone received individually £75,342
16s. 4d. for 1,609 slaves, apart from his share in the several
partnerships in which he was engaged.

One episode of 1837 is of more pleasing interest.
During the summer, Mr. Gladstone presented a petition
from certain electors of Ross and Cromarty
complaining that a voter, one John Gibson,
had been abducted by his political opponents

*July, 1837:
Mr. Gladstone
presents a curious
petition.*

during a recent bye-contest. They alleged that Gibson had
been induced to repair to the town of Cromarty; that
while there he became suddenly intoxicated; that he was in
that state carried out of the town, and in a fisherman's boat
across to Nairn, whence he was taken further southward
and detained; and that he was rescued by his friends barely
in time to tender his vote. Such Radicals as Wakley and
Hume were duly shocked at a drunken plaint being received; but Mr. Gladstone urged that the allegations, if
proved, involved a breach of privilege; and upon
his motion the petition was printed.[2] Four days later,
he moved for copies of the depositions taken in the
matter; and, having satisfied himself by inquiry that
Gibson was a proverbially sober man, he suggested that
the toddy had been drugged, arguing, however, that,
even if it were a case of ordinary intoxication, it was a
breach of privilege to try to prevent his voting. The Lord

[1] *Ibid.*, pp. 392, 632, and 357.
[2] 'Mirror of Parliament' (1837), pp. 2153, 2154.

Advocate replied that to adopt the motion would be against all precedent; Wilson Patten remarked that the object of the petitioners had evidently been to prevent the recurrence of such an outrage; Mr. Gladstone withdrew his proposal; and John Gibson his toddy, and his abduction vanished for ever from the parliamentary scene.[1] And with this quaint episode, save for the opposition to the slave compensation return already noted, Mr. Gladstone's parliamentary efforts in a House of Commons elected under William IV., came to an end; for by this time the King had died, Princess Victoria had ascended the throne, and Parliament was only awaiting the dissolution then enforced by law upon the demise of the Crown.

[1] July 10: *Ibid.*, pp. 2182, 2183.

XI.—Apprenticeship and the Aborigines.

Scarcely a session at this period passed without the question of slavery coming in some form before Parliament. The Act of 1833, by which the negroes were apprenticed for seven years to their former owners, who were empowered

The Negro Appren-
ticeship System.

to exact from them three-fourths of their time, with the whip as the allotted penalty for disobedience, was a compromise which satisfied neither the planter nor the abolitionist. The former, therefore, exerted his power to exact an undue amount of work from the so-called apprentice; the latter commenced to pour in petitions upon the Legislature praying for the system to be destroyed. Tales came to England from colony after colony, and especially from Jamaica, declaring that the negroes were treated more harshly and with an even greater refinement of cruelty under apprenticeship than during slavery: and early in the session of 1836, and on the night that several petitions had been presented, asking for the abolition of negro apprenticeship and the grant of unconditional freedom to the inhabitants of every British colony without distinction of colour, Buxton moved for a select committee to inquire into the working of the system and the condition of the apprentices. In his speech, he personally appealed to Mr. Gladstone to say whether his family had not been perfectly satisfied with their very consider-

March 22, 1836.
Mr. Gladstone and
compensation.

able share of the compensation money, and whether that compensation, so far from reducing the whole of the proprietors, had not saved them from absolute ruin. Mr. Gladstone, called up by this, disputed Buxton's contention that the twenty millions grant was enormous and exorbitant, though willing to admit that it was generous and disinterested. He expressed a doubt whether the committee, which had been promised by the Ministry, would effect any good, as he regarded colonial committees as very inexpedient instruments of government. The apprenticeship system had worked better, in his opinion, than they had had any right to expect; but he denied with emphasis the assertions of the Anti-Slavery Society that there had been under it an access of cruelty to the negroes, assertions made with 'the most awful adjurations in the solemn name of God, a name I do not wish to exclude, because I do not consider any one can consider a subject of such importance as this without an inward feeling of reverence to the sacred name of that Being to whom we are indebted for the success of the experiment as far as it has gone.' 'Let us not be too sanguine,' he concluded, 'in the midst of that thankfulness which we ought to feel. The greater portion of the transition from slavery is not past, but future. Apprenticeship is a modified form of slavery rather than a species of freedom, while it is purged in principle from the abuses of private and arbitrary power. Thus far it has proceeded well beyond our hopes, under all the circumstances of the case; but let me remind the House that incautious and precipitate anticipations of entire success before it has arrived, may themselves be among the actual and efficient means of final disappointment. May the measure proceed and prosper.'[1]

Six days later the committee was nominated, and upon it, in addition to Buxton, Howick, Sandon, Graham, O'Connell, and Grey, was placed Mr. Gladstone,[2] it being specifically instructed to inquire into the working of the apprenticeship

March 28. Nominated on an Apprenticeship Committee.

[1] 'Mirror of Parliament' (1836), pp. 726-35.   [2] *Ibid.*, p. 838.

system, the condition of the apprentices, and the laws and regulations affecting them. As it was found impossible to investigate the whole subject in one session, it was determined to limit the immediate inquiry to Jamaica, the colony regarded by the abolitionists as the chief offender. The member for Newark, who was in daily attendance, obviously watched the case for the planters, and a study of his questions is almost necessary to a full understanding of the quality of his mind. As might be gathered from his speech upon Buxton's motion, he approached the inquiry with the belief that the stories related by the abolitionists were grossly exaggerated where they were not palpably untrue ; but he could not have concluded his questioning with the same complacent conviction. Jamaica, in fact, had had a specially bad record in regard to its treatment of the negro : and the facts revealed before this committee strengthened the evil impression that the obstinacy of its planters and the callousness, even when not the cruelty, of its overseers had caused. The negroes complained that there had been more 'flog ! flog !' to use their own term, since the King had given them ' free ' than there had been before ; they had little confidence in the special magistrates who had the power, if they thought the blacks had made an improper complaint, to have them whipped : and, in the opinion of one witness, who had lost his seat in the House of Assembly in consequence of having proposed to abolish the flogging of females, it was impossible for a special magistrate, who depended entirely upon the overseers or managers, to avoid either becoming in his feelings a planter or quarrelling with that class. The planter

The Jamaica planters.

witness who solemnly complained that, since the passing of the Abolition Act, the little negroes went and basked on the sea-side, climbed the mango-trees, and scampered over the country in idleness instead of weeding the cane-fields, owned to having no school on his estate, though he hoped soon to have one, which might tempt them from these wicked pursuits. He had been accustomed to put children of between five and six to work during the time of slavery; but now, he sadly observed, 'I have a fine young gang on my estate; I say, "Let me see them in the yard," but they are so independent they will not come.' Another planter, however, praised the system of apprenticeship, and observed that the majority of the people of the island were favourable to it. 'Do you mean by that to include the negroes?' asked Buxton. 'I mean the managers and proprietors,' was the reply. Mr. Gladstone followed up the query: 'Should you include the negroes or not?' 'I dare say the negroes would wish to dispense with the apprenticeship,' was the rejoinder, 'they are fond of any change,' except, as he afterwards admitted, back to slavery, which, under the circumstances, will scarcely strike the observer as singular.

But the real point for the committee's consideration— apart from how many females had been flogged, how few wielders of the whip had been punished, and the number of hours the negroes were being illegally worked—was concentrated in two questions, the one put by Buxton and the other by Mr. Gladstone, each with an obvious side-glance at the other. 'It was held by a body of persons in this country, and almost universally in the West Indies during the time of slavery, that it was a romantic and foolish notion that negroes would work for wages; do you think,' asked Buxton of a planter, 'that that notion has proved absurd, or that it is well-founded?' 'I always thought,' replied the planter, 'it was absurd to suppose that negroes would not work for wages.' It was then Mr.

Gladstone's turn : 'Are you aware whether there were also a class of persons in this country, those most favourable to the interest of the negro, who maintained that the establishment of an intermediate state, like the system of apprenticeship, was a plan of all others the most chimerical and the most impossible to carry into execution ?' The answer must have been disappointing: 'No, I was not aware of that.'

The report presented by the committee at the end of the session referred, of course, only to Jamaica ; and, while pointing out various improvements in detail that might be made, and especially deprecating the flogging of women and the placing them in chains, asserted the belief that the apprenticeship system was working in a manner not unfavourable to the momentous change from slavery to freedom.   The conviction was added that nothing could be more unfortunate than any occurrence which had a tendency to unsettle the mind of either the planter or the negro regarding the fixed determination of the Imperial Parliament to preserve inviolate the system destined by law to expire in 1840 ;[1] and the report was, in brief, a triumph of the official mind, though not found convincing by the outside public.

In the next session, but not as early as might have been expected, the committee was reappointed ; but this time

May 19, 1837.
The committee re-
appointed.

the singular course was adopted of declining to print the evidence or even to mention the witnesses' names.   The reason may be guessed from the fact that although, when Buxton proposed that, in order to secure from punishment the negroes who had afforded information, the evidence in the first instance

---

[1] 'Parliamentary Papers,' 1836, vol. vii.

should be given without names, dates, or places, he was supported by only one other member, and opposed by Mr. Gladstone, the testimony furnished caused the committee to declare that there ought to be instituted without delay a strict and searching examination into the state of the workhouses in the West Indian colonies, and especially into the construction and use of the treadmills employed in them, and the nature of the coercion adopted to ensure labour among the prisoners,[1] a recommendation which the Melbourne Government at once adopted.

While the member for Newark was thus working in committee, his father was concerned with another phase of the slavery question; for, as the date for full emancipation drew near, the planters commenced to prepare for a possible lack of labour, and with the early result of arousing another storm of popular and parliamentary indignation against them. The idea of supplementing servile labour by hired immigrants was just then being revived. As far before as 1811, a committee of the House of Commons, appointed to consider the practicability and expediency of supplying our West India colonies with free labourers from the East, had reported generally in favour of this being permitted, it being 'very desirable that the Executive Government should bear in mind the advantages which might follow in the West Indies from the introduction of a new class of free people;'[2] while the Colonial Lands Committee of 1836, of which William Gladstone had been a member, indicated its idea that some system of colonisation in the West Indies was desirable.[3]

The coolie labour question.

[1] *Ibid.*, 1837, vol. vii., p. 749.
[2] *Ibid.*, 1810-11, vol. ii., pp. 409, 410.
[3] *Ibid.*, 1836, vol. xi., p. 502.

Early in 1837, therefore, John Gladstone wrote to Sir John Cam Hobhouse (then President of the Board of Control, and virtually Minister for India) that, being deeply interested in plantations situated in Demerara and Jamaica, he wished, in conjunction with John Moss, of whom mention has already been made, to send to Calcutta a ship to convey about 150 hill coolies from Bengal to the former colony.[1] Experiments of importing labourers from Germany, Madeira, Ireland, and elsewhere had failed, ' the influence of the climate generally producing reluctance to labour, and increasing the desire for spirituous liquors, which the low price and abundance of new rum enables them to gratify '; and he wished to know, before the ship was sent, whether an Order in Council or any other authority was necessary for carrying the coolie experiment into execution.   Hobhouse immediately replied that there was no reason to apprehend interference; but, as there still seemed some doubt, John Gladstone forwarded the correspondence to the Colonial Secretary (Lord Glenelg).   The latter confirmed the opinion of his colleague, but added, for the prevention of misconception, that, as the experiment would be of a very novel kind, the Government held itself free to originate any law necessary for protection of the coolies.   An interview between Glenelg and John Gladstone soon afterwards resulted in the Ministry agreeing to issue an Order in Council, which allowed the shipping of the coolies on the planters' terms, and this was approved by the Queen within three weeks of her ascending the throne.   The Governor of British Guiana (Sir James Carmichael Smyth), who had proved an excellent friend of the negro during the trying transition period, was

1837.
John Gladstone and the coolies.

---

[1] Two-thirds of the coolies were to be sent for John Gladstone, and the other third for Moss.

not so complaisant as his chief. He wanted to know what would happen to the coolies if John Gladstone and his colleagues (four firms now being involved) failed or died during that term ; and he suggested that the importer should be compelled to deposit a sum of money for each individual labourer, equal to the expense of the return passage.   But Glenelg, 'convinced by the elaborate calculations produced by Mr. Gladstone,' and unhappily both for himself and the coolies, adhered to all his terms.[1]

This arrangement was highly distasteful to the abolitionists ; and a circular was issued by a prominent one among them, named Crewdson, calling the Christian public's attention to the Order in Council, and declaring it tantamount to a revival of slavery.   A somewhat similar contract was brought under the notice of the House of Commons two days before John Gladstone's desired Order in Council was royally approved.   This concerned a number of labourers taken from Bengal to the Mauritius ; and Buxton, in one of his last efforts at Westminster, called them slaves.   Hobhouse retorted that they were 'neither more   Slaves or free nor less than free labourers, and no more   labourers? slaves than we are.'   And the member for Newark, who evidently knew much that was proceeding in the matter, mentioned that, while it was 'a highly respectable gentleman' who had engaged these men to serve for five years, the Colonial Office would not allow a longer term than three.[2]

Much more was to be heard in the following spring of the concession made to John Gladstone.   Communications were resumed between Glenelg and himself; planter and politician met on February 27th; and, on the

---

[1] *Ibid.*, 1837-38, vol. xvii., pp. 24-37.

[2] July 10, 1837 : ' Mirror of Parliament ' (1837), p. 2180.

following day, the former sent to the Colonial Secretary various documents giving a history of the transaction from the beginning, with details of the arrange-

1838.
The matter brought
before Parliament. ments he had made.[1] The abolitionists in the Commons contented themselves with moving for the production of this correspondence, through Joseph Pease, who had taken up the Parliamentary mantle which defeat at Weymouth had drawn from the shoulders of Buxton; but this mild fashion of dealing with the affair did not commend itself to Brougham. On March 6th, after a preliminary skirmish some weeks before, he initiated a formal debate in the House of Lords, demanding the repeal of the Guiana Order in Council. He enforced his points in a highly-coloured speech, which he immediately re-published, with a dedication to Wellington, who, by moving 'the previous question,' had extinguished the discussion. But, though he denounced the Government and its 'West India confederates'—'respectable men, whom I personally know,' he was as silent regarding John Gladstone as he had been in the debate upon Missionary Smith fourteen years before, a fact only to be accounted for by long acquaintance. It was, indeed, Wellington who first brought John Gladstone by name into the debate, while Melbourne and Ellenborough also mentioned him, the latter especially praising him for having expressed the wish that not less than one-half of those sent from the East Indies under the scheme should be women. But Brougham would not be drawn into directly attacking his old Liverpool friend; and it was with a flourish about his intention not to suffer the Upas tree to be transplanted that he took the Peers to a

[1] 'Parliamentary Papers,' 1837-38, vol. xvii., pp. 143-51. Another history of the transaction, from a critical point of view, is to be found in *Ibid.*, 1842, vol. xiii., pp. 316-18.

division, in which he was decisively beaten, though among the minority was Canning, Mr. Gladstone's Eton school-fellow.[1]

This, however, was but the beginning of a long fight. As it happened that the Whig Administration had sanctioned the Order in Council, the ethics of partisanship, aside from all other considerations, demanded that the Tories should attack it. The *Times* took up the case of the coolies as against the Government; and the Ministers, affrighted at the protests that had been raised, agreed at the end of the session that the Indian Government should prevent any further emigration of coolies to the West Indies until there had been a full investigation of the circumstances under which certain of them had already gone. To this course, and to the consequent revocation of the Guiana Order in Council, they were, indeed, pressed by Peel and Graham, the Tory leader treating the question as one of the greatest importance.[2]

Peel's prescience was soon proved; but, meanwhile, an incident had occurred which served to fan the flame that was steadily being aroused. Smyth, as Governor of British Guiana, had issued, on April 24th, 1837, a proclamation raising the quantity of corn-meal to be given to the apprentices, and various of the planters protested, John Gladstone specially seeing Glenelg on the subject. Stephen, as Permanent Under-Secretary to the Colonial Office, communicated to John Gladstone *The apprentices' food.* the desire of his chief, who was always complacent to the planters, to consider any proof that the previous allowance was sufficient; and on August 26th a reply was sent from Fasque, giving figures to show that the proposed increase

[1] 'Hansard,' 3rd series, vol. xli., ff. 416-76.
[2] July 20, 1838: *Ibid.*, vol. xliv., ff. 382, 383.

would be most injurious, and even ruinous, to the planters, while it would be hurtful to the apprentices, as causing them to waste food which they could not individually consume. Glenelg forwarded the correspondence to Smyth, who, before receiving it, had written to the Colonial Office, pointing out that, in John Gladstone's proposed agreement with the coolies, a distinctly larger allowance was provided than the Demerara planters asserted to be sufficient for a labouring negro; and later, Smyth adhered to his point, though, as before, he could not entirely carry Glenelg with him.[1] But, when Smyth shortly afterwards presented gold medals to those twelve managers of estates in British Guiana who had been recommended by the special justices for their kindness and good conduct towards the apprentices, it was not upon the Gladstone manager that such a distinction was conferred.[2]

Smyth's term of office expired before his doubts as to the coolie experiment could be tested; but Henry Light, the new Governor of British Guiana, took, at the outset, the usual officially optimistic view of the scheme. The coolies, whom he appears to have looked upon as productive and marriageable animals, were much better off, in his opinion, than they had ever been; while those 'on Mr. Gladstone's property are a fine healthy body of men: they are beginning to marry or cohabit with the negresses, and to take pride in their dress; the few words of English they know, added to signs common to all, prove that "Sahib" was good to them.'[3] That was in the January of 1839, but the note was soon changed; and, although Light did his best to put a better face on the matter than the facts permitted,

---

[1] 'Parliamentary Papers,' 1837-38, vol. xlix., pp. 460-500.

[2] *Ibid.*, p. 567.

[3] *Ibid.*, 1839, vol. xxxix., p. 128.

even he had in the April to own that the coolies had
suffered much from sickness and were in a very bad condition. The two worst estates were Bellevue and Vreed-en-
Hoop (the latter, which Howick had attacked in 1833,
being still John Gladstone's, as was also Vreedestein, where
other coolies were placed); and it was proved
that the coolies at Vreed-en-Hoop had been
beaten by the interpreter, and that several
of them, having fled to avoid further ill-treatment, were
captured and severely flogged, while it was also averred
that two others had died in the bush after having made
their escape. Sanderson, John Gladstone's manager, protested against the Governor's investigation of the affair,
though professing himself ready to appear in open court to
answer any charge; and Light replied by asking Stuart, the
attorney of the plantation, to dismiss both the manager and
the interpreter. This, as far as the former was concerned,
Stuart declined to do; and, while Light forwarded the
details to Normanby (now Colonial Secretary in place of
Glenelg), the attorney proceeded to England to confer with
his employer. That was the more necessary because,
immediately upon receipt of the despatches from British
Guiana, Normanby (through Henry Labouchere, then
Colonial Under-Secretary, and afterwards Lord Taunton), sent them to John Gladstone, who, six days later,
and on July 15th, replied that 'it fortunately happened'
that Stuart—'a person of the first respectability in
the colony, where he has resided for the last 30
years, and in whom I have the fullest confidence'—
was in London, and his explanation was enclosed. This
averred that the manager knew nothing of
the interpreter's conduct; that the interpreter
'erred in a great measure from ignorance of the laws of

The ill-condition of John Gladstone's coolies.

His agent's explanation.

the colony;' and that effectual steps had been taken to prevent a recurrence of the incident.[1]

Early in the session, Baines, as an abolitionist, had obtained from the Government an assurance that no more coolies were being sent from India;[2] and a few weeks later, evidently as a counterblast, Mr. Gladstone asked Labouchere whether there was any objection to produce Light's official account of the condition of those in British Guiana. The Ministry had no objection,[3] for this was the optimistic report already referred to; but, just after the question had been put, the floggings at Vreed-en-Hoop were being investigated, and when the news reached this country there was an outburst of indignation, which speedily penetrated Vreed-en-Hoop once the walls of Westminster. Mr. Gladstone
more. was on his honeymoon when the storm broke, for it was on July 23rd, or only two days before his marriage, that the *Times* published a startling account of the manner in which the coolies had been treated on the voyage, and especially later on the estate of Bellevue. Ellenborough the The matter before same evening brought the matter before the Parliament. Lords, Normanby promised the greatest attention, and Brougham prided himself upon his prophesies of evil having been so speedily fulfilled.[4] The next day Graham, in the Commons, pressed for fuller information, but Labouchere asked for a suspension of judgment until the production of the papers; and, in the usual official manner, he argued that, while there had been cruelties and hardships, their relation had been exaggerated.[5] But Ministers, perceiving that the parliamentary

---

[1] *Ibid.*, pp. 129-152.

[2] Feb. 15, 1839: 'Mirror of Parliament' (1839), p. 275.

[3] March 27: *Ibid.*, p. 1597.

[4] July 23: *Ibid.*, pp. 4193, 4194.   [5] July 24: *Ibid.*, p. 4244.

temper was rising, hastened their operations in an unaccustomed degree; and, Normanby having promised the papers within two days, Labouchere laid them before the Commons on the 26th, at the same time correcting his previous minimising statement, and admitting that the condition of the coolies was worse than at first he had thought.[1]

Three days later, and before the question came up in Parliament again, the *Times* had a savage attack upon the promoters of the immigration, and the Whigs for having aided them. It denounced the scheme as inevitably generating 'a system of Jew jobbing and crimping, which, though studiously renouncing the name and objects of slavery, would practically revive all its most odious horrors'; thanked Peel for having the previous year 'successfully blown up the Hill Cooly plot'; assailed the Whig Government in violent terms for having allowed it to proceed; described the process as one of 'Colonial blood-guiltiness'; and exclaimed, 'The blood of these men is crying from the ground. We ask, who shall answer for it, and who shall avenge it?' And it specially emphasised a statement that, on the voyage from India to Demerara, 'the old abominations of the Guinea slavers have been reproduced with modern refinements and aggravations.'

The Times' denunciation.

On August 3rd, and in consequence of what had passed in both Houses, as well as after this attack on the *Times*, John Gladstone felt it necessary for the vindication of his character to make public all the facts and to court the fullest investigation; and he did this in a letter to Normanby, written by his eldest son, Thomas, who was not at the moment in Parliament, having been beaten when seeking re-election for Leicester. In this it was declared that

[1] *Ibid.*, p. 4370.

the *Times'* accusations about the voyage were unfounded,
John Gladstone's and that, although eleven coolies died
reply. within six days after the ship leaving Calcutta, it was mainly because of repletion, they never before
having had enough to eat. Twelve had since died on the
Gladstone estate, but chiefly from complaints the seeds of
which they had brought from Bengal; and the rest 'continued cheerful and contented, but evil-disposed persons
have recently gone among them, and have endeavoured to
create a bad and dissatisfied feeling, in which they may
have partially succeeded, as it is at present too generally
the case in England, where similar effects are produced by
the Chartists and others among the lower classes.' Regarding the flogging, Stuart's explanation was repeated; and,
although it was admitted to be unjustifiable, it was declared
to have been 'proved in court to have been of a very trifling nature '—which was not the opinion of Governor Light,
who described the punishment as revolting, a conclusion
which will be endorsed by any who may now care to read
the evidence. And it was offered that, if Parliament liked
to reimburse John Gladstone the expenses he had incurred
over the coolies, he was ready to relinquish their services,
and to allow to return to Calcutta such of them as wished [1]
—a suggestion at which Graham had hinted in Parliament,
but which the *Times* had stigmatised as inadmissible : 'the
expense must be borne, exclusively, by those who lured them
away.' Thomas Gladstone's attempted defence would have
been more effective if he had known, when writing, that a
further despatch from Light was on the way, giving the
result of the inquiry made by three special commissioners
at the end of May, and saying of the coolies on Vreedestein,

[1] 'Parliamentary Papers,' 1839, vol. xxxix., pp. 158-60.

They appear contented and happy on the whole; no one has ever maltreated or beaten any of them, excepting in one instance:' and of those on Vreed-en-Hoop, 'These people appear perfectly contented, and express themselves in high praise of their manager, Mr. Sanderson, who, they state, "give not only all our allowances of food and clothing, but he supplies us with many other articles, such as tobacco, flour, and pipes,"' it being, indeed, only of the interpreter whom they complained, and he had already been dismissed, after being both fined and imprisoned for his conduct.[1] Complaints continued to be made, however, during this same summer concerning the treatment of the coolies on Vreedestein, and these were much pressed by John Scoble, a friend of abolition; but Light wrote to Normanby that Scoble 'had raked up every incident connected with the coolies, with a perseverance which I trust proceeds from worthy motives. The investigation does not bear out his charges.'[2] By the time the despatch arrived in Downing Street, Russell had succeeded to the Colonial Secretaryship, and he rejoined concerning the Vreedestein coolies, 'Some irregularities appear to have occurred in the treatment of these people; but it is satisfactory to find that they have no reason to be discontented with their condition, nor any disposition to complain of it.'[3]

It was upon a motion by Mr. Gladstone himself that these despatches were laid before the House of Commons

[1] *Ibid.*, pp. 167, 179.

[2] *Ibid.*, 1840, vol. xxiv., p. 184.

[3] *Ibid.*, p. 187. On pp. 218-20 are given official reports of the condition of the coolies on John Gladstone's two estates, in January and February, 1839, and on pp. 231, 232, similar returns of November, 1839: in all cases the management is spoken well of, and no complaints against the employer are recorded.

S

in 1840,[1] and in the course of a session which heard much of the coolie question.   The West India merchants, both in London and Liverpool, had expressed at the end of 1839 a strong desire that immigration should be again allowed; but Russell wrote to Light that he was not prepared to encounter the responsibility of a measure which might lead to either a dreadful loss of life or a new system of slavery.[2]   This decision he announced in the House of Commons soon after the session opened,[3] but it did not suffice to satisfy the abolitionists, from whom a steady stream of petitions flowed throughout the year, some presented by Macaulay, some by Charles Villiers, and some by Strickland, of whom more will be heard, all praying that the traffic should definitely be put an end to.   An unexpected opportunity offered itself for a manifestation of the prevalent feeling.   The Ministry brought in a Colonial Parliamentary action Passengers Bill, amending that passed at on the coolies. the original instance of Mr. Gladstone in 1835; and in this Russell inserted clauses for promoting the emigration of coolies to the Mauritius.   The abolitionists

---

[1] The only specific reference Mr. Gladstone made in Parliament to the subject was on May 14, 1841, when, replying to an attack from Vernon Smith, the Whig Under-Secretary for the Colonies, he stated that he had never heard of any mortality among the coolies on his father's estate beyond what was natural after the period of their landing, or of any serious complaints, except in one instance, when it was brought by one of them against another.   'These hill coolies,' he added, 'were, to a man, satisfied with the treatment they received, and themselves declared, in the presence of a stipendiary magistrate, that, instead of claiming an immediate passage back to India or taking their chance for labour in the colony, they preferred continuing in the employment they were then in': 'Mirror of Parliament' (1841), p. 1720.

[2] 'Parliamentary Papers,' 1840, vol. xxiv., pp. 166-71.

[3] Feb. 4, 1840: 'Mirror of Parliament' (1840), p. 741.

were up in arms against the project which Macaulay, then Secretary-at-War, defended, largely on the ground that the Mauritius was not the West Indies, a speech to which O'Connell replied by proposing a motion hostile to the progress of the Bill. This he subsequently withdrew, and Mr. Gladstone thereupon supported the measure, though he considered it nugatory as well as harmless, but he thought the question of great importance, not only to the planters and labourers but to the cause of humanity.[1] The abolitionists, however, waited their chance; upon Russell moving the third reading, Howick joined with Graham and O'Connell to speak against the measure; and the Government was defeated on its Mauritius proposal by forty-nine votes, for, although Mr. Gladstone voted with Ministers, Peel was in the other lobby with Lincoln and Sir Stephen Glynne, among the member for Newark's closest friends, as well as Disraeli.[2]

Before the session ended, Mackinnon, the Tory member for Lymington, moved for a select committee on the whole subject, but he was opposed by the Government and the House was counted out,[3] the same fate awaiting him the next year upon a similar attempt.[4] The select committee, which had thus twice failed to be appointed in the Whig Parliament, was chosen soon after the Tory House of Commons got into working order; and it reported in favour of allowing immigration under the authority, inspection, and control of free men.[5] Stanley and Howick were alike on this body, and both, as well as Mr. Gladstone himself, had

[1] June 4 : *Ibid.*, p. 3571.
[2] June 22 : 158-109 : *Ibid.*, pp. 3933-48.
[3] July 14 : *Ibid.*, pp. 4571-74.
[4] March 11, 1841 : *Ibid.* (1841), p. 678.
[5] 'Parliamentary Papers,' 1842, vol. xiii.

later to give practical effect to the recommendation.
Immigration once more allowed. Stanley, as Secretary for the Colonies under Peel, wrote in November, 1843, to the Commissioners for the Affairs of India that certain of the coolies were returning from British Guiana, and indicated the opinion that the prohibition of immigration might be removed, the original abuses having arisen chiefly from defects in the mode of engaging and inexperience in the proper manner of treating the labourers.[1]   In the next summer he forwarded to Light, who was still Governor of British Guiana, a guarantee from a body of proprietors and merchants connected with that colony, which enabled him to assent to the immigration of five thousand coolies.[2]   Twelve months later he sanctioned the introduction of another similar number ; during the closing days of the Peel Administration, when Mr. Gladstone had succeeded Stanley as Colonial Secretary, the request of the Committee of the West India Proprietors to forward a further six thousand was granted ; while a year afterwards, and as showing that all parties had now agreed to the idea, Howick himself (who had become Earl Grey and Secretary for the Colonies) authorised the introduction of five thousand more.[3]   And, as a result, half-a-century after the fierce debates which have been recorded, a special recommendation, at sales of sugar plantations in British Guiana, was a good supply of immigrant labourers.[4]

Another phase of the black question was under earnest
The treatment of the Aborigines. consideration throughout this period, and was by none more closely studied than by the member for Newark.   In the opening days of

---

[1] *Ibid.*, 1844, vol. xxxv., p. 590.

[2] *Ibid.*, 1847-48, vol. xliv., p. 3.

[3] *Ibid.*, pp. 10, 11, 17.

[4] Advertisement in *Daily News*, November 26, 1891.

the session of 1836, a select committee was appointed by the House of Commons 'to consider what measures ought to be adopted with regard to the native inhabitants of countries where British settlements are made, and to the neighbouring tribes, in order to secure to them the due observance of justice and the protection of their rights, to promote the spread of civilisation among them, and to lead them to the peaceful and voluntary reception of the Christian religion.' Of that body, as originally constituted, Mr. Gladstone was not a member ; but a week after its appointment, and when it had sat twice, he was added in the room of John Hardy, father of the first Earl of Cranbrook, and then member for Bradford. Buxton was the chairman, as he had been of a similar committee which had sat during the previous year ; and Mr. Glad- Feb. 9, 1836.
stone, from the time of his being added, Mr. Gladstone on the Aborigines
was a constant attendant and a frequent Committee.
questioner, especially with regard to the treatment of the natives during the then recent Caffre War. A Caffre chief, named Jan Tzatzoe, who had been educated by the missionaries, and who desired to vindicate the character of his countrymen and expose the cruelty and injustice with which he asserted them to have been treated, was called as a witness ; but, before he could be examined, Mr. Gladstone proposed that he should not be questioned concerning any grievances he might allege he had endured, unless it should appear that these had been communicated to the Government without effect. This was defeated by the casting-vote of the chairman, and Tzatzoe told his tale, showing his degree of education by writing 'God save the King' in Dutch for the committee's inspection, and proving his intelligence by the shrewd answers he gave during a three days' examination. Having a grievance, for instance, that his land had

been taken away, he had not complained of it to the Governor of the Cape, but had journeyed to England to state his case. 'How came you to think,' asked Mr. Gladstone, 'that the Government in England would be more ready to do you justice than the Government at the Cape?' 'Because,' replied the Caffre, 'the missionaries used to tell us that the good people and right people were here, and that justice was here.' 'Had you not heard,' pursued Mr. Gladstone, 'that the Governor of the Cape was very anxious to do justice to all the native people?' 'Yes,' was the rejoinder, 'I heard so, but he did me no justice,' and from that position the chief would not swerve. With the same native shrewdness, he answered a question of Sir Rufane Donkin, a member of the committee, who in earlier years had been Governor of the Cape, 'Do you appear before the committee here as a missionary to advocate the cause of the Caffres?' 'I sit here as an assistant missionary and a Caffre chief;' and when Mr. Gladstone immediately asked, 'Who desired you to preach?' he made reply, 'When I felt the power of the Word of God, I went to the Boers and to the Hottentots, and I preached what God had done unto me; and so the missionaries engaged me, and said, "You can do that work."'

He questions a Caffre chief

Another native witness, Andrew Stoffel by name, and this one a Hottentot, proved equally cunning of fence. He described himself as having lived in the mountains until the missionaries visited his people; 'then I came amongst human beings . . . we put off our skins and put on clothes.' He had been taught by them to thank the English people for having sent the Bible, but now 'the Hottentot has no water; he has not a blade of grass; he has no lands; he has no wood; he has no place where he can sleep; all that he now has is the missionary and the Bible; and now that we are taught, the Bible is taken away from us, and they want to remove the missionaries from amongst us.' 'How,' queried Mr. Gladstone, 'have they removed the Bible away from you?' and a Hottentot. 'There is no one that gets up on Sunday to speak and to explain the Bible, and to preach to us.' 'Have you not got your Bibles as you had them before?' The reply was instantaneous: 'If you had no English preachers in this country, what would you do with the Bible?' Mr. Gladstone tried another tack: 'What redress would you wish to have for the injuries you have described?' 'In the first place, I want my schools back and my missionaries; the children must be taught. We want education among the Hottentots.' 'Do you want the land and the water and the wood back?' This time the answer was diplomatic: 'I am not man enough, and I do not know where it would lead me, if I were to speak about the land and the water; but I would speak about the other first.'

Mr. Gladstone did not attend as regularly during the closing sittings, and he missed being at the examination of the two witnesses who remain of interest to many of to-day —Captain Allen Gardiner, who testified to the murders and cruelties of Chaka and Dingaan, successive kings of the Zulus, in words which summarise the hideous facts narrated in detail by Mr. Haggard in 'Nada the Lily,' and the Rev. John Williams, the famous Congregationalist missionary to the South Sea Islands, who declared, as a result of his long experience, that, in attempting to introduce Christianity among a people, he would rather by far go to an island where they had never seen a European than to a place after they had had intercourse with such. But, when the chairman produced a draft report recommending the reappointment of the Committee in the next session, Mr. Gladstone was there to move an amendment. 'Your Committee,' wrote Buxton, 'are prepared at present to say no more than that the question is one which merits the most careful attention, and that they believe it will not be difficult to devise a system of intercourse with uncivilised nations more consonant to justice and humanity, more in unison with the high character which Great Britain ought to maintain, and more conducive to her real interests than that which has been hitherto adopted.' Mr. Gladstone wished to strengthen this into an expression of absolute belief that it would be 'practicable to, devise a system of intercourse with the uncivilised tribes, consonant to justice and humanity, and in unison with the high character of Great Britain;' but he was defeated by a single vote.[1]

Early in the following session the committee was re-appointed, Mr. Gladstone being named second on the list; and it at once resumed the taking of evidence. The member for Newark was by no means as constant in attendance at the examination of witnesses as he had been during the previous year, and his questions were few and relatively unimportant. When it came to preparing the full report, he was in cordial assent with his colleagues in the declaration that the moment had arrived 'for the nation to declare that, with all its desire to give encouragement to emigration, and to find a soil to which our surplus population may retreat, it will tolerate no scheme which implies violence or fraud in taking possession of such a territory; that it will no longer subject itself to the guilt of conniving at oppression; and that it will take upon itself the task of defending those who are too weak

*1837.
The Aborigines Committee reappointed,*

and Mr. Gladstone agrees with Buxton's report.

[1] 'Parliamentary Papers,' 1836, vol. vii.

and too ignorant to defend themselves.' 'The British empire,' continued the report in terms seldom to be found in blue-books, 'has been signally blessed by Providence, and her eminence, her strength, her wealth, her prosperity, her intellectual, her moral, and her religious advantages, are so many reasons for peculiar obedience to the laws of Him who guides the destinies of nations. These were given for some higher purpose than commercial prosperity and military renown. . . . He who has made Great Britain what she is, will inquire at our hands how we have employed the influence He has lent to us in our dealings with the untutored and defenceless savage; whether it has been engaged in seizing their lands, warring upon their people, and transplanting unknown disease, and deeper degradation, through the remote regions of the earth; or whether we have, as far as we have been able, informed their ignorance and invited and afforded them the opportunity of becoming partakers of that civilisation, that innocent commerce, that knowledge and that faith with which it has pleased a gracious Providence to bless our own country.' And, passing from the general to the particular, the committee recommended that the protection of the aborigines should devolve on the Executive Government; that all their contracts for service with the colonists should be expressly limited to within a year; that the sale of ardent spirits to them should, as far as possible, be prevented, there being 'for the extermination of men who are exempt from the restraints both of Christianity and of civilisation, no weapon so deadly or so certain as the produce of the distilleries'; that new territories should not be acquired without the sanction of the Home Government; that crimes against the natives should be more effectually punished; that religious instruction and education should be provided; and that missionaries,

'these gratuitous and invaluable agents,' should be pro-
tected, assisted, and countenanced.[1]

His work on the Aborigines Committee appeared to
impress Mr. Gladstone more than any parliamentary duty
in which up to that time he had been engaged, and his
references to it were frequent.   Soon after it was appointed,
he joined with Howick, then Secretary-at-War, in contending, as against Hume, that, while not in any sense a judicial
committee, its powers were sufficient to enable it to determine the policy which ought to be pursued with reference
to the native inhabitants in, and on the borders of, our
colonies.[2]   The next year, however, Hume was with him
on a point that incidentally arose out of the committee's
proceedings.   Mr. Gladstone presented a petition to the
Commons from freeholders and other residents at the
Cape, praying that a commission might be appointed to
investigate on the spot the charges that had been made
against the colonists, as regarded their relations with the
aborigines.   He considered the petition to be justified both
by the action of the Government and the report of the
committee censuring the colonists, the latter especially
as, without intimating any suspicion of its fairness, he
thought it a very unfit tribunal to adjudicate upon matters
whereon great excitement prevailed and character was
intimately concerned.   Accordingly, he moved for the
appointment of a commission as prayed ; but this, though
supported in principle by Hume, was opposed by the Government as well as by Buxton, who declared that, so far from the
report of the Aborigines Committee having been couched
in severe terms, there was never more indulgence shown

[1] *Ibid.*, 1837, vol. vii.
[2] April 11, 1836 : ' Mirror of Parliament ' (1836), pp. 894, 895.

than in that document ; and the matter was allowed to drop.[1]
Even yet Mr. Gladstone had not done with the question ;
but, before it was again prominently brought forward,
Victoria had for some time been seated on the throne.

[1] July 5, 1837 : *Ibid.* (1837), pp. 2139, 2140.

XII.—The Contest at Manchester.

WHILE all men were talking of the death of William IV.
and the accession of Victoria, politicians had to turn their
thoughts to that provision of the Constitution, since done
away with, which secured the summoning of a new Parliament within six months of the demise of
the Crown. Among these was Mr. Gladstone,
who, writing to Milnes, observed : ' We are
now beginning to feel tickled by the approaching dissolution. . .   The Ministers have, you see, pretty well surrendered their ostensible ground about the Irish Church, so
I hope that you and I, should we sit in the approaching
Parliament, shall not be found in different lobbies on any
material divisions.   At Newark I have as yet no ground to
anticipate a contest.'[1]   This anticipation proved correct,
but the ensuing dissolution saw Mr. Gladstone concerned
in an electoral struggle elsewhere which presented special
points of interest.

It was at once assumed at Newark, despite rumours of a
possible second Conservative candidate being started, that
no real opposition would be raised to the re-choosing of the
old members ; and, as the proceedings in that borough
promised to be of the tamest, Mr. Gladstone did not
consider it necessary even to advertise his address
seeking re-election.   But after he had gone thither
from London, a curious circumstance took place.
A meeting of the Conservatives of Manchester was

1837.
Accession of
Queen Victoria:

[1] June 26, 1837 : Reid's ' Houghton,' vol. i., p. 99.

hurriedly called for July 15th, to choose two candidates
in opposition to the retiring representatives, both of whom
had sat since that place had been given members by
the Reform Act, Charles Poulett Thomson (then President of the Board of Trade, and afterwards Governor-
General of Canada and Lord Sydenham), and Mark Philips,
a local magnate ; and, on the morning that it was held, it
was announced in advance by a local paper that one of
these had been already named in the person of Mr. Gladstone.[1]   He, in fact, was the only one chosen, and a deputation of three was appointed to wait upon him ; but it was
at first rumoured in the town that he had de-   July,
clined to fight so forlorn a hope, as his   Mr. Gladstone
                                              invited to contest
friend, Mahon, had done before him.   The   Manchester,
deputation, it appeared, when it reached London, learned
that Mr. Gladstone had gone to Newark, and, on following
him thither, found him engaged in his canvass.   ' I felt the
honour,' he wrote a few days later, 'but I answered un-
equivocally, and at once, that I must absolutely decline the
invitation.'   This was on July 19th, but the next day,
when the deputation had returned to Man-   and, although he de-
chester, the Conservatives of that place   clines, is brought
                                            forward.
determined to bring him forward on the
idea, which some of them considered he had countenanced,
that, if he chanced to be chosen without a personal canvass or an appearance on the hustings, he would elect to
sit for the more important constituency—a course which
was the signal for an outburst of praise from the Tories and
disparagement from the Whigs and Radicals that furnishes
instructive reading.   Most noteworthy among the former
was a document circulated in support of the candidature by
the Conservative Committee, and which deserves lengthened

[1] *Manchester and Salford Advertiser*, July 15, 1837.

quotation as a friendly estimate of Mr. Gladstone's qualities,
claims, and political prospects before he had reached the
age of eight-and-twenty.

'Electors of Manchester,' this appeal ran, 'at length
is introduced to your notice a candidate deserving
of your strongest support, and who, if
elected, will do honour to the great constituency which returns him.   Mr. W. E. Gladstone is, by
universal admission, one of the most useful members in the
House of Commons, and perhaps the most promising young
statesman of the day.   The high honours he took at the
university first fixed public attention upon him, which has
not been disappointed by his subsequent distinguished
parliamentary career.   Mr. Gladstone is of your own
county, of a family who have risen by commerce, and is
thoroughly conversant with those important commercial
questions which are of such vital consequence to our constituency.   He is in the prime of life and vigour, and capable of undergoing all the labour and mental fatigue which
the onerous duties attaching to your representative impose.
Without having been a very frequent speaker in the House,
or one of those who have obstructed the progress of business by endless harangues, whenever he has taken a part in
debate he has fully supported his high reputation.   Under
the administration of Sir Robert Peel, he took office as a
lord of treasury, and subsequently held the responsible situation of under secretary in colonial matters; and has,
throughout his public life, followed the steps of that distinguished statesman.   He is a conservative in principle,
without being indisposed to correct abuses where proved
abuses exist, and a thorough supporter of our church
establishment, without seeking to deprive conscientious dissent of its rights and immunities.   His votes in parliament

A Tory estimate of Mr. Gladstone.

on every important question are before you, as the record
of his political opinions ; and, with that evidence, we now
call upon you to support him.   Though circumstances will
render his absence from Manchester, during the canvass,
unavoidable, yet you will recollect that he is no new or untried man, and that his public life has afforded the fullest
means of adjudicating on his fitness to represent your
borough.   If elected, there cannot be a doubt but that his
devotion to the cause, in which he has been engaged, and
his strong desire to increase his public usefulness, will, at
whatever sacrifice, impel him to accept the high and honourable trust of your representative.   Electors of Manchester
who wish to see this great metropolis of commerce duly represented, give your support to one in whose ability, station,
commercial knowledge, and general character, you have the
strongest guarantee that your interests, various and important as they are, will be guarded over, attended to, and
secured.'   And the document ended with an appeal to the
Manchester electors to ensure a triumph which would assist
to ' give to your queen patriotic and conservative ministers,
who, supporting our national institutions, will uphold the
constitution in its integrity '—a curious anticipation by six
years of Disraeli's creation of the Taper-and-Tadpole Tory
cry, ' Our Young Queen and our Old Institutions ! '

This document was dated July 21st, and the next day
the chief Tory organ, the *Manchester Courier*, echoed it.
Another, the *Manchester Chronicle*, was more detailed in
its encomium. ' To those who have not paid much attention to the proceedings in Parliament,' the latter observed,
' it may be necessary to state that Mr. Gladstone is one of
the most promising young statesmen of the day, and that
he holds precisely the same rank as to ability, in the estimation of all politicians, **as** Sir Robert Peel held some

fifteen or twenty years ago. . . . In his early life he was "a most distinguished debater at Eton, and afterwards was most favourably known at Christ Church, Oxford, for the prompt readiness of his replies." At college he attained the highest honours, having been a double first-class man, and when he entered Parliament, in 1832, a Radical paper said of him, "His maiden speech was one of the best delivered within our remembrance." [1]   His career in Parliament has been a most brilliant one, and he has acquired a degree of influence in the House of Commons which few men of his years have been able to achieve, and which nothing but superior powers of intellect, and superior acquirements can give.   His first great effort as a debater was on the motion for the third reading of Mr. G. W. Wood's Bill for pulling down the religious system of education established in the universities,[2] and it is really amusing to see the admirable style in which the youthful statesman of that day scattered to the four winds of heaven the flimsy arguments of the ex-member for South Lancashire. . . . Since that memorable debate, Mr. Gladstone has eminently distinguished himself both publicly and privately as the opponent of all rash innovations, and as the staunch defender of the established principles of the constitution. In the session just closed he is admitted to have made incomparably the best speech that was made on the church rate question, and we had the testimony of Mr. Thomson himself on this point, when he attempted to reply to him. So far as our candidate is concerned, therefore, we have

[1] No indication is given of the source from which either of these quotations is taken.

[2] The *Times* of July 25, 1837, in a paragraph about the Manchester election, similarly refers to this speech as Mr. Gladstone's 'first great effort as a debater.'

nothing to fear. His local and commercial knowledge, his high attainments, his powers of oratory, and his influence in the House of Commons, all conspire to fit him for the honourable office in which we wish to see him placed.'

It was in very different terms that the Whig *Manchester Guardian* dealt with the young politician. 'Since Mr. Gladstone's name has been brought forward,' it wrote, 'we have taken the trouble to refer a little to the records of his parliamentary career; and we find him, on A Whig criticism. every one of the questions which now press for the decision of public men, voting with the highest tories.' It mentioned several of his votes, by which he was asserted, among other things, to have pertinaciously sought to insult the Dissenters and to have 'acted like a true Cumberlander,'—'God save Queen Victoria, and preserve us from the Duke of Cumberland,' it is to be remembered, was a popular cry just then; and it was added, 'They sufficiently mark the man; they show him obstructing every useful reform, and carrying his exclusiveness so far as to wish to subject even the poor negroes of his father's estates to the slavery of a dominant church. It is indeed an insult that, in Manchester, where the anti-slavery feeling is so strong and general, the person put forward by the tories as their chosen instrument should be one, the whole wealth and consequence of whose family has [*sic*] been derived from holding his fellow-creatures in bondage. But the insult will be repelled by a summary rejection of the candidate.' Another Whig journal, the *Manchester Times*, took more local ground for its denunciation. It warned Mr. Gladstone that, if he visited the town, some awkward questions might be put to him, 'especially as to his opposition, in his capacity of a Liverpool merchant, to Manchester being made a bonded port'

T

—though it was not until January 1st, 1894, that, on the opening of the Ship Canal, Manchester was formally constituted a port, and even then Lord Rosebery, as Foreign Secretary in Mr. Gladstone's last Administration, declined to officially advertise the fact to the nations of the world. But in this matter and on that occasion, the son was evidently being confused with the father, who at the moment was fighting a forlorn Tory hope at Dundee, some of the more heated citizens of which burgh received him with physical as well as political opposition. And this confusion was repeated at a Liberal meeting, where the younger man was characterised not only as a Tory of the worst description, but as 'an old borough-monger from Liverpool.'

On the day upon which appeared the varying estimates of the Manchester journals, already quoted, the *Notting-ham and Newark Mercury* called the attention of the old constituents of Mr. Gladstone to what was going on in Lancashire; and that gentleman at once issued a handbill saying that he had declined the Manchester invitation, and stating, 'in terms as explicit as I can command, that I hold myself bound in honour to the electors of Newark, that I adhere in every particular to the terms of my late address, and that I place my humble services during the ensuing Parliament entirely and unconditionally at their disposal.' This document somewhat upset the calculations of the Manchester Tories, who published a placard implying a doubt as to its genuineness, and adding, 'The decided impression of his committee is, that, should Mr. Gladstone be elected here, he will be able to accept the trust, without breaking any pledge made to his friends at Newark.'

This was too feeble to carry a candidate upon; and the

July 22.
Newark alarmed.

proceedings at the nomination sufficiently prognosticated the crushing defeat the Manchester Tories were to undergo. Mr. Gladstone's proposer The Manchester nomination. praised him for the rare versatility of talent which had recommended him to the notice of Peel ; but the man by the hustings who held up a bundle of straw as an emblem of the Conservative candidate's place in the representation of the borough, was more to the taste of the crowd, which showed its hands overwhelmingly in favour of the two Liberals. Both these gentlemen were polite in reference to their invisible opponent. Philips considered Mr. Gladstone a worthy gentleman, whom it would be no disgrace to meet face to face on the hustings ; while Thomson observed that he could have praised him personally more than his proposer and seconder had done, but politically he was an honest and consistent politician of the ultra-Tory school, one of the small minority of that party which acknowledged as its head the King of Hanover, who had just before been Duke of Cumberland, and which was far beyond those more discreet and far-seeing Tories who were willing to assume a semblance of liberality—a description which singularly forecasted the more famous one of Macaulay a year and a half later. 'Mr. Pig-in-a-Poke Gladstone,' (as a well-known and somewhat rabid London Radical of the day nicknamed him, in a speech he seized the opportunity of making, in company with Feargus O'Connor, after the nomination), was heavily beaten at the poll, Thomson having 4127 votes, Philips 3759, July 27. and Mr. Gladstone only 2324, the mistaken The Manchester poll. tactics of the Tories having largely increased their opponents' majority in comparison with the contest at the previous general election. The *Chronicle* was so chagrined that it said nothing in comment upon the result ; but the other Tory organ, the *Courier*, put a better face on the matter, attributing the crushing nature of the defeat to lack of organisation.

Meanwhile Mr. Gladstone, with Wilde once more as his colleague, had been re-elected without opposition for Newark.

July 24.
Re-elected for
Newark.
In his speech of thanks, he congratulated his constituents that the slavery question was practically disposed of, though there remained much to be done for the improvement of both the physical and the moral condition of the blacks, and in this it would be his pride and pleasure to assist. The remainder of the address was devoted to a general approval of the principle of the new Poor Law, a defence of Church rates, an attack upon the Whig Ministry, and a compliment to Wilde— a compliment which was repaid with interest : ' My honourable colleague,' said the Serjeant, 'has to pride himself upon the honourable situation in which he is placed, and upon which no man has a right to pride himself more, from the merit both in his public and private station, and from the talents he possesses, and grace all the objects that he enters upon.' The usual ' chairing ' followed, and the Conservatives enjoyed a dance, but the local Whigs were not satisfied. Their organ sneered at the ' nice young man,' and solemnly recorded that ' the Ducal nominee, whose duplicity is now manifest in his suffering himself to be put in nomination at Manchester, left the town without spending one shilling more than the necessary expenses,' a remark which throws a vivid light upon the ethics of electioneering as they were then understood in small boroughs.

Not at all dismayed by being assured by the same authority that the contempt with which he had treated the Newark Conservatives had made fresh converts to the

Liberal cause, Mr. Gladstone speedily accepted an invitation to a dinner at which the Manchester
Tories celebrated their defeat.   There he
responded to the toast of his health, drunk,

August 9.
Is entertained by the
Manchester Tories.

in accordance with the lusty custom of the time, with 'four times four, repeated'; and, in an hour's speech of what a local reporter described as quiet and surpassing eloquence, he briefly referred to the circumstances of the contest; defended himself and the Conservatives generally from the charge of having opposed negro emancipation; denied that he was in alliance with what had been termed the Hanoverian party; and claimed that whenever the Whigs had introduced a useful measure the Conservatives had supported it.   But, as was usual with him at that period, his main topic was the Church.   No question, he asserted, could be put in comparison as to importance, not even if it touched the throne.   He charged Ministers with tampering with that fundamental institution, and with having sacrificed their principles in its support to the exigencies of their party; and he waxed especially warm in denunciation of the electioneering use to which the Whigs had put the name of the young Queen.   He ridiculed the idea that her Majesty, as had been asserted by Sir Henry Parnell (then Treasurer of the Navy and Ordnance, and afterwards Lord Congleton), had definite and firm opinions on all the questions of the day.   'What!' he exclaimed, 'does Sir Henry Parnell conceive that amidst the shades of Kensington Gardens the Princess Victoria has been studying the question of Irish Municipal Corporations; that she has taken her morning walks with the division list in her hand, and has, over her evening tea, discussed the probability of Tory or Whig ascendancy?' There was sufficient evidence, he held, to know that she

had never meddled with party politics; and he expressed the firm belief that her Majesty—who had been given a
Compliments the young Queen. sound and careful education, who had been versed in all becoming accomplishments, made intimately acquainted with the history of her country, and brought up in the knowledge and fear of God—would be found to unite, with female delicacy and grace, a masculine vigour of understanding, and that determined tone of character which had so honourably distinguished so many members of her illustrious house. And, with a warm appeal to all upholders of the rights of property to stand by the Conservatives, and a glowing defence of the British Constitution, Mr. Gladstone concluded, amid enthusiastic demonstrations again and again repeated and echoed in the subsequent speeches.

Local criticism was generally favourable concerning the manner, if not the matter, of the address. The Conservatives
Local opinion on the speech: were so impressed that they suggested it should be reprinted and extensively circulated throughout the kingdom, while a Radical comment was that Mr. Gladstone was a very fluent speaker and seemed to possess the qualities of a ready debater. The *Guardian*, however, was not in the mood for compliment. The speech, 'taken all together, was a very dull and commonplace harangue on the commonplace topics of the day; and, as such, we may dismiss it.' It was the same address which the *Chronicle* considered 'one of the most eloquent expositions of Conservative principles and policy that it has been our good fortune to listen to;' and which the *Courier* thought was a powerful oration, 'calculated to do much good by removing the prejudices which it has been the constant endeavour of the Whig-Radical party to infuse into the minds of the public.' Mr. Gladstone, if

he had not learned the lesson already, must by this manifestation have been impressed with the main hardship of the politician's life—that not a single thing he does is impartially judged by friend or foe. And it may have been a semi-consciousness of this which, two days after the Manchester festivity, impelled him to write from Liverpool to his friend Milnes that he was sick and weary with his election peregrinations, and that he was taking passage for Fasque in time for grouse and the Twelfth.[1]

[1] Reid's ' Houghton,' vol. i., p. 200.

XIII.—CHURCH AND STATE.

ONCE more an occupant of what was now a safe seat, Mr. Gladstone, while continuing to take a prominent part in debate, became absorbed in a controversy other than partisan, but one which, though marking him out more clearly than ever as certain to play a prominent part in affairs, seemed for the moment little calculated to help him to the Premiership already in anticipation associated with his name. Everyone, however partially acquainted with his career, has heard of, few have seen, fewer still have read, his work upon the relationship between the Church and the State. The widespread knowledge that such a book proceeded from his pen is mainly due to the fact that Macaulay, in reviewing it, used a phrase in description of its author which was sufficiently paradoxical to be remembered by even the most careless. But a study of the circumstances under which the work was written, the influences surrounding its writer, and the immediate consequences of its production, is essential to an understanding of all the book meant to its author, not merely as a devoted son of the Church but as a young politician who promised to achieve great things.

Mr. Gladstone on Church and State.

There has been described the tendency of Mr. Gladstone to be associated, rather than allied, with the Tractarian party; but one great influence in shaping his theological views was his close friendship with James Hope, which, commenced in 1836, was intimate for the fifteen years that elapsed before the latter joined the Roman Communion, and in essence was unbroken through life. They had been contemporaries at Eton and Oxford; but, as Hope was nearly three years the younger, they were only acquaintances His friendship with at Eton, and, though both at Christ Church, Hope-Scott. were in different 'sets' at Oxford, yet going together to hear Chalmers and Rowland Hill.[1] It was not, however, for some years after this—about 1836, is Mr. Gladstone's remembrance—that they again met; and by that time the one was a promising barrister, the other a rising politician. The consequence of the renewed converse—of the first conversation, indeed—was of momentous importance to Mr. Gladstone: it not only secured him the warmest of all his friendships; it definitely linked him to the Oxford Movement.

Another and an earlier friend was somewhat later to give Mr. Gladstone a significant indication of the estimation in which was held any effort of his to strengthen the Church. In the spring of 1838, George Selwyn published a pamphlet, 'Are Cathedral Institutions Useless? A Practical Answer to this Question, addressed to W. E. Glad- 1838. George Selwyn stone, Esq. M.P.'; and in an introductory and Mr. Gladstone. letter dated 'Eton College, April 5, 1838,' the author observed to 'My dear Gladstone,' 'If I were required to give a reason for addressing you on the present occasion, it would be sufficient to say, that, as I am writing from the birth-place of many lasting friendships, and, The Cathedral Question. amongst the rest, of that which has now subsisted between us during fifteen years; the scenes with which I am surrounded naturally remind me of one of my earliest and most constant friends. But, among the many

[1] Hope-Scott's 'Memoirs,' vol. ii., p. 274.

advantages which I have derived from that intimacy, there is no one which I value so highly as the opportunity that it has given me of corresponding with you from time to time on the state and prospects of the Church.' That correspondence, indeed, had furnished the initiative for Selwyn's work, it being a letter from Mr. Gladstone at the beginning of the year which contained a suggestion that led his friend to inquire into the uses of cathedral institutions. Before the pamphlet was published for general reading, it was circulated privately at the Universities and elsewhere; and in this task Mr. Gladstone specially assisted, sending copies to Bishop Phillpotts of Exeter, Pusey, Manning, Inglis, Ashley, Acland, and Mahon among others of his acquaintance.[1]

Another proof of how widely Mr. Gladstone was regarded as the coming man of the Church-and-Conservative party, is afforded in a letter of April 20th of the same year written to him by Samuel Wilberforce (afterwards Bishop in succession of Oxford and Winchester), when the one was Samuel Wilberforce no more than rector of Brighstone and the and Mr. Gladstone. other a politician who, in a subordinate position, had held office for some weeks. ' It would be an affectation in you, which you are above,' wrote Wilberforce, ' not to know that few young men have the weight you have in the House of Commons and are gaining rapidly throughout the country. Now I do not wish to urge you to consider this as a talent, for your use of which you must render an account, for so I know you do esteem it, but what I want to urge upon you is that you should calmly look far before you ; see the degree and weight of influence to which you may fairly, if God spares your life and powers, look forward in future years and thus act *now* with a view to *then*.

[1] H. W. Tucker's ' Memoir of Bishop Selwyn,' vol. i., p. 40.

There is no height to which you may not fairly rise in this country. If it pleases God to spare us violent convulsions and the loss of our liberties, you may at a future day wield the whole government of this land; and if this should be so, of what extreme moment will your *past steps* then be to the real usefulness of your high station? If there has been any compromise of principle before, you will not then be able to rise above it; but if all your steps have been equal, you will not then be expected to descend below them. I say this to you in the sad conviction that almost all our public men act from the merest expediency; and that from this conventional standard it must be most difficult for one living and acting amongst them to keep himself clear; and yet from the conviction, too, that as yet you are wholly uncommitted to any low principles of thought or action. I would have you view yourself as one who may become the head of all the better feelings of this country, the maintainer of its Church and of its liberties, and who must now be fitting himself for this high vocation.'

To this exhortation, Mr. Gladstone speedily made a long reply. 'I fear,' he wrote, 'entering on the subject to which you have given the chief part of your letter, because I know how large it is, and how oppressive, how all but intolerably oppressive, are the considerations with which it is connected. I have not to charge myself inwardly with having been used to look forward along the avenues of life rarely or neglectfully: but rather with that weakness of faith, and that shrinking of the flesh, of which at every moment I am mournfully conscious, but most so when I attempt to estimate or conjecture our probable public destinies during the term to which our natural lives may extend—a prospect which I confess fills me with despondency and alarm. Not that these feelings are unmixed: they are tempered

even as regards the period of which I speak with the confident anticipations of new developments of religious power
which have been forgotten in the day of insidious prosperity,
and seem to be providentially reserved for the time of our
need, for the swelling of Jordan; and of course there lies
beyond that period, for those who are appointed to it, a
haven of perfect rest; but still the coming years bear to my
view an aspect of gloom for the country—not for the Church:
she is the land of Goshen. Looking, however, to the
former, to the State as such, and to those who belong to it
as citizens, I seem unable to discern resources bearing a
just proportion to her dangers and necessities. While the
art of politics from day to day embraces more and more
vital questions, and enters into closer relations with the
characters and therefore the destinies of men, there is, I
fear, a falling away in the intellectual stature of the generation of men whose office it is to exercise that art for good.
While public men are called by the exigencies of their position to do more and more, there seems to be in the
accumulation of business, the bewildering multiplication of
details, an indication of their probable capacity to do less
and less. The principles of civil government have decayed
amongst us as much, I suspect, as those which are ecclesiastical; and one does not see an equally ready or sure
provision for their revival. One sees in actual existence
the apparatus by which our institutions are to be threatened,
and the very groundwork of the national character to be
broken up; but upon the other hand, if we look around for
the masses of principle, I mean of enlightened principle,
blended with courage and devotion, which are the human
means of resistance, *these* I feel have yet to be organised,
almost to be created.' [1]

[1] 'Life of Samuel Wilberforce,' vol. i., pp. 133-6.

Special significance attaches to that portion of the letter which deals with the ecclesiastical problem, for, at the moment of its writing, Mr. Gladstone was engaged upon his first important work, 'The State in its Relations with the Church.' It has been seen how, Mr. Gladstone ever since he came to manhood, he had writes upon the Relations of Church warmly placed himself on the side of and State. the Church ; and the dedication to him of Selwyn's pamphlet upon cathedrals and the communication from Wilberforce, as well as one on religious education, later to be noticed, from Hook, and all in this same spring of 1838, indicate how highly he was regarded by the younger and more energetic champions of the Establishment. At that time, as Mr. Gladstone not long afterwards explained, the sentiment in favour of that institution was very powerfully aroused, and it appeared to him 'a contingency greatly to be feared, that the affections then called into such vivid action, in a great degree through political circumstances, might satisfy them-selves with a theory which teaches, indeed, that the State should support religion, but neither sufficiently explores the grounds of that proposition, nor intelligibly limits the re-ligion so to be supported ; and which also seems relatively to assign too great a prominence to that kind of support which taxation supplies.' As such a theory, in his opinion, would probably be found to guarantee neither purity of faith, nor harmony or permanence of operation, he wrote his book.[1] But another moving impulse of the work came from out-side, and from one who was to be historic as leader of the disruption of the Church of Scotland, for Mr. The influence of Gladstone has recorded that it was 'a Chalmers. series of lectures which Dr. Chalmers delivered in the

[1] 'The State in its Relations with the Church,' preface to the 4th edition, pp. v., vi.

Hanover Square Rooms, to distinguished audiences, with a profuse eloquence, and with a noble and almost irresistible fervour [which] drove me upon the hazardous enterprise of handling the same subject upon what I thought a sounder basis.'[1]   To the many other claims which Chalmers has upon the national memory is thus to be added the original inspiration of Mr. Gladstone's first and best known politico-theological work.

The book was for some time in incubation, and it was in July, 1838, that the author communicated to John Murray that he thought of publishing some papers on the relationship of the Church and the State, which would probably fill a moderate octavo volume.   Murray showed himself inclined to issue the work;[2] but, before any arrangement was arrived at, Mr. Gladstone entered into a detailed correspondence regarding the book with Hope.   This commenced with a letter from the House of Commons on July 18th, in which the hope was expressed that the general tendency would meet with his friend's approval; 'but a point about which I am in great doubt, and to which I request your particular attention is, whether either the work or some of the chapters are not so deficient in clearness and arrangement as to require being absolutely re-written before they can with propriety be published.'   'Between my eyes and my business,' he added, with a pathetic touch much later recalled, 'I fear it would be hard for me to re-write;' but he urged Hope to tell him 'the amount of the disease and the proper kind of remedy.'

July.
Mr. Gladstone arranges to publish.

Submits the manuscript to Hope.

Hope undertook the duty with zeal, 'using the pencil

[1] Hope-Scott's 'Memoirs,' vol. ii., pp. 276, 277.
[2] Samuel Smiles' 'John Murray,' vol ii., p. 437.

very unscrupulously,' and giving many a hint, while the first
suggestion of the title came from Mahon.

The title.

This was 'Church and State considered in
their connection,' which Mr. Gladstone first modified to
'The State viewed in its connection with the Church,' and
finally, in accordance with a hint from Hope, 'The State in
its Relations with the Church.' Mr. Gladstone worked hard
to meet Hope's various criticisms, which were both subtle
and voluminous; [1] and in the course of August the revision
was completed, and Murray furnished with the manuscript; [2]
but, just as the proofs were ready, the author left England
for the Continent. He had resolved upon going to Ems
when the House rose, but on July 26th he indicated to Hope
a change of intention, adding, 'I am very

August.

desirous to set both my mind and eyes at
liberty before I go to the Continent, which

Mr. Gladstone goes
to the Continent.

I can now hardly expect to do before the first week in
September.' His holiday, however, was earlier commenced.
Parliament was prorogued on August 16th; and Mr. Gladstone on the next day was writing to Murray 'a line from
Rotterdam to say that sea-sickness prevented my correcting
the proofs on the passage.' But, even when he reached
Ems, where he received further suggestions from Hope, he
was not content to let the proofs pass without his friend
seeing them. Writing from that place on September 7th, Mr.
Gladstone told him he had asked Murray to request
him to look at the corrected proofs; and Hope, in replying
five weeks later that he had done so, added of the work,
'She is a noble vessel, freighted with the riches of a true
wisdom, directed by a spirit of pure and fervent piety, furnished out with knowledge and a practical experience.

[1] Hope-Scott's ' Memoirs,' vol. i., pp. 142-64.
[2] Smiles' 'Murray,' vol. ii., p. 437.

May God's blessing be with her, and may she so sail upon the troubled and uncertain sea of men's opinions, that through her we may in some degree be brought on our voyage towards "the haven where we would be!"' [1]

Before this letter could reach him, Mr. Gladstone had travelled still further to the South; and by the end of October he was in Sicily, where, having previously visited Vesuvius, he saw the commencement of a slight eruption of Etna, of which he recorded in his diary a long account, subsequently published in Murray's 'Handbook for Sicily.' It was in the last two days of October that he made the ascent, listening as he went to the distant booming of the mountain; and, as he neared the top, 'light fleecy clouds lay upon the sea below us, which I would compare to those of Guido's Aurora in the Rospigliosi Palace at Rome.' The crater was found to be filled with lava to within a few feet of the brim, a circumstance which aroused the enthusiasm of the guide, and which caused Mr. Gladstone to remark: 'We were indeed extremely fortunate, and actually the first spectators of this great volcanic action.' Even at that moment of keen enjoyment, he characteristically 'could not help being struck with the remarkable accuracy of Virgil's account;' [2] and, in his diary, he proceeded to give illustrative extracts from the third book of the 'Æneid,' exclaiming: 'And this is within the limits of 12 lines. Modern poetry has its own

October.
Visits Sicily.

Ascends Etna when in eruption.

[1] Hope-Scott's 'Memoirs,' vol. i., pp. 165, 166.

[2] In the same way he wrote: 'One finds the precepts of Virgil in some respects observed in Sicilian agriculture, contrary to modern, at least, to our northern practice;' and he quoted lines from the 'Georgics' in proof: Murray's 'Handbook for Travellers in Sicily' (1864), p. xvi.

merits, but the conveyance of information is not, generally speaking, one of them. What would Virgil have
thought of authors publishing poems with explanatory notes
(to illustrate is a different matter), as if they were so many
books of conundrums? Indeed this vice is of very late
years.'

'Our position was not quite secure,' Mr. Gladstone
added, 'as the winged lava every now and then hissed and
whistled past our ears; and we sorrowfully turned away
from a scene which, with the combination of features it exhibited on this happy morning, may well be termed one of
the wonders of the world, and of itself amply repays the
pains of our journey to Sicily, and obliterates from recollection the vermin and the mules.'[1]   Concerning the
former, no details are given; as to the latter, Mr. Gladstone
wrote: 'The acquaintance which it gives you with this race
is one of the characteristic features of Sicilian travelling.
The mule seems to have no sense of fatigue, of kindness, or
of emulation; a light or a heavy load, a long or a short distance, a good or a bad road, provided only the pace be not
rapid, are all without the slightest effect upon the physical
composure of the mule.   The wiry beast works in his own
way, and in no other, resenting punishment, but hardly
otherwise affected by it, and still less accessible by any
other means of influence.   Michael calls his mules "Porco"
when they stumble.   But they really seem like Franken-
steins[2] of the animal creation.   Sympathy, however, they
have; and with a faint yet wild and unnatural neighing
they will sometimes recognise relationship.'[3]   Other more

[1] *Ibid.*, pp. 442-6.

[2] Mr. Gladstone here fell into the common error of confounding the
hero of Mrs. Shelley's tale with the monster he created.

[3] *Ibid.*, p. xlvi.

U

characteristic remarks, the fruit of this journey, are these:
'The temples enshrine a most pure and salutary principle
of art, that which connects grandeur of effect with simplicity
of detail; and retaining their beauty and their dignity in
their decay, they represent the great man when fallen, as
types of that almost highest of human qualities, silent, yet
not sullen endurance;'[1] and the not dissimilar thought:
'It seems as if the finest of all soils were produced from
the most agonising throes of nature, as the hardiest characters are often reared amidst the severest circumstances.'[2]

A quarter of a century later, Mr. Gladstone recounted
in a lecture at Hawarden some of his Sicilian experiences,
which seem to have had a bearing upon an important after-
development of his views on Italy. Shortly before he
visited the island, the cholera had ravaged it; and the
people were possessed of the feeling that
the epidemic had been introduced by the
Government of the Two Sicilies, under which they were at
that time placed. The belief was that this had been done
in order to check the revolutionary spirit and thin the
people, and that, as the Cardinal Archbishop had refused
to have anything to do with such a plan, the cholera had
been given him in a pinch of snuff by one of the royal
generals. Mr. Gladstone noted this in writing at the time,
and afterwards expressed his impossibility to conceive anything more illustrative of the unhappy and bad system under
which the Sicilians lived at that period.[3] And it may be
that this experience with these cruelly superstitious folk led
him in 1851, when arousing Europe to the enormities of
Bourbon rule in the Two Sicilies, to make no reference to

The cholera in Sicily.

---

[1] *Ibid.*, p. xxvi.
[2] *Ibid.*, p. 454.
[3] Lecture at Hawarden, Jan. 5, 1863.

the successful subjugation by the King of his Sicilian subjects, but to confine the protest to his conduct towards his Neapolitan subjects, through whose fidelity and courage that subjugation had been effected.

While its author was travelling in Italy, and early in December, the work on Church and State appeared, and at once passed into a second edition. In the previous month, Bunsen (the Prussian Minister to England, who had long known and admired Mr. Gladstone) while visiting Sir Thomas Acland at Killerton, had announced to his wife, 'Gladstone's book is coming out;' and on December 13th he thus recorded for the same correspondent the effect it caused: 'Last night, at eleven, when I came from the Duke [of Wellington], Gladstone's book was on my table, the second edition having come out at seven o'clock. It is the book of the time, a great event —the first book since Burke that goes to the bottom of the vital question; far above his party and his time. I sat up till after midnight, and this morning I continued until I had read the whole, and almost every sheet bears my marginal glosses, destined for the Prince,[1] to whom I have sent the book with all despatch. Gladstone is the first man in England as to intellectual power, and he has heard higher tones than anyone else in this island.'[2]

December. The book appears.

Bunsen's opinion.

How greatly Bunsen was impressed appears from a letter he wrote to Dr. Arnold on the Christmas Eve :—'I read in London Gladstone's book, in the night and following morning of the day it was published. It appears to me the most important and dignified work which has been written on

[1] William, Crown Prince of Prussia, afterwards King of Prussia and German Emperor.

[2] 'Memoir of Baron Bunsen,' pp. 481-90.

that side of the question since Burke's "Considerations." Gladstone is by far the first living intellectual power on that side.   He has left his schoolmasters far behind him, but we must not wonder if he still walks in their trammels—his genius will soon free itself entirely—and fly towards heaven with its own wings.   I have sent my copy with some hundred marginal notes and effusions of heart to the Crown Prince of Prussia.   You will see my thoughts run in the same channel as Gladstone's; his Church is my Church, that is, the Divine consciousness of the State,—a Church not profaned and defiled either by Popery or the unholy police regulations of the secular power.'   And, after sug· gesting several points upon which he wished further information from Mr. Gladstone, he added: 'These and similar questions I have a mind to ask him, in one way or other.   I know him personally, from the time of his visit to Rome.' [1]   Writing to yet another correspondent two days later, Bunsen reiterated his praise.   'I have sent Gladstone's work with my *postilla* to the Crown Prince.   It is—in its principal bearings—second only to Burke's "Considerations" in my opinion; still he walks sadly in the trammels of his Oxford friends in some points. . . . I wonder Gladstone should not have the feeling of moving on an *inclined plane*, or that of sitting down among ruins, as if he were settled in a well-stored house.   The reason of these defects in his book I ascribe to the want of a deeper philosophy.' [2]

'The State in its Relations with the Church, by W. E. Gladstone, Esq., Student of Christchurch, and M.P. for Newark,' thus glowingly extolled by one of the most experienced authors and diplomatists of Europe, was

[1] *Ibid.*, pp. 492, 493.   The last sentence obviously refers to Mr. Gladstone's first visit to Rome in 1832.

[2] *Ibid.*, pp. 493, 494.

'Inscribed to the University of Oxford; tried, and not found wanting, through the vicissitudes of a thousand years; in the belief that she is providentially designed to be a fountain of blessings, spiritual, social, and intellectual, to this and to other countries, to the present and future times; and in the hope that the temper of these pages may be found not alien from her own.'[1] It was an octavo book of 324 pages, divided into eight chapters. The first consisted of introductory explanations and a statement of several published theories, including those of Hooker, Warburton, Paley, Coleridge, Chalmers, Hobbes, Bellarmine, and the Ultramontanes. In the second the theory of the connection between the Church and the State was examined; and in the third the author discussed the influence of that connection upon the tone of personal religion in the Church. After a sketch of the ecclesiastical supremacy of the Sovereign in England, which filled the fourth chapter, the fifth was occupied with a consideration of the Reformation, as connected with the use and abuse of private judgment, and the sixth with that use and abuse as related to the principle of union between Church and State. The seventh dealt with the existing constitutional and administrative practice, in which was included a declaration concerning the Government grant to the Roman Catholic College of Maynooth, which had an important bearing upon the author's political future; and the eighth with the ulterior tendencies of the movement towards the dissolution of the connection between Church and State, in which it was contended that the existence of the former was independent of that connection, and that it was the State which demanded solicitude, for 'we may

The book described.

---

[1] This dedication was dated, 'London, August, 1838.'

tremble at the very thought of the degradation she would undergo, should she in an evil hour repudiate her ancient strength, the principle of a national religion.'

It is not only of interest, it is in itself fair, to adopt Mr. Gladstone's own idea of the plan and purpose of his book.

Mr. Gladstone's description of its purpose. 'The work,' he wrote thirty years after its publication,[1] 'attempted to survey the actual state of the relations between the State and the Church; to show from history the ground which had been defined for the National Church at the Reformation; and to inquire and determine whether the existing state of things was worth preserving, and defending against encroachment from whatever quarter. This question it decided emphatically in the affirmative. . . . Faithful to logic, and to its theory, my work did not shrink from applying them to the crucial case of the Irish Church. It did not disguise the difficulties of the case, for I was alive to the paradox it involved. But the one master idea of the system, that the State as it then stood was capable in this age, as it had been in ages long gone by, of assuming beneficially a responsibility for the inculcation of a particular religion, carried me through all. My doctrine was, that the Church, as established by law, was to be maintained for its truth; that this was the only principle on which it could be properly and permanently upheld; that this principle, if good in England, was good also for Ireland; that truth is of all possessions the most precious to the soul of man; and that to remove, as I then erroneously thought we should remove, this priceless treasure from the view and the reach of the Irish people, would be meanly to purchase their momentary favour at

---

[1] 'A Chapter of Autobiography,' sects. 13, 16.

the expense of their permanent interests, and would be a high offence against our own sacred obligations.' And this was the effort which without delay was to bring upon its author's head a torrent of adverse criticism, slightly checked by recognition of honest aim.

XIV.—MR. GLADSTONE AND HIS CRITICS.

MURRAY had announced 'The State in its Relations with the Church' in good company, for, in the *Times'* advertisement, Hallam's 'Introduction to the Literature of Europe' was placed immediately above, Mahon's concluding volume of the 'History of England' immediately below, and Milnes' 'Poems' close to its side. The notice it had excited among politicians soon passed to the Press; and on December 19th the *Times* devoted a leading article to the book, which, it explained, had been in its possession several days, but, from various causes, the editor had not been able until then to command the requisite leisure to examine it. The review was distinctly favourable,

December 19, 1838.
The *Times'* first
notice,

opening with personal compliment and ending with hearty commendation. 'The announcement of this volume, we own, excited our most sanguine anticipations; and whether we consider the essential importance of the question it treats of, or the extrinsic interest attaching to that question under existing circumstances, or the high estimation in which the honourable author is held both by friends and opponents, it has seldom been our lot to engage in the perusal of any book with a stronger presentiment in its favour, or with a more thorough persuasion that the writer's acknowledged sobriety of judgment would not have committed him to undertake a task for which his talents and resources were inadequate. . . . All things considered, the moral and mental qualifications of Mr. W. E. Gladstone appeared to us to fit him very eminently for the successful achieve- <small>which is favourable.</small> ment of his task; and, although we are un- able to give an unqualified approbation to the whole of his assumptions and reasonings, it is not too much to say that he has acquitted himself with transcendant ability through- out, and has produced, indeed, one of the most profound, eloquent, and unanswerable demonstrations that we ever remember to have read.'

While the *Times* considered that, in occupying his first chapter with a statement of the theories put forth by former writers touching the connexion between Church and State, Mr. Gladstone had swelled the size of his book without materially increasing its value, it held that the theory set forward in the second, concerning the relation- ship between the civil magistrate and religion, was so in- genious and satisfactory that nothing short of quotations would serve.   Even more impressed was the *Times* with the portion regarding the religious responsibilities of nations, the points being ' reasoned out with a force and conclusive- ness which, while putting the poor voluntaries into a most piteous plight, change our contempt for them into some- thing like compassion.'   The next sentence sounds of a sigh even now :   'We regret that our limited space compels us to relinquish several passages which we had marked for quotation; but the following [alleging "the radical defects of the voluntary system "] is too good to be omitted.'   And the article proceeded to its eulogistic conclusion :   'Ex- cellent as all this is, Mr. Gladstone improves as he advances. In the third chapter, we scarcely know which most to admire, the originality and depth of his views, or the precision and splendour with which they are developed.   Our extracts from the work shall therefore be continued; and the rather

as we have not yet arrived at those portions of it whereon
we must very decidedly differ with him.   Meanwhile, every
person interested in this great argument ought, if possible, to possess himself of Mr. Gladstone's ingenious
book.'

A week later—on the morning after Christmas Day—the
Times gave a further series of extracts.   It still thought that,

Dec. 26.
The *Times'* second
notice,

although the author had 'expressed himself
with somewhat more of the Clockmaker's[1]
" soft sawder " than we have cared to imply,
his refutation of Dissenting calumnies against the church,
particularly as regards her alleged tendency to "ruin more

which is qualified.

souls than she saves," is bold, trenchant,
and complete.'   And in the remainder of
the article Mr. Gladstone's reasoning was described as dex-
terous, profound, and striking.

But a change was soon to come.   A leading article of
January 4th, 1839, thus commenced : ' In a former notice of

January 4, 1839.
The *Times'* third
notice,

Mr. W. E. Gladstone's work *On the State
in its Relations with the Church*, we mentioned that there were certain points on
which we should be constrained to differ from him.   Such
points appeared to us, in the first instance, to lie upon the
surface, and to admit of an easy adjustment ; but, on
divesting them of the verbal garniture in which they are
muffled up, and on subjecting them to that stricter analysis
which their apparent harmony with divers dogmas of the
Pusey school seemed to force upon us, we must own, with
the deepest regret, though not retracting a particle of our

which is hostile.

homage to the general ability of Mr. Gladstone's volume, that these points are much
more vital and important than we had formed any idea of.'

[1] ' Sam Slick,' T. C. Haliburton, afterwards member for Launceston.

A violent attack followed upon those who had circulated 'certain stupid and perfidious pamphlets, entitled "Tracts for the Times"'; they were informed that 'as long as, with their present *anti-Protestant* sentiments, they persist in retaining Protestant benefices and obligations, their pretences to conscientiousness can deserve nothing but unmitigated contempt'; 'until they purge their consciences from the guilt of compounding them for filthy lucre's sake, we must sternly deny to Dr. Pusey and his associates the smallest credit for moral integrity in their innovations'; and they were roundly told that 'the infamy of perjury as identified with the violation of their Protestant vows, is adhering to them in its most obvious form.'

'It is time for us to speak out upon this subject,' the *Times* observed; and from general denunciation it proceeded to particular. 'It is quite clear to us, from many passages in Mr. W. E. Gladstone's recently published volume that that able and accomplished person is deeply, and, we fear, irrecoverably contaminated with these new-fangled Oxford bigotries: and, after having successfully enthralled such a mind as his, their progress must be looked to with jealousy and alarm by every sound Protestant in the kingdom. Among the more objectionable sentiments put forth by Mr. Gladstone are the following, which we give in their fair contextual meaning, without any other view at present than merely to show the *Popish biases* wherewith on several important points his mind is unhappily imbued. Those of them which tend to the discredit and ruin of our noble Protestant church we shall deal with afterwards.' Eight points put forward in the work, mainly concerning 'the one Catholic Church,' were then attacked, and the article concluded: 'We must painfully declare that our further acquaintance with the opinions of this writer has greatly shaken our confidence in his judgment. The fact is, he leaves us to infer that Popery has a better right to be established in Ireland than Presbyterian Protestantism has in Scotland.'

Even with this assault the *Times* was not satisfied, and a fortnight later it returned to the attack. All trace of compliment now disappeared. 'Whether from an accidental ignorance of what had previously been written on the subject, or from conscious inability to overcome certain embarrassments in his argument, which deeper thought and better information might have satisfactorily removed, the hon. gentleman, with the best intentions in the world, has advanced divers principles in defence of our established church not only untenable in themselves, but which, if practically followed out, would render that church an unendurable nuisance, and involve it in universal odium.'   Later it was observed that 'our youthful author has taken refuge in an exploded Popish absurdity'; he was told that his estimate of the position of the Church of Scotland was 'flippant and irreverent,' and that 'this puerile bigotry is discreditable.' The bludgeon, possibly 'from an accidental ignorance of what had previously been written on the subject,' was wielded to the end.   'We cannot accompany Mr. Gladstone any further.   With his abilities and acquirements he might have written a book that would have been essentially serviceable to the church as well as creditable to himself. But, notwithstanding the many excellent passages which occur in it, he has done little else than disturb questions which, under the present temper and settled arrangements of society, no discreet Christian or constitutionalist should have ventured to revive, much less in the spirit of slavish mysticism with which his work is

Marginal notes:

January 21.
The *Times'* fourth notice,

which is savage.

unhappily imbued. If this gentleman's views of the church of England, as a tame dilution of Romanism, could be supposed to obtain extensive credit, she may henceforth write *Ichabod* upon all her gates, for assuredly her doom were sealed.'

This overwrought fashion of denouncing an author who so recently, and for the same book, had been extravagantly praised, naturally excited comment. It was to be expected that Newman would not appreciate ;it, for only on January 14th he had exclaimed to Frederic Rogers, 'What a fine fellow Gladstone is !' Curiously, however, it is to be found in a letter eight days later—or a day after the second attack—that, although Newman could tell Rogers that 'the *Times* is again at poor Gladstone,' and could observe, 'Really I feel as if I could do anything for him,' he had not troubled to glance at the work which had aroused the storm. 'I have not read his book, but its consequences speak for it,' he wrote, adding the pitying words : 'Poor fellow ! it is so noble a thing.'[1] But as competent a critic—though, as he was in Rome and not at Oxford, he likewise, though for a better reason, had not seen the book— condemned the attitude of the *Times ;* for John Sterling, writing in the course of the same month, remarked : 'I have not yet seen Gladstone's *Church and State ;* but as there is a copy in Rome, I hope soon to lay hands on it. . . . I saw yesterday in the *Times* a furious, and I am sorry to say, most absurd attack on him, it, and the new Oxonian school.'[2]

The Times attack condemned by Newman

and John Sterling.

Sterling was a keen admirer of Mr. Gladstone at this

[1] Anna Mozley's 'Letters, etc., of Newman,' vol. ii., pp. 278, 279.

[2] Carlyle's 'John Sterling,' p. 142.

period, showing himself 'much delighted' with him; but Maurice, who recorded this in a letter to Trench on February 12th, was not so impressed. 'Gladstone's book,' he said, 'has disappointed me more than I Opinions of F. D. like to confess, but he seems to be an ex- Maurice, cellent and really wise man.' [1] Arnold, of Rugby, who looked at Church affairs from a very different standpoint to that adopted by Mr. Gladstone, Arnold of Rugby, also in the main spoke favourably of the book, though with qualifications later to be noted. 'I quite agree with you,' he wrote to a clerical friend on February 25th, 'in my admiration of its spirit throughout; I also like the substance of about half of it; the rest of course appears to me erroneous. But it must be good to have a public man writing on such a subject, and it delights me to have a good protest against that wretched doctrine of Warburton's, that the State has only to look after body and goods.' [2]

The work, indeed, was read with sympathy in a great variety of circles. Henry Taylor, whose favourable opinion of Mr. Gladstone while at the Colonial Office has been noted, had written of it on New Year's Day to Southey: 'It is closely and deeply argumentative, perhaps too much in Henry Taylor, the nature of a series of propositions and corollaries, for a book which takes so very demonstrative a character leads one to expect what is impossible and to feel thrown out by a postulate. But it is most able and most profound, and written in language which cannot be excelled for solidity and clearness. It is too philosophical to be generally read; but it will raise his reputation on the authority of those who do read it, and

[1] 'Life of F. D. Maurice,' vol i., p. 257.
[2] Stanley's 'Life of Dr. Arnold,' vol. ii., p. 144.

will not embarrass him so much in political life as a popularly quotable book on such subjects might be apt to do. His party begin to speak of him as the man who will one day be at their head, and at the head of the Government, and certainly no man of his standing has yet appeared who seems likely to stand in his way. Two wants, however, may lie across his political career—want of robust health, and want of flexibility.'[1]   When politicians recall Mr. Gladstone's succession of Liberal Premierships and all men know of the physical strength of his later years, these wants may arouse a smile, but no one would have foretold either in 1839.

Taylor was on safer ground than prophecy when remarking in a letter of this same month of January to Miss Fenwick, a much-valued friend of Wordsworth : 'Gladstone's book is variously spoken of. Some people say it is crazy and nonsensical ; others, that it will ruin him in political life ; many, that it is bigoted and papistical ; [Sir James] Stephen, that it is a book of great majesty, dignity, and strength.'[2]   'What says *James Stephen,* Wordsworth ?' he added, 'and what you?' and to the former question the lady was able to reply, for the work was at the moment the main subject for conversation at Rydal Mount.   Henry Crabb Robinson was visiting there ; and on the first Sunday in the New Year, after listening to a sermon by Arnold, he perused part of Mr. Gladstone's book ; on the next day, Wordsworth, Arnold, and himself 'had an agreeable evening, divided between whist, Carlyle, and Gladstone' ; on the Tuesday, the poet being ill in bed, Robinson read the book to him ; and six days later the diarist's record ran, 'The afternoon and evening spent as

---

[1] Henry Taylor's 'Correspondence,' pp. 108, 109.

[2] *Ibid.*, p. 112.

usual—whist and Gladstone.'[1]   The result of all this cogita-
tion was much free criticism.   Robinson, on the first evening of perusal, had questioned the assumption which under-
lay the work that there is a moral duty on the part of a
Government to support what it deems the truth ; and a

Crabb Robinson, fortnight later he wrote of the book that ' it
will delight the High-flying, Anglo-papistic,
Oxford party, but only alienate still further the conscientious
Dissenters and displease the liberal Churchmen.   Even
Wordsworth says, he cannot distinguish its principles from
Romanism.   Whilst G. expatiates with unction on the
mystic character of *the Church*, he makes no attempt to
explain *what is the Church of England ;* though, to be
candid,' he slyly added, ' even Dr. Arnold is not able to
make that clear to me.'   And in his diary, he further recorded his gladness at finding that neither Wordsworth nor
Arnold could 'accompany Gladstone in his Anglo-papistical
pretensions.'[2]

It is little wonder, therefore, that Miss Fenwick, replying
to Taylor on January 26th, while Robinson was still at Rydal,
had to explain that she had not yet read the work, because
it had been in such great request, first at the Mount and
then at Arnold's.   ' Wordsworth,' she added, ' says it

and Wordsworth. is worthy of all attention, and it seems to
have his approval, though not his entire
approbation.   He seems to think that Gladstone goes too
far in his idea of the authority of the Church as derived
from apostolical descent ; but at the same time he says that,
to be decided in his opinion on this point, he ought to
know a great deal more of ecclesiastical history than he

[1] H. C. Robinson's 'Diary, Reminiscences, and Correspondence,'
vol. iii., pp. 163-5.

[2] *Ibid.*, pp. 168-70.

does, and be more deeply read in the Fathers than he is ; and also that he must read Mr. Gladstone's book again, before he can see clearly what he *does claim* for the Church.'[1] A certain lack of clearness, indeed, had been detected by Hope when revising the proofs, and had been endeavoured by him to be obviated by an occasional alteration of a word or arrangement of a sentence ;[2] but such defect as in this respect existed lay too deep to be so easily cured.

A point of more than merely critical interest, however, was simultaneously being raised. 'Have you seen Gladstone's book ?' asked James Mozley of his sister from Oxford, in the middle of January. 'It is a very noble book, I believe, and has damaged, if not destroyed, his prospects with the Conservatives. People are now saying, "Poor fellow," and so on. Hope of Merton told Newman this as what he heard in town, and also said persons out of the political world could not understand the sacrifice Gladstone had made.'[3] 'If I go on and publish,' Mr. Gladstone himself had written to Hope when the book was in embryo, 'I shall be quite prepared to find some persons surprised ;'[4] but he could scarcely have anticipated in how many quarters the question would be put, 'What effect will the book have upon its writer's career?' and, if the every-day politician had known Peel's opinion concerning it, that question would have been answered in the one word, 'Disastrous.' It is related in the biography of Lord Houghton that he was staying at Drayton Manor, Peel's country seat, when the essay reached the statesman's hands. 'Peel turned over the

The effect upon Mr. Gladstone's prospects.

Peel's opinion.

---

[1] Henry Taylor's 'Correspondence,' pp. 114, 115.

[2] Hope-Scott's 'Memoirs,' vol. i., p. 166.

[3] 'Letters of the Rev. J. B. Mozley, D.D.,' vol. i., p. 87.
 Hope-Scott's 'Memoirs,' vol. i., p. 143.

pages of the book with somewhat scornful curiosity, and after a hasty survey of its contents threw the volume on the floor, exclaiming as he did so, "That young man will ruin his fine political career if he persists in writing trash like this."[1] Houghton supplied Mr. Gladstone himself with a variant of this idea in a letter nearly thirty-five years later: 'My shrewd father called every book of mine a nail in my political coffin, and I well remember Sir Robert Peel's annoyance at your literary productions. "With such a career before him," he said, "why should he write books?"'[2] And in that connection, it is significant that in this January of 1839, when all the talk was of Mr. Gladstone's essay, Peel, writing to Ashley from Drayton, thanking him for calling attention to a *Quarterly* article upon 'Papal Usurpations and the Spirit of Popery,' took occasion to strongly deprecate the Oxford Movement.[3]

Bunsen, whose enthusiastic praises of the work have been given—and who later in the spring desired Abeken, his closest friend, to translate it into German, with a preface dedicated to the future William I. of Germany, from the pen of the diplomatist himself[4]—was evidently afraid that it might retard Mr. Gladstone's political advancement. On February 7th, he told his wife that, with Thomas Acland, one of the author's old Oxford companions, and just as ardent a supporter of the Church,[5] he had gone to see Mr. Glad-

Bunsen's prophecy.   stone, 'and was delighted with the man, who is some day to govern England, if his book is not in his way.' He added the singular phrase,

---

[1] Reid's 'Houghton,' vol. i., p. 316.   [2] *Ibid.*, vol. ii., p. 279.

[3] Hodder's 'Shaftesbury,' vol. i., p. 242.

[4] Bunsen's 'Memoir,' vol. i., p. 523.

[5] Eldest son of the Sir Thomas Acland previously mentioned, afterwards succeeding to the baronetcy, and father of Mr. Arthur Acland, Vice-President of the Council in Mr. Gladstone's fourth Cabinet.

'We are soon to meet *under four eyes*, which is the only way for becoming known to each other;' but the explanation was soon afforded. 'On Sunday [February 11th] I went at eleven with Gladstone to his parish church, after which we began our conference, closeted in his room. He said it had been his wish that I should be prevailed upon to write a book on the present state of the Church of Rome—if not of the whole Church. I answered that the first of a series of letters with which his work had inspired me, had exactly that title and import ; but I had rather begin with the second, the apostolical succession. This led to my *declaration of love* to him for having consciously thrown a stumbling-block in his own way as a statesman, and excited censure, because he came conscientiously to those consequences for which he was so violently attacked; and that I admired him (with permission for saying so), particularly as to the point on which I differed from him.' And then came an agreeable personal touch : ' At five minutes before three, he stopped me in order to introduce me to his father, who was pleased to hear from me what I was so happy to express to him about his admirable son. Then we went together to church, and heard a very good sermon from the Bishop of London [Blomfield] : then returned, and again had a conversation alone together.' One fruit of this was that two days later Bunsen could record : ' This morning I found a note from Gladstone, with three copies of his work. This man's humility and modesty make me ashamed ; I hope and trust I shall profit by it : but in his kindness I delight. He always speaks as if he had only to learn from me.' [1]

Within a week, Bunsen was endeavoured to be made an indirect assistant in the incubation of that historic review by

[1] Bunsen's ' Memoir,' vol. i., pp. 501-4.

Macaulay, mainly owing to which Mr. Gladstone's 'Church
and State' is now more than a name to the English-speaking
world.   While the younger man had been in Rome during

December, 1838.
Macaulay first meets
Mr. Gladstone. the winter, Macaulay had seen him.   'On
Christmas eve,' he wrote home, 'I found
Gladstone in the throng, and I accosted
him ; as we had met, though we had never been introduced
to each other.   He received my advances with very great
empressement indeed, and we had a good deal of pleasant
talk.' [1]   Within a very few days of his return to London, in
the first week in February, he bought a copy of the second
edition of the book, and at once saw the opening for a

February, 1839.
Determines to review
the book. telling review.   'A capital shrovetide cock
to throw at,' he exclaimed in his diary ;
'almost too good a mark.'   This, it is well
to note, was his opinion after a glance at the work, for it
was not for another five days that he could say, 'I read,
while walking, a good deal of Gladstone's book.'   'The
Lord,' he went on, 'hath delivered him into our hand.   I
think I see my way to a popular, and at the same time
gentlemanlike, critique.'   And he closed the day's entry
with 'Home, and thought about Gladstone.   In two or
three days I shall have the whole in my head, and then my
pen will go like fire.' [2]   This was on February 13th, and it
may be taken that he immediately arranged with Macvey
Napier, the then editor of the *Edinburgh*, to furnish the review, for a week later Bunsen was telling his wife of a breakfast
at Henry Hallam's, at which he sat between the host and
Macaulay, 'who is the Demosthenes and Cicero of the
Whigs.'   'The conversation was very lively and instructive;
after breakfast its course was turned to what is now in

[1] Trevelyan's 'Macaulay,' p. 367.
[2] *Ibid.*, pp. 373, 374.

everybody's mind—the Church. It was evident that Macaulay is writing the article in the "Edinburgh" on Gladstone's book; he spoke with all the power of his mind (or rather *esprit*) on the subject. They wanted to draw me into the debate, but I slyly departed, not wanting to tell them all I knew on the matter, and desiring neither to give them arms against my friends, nor to withhold my opinion.'[1]

Macaulay was speedily at work on his article; and on February 26th he promised it to Napier 'in a week or ten days at furthest. Of its length I cannot speak with certainty. I should think it would fill about forty pages;[2] but I find the subject grow on me. I think that I shall dispose completely of Gladstone's theory. I wish that I could see my way clearly to a good counter theory; but I catch only glimpses here and there of what I take to be truth.' The touch of diffidence in this confession is not made the less pleasant by a subsequent portion of the same letter : ' By the bye, I met Gladstone at Rome. We talked and walked together in St. Peter's during the best part of an afternoon. He is both a clever and an amiable man.' Napier was delighted with the review, and, in sending its writer the proofs, 'he magnified the article prodigiously.' 'In a letter to Empson,' Macaulay told his sister, 'he calls it exquisite and admirable, and to me he writes that it is the finest piece of logic that ever was printed. I do not think it so; but I do think that I have disposed of all Gladstone's theories unanswerably ; and there is not a line of the paper which even so strict a judge as Sir Robert Inglis, or my Uncle Babington, could quarrel at as at all indecorous.'[3]

[1] Bunsen's ' Memoir,' vol. i., p. 507.
[2] It filled just 50 pages.
[3] Trevelyan's ' Macaulay,' pp. 374, 375.

The essay is too well-known to need even a summary. Mr. Gladstone himself, writing in 1868, ex-

Macaulay's review. pressed the belief that the book had lived until then only because of this 'vigorous and brilliant, though not (in my opinion) entirely faithful picture;' [1] and, although that would be as true now, it is probable that even Macaulay's striking attack would not have been so widely remembered if it had not been for his description of the author, since quoted on ten thousand platforms and in a myriad leading articles, as 'the rising hope of those stern and unbending Tories, who follow, reluctantly and mutinously, a leader [Peel] whose experience and eloquence are indispensable to them, but whose cautious temper and moderate opinions they abhor.' It was, indeed, as 'a young man of unblemished character, and of distinguished parliamentary talents . . . [whose] abilities and demeanour have obtained for him the respect and good-will of all parties . . . [and] who is rising to eminence in the House of Commons' that Macaulay treated the author; and the closing sentences were chivalry itself. 'We have done; and nothing remains but that we part from Mr. Gladstone with the courtesy of antagonists who bear no malice. We dissent from his opinions, but we admire his talents; we respect his integrity and benevolence; and we hope that he will not suffer political avocations so entirely to engross him as to leave him no leisure for literature and philosophy.' [2]

This review in the *Edinburgh* was at once the talk of the town; and on April 16th Bunsen informed his wife that 'you and mamma ought to get the "Edinburgh" and "Quarterly Reviews" of March—the former contains Macaulay's article

---

[1] 'A Chapter of Autobiography,' sec. 12.

[2] *Edinburgh Review*, April, 1839; pp. 231-80.

on Gladstone—contradictory, but very respectful : Gladstone has written him a note of thanks.'[1] That, indeed,
Mr. Gladstone had done a few days previously, and in a
letter with which Macaulay was so pleased that he kept it
unburned, 'a compliment,' says his biographer, Sir George
Trevelyan, 'which, except in this single instance, he never
paid to any of his correspondents.' The letter thus distinguished, written on April 10th, offered the essayist very
cordial thanks for his review. 'In whatever you write,'
said Mr. Gladstone, 'you can hardly hope for the privilege
of most anonymous productions, a real con- Mr Gladstone
cealment; but, if it had been possible not thanks Macaulay.
to recognise you, I should have questioned your authorship
in this particular case, because the candour and single-
mindedness which it exhibits are, in one who has long been
connected in the most distinguished manner with political
party, so rare as to be almost incredible . . . In these
lacerating times one clings to everything of personal kindness in the past, to husband it for the future ; and, if you
will allow me, I shall earnestly desire to carry with me such
a recollection of your mode of dealing with a subject upon
which the attainment of truth, we shall agree, so materially
depends upon the temper in which the search for it is
instituted and conducted.' And Macaulay's reply was
equally full of warmth. 'I have very seldom,' the essayist
told Mr. Gladstone, 'been more gratified than by the very
kind note which I have just received from you. Your book
itself, and everything that I heard about you, though almost
all my information came—to the honour, I must say, of our
troubled times—from people very strongly Macaulay's acknow-
opposed to you in politics, led me to re- ledgment.
gard you with respect and good-will, and I am truly glad

[1] Bunsen's 'Memoir,' vol. i., p. 519.

that I have succeeded in marking those feelings. I was half afraid, when I read myself over again in print, that the button, as is too common in controversial fencing even between friends, had once or twice come off the foil.' [1]

So shrewd an observer as John Sterling was somewhat unfavourably impressed with the *Edinburgh* essay. ' I suppose,' he wrote in May to Trench, 'you have read Macaulay's article, and probably consider it, as I do, the assault of an equipped and practised sophist against a crude young Platonist, who happens by mere accident to have been taught the hard and broken dialect of Aristotle rather than the deep, continuous, and musical flow of his true and ultimate master.' [2] Sterling, as has been noted, had a high opinion of the young author. Just before his letter to Trench, he had called upon him, in company with Bunsen; and, while he thought the German to be one whom he could not but like and gain information from, he considered Mr. Gladstone, though possessed of far less knowledge and speculative insight, a man of nobler type. It may be that a consciousness of this on the part of the former accounts for there being no mention of this meeting, or indeed of Sterling at all, in Bunsen's ' Memoir.'

Sterling's opinion of Macaulay's review.

It was not until the following December that the *Quarterly Review* noticed the work; and then, from the pen of the Rev. William Sewell, it devoted no fewer than fifty-six pages to the third edition. Like the rest of the published criticisms, this commenced with personal eulogy. ' If Mr. Gladstone were an ordinary character, we should be inclined to speak most strongly of the singular vigour, depth of thought, and eloquence, which he has displayed in his

*December.
The Quarterly reviews the book.*

[1] Trevelyan's ' Macaulay,' pp. 375, 376.
[2] Trench's ' Letters, etc.,' vol. i., p. 237.

essay. But he is evidently not an ordinary character . . . and the highest compliment which we can pay him is to show that we believe him to be what a statesman and philosopher should be—indifferent to his own reputation for talents, and only anxious for truth and right.' After compliment, criticism. 'When Mr. Gladstone has written more on these subjects—as it is to be hoped he will—he will write with greater ease and clearness. At present his language is the natural expression of a high-toned and powerful mind labouring to reach a truth deeply felt, but indistinctly discerned, through a complication of popular errors. Men cannot carry on a resolute struggle against sophistry with the same smoothness and simplicity with which they enunciate truisms. And perhaps even the occasional obscurity of his style may do good, if it compel those who read, and, still more, those who propose to apply his theory, to examine it very carefully before they pretend to understand it.' 'Even if he stood alone,' exclaimed the reviewer, 'yet with his talent and position in the country, this movement to escape from the low ethics of the eighteenth and nineteenth centuries would be of great importance.' And then the article went on to deal, from a Tory and High Church standpoint, with the various phases of the argument for a State recognition of the Church, and to conclude with a violent denunciation of the Whig Ministers.

For the *British Critic*, Newman, its editor, asked Hope to do the review; but, from considerations both of health and occupation, the latter declined, recommending, however, that no one should undertake it without having read Coleridge's 'Church and State,' 'a work which has evidently had a great deal to do with Gladstone's fundamental ideas of the subject, and to which I am disposed to impute the

adoption of at least one of his views from which I dissent.'[1]
This letter was dated March 1st; but it was not until the
October number of the magazine that a review of the third
edition from the pen of Keble appeared, this extending to
forty-two pages. 'Here,' Keble exclaimed, 'we have no village theoriser, no cloistered alarmist, but a public man, and a
Keble's review in the man of the world, a statesman of the highest
British Critic.   talent for business, an orator who commands the ear of the House of Commons; so deeply
impressed with the perils of our Church's position at this
moment, that he makes time to develop and express his
views, deep and manifold, and brought out with serious
labour, of the very sacred nature of her connection with the
State; if haply he may lead any to think earnestly of it, who
have hitherto treated it as a mere party question.' And,
notwithstanding that 'we find him writing in a tone, not
indeed of despondency, but of very deep and serious
alarm; not as one who gave up the defence of a place, but
as one who thought the time was coming for making a last
effort, and calling out those who would not shrink from a
forlorn hope': despite this, 'Mr. Gladstone's publication is
most encouraging from the earnest it gives us that even in
high places of the State there are those who never will for-
sake the City of God, and still more from the rare and
noble specimen which it exhibits of what sound religious
(in which term we include sound ecclesiastical) principles
can do for a person in the most dangerous walks of life:
how neither political nor intellectual importance can mar
the freshness, the simplicity, the generosity, and (more
than all, for it lies at the root of all) the reverential spirit,
with which the Church's true scholars enter on these high
and delicate practical discussions.'

[1] Hope-Scott's ' Memoirs,' vol. i., pp. 169, 170

But, notwithstanding 'the uncompromising desire which Mr. Gladstone evidently feels to stand in all events irrevocably committed to the cause of primitive truth and order,' Keble was of opinion that there was in his reasonings 'an unconscious tinge, we will not say of Erastianism, but of State as distinct from Church policy.' His theory, in fact, 'seems hardly to come up to our own view of the relations of Church and State ;' he 'has not been quite able to keep his language clear of a certain utilitarian tone ;' and, as to some of his statements, 'we wish it to be well considered, how they appear when placed side by side with certain clear injunctions of our Saviour, as explained by the recorded practice of his Apostles.' And, therefore, though Mr. Gladstone was referred to as 'the Christian statesman,' 'the high-minded writer,' and 'the excellent author,' his argument described as clear and his style as condensed— compliments concerning argument and style which Macaulay would not have endorsed—the review was somewhat grudging as to the merit of his reasonings : one of these was desired, 'on the whole,' to have been 'so expressed as to give less encouragement to the enemies of Christian discipline ;' in another his wish was declared to have been father to his thoughts ; while, concerning a third, it was bluntly said, 'we confess ourselves unable to comprehend this line of argument.' Close upon thirty years later, when Keble had passed away and Mr. Gladstone was called to the Premiership for the express purpose of disestablishing and disendowing the Irish Church, this review was reprinted in pamphlet form with a preface by Liddon, Pusey's greatest disciple. Mr. Gladstone had asserted the acknowledgment by Keble of the justice of such a disestablishment ; [1]

[1] 'A Chapter of Autobiography,' p. 52, note ‡.

Newman had corroborated this; [1] but Liddon, considering the assertion, in its naked form, to be too unqualified to convey a true impression of Keble's general mind on the subject, exhumed the review, pointing out that its author was nearer to Mr. Gladstone's later position on the subject than, at the time of its writing, was Mr. Gladstone himself.

Perhaps the only completely ungrudging notice of the work appeared in the *British Magazine*, a Tractarian monthly, which had been edited by Hugh James Rose, and which in its issue of February, 1839, said: 'It will be curious if, after all the books which have been written by our divines on the connexion between the church and state, we should be indebted for the soundest work on that important subject to a layman. Yet this seems likely to be the case. Admirably as the nature and constitution of the church have been discussed by the great Anglican writers, the relations in which our church stands to the state have hitherto been examined only superficially and upon false principles. Mr. Gladstone has entered upon a subject which has long been the prey of ignorance and error. He has communicated a large quantity of most valuable information. And it is a matter for sincere thankfulness to find that the Church has such an accomplished advocate in the branch of the legislature which has shewn itself least disposed to treat her with favour.' [2]

February.
The *British Magazine's* notice.

There was at that time struggling through a twelve-month's existence in the constituency Mr Gladstone represented, an ambitious little literary magazine, the *Newark Bee*, the bulk of which was written by the Rev. S. Reynolds Hole; and its very last

Reviewed in the *Newark Bee*.

[1] J. T. Coleridge's 'Life of Keble,' p. 518.
[2] *British Magazine and Monthly Register*, vol. xv., pp. 203, 204.

number, published the month after the issue of 'The State in its Relations with the Church,' contained a review of the work. This was cast in the form which had been made popular by 'Christopher North,' and it formed the second of 'Noctes Apianæ,' participated in by a set of somewhat dull puppets, labelled the Editor, Clericus, and Reformator. In the opinion of Clericus, the work, 'the first offering of a mighty mind to its parent university, written by our member, Mr. Gladstone, a student and a statesman, distinguished for his learning, his principle, and his worth,' was 'not only a credit and an ornament to the literature of the age, shining like a star through the gloom which so long has darkened over our intellectual world, but is calculated to be a means of the highest advantage to our community.' Reformator pooh-poohed this enthusiasm, for he had been 'told, in the first place, that the work is a paradox, and unintelligible throughout; and, in the next, that its author is a Puseyite, double-distilled.' To which the Editor solemnly rejoined : 'They who tell you that the book is unintelligible, pay a sorry compliment to their own capacity ; yet yours is by no means an isolated case. Every one is *told* that the work is a failure, but I have scarcely met an individual who has really read it.'

Among the most interesting of the contemporary references was not that of either friend or reviewer, but of Carlyle to Emerson in a letter of the February after the book appeared. Mr. Gladstone had quoted 'a striking and almost an indignant' argument from an oration 'delivered by Mr. Emerson, an American, at an American Cambridge ;' and Carlyle wrote to his friend : 'One of the strangest things about these New England Orations is a fact I have heard, but not yet seen, that a certain W. Gladstone, an Oxford crack Scholar, Tory

Carlyle's Opinion.

M.P., and devout Churchman, of great talent and hope, has contrived to insert a piece of you (*first* Oration it must be [1]) in a work of his on *Church and State,* which makes some figure at present! I know him for a solid, serious, silent-minded man; but how, with his Coleridge Shovel-Hattism, he has contrived to relate himself to *you,* there is the mystery. True men of all creeds, it *would* seem, *are* Brothers.' [2]

Of all commentators upon the book, none evinced a more decided disbelief in its theory than the Duke of Sussex, an uncle of Queen Victoria. The youngest son of George III., unlike his brothers, and especially those of Cumberland and York, was a pronounced Whig in politics, while he was a sympathiser with Hampden in religion;[3] and his views, therefore, were widely separated from those of a High Church Tory.[4] Possessing himself of a copy of the first edition, now to be seen in the British Museum, he not merely read it with care but made frequent marginal notes. Some of these resemble in ejaculatory commonplace the pencillings on novels in a circulating library, but others are sufficiently shrewd. In the very first he hit the cardinal defect of the book—that it lacked definition—for, appended to Mr. Gladstone's assertion, 'We know of no effectual preservative principle [for the State] except religion; nor of any permanent, secure, and authenticated religion, but in the

Comments of the Duke of Sussex.

---

[1] This surmise was correct; the quotation, given on p. 30 of 'Church and State,' was from 'The American Scholar,' an oration delivered before the Phi Beta Kappa Society, at Cambridge (U.S.), August 31, 1837.

[2] 'The Correspondence of Carlyle and Emerson,' vol. i., pp. 217, 218.

[3] 'Memorials of Bishop Hampden,' p. 81.

[4] It may be noted that Wilde, Mr. Gladstone's colleague at Newark, married some years later a daughter of Sussex.

church,' was the query, 'What means the word Church?' Similarly, when the author observed, 'Governments are by "dutiful necessity" cognizant of religious truth and false-hood, and bound to the maintenance and propagation of the former,' Sussex wrote: 'I doubt the Position. Government is bound only to the preservation of Peace, and in as much as this is likely to be broken or disturbed It is called upon to interfere.' And when Mr. Gladstone went on to argue that 'toleration promotes truth; but *exclusion* may perhaps be defended where disaffection happens to be connected with certain religious distinctions,' the duke pertinently asked, 'Who is the fair and impartial Judge on this Point?' the same idea being embodied in his note, after Mr. Gladstone had quoted Coleridge's lectures on Church establishments in favour of a Church of one given denomination, 'The Principle is decidedly one of Persecution, and not admissible in the present State of Society.'

A touch of special interest in these annotations is given where Mr. Gladstone had quoted, as an argument in favour of one of his propositions, the fact that in Saxony the Royal Family was Roman Catholic while the nation was Lutheran, and Sussex remarked, 'The Royal Family of Saxony changed their religion from Protestant to Catholic for the sake of becoming Kings of Poland.' The Duke's own view was the broadest of the broad: 'Catholic,' he wrote on a page in which Mr. Gladstone, in defining the general doctrine em-bodied in the phrase 'Church and State,' referred to 'the Catholic church of Christ,' 'Catholic means universal, and therefore when talking of one division it is a sect or portion of a whole, and I believe the Church of England to be one of the smallest.' 'All this,' he admitted on another, 'is very proper and very true, but this is no proof of the necessity of a State Religion.' And on a third he asked, 'Is not God the God of all Nations, and of all religious Persuasions?' But the majority of the notes were critical rather than philosophic. 'What do you mean?' he queried, where Mr. Gladstone had referred to spiritual courts regulating spiritual causes, 'by the word Spiritual, for there is sad Confusion on that subject?' 'What right have you to assume this?' he asked, when the author had laid it down that 'there are men even among us who view religion, and especially State religion, as a deceit intended to tame and subdue the people.' And sprinkled over the pages are such notes as 'This is not the Reasoning either of a Philosopher or a Statesman'; 'This is begging the Question at issue by an assumption which I very much doubt'; and 'This is an Argument which demands much consideration as well as much discussion and argument, which the Author gets rid of by assuming it as a fact and then drawing his conclusion.' But enough has been quoted to indicate the bent of these hurried, and some of them almost illegible, criticisms.

It will have been gathered from a consideration of the leading reviews, as well as of the other contemporary comments, that no section of political or ecclesiastical thought was satisfied with Mr. Gladstone's book. All united in thanking him for addressing himself to so important a subject; all agreed that as a writer he was high-minded, and as a statesman promising; but Whig and Tory, Low Churchman and Puseyite alike had fault to find with his reasoning. If it went too far for Arnold, it did not go far enough for Keble; Peel liked it as little as Macaulay; political friends were even more outspoken in denunciation than political foes; and the fears of his intimates that Mr. Gladstone had prejudiced his

The book satisfies no party.

career by indiscreet outspokenness, seemed for the moment to have foundation.

That this might well have been concluded by the Tapers and the Tadpoles of politics may be taken from a parliamentary episode of the year after the book was published. Mr. Gladstone had been participating in a House of Commons discussion upon national education, yet to be described; and Russell, in reply, taunted him with the assertion that his writings The book used against him. made it clear that he objected to the religious liberties already established, and added that, while the member for Newark might take pride in victories won by burnishing up afresh the 'No Popery' cry, he would not succeed in reimposing the fetters which had been struck off. Peel, who immediately followed, was obviously annoyed at this introduction into debate of a book he disliked; and he told the House that he meant to confine himself rather to the discussion of the practical merits of the Ministerial proposal they were called upon to decide, than to consider whether the views advanced by Mr. Gladstone, or any other speculative opinions, were sound.[1]

It may fairly be assumed, however, that, with the fears of his friends and the rejoicings of his foes thus plainly before him, Mr. Gladstone would willingly have set against every risk of political check, the approval of his conscience. And he must have been strengthened by the testimony of the personal influence of his book upon his dearest friend, accorded by Hope after reading the last proof. 'The intercourse which I have had with you upon this occasion,' wrote Hope, 'and the tone of mind in which your work has been conceived, carried on, and finally prepared for the

---

[1] June 20, 1839 : ' Mirror of Parliament ' (1839), pp. 3185-88.

world, and which I have had an opportunity of considering more closely than my previous acquaintance with you had allowed, have given me feelings towards you which are Hope-Scott's opinion either not generally natural to me, or which of its author. have found few objects on which to rest, and I do not scruple to say that on looking forward into that confused and dangerous period upon which we appear to be entering there is no one upon whom I so much rely for guidance and encouragement, no one with whom I would so gladly act or suffer as yourself. . . . Whenever or wherever you may think that a willing labourer may be of use, you may reckon upon finding one in me ; and, should I grow careless or draw back, there is no service you can render me which can deserve half that gratitude which I shall owe to you for rousing me to a more consistent sense of my duty.'[1]   It was no ordinary character which, within a period of no more than six months, earned a testimony to personal power for good from George Selwyn, Samuel Wilberforce, and James Hope, and which was soon afterwards to receive proof, from so promising a politician as Cornewall Lewis, that his arguments were regarded in the regions of statesmanship as of weight.[2]   One who, before he had reached the age of thirty, could influence to higher things or broader views four such men as these might well be content to be for a moment misunderstood.

'Scarcely had my work issued from the press,' confessed Mr. Gladstone in later years, 'when I became aware that there was no party, no section of a party, no individual person probably in the House of Commons,

[1] Hope-Scott's 'Memoirs,' vol. i., pp. 166, 167.
[2] See G. C. Lewis' 'Essay on the Government of Dependencies,' edition of 1841, p. 278.

who was prepared to act upon it. I found myself
the last man on the sinking ship. Exclu-
sive support to the established religion Mr. Gladstone ac-
knowledges his soli-
tariness of opinion.
of the country, with a limited and local
exception for Scotland under the Treaty of Union with that
country, had been up to that time the actual rule of our
policy; the instances to the contrary being of equivocal
construction, and of infinitesimal amount. But the attempt
to give this rule a vitality, other than that of sufferance, was
an anachronism in time and in place. When I bid it live,
it was just about to die. It was really a quickened, and
not a deadened conscience in the country, which insisted
on enlarging the circle of State support, even while it tended
to restrain the range of political interference in religion.
The condition of our poor, of our criminals, of our military
and naval services, and the backward state of popular
education, forced on us a group of questions, before the
moral pressure of which the old rules properly gave way.'[1]

But, despite the knowledge that he was fighting for a
lost cause, Mr. Gladstone determined to persevere with the
endeavour to make his views understood. The lack of
clearness which even friendly commentators had found in
the book was perceived by himself; and, after three identical
editions had been printed, but the third not entirely disposed
of, he prepared a fourth and considerably
enlarged one. In the preface to this, dated 1841.
He publishes
a revised edition.
April 3rd, 1841, Mr. Gladstone observed
that, while not repenting his effort, he did repent its
numberless imperfections; and, being fully aware of ob-
scurities that required to be cleared up and omissions it
was needful to supply, he had given his best care and
labour to the task. The idea thus formally expressed to

[1] 'A Chapter of Autobiography,' sec. 26.

the world, was privately conveyed to the publisher. 'I am
not a fair judge of its merits even in comparison with the
original form of the work,' wrote Mr. Gladstone, 'but my
idea is, that it is less defective both in the theoretical
and in the historical development, and ought to be worth
the notice of those who deemed the earlier editions worth
their notice and purchase : that it would really put a reader
in possession of the view it was intended to convey, which
is more than can with any truth be said of its predecessors.'[1]
Yet, as the author himself subsequently said concerning
the publication of this edition of the book, 'all interest in
it had, even at that time, long gone by;'[2] and, if it had
not, the elaborations of the fourth edition were not calculated to sustain it.　Chapters were broken into more
chapters, sentences were involved in further involutions,
words were added where no one but the author would
have considered them to be required, and the whole effect
was to confuse still further the reader who turned to the
pages in search of light.　It illustrated once more the fact
that Mr. Gladstone's very desire to make his contentions
perfectly clear was a cause of stumbling.

Many things had contributed to draw public attention to
'The State in its Relations with the Church ;' but Mr.
Gladstone's next politico-theological work, published in
1840, was little noted by the public, and is now best known
in catalogues of second-hand books.　'Completed beneath
the shades of Hagley,' in August, 1840,
1840.
Writes another book 'and dedicated, in token of sincere affec-
on the Church,
tion, to the Lord Lyttelton,' by this time
his brother-in-law, 'Church Principles considered in their
Results' sought to set forth the bearings of particular

---

[1] April 6, 1842 : Smiles' 'John Murray,' vol. ii., p. 438.

[2] 'A Chapter of Autobiography,' sec. 12.

truths of religion with respect to the shifting circumstances of the world from time to time, and to the different degrees and modes in which those truths are apprehended. Mr. Gladstone attempted a representation of the doctrine of the visibility of the Church, the apostolical succession in the ministry, the authority of the Church in matters of faith, and the things signified in the sacraments; and he strove to show the practical results of these principles upon the relations of members of the Anglican Church with one another and with those of other communions. These varied points were discussed at great length, and the lesson was enforced with much copiousness of argument and illustration that, although the English Reformation, as tested by its results upon the national destinies, was open on certain points to animadversion, the historical identity of the Church was unbroken, and her principles were the specific barrier against Romanism. Permanence of the faith, comprehensiveness of communion, and liberty of thought were, Mr. Gladstone held, the conditions requisite for the general efficacy of Christianity; while, as a sentiment of the necessity for religious union was growing among serious persons, he saw no reason why the peculiar strengths of Romanism and Protestantism should not be combined, or anything in the Church of England to disqualify her from fully combining them.

But this utterance fell almost stillborn from the press. Macaulay's review had done much to give popular vogue to the earlier work, but none such was forthcoming for the later. This did not arise from want of will, for the essayist, a month before the new publication was which fails to attract issued, had written to the editor of the *Edin-* attention. *burgh Review*, 'Gladstone advertises another book about the Church. That subject belongs to me; particularly

as he will very probably say something concerning my
former article.'[1]   But, when he had read the work, he observed : 'I do not think it would be wise to review it.   I
observed in it very little that had any reference to politics,
and very little, indeed, that might not be consistently said
by a supporter of the Voluntary system.   It is, in truth, a
theological treatise, and I have no mind to engage in a con-

Macaulay declines troversy about the nature of the sacraments,
to review it.   the operation of holy orders, the visibility
of the Church, and such points of learning; except when
they are connected, as in his former work they were connected, with questions of government.   I have no disposition to split hairs about the spiritual reception of the body
and blood of Christ in the Eucharist, or about baptismal
regeneration.   I shall try to give you a paper on a very
different subject—Wycherley, and the other good-for-nothing
fellows, whose indecorous wit Leigh Hunt has edited.'[2]
And thus it was that to the *Edinburgh Review* for January,
1841, Macaulay contributed an essay, not on 'Church
Principles considered in their Results,' but that which
appears in his collected works on ' The Comic Dramatists
of the Restoration.'

The newspapers and magazines alike, indeed, steadily
ignored the book, with the exception of the *Spectator*,
which, though it had not noticed the earlier, gave a long
review of the later work.   In unconscious agreement with
Macaulay, it admitted that the volume placed the reviewer
in a difficulty, as the generic subject was scarcely fit for lay
discussion : yet the task had to be undertaken, not alone
because of the increasing prominence of the Oxford
Movement, but because ' Mr. Gladstone himself is not only

[1] Oct. 14, 1840 : Trevelyan's ' Macaulay,' p. 394.
[2] Nov. 13 : *Ibid.*, p. 395.

a rather distinguished Member of Parliament, and a sort of second hope of the religious party there, but he is also considered a rising man who is pretty certain of office on the accession of the Tories to the government : he is one, therefore, whose religious views have a more than theological interest, and may possibly produce heats and divisions in his party, and inconvenience in the state itself, should his conscience impel him to act upon his belief when he has the power.' The principles of the book were declared to be essentially Romish ; its author ' maintained precisely the same views which characterised the Romish clergy in the darkest ages ; ' and ' though every one will readily admit that Mr. Gladstone is well-meaning, we are afraid he must be pronounced weak - judging in this publication.' And, while it was allowed that ' the writer's meaning is for the most part clearly expressed,' ' the meaning itself might have been shorter and better.'[1]

The reception of the book even by personal friends was lukewarm. ' Mr. Gladstone's volume,' wrote Mahon to John Murray, ' has of late engaged much of my attention. It is difficult to feel quite free from partiality where so amiable and excellent a man is concerned ; but, if my friendship does not blind me, I should pronounce his production as marked by profound ecclesiastical learning, and eminent native ability. At the same time I must confess myself startled at some of his tenets ; his doctrine of Private Judgment especially seems to me a contradiction in terms, attempting to blend together the incompat- Mahon's opinion ible advantages of the Romanist and of the of it. Protestant principle upon that point."[2] Newman's criticism, conveyed in a letter to Frederic Rogers, was half-hearted

[1] *Spectator*, November 28, 1840.
[2] Dec. 7 : Smiles' ' John Murray,' vol. ii., p. 440.

and cold : 'Gladstone's book is not open to the objections I feared ; it is doctrinaire, and (I think) somewhat
self-confident, but it will do good.'[1]

The book, thus frigidly received by theological friends, was
cordially disliked by certain of Mr. Gladstone's ecclesiastical
opponents, Arnold, for instance, finding in

Arnold denounces it.

it 'incredible errors ; '[2] but Maurice was of
opinion that it was a better work than its predecessor.
Writing to Archdeacon Hare, he agreed 'as to the
ponderousness of Gladstone's style,' but he asked, 'is it not
very much improved since his last volume ?   It struck me
that it had become really grave and laden with earnest
thoughts ; not as before, oppressed with the phrases and
notions of the House of Commons and the Debating
Society.   His Aristotelianism is, however, it strikes me,
more deeply fixed in him than before, and, on that account,
I do not see how he can ever enter enough into the feeling
and truth of Rationalism to refute it.   His notion of attacking the Evangelicals by saying, "Press your opinions to
their results and they become rationalistic," is ingenious,
and wrought out, I think, with great skill and an analytical
power for which I had not given him credit ; but after all
it seems to me an argument which is fitter for the courts
than for a theological controversy.   The two sets of principles have evidently a different origin, and appeal to
different habits of mind ; how much better, then, to take
each upon its own ground and to show what each means
than to prove, ever so clearly, that some day or other they
will become identical.   I do not think men can be jostled
away from their standing-point by any such logic as this,

[1] Dec. 26 : Anna Mozley's 'Letters, etc., of Newman,' vol. ii., pp.
321, 322.

[2] Dec. 4 : Stanley's 'Arnold,' vol. ii., p. 233.

or, indeed, by any logic at all.'[1]   In the following spring, a more striking testimony to the divers feelings aroused by the work was given, for Charlotte Williams-Wynn (eldest daughter of Charles Wynn, a veteran member of the House of Commons, and sister of Mrs. Milnes-Gaskell), in telling Baron Varnhagen von Ense that Bunsen had written to Thomas Acland respecting the Tractarian doctrines, ' Your new faith seems to me to be Popery without infallibility, Catholicism without universality, Evangelism without spirituality, and Protestantism without liberty,' added, ' Their most dangerous tenet, however, seems to me to be that of mental reservation. . . . I hear [they] are very angry with Mr. Gladstone's book, and say, " Here are mysteries, which we never discuss but amongst ourselves, thrown open by a layman to be commented upon by every fool who can read." '[2]   Henry Alford, afterwards Dean of Canterbury, was, indeed, about the same time recording in his journal that he ought not to leave unread the contemporary publications touching the question of Church and State : ' Gladstone pleases me as much as any of the authors now writing ;'[3] but ' Church Principles ' proved far from a success.   It did not even bring its author the satisfaction of public attack ; and, fifteen months after its issue, it was his lot to suggest to Murray that it might be well to advertise it a little in order to revive the sale, though he took comfort from thinking that copies did not find their way much into the second-hand shops.[4]   They did in later days ; and with this record of partial failure the chapter of Mr. Gladstone's literary defence of the Establishment was closed.

[1] Dec. 28 : ' Life of F. D. Maurice,' vol. i., pp. 302, 303.

[2] March 4, 1841 : ' Memorials of Charlotte Williams-Wynn,' pp. 7, 8.

[3] ' Life, Journals, and Letters of Henry Alford, D.D.,' p. 133.

[4] April 6, 1842 : Smiles' ' John Murray,' vol. ii., p. 437.

XV.—EDUCATIONAL AND PHILANTHROPIC ENDEAVOUR.

FROM his earliest days in the House of Commons, Mr. Gladstone displayed special interest in the education of the people. It was a time when the voluntary system, imperfect as it was, seemed the only probable one to be permanently adopted, and when State aid was so obviously likely to be turned mainly to the advantage of the Church that it was strenuously objected to by an influential section of the Nonconformists. Two great organisations, the National Society for the Education of the Poor and the British and Foreign School Society (known also at that time as the Lancasterian Society) represented the respective voluntary efforts of the Church and what may be called Congregational Nonconformity, while the Roman Catholics and the Wesleyans had schools of their own. But, although it was long before it was clearly perceived that the education of a whole population was a task at once too large in itself and too important to the community to be left to the rival efforts of religious bodies, the feeling developed speedily after the Reformed Parliament had assembled that the existing system was incomplete, and that it needed strengthening though only, as was believed, at some trifling cost.

Mr. Gladstone and education.

Education had been the theme of Mr. Gladstone's maiden speech at the Eton Debating Society; and in his second parliamentary session, and in company with Peel and

Graham, Russell and Spring Rice, Morpeth and Roebuck, he was nominated upon a Select Committee to inquire into the existing state of the edu- cation of the people in England and Wales,

June 4, 1834. On an Education Committee.

the application and effects of the grant made in the previous year for the erection of schoolhouses, and the expediency of further grants. The committee sat for two months; but, after having examined several witnesses, and obtained information respecting the system then prevailing in the United Kingdom generally as well as in some foreign countries, it found that the lateness of the session prevented the completion of the inquiry. It, therefore, contented itself with reporting the evidence, adding a hope that the House would direct early in the next year a further prosecution of investigation upon a subject which it deemed of the highest national importance.[1] A new Parliament was elected before the recommendation could be carried out, but it was adopted during the brief-lived Peel Ministry; and the committee now included Grote and Bowring, Ashley and Lincoln, as well as Mr. Gladstone. Again, however, there was little ob-

March 3, 1835. The committee re-appointed

vious result, for once more, as August came round, the committee observed that, ' at the present late period of the Session, they find themselves unable to report their opinion to the House ; they will therefore content themselves with laying the Evidence before the House, with the Hope that the House will, early in the next Session, direct the further prosecution of the inquiry upon a subject of such high national importance.'[2] But this

but again proves abortive.

seemed like reducing the matter to a farce, and the recommendation was unattended to.

[1] ' Parliamentary Papers,' 1834, vol. ix.
[2] Ibid., 1835, vol. vii.

The reports of the proceedings before select committees
at that time did not show which members put questions to
witnesses, and, therefore, it is not possible to judge from
them the special part Mr. Gladstone took in these inquiries;
but as to his interest in the education question generally
during the earlier portion of his career there exists material
in proof.   Being convinced that to the question, 'Who is to
teach the nation with authority?' the answer was, 'The
Church,' he laboured to secure that the Establishment
should do worthy work in that direction.   This was especially shown, early in the new reign, in his association with
his friend Acland and some kindred spirits, including
Ashley, Sandon, Praed, and Henry Nelson Coleridge, to
assist in carrying on an educational work set on foot by
Gilbert Mathison in connection with the National Society.
A Committee of Inquiry and Correspondence was formed
to prepare plans to this end, the special objects being
(1) to establish training colleges for giving education to
schoolmasters instead of employing men of little learning ;
(2) to appoint inspectors under episcopal

<small>1837-38.
The Acland-Mathi-
son movement.</small> authority ; and (3) to found middle-class
or commercial schools on Church principles,
as a means of promotion for the masters of elementary
schools.   The founders of the movement worked hard :
they organised diocesan and archidiaconal boards with a
view to strengthening the united action of the Church as a
whole, and to secure its recognition as the teacher of the
nation, such lords-lieutenant of counties and mayors of
towns as were Churchmen (and most of them were) being
invited to join.   Mr. Gladstone threw special energy into
that portion of the work which would have made the
cathedral bodies more efficient in assisting education; while
Mathison, though his brain was for a time overtaxed,

raised, with Ashley's aid, various large sums to found St. Mark's College and training institutions, as well as to establish factory schools. A powerful stimulus was thus given to the work of education upon a Church basis; and in the spring of 1838, John Sterling could write to Trench, 'The best intelligence I have heard is that Mr. Gladstone has taken up zealously the task of improving the National School Society system, and has met with much support in a work which I regard as the most religious and patriotic any man can enter on.'[1]

Earlier in that same year Hook (afterwards Dean of Chichester, who had not then long been Vicar of Leeds) wrote to Mr. Gladstone : 'What we want in manufacturing towns is the appointment of some well-educated energetic man in each town to act as catechist-general under the clergy; and the National Society ought to be in fact what it is in theory, a grand normal school for the education of such persons. . . . In country parishes the present system, when properly acted upon, answers admirably; the clergyman superintending the schools and regularly catechising the children, the master is only required to direct the details of business, for which an inferior man will suffice.'[2]   The 'inferior man' point deserves the more note because Mr. Gladstone differed upon it from the majority of the clergy, who did not specially sympathise with that one of the objects of the Acland - Mathison movement which was to educate and elevate the schoolmasters.   But, before he could specially show this, there was much to be done.   Ireland had furnished the first fighting-ground for rival systems of national

Hook consults him on education.

[1] May 7, 1838 : Trench's 'Letters, etc.,' vol. i., p. 227.
[2] March 26, 1838 : W. R. W. Stephens' 'Life and Letters of Walter Farquhar Hook,' 7th ed., p. 285.

education; and in 1832, Stanley, while Chief Secretary in
the Whig Government of Grey, had introduced there an
unsectarian plan which provoked the bitter hostility of the
bigots, Protestant as well as Roman Catholic. It has been
seen how Mr. Gladstone, in his first session, obtained a
series of returns regarding the Irish Board of Education
which Stanley had established; and four years later, early
in the session of 1837, and in reply to continuous and
contumelious attacks from such rival ex-
tremists as M'Hale, the Roman Catholic
Archbishop of Tuam—O'Connell's 'Lion of
the Tribe of Judah'—and Philpotts, the Anglican Bishop
of Exeter, when the Melbourne Administration assented to
the appointment of a Commons' committee to inquire into
the progress and operation of the Irish plan, the member
for Newark was placed upon it in company with Stanley
himself, as well as with Spring Rice, Graham, Sandon,
Lord Leveson (afterwards one of Mr. Gladstone's most
faithful political friends and colleagues as the second Earl
Granville), and Sheil. Association in such a matter with
the distinguished Irishman last named could not but have
recalled to Mr. Gladstone their first meeting in private life
some two years before, for it was during that
earliest conversation that Sheil described, in
terms which left upon his most famous hearer an indelible
impression, the scene at an Irish election when 'the
colonels in black,' as he termed the priests, marshalled
the voters and led them on horseback to the poll.

Of these 'colonels in black,' something was heard during
the sittings of the committee, at which Mr. Gladstone was a
constant attendant and a frequent questioner. He was
particularly anxious to know whether the Irish Board of
Education considered that the Government ought to give

Marginal notes:
March 7, 1837.
Mr. Gladstone and
Irish education.

His acquaintance
with Sheil.

secular instruction where it could not religious; he was much interested by the account which the Protestant Dean of Ardagh told of the system of 'exclusive dealing' practised towards those Roman Catholics who had joined the Establishment; and he voted in *His work on the Irish Education Committee.* a small minority which favoured the calling of 'Henry of Exeter,' before the committee. But, after voluminous evidence had been taken, the course of the inquiry was broken by the sudden dissolution, and it was never resumed.[1]

Very soon, however, more tangible work was to be done in another direction; for, speedily after the new Parliament had assembled, a select committee of the Commons was ordered 'to consider the best means of providing useful Education for the Children of the Poorer Classes in large Towns throughout England and Wales.' As first nominated, *December. Upon an English Education Committee.* it included Peel and Ashley, Sandon and Stratford Canning, but not Mr. Gladstone, who with Philip Pusey, the Tory member for Berkshire, was added on December 12th, Acland being placed upon it in the following March. The member for Newark attended every day, except two, while the committee sat, it not concluding its labours until July; and some of his questionings remain of permanent interest. During the examination of James Phillips Kay, an Assistant Poor Law Commissioner,[2] who was a leading advocate of the Lancasterian or unsectarian system, and who was opposed to gratuitous instruction, Mr. Gladstone asked, 'Is your

[1] 'Parliamentary Papers,' 1837, vol. ix.

[2] Afterwards Sir James Kay - Shuttleworth, Secretary to the Committee of the Privy Council on Education, and father of Sir Ughtred Kay - Shuttleworth, Parliamentary Secretary to the Admiralty in Mr. Gladstone's fourth Administration.

reason for forming that opinion the idea that it may render
the parents less alive to the value of the means that may be
offered, than they would be if they were called upon to make
some payment?'—and this embodied a leading objection to
free education which prevailed for more than another fifty
years. One of the difficulties which then had to be faced
was the obtaining of competent and trained schoolmasters;
and Mr. Gladstone was insistent in his questions upon this
point. The supply, Kay said in answer to him, was
abundantly sufficient in quantity but not in quality, while

His opinion .
of Elementary
Schoolmasters,

the status of the schoolmaster was low. Mr.
Gladstone asked whether he meant that, in
addition to the extremely harassing nature of
the labour and the smallness of the stipend, the social position of the masters was very much lower than, with reference
to their character, it ought to be; and the reply was in the
affirmative. Henry Ashworth, of Bolton, one of Kay's colleagues in educational work, confirmed this statement; while
a clergyman, named Wigram, who was then Secretary of the
National Society, could compare them only with mechanics,
telling Mr. Gladstone that he thought they were generally
regarded by such as people who had a very comfortable
situation: 'they have so much time to themselves out of
school hours; they have more time at their own disposal
than any class of mechanics.' Wigram added to Sandon
that there was no losing caste in becoming a schoolmaster;
but Mr. Gladstone evidently thought this was very negative
praise, and, having received an affirmative reply to his
query, 'If the qualification of schoolmasters was made
higher, is it not to be expected that a still further increase
of reputation would follow?' he had another to the question, 'Should you not say that the greatest obstruction in
the way of extending popular education, in conjunction with

the National Church, is at this moment the difficulty of finding suitable schoolmasters?' And Mr. Gladstone indicated in further questions higher salaries as one means of obtaining better men and raising the schoolmaster's status.

Points regarding the religious instruction given in the schools necessarily occupied much of the committee's attention, and Henry Dunn, the Secretary of the British and Foreign School Society, was specially examined by Mr. Gladstone concerning them. Asked by the member for Newark whether he would entertain any objection to the Government giving grants to schools in which the Scriptures were not read, Dunn replied that he thought they should be read, although Roman Catholics *and of religious* and Jews ought to be exempted, adding, *instruction.* 'I cannot think that, under any circumstances, requiring the Scriptures to be read as the price of education can act beneficially.' But he accepted Mr. Gladstone's definition of his opinion that a man who did not believe in revelation had no fair plea to which the Government ought to defer against the introduction of the Scriptures into the schools. Concerning the glimmering of the earliest form of conscience clause in the workhouse schools and in the discretionary power of the National Society, only rarely exercised, exempting the children of Nonconformist parents from attending church as an equivalent for their being educated, Mr. Gladstone was also anxious for information; while he anticipated the ideas of to-day by his suggestive questions respecting the teaching of singing in schools.

When the report was drawn up, the committee unanimously agreed to declare that, in the metropolis and the large towns of England and Wales, there existed a great want of education among the children of the working

classes, and that means of daily education, within their
reach, ought to be provided for not less than one-eighth of
the population. It was further recommended that Government assistance to such schools, established on the principles
of either of the two rival societies, should be continued
and extended, but no other suggestion for meeting the
His action on the deficiency was made; and Mr. Gladstone
report. was one of a majority of five to four which
declined to suggest 'That it is desirable a Board or Office
of Education should be established under the control of
Parliament.' He also was in a majority which refused to
state 'That your Committee do not believe that the
difficulties attendant on the framing a general system of
Education for the children of the humbler classes (difficulties almost wholly arising from differences of religious
opinion) are such as the well-directed efforts of the Executive Government, under the sanction of the Legislature,
might not successfully remove.' As against the opposition
of Ashley and Acland, however, he secured that the
resolutions agreed to should be preceded by a short
statement of facts, and this summary is of distinct
value in the history of national education.[1] This report,
it may be noted, was agreed to on July 12th; and a fortnight
later Mr. Gladstone was nominated on another committee,
that being instructed to inquire into the state of education
July 27, 1838. in Scotland; but it took no evidence
On a Scotch Educa- owing to the late period of the session,
tion Committee. and, having called for some returns, recommended its own reappointment the next year,[2] a suggestion which was unattended to.

By this time, Mr. Gladstone was in the throes of preparing

[1] Parliamentary Papers, 1837-38, vol. vii., pp. 157-343.
[2] Ibid., pp. 437-51.

for publication his work on Church and State; but the seed he had sown was bearing fruit. Early in December, and while the member for Newark was in Rome, Samuel Wilberforce, in a letter to (Sir) Charles Anderson, observed: 'We are now very busy ordering a Diocesan Board for National Education after the notions of Acland, Wood, Gladstone, and all that party of young men who have been moving the subject in London. . . . It is, I believe, a vital question for the Church.'[1] *Wilberforce on Mr. Gladstone's educational work.* The future bishop was not alone in so thinking, for at the end of the same month Mrs. Austin, a woman keenly interested in the education question, thus described the movement to Victor Cousin, the French economist: 'There is a certain party of young men (clergymen and others), all Tories and High Churchmen, who have, it seems, had the sense to see that the schools of the National School Society (which as you know have long represented the bigoted party) are bad enough and ridiculous enough to discredit their supporters. From what I hear, they are going to try and reform the church schools, to insist upon better instruction, and to try and place them on a par with the best liberal schools; always retaining religion (Anglican of course) as the principal thing. These gentlemen appear to me to have faith in their religion, and not to be afraid of a little *Mrs. Austin's prophecy.* secular teaching. The man who is at the head of this movement is Mr. Gladstone, a Member of Parliament, who is regarded as the probable successor of Peel, i.e., the leader of the Tory party.'[2]

This letter was dated December 31st, 1838, just at the

[1] 'Life of S. Wilberforce,' vol. i., p. 130.

[2] Janet Ross' 'Three Generations of Englishwomen, vol. i., p. 125.

time that Macaulay was meeting Mr. Gladstone in Rome and was preparing to prophesy for him a like position; and the moment was one of anxiety to all his friends. 'Gladstone is on his way home,' wrote Newman to Frederic Rogers on January 22nd: 'Is he prepared for the tempest?'[1] Presumably he was, and, in any event, when nine days later with Charles Marriott, a well-known Tractarian clergyman of the time, as his travelling companion, he returned to London from the Continent, he not only found the controversy concerning his 'Church and State' in full blast, but he was invited to plunge at once into another discussion, involving both religious and political issues. On his table, when he came back, was a letter from Abraham Hayward—the busy writer and critic with whom he was afterwards so frequently to correspond—asking for information and assistance in Abraham Hayward's preparing an article upon the education request. question. To the application, which was a natural one seeing how earnestly Mr. Gladstone had applied himself to this theme before he left England, the member for Newark, replying two days after his return, observed : 'Six months of absence on the Continent have interrupted my acquaintance with the state of the measures respecting education which have been in progress among the members of the Church ; during the last spring and summer I was very much occupied about them, and in the course of a short time I hope to be *au courant* of their present state.'[2]

There was no lack of friendly suggestion to that end. 'I believe that he and I shall suit each other,' Mrs. Austin had told Cousin concerning Mr. Gladstone in the previous December; and, very soon after his return from the

[1] Anna Mozley's 'Letters, etc., of Newman,' vol. ii., p. 279.

[2] 'Correspondence of Abraham Hayward, Q.C.,' vol. i., p. 67.

Continent, she had asked him for some documents bearing upon his work on the National Society and in connection with diocesan training seminaries. 'Allow me,' he wrote in sending her the papers, 'to request your continued and, if possible, active interest in furtherance of these designs'; and she triumphantly replied that she had Mr. Gladstone's correspondence with Mrs. Austin. had the pleasure of making two inexorable Liberals waver, and at last confess that there was a great deal that was good in the scheme. But she sounded a needful warning: 'My fear is, my dear Mr. Gladstone, that your own earnest and, to me, affecting view of the duties and rights attached to the character of Christian teacher, leads you to over-estimate, and alas! greatly, the aid we have to expect from the clergy. Shall I say more?— that they will thwart you—not all, God forbid, but many.' An even more sagacious hint was later to come: 'With regard to the thing which makes the great clamour—the exclusion of the Dissidents—I think little of that; that is not your affair or the Church's. If the State gives money, that is another thing. It must give to all, and for all, from whose pockets it is taken. That is just.' And she emphasised the point that '*all* must be taught,' with a special plea for the education of girls.[1] This correspondence was supplemented by an interview; and Mrs. Austin, in immediately sending Cousin some information which Mr. Gladstone wished him to have, observed: 'I have seen young Gladstone, a distinguished Tory, who wants to re-establish education based on the Church in quite a Catholic form. He has, however, clear ideas, zeal and conscientiousness. We get on extremely well together.'[2]

[1] Letter of Mr. Gladstone, Feb. 16, 1839; letter of Mrs. Austin, Feb. 18: 'Three Generations of Englishwomen,' vol. i., pp. 127-9.

[2] *Ibid.*, pp. 129, 130.

It was, indeed, upon this question of national education that Mr. Gladstone's most striking speech of 1839 was delivered. He had not been home a fortnight, and Parliament had been opened only a week, when he commenced questioning the Government as to its plans. Russell had proposed that the annual grant of £20,000, which for the previous six years had been made by the State towards the promotion of education, should be raised by one-half, the money to be distributed by a Central Board, which in effect was to be an unpaid committee of the Privy Council. At first, even the extremest members of the Church party did not see reason to object; but, by the time an Order in Council had been drawn up to carry out the Ministerial plan, antagonism had commenced to be aroused among their adherents in the country; and, although the Cabinet threw overboard that part of their scheme which would have established a Normal School for the training of teachers, and which it was thought might possibly aid the Nonconformists, an attack along the whole line, led by Stanley and backed by the united strength of the Tory Opposition, was made upon the plan.

1839.
The new Ministerial plan of Education.

On the third night of the set debate in June, Mr. Gladstone rose. It was with reluctance that he did so, for, as he declared, he was profoundly impressed with the knowledge that the vital principles upon which the controversy of the moment turned were deep and abstruse principles of religion which could never be discussed in Parliament with advantage. But O'Connell (who, having immediately preceded him, had left the House as soon as his speech was ended) had challenged Mr. Gladstone in a question upon the authority of tradition; Morpeth, on the opening night, had taunted him with the principles advocated in his now famous book; and Charles Buller, on the second evening,

June 20.
Mr. Gladstone upon it.

had likewise brought that effort into the field. 'All will admit my candour, I trust,' Buller had said, 'in taking for the object of my attack the able work which has emanated from so respectable a source, and endeavouring to excite the reprehension of doctrines supported by a gentleman, of whom I cannot speak without congratulating him that he, almost alone of his age, has the fearless intrepidity to avow unpopular doctrines, and exhibits an intrepidity of logic, very little imitated by other gentlemen on the same side.'[1] Mr. Gladstone faced all his critics at once. To O'Connell's parade of statistics, he replied with an observation of Canning that he had a great aversion from hearing 'a fact' in debate, but that which he distrusted most was a figure. Morpeth received a hint that he had probably never been able to spare time to read the work he had attacked, and an avowal that its writer would not flinch from a word he had uttered or a syllable he had written upon religious topics. And to Buller's contention that Mr. Gladstone's doctrines, if pushed a step further, would lead of necessity to persecution, it was retorted that those of Buller destroyed the means of discerning between truth and falsehood, and would lead, if carried out to their next stage, to nothing less than national infidelity.

Mr. Gladstone turned from these personal aspects of the debate to a defence of the Wesleyan Methodists from an attack of O'Connell, because in this controversy they were supporting the Established Church. The Irish leader had taunted them with being inconsistent, and had told them they ought to return to the fold; and Mr. Gladstone exclaimed, 'I—who have always lamented their secession from the Church, and have always been of opinion that the fault was more on the side of those who caused that

[1] 'Mirror of Parliament' (1839), p. 3123.

secession than on the side of those who made it—join
His eulogy of the
Wesleyans. cordially in the hope that the union, so
unfortunately broken, will ere long be
resumed.' He went on to defend the Wesleyans from
O'Connell's further charge that they had been the most
persevering enemies of civil and religious liberty. ' It is,
indeed, extremely harsh and unjust to say that they have
never given proofs of their attachment to the enlarged
rights of humanity, after all their long years of exertion to
bring about the abolition of negro slavery. No sect has been
more prominent than they have been in pursuing to its
consummation that great object, nor have more assiduously
kept the interests of humanity in view, while they were
acting as vigilant guardians of all the best laws and interests
of society. It is unjust in the extreme to designate men
who have been most zealous and untiring in their exertions to obtain the liberty of the negroes, as parties
perseveringly, if not malignantly, hostile to freedom.'

From defence of the Wesleyans, the member for Newark
proceeded to a discussion of the general questions involved.
The Government had defined its intention as one to
secure 'an education in which religion is combined with the
whole manner of instruction, and is to regulate the whole
system of discipline.' These words Mr. Gladstone accepted
as satisfactory, but he held that, if the religion was to be
that of all forms indiscriminately, the principle was both
new and unconstitutional. If the State was to be regarded
The State and re-
ligious instruction. as having no other function than representing the mere will of the people as to re-
ligious tenets, the principle might be admitted, but not so
if the State was capable of duties and possessed a conscience. Warming to his work as he proceeded, Mr.
Gladstone asked to what the Government was bringing the

country. Russell threw in the answer, 'At least, not to bigotry and intolerance,' to which his young antagonist retorted, 'The noble lord would be more accurate if he said to latitudinarianism and atheism'; and Russell, replying later in the evening, admitted his interruption to have been somewhat irregular, though claiming that it represented not only what Mr. Gladstone had said but what he had written. The member for Newark having further condemned the Ministerial plan both in outline and detail, as being insidiously hostile to the Church and not agreeable even to the Dissenters themselves, described it in subsequent sentences as bad in principle, as polluting and desecrating to the commonwealth, as not even possessing the temporary and partial recommendation of popularity, and as being certain to excite greater indignation throughout the country than had been known for many years in the history of the Empire.[1]

Spring Rice, the Chancellor of the Exchequer, commenced his reply with a compliment. 'I differ from the honourable gentleman,' he observed, 'with the most entire respect, because I am perfectly sure that, whether as a writer or as a Member of Parliament, no individual comes forward with more frank avowals of what he believes to be right, and no one places his case on a higher or fairer basis —and I believe no one is more ready to expose himself to obloquy in maintaining *Spring Rice's compliment* his own opinions.' But after this tribute to Mr. Gladstone's courage, Spring Rice went on to denounce his principles as not only inconsistent with the English Constitution but with all received notions of civil and religious freedom. The contention that the State had a conscience and, like an individual, was not justified in propagating error, Spring

[1] *Ibid.*, pp. 3164-71.

Rice answered by touching Mr. Gladstone on the tender point of whether he would refuse the then annual vote for Maynooth.   He pressed the point further home by reminding the member for Newark that he once was Under-

and reply.   Secretary for the Colonies, and that in our possessions the State supported by grants of money not alone the Church of England but that of Scotland, the Lutherans, the Roman Catholics, and the Jews.   'What becomes of the State conscience now?' he asked amid triumphant shouts from the Whigs—'the State conscience bound only to disseminate truth?   The honourable gentleman says truth is single.   Which, then, of these various forms is the truth?   All cannot be the truth, and yet you support all.'   The final blow was to come.   Aberdeen, as Colonial Secretary in February, 1835, had endorsed a plan for the endowment of certain Roman Catholic clergy in New South Wales ; and the Chancellor of the Exchequer, with a second reminder that Mr. Gladstone was the Under-Secretary at the time, asked what became of the scruples of the State conscience on that occasion.[1]   Russell later in the debate, as has already been noted, brought in a further reference to the member for Newark's published writings, but Peel declined to continue that portion of the controversy ; and Stanley's motion, after all this heat, was defeated by no more than five votes.[2]

Mr. Gladstone's 'excellent speech,' as the *Times* called it the next day, was declared to be 'inimitable' by the *Standard*, and 'the best perhaps that ever even he delivered.'   The *Morning Herald* praised its 'singular power and eloquence,' and averred that in Spring Rice's 'attempt to answer the irresistible arguments,' there was considerable

[1] *Ibid.*, pp. 3171-74.
[2] The numbers were 280 to 275.

boldness but very slender success; and *John Bull* was even more enthusiastic: 'Mr. Gladstone, in a speech to the excellence of which no words of ours can do justice, not only overthrew all O'Connell's arguments, but exhibited the fallacy of his statistical illustrations in the most masterly manner.' Even the Whig organs forbore to denounce; and, while the *Globe* merely chuckled over Spring Rice's retort to 'the new apostle' on the State-conscience point, the *Morning Chronicle* declared that Peel, though wishing to avoid the inconvenience of appearing to agree with his young follower, 'means the very same thing that Mr. Gladstone means; but it is not his nature to go to work in the same direct manner.' The 'rising hope,' in fact, had by this time well-nigh risen.

Press opinions upon Mr. Gladstone's speech.

In the May, and before the great debate, Mrs. Austin had asked Mr. Gladstone to read the proofs of a reprint of a magazine article by her upon public instruction. She sought his advice because she looked with anxious expectation to him and the small knot of friends with whom he acted; and she pointed out that he would see in her work a sort of prophetic longing for that very movement in the Church which he had excited. In his reply, which was written on June 18th, Mr. Gladstone, though echoing Mrs. Austin's idea that her point of view upon the whole subject was different in a considerable degree from his own, observed: 'You are for pressing and urging the people to their profit against their inclination: so am I. You set little value upon all merely technical instruction, upon all that fails to touch the inner nature of man: so do I. And here I find ground of union broad and deep-laid, and I should indeed rejoice to see a portion of your benevolent energies lent, as I am sure they would freely be, to aid in the work of

Mr. Gladstone and Mrs. Austin's theories.

popular education within the bosom of the Church.   As to that subtle and ulterior question which respects the duty of the State at a moment when it seems to be losing in great measure the capacity and even the idea of duty properly so-called, I can tremble and hope, but little more. I more than doubt whether your idea, namely that of raising man to social sufficiency and morality, can be accomplished, except through the ancient religion of Christ ; or whether, overlooking what severs professing Christians, we can secure a residue such as shall produce an adequate effect upon the heart and affections of man ; or whether the principles of eclecticism are legitimately applicable to the Gospel ; or whether, if we find ourselves in a state of incapacity to work through the Church, we can remedy the defect by the adoption of principles contrary to hers.   On these questions, or forms of the same question, I am quite unable to fix myself in the affirmative conclusion.'

A personal reference of more than ordinary importance immediately followed and closed the letter : ' But indeed I am most unfit to pursue the subject ; private circumstances of no common interest are upon me, as I have His engagement become very recently engaged to be married to Miss Glynne, and I hope your recollections will enable you in some degree to excuse me.'[1] Miss Catherine Glynne, the lady here referred to, and who for more than fifty years has been known to the English people as Mrs. Gladstone, is the elder daughter of Sir to Miss Glynne. Stephen Richard Glynne, eighth baronet of Hawarden, who died when she was little more than an infant ; and they had been much in each other's company during the continental journey of the previous autumn.   Her sister, Mary, became betrothed

[1] ' Three Generations of Englishwomen,' vol. i., pp. 135-7.

about the same period to George, fourth Lord Lyttelton; and although, owing to the fact that an attack had been made by some Chartists upon Lyttelton's Worcestershire mansion at Hagley, there seemed a chance that the marriages might be postponed, it was determined to proceed with them on the date originally fixed, Thursday, July 25th. The bridegrooms had been staying in the district of Hawarden for some days, and on the Monday, with their *fiancées*, had attended a bazaar at Soughton Hall, in aid of the restoration of Northop Church. The Thursday found the whole neighbourhood early awake and actively rejoicing. Even at five in the morning the countryside was hastening to the wedding; cannon boomed and bells rang; flags and bridal favours were displayed on every house; the village was festooned with laurel; and the Hawarden Castle Lodge of Odd Fellows by parade with bands and banners added harmony and colour to the scene.

July 25.
The marriage.

The marriage procession from Hawarden Castle to the church was long and varied: Odd Fellows and members of temperance societies with 'tradesmen in large numbers' preceded the carriage of Sir Watkin Williams Wynn, the chariot of Lord Delamere, and the barouche of Lord Wenlock. In Lady Glynne's chaise rode four of the bridesmaids, including Mr. Gladstone's sister; then came Sir Stephen Glynne with his sisters, the two brides; Lord Lyttelton followed with his groomsman; Mr. Gladstone rode next with his father, while his eldest brother, Thomas, came later with Doyle; and the second brother, Robertson, with his wife, was also in the procession. At the crowded church, which was reached amid loud plaudits from the multitude outside, and the path to which was bestrewn with flowers, the wedding party was received with an anthem,

rendered by a choir of children; and Sir Stephen Glynne
led his elder sister to the altar rails, his brother, Henry,
attending the younger. The ceremony was performed by
Neville Grenville, Dean of Windsor, and uncle of the brides
—who, it may be recorded, wore peach-white satin dresses,
trimmed with Brussels flounces, and orange blossom
wreaths having a diamond in the centre; while the bridesmaids were attired in mulled muslin dresses, with trimmings
of blonde and peach colour, head-wreaths similar to the
brides, and crape lace bonnets. 'On quitting the church,'
said the *Chester Gazette*—the *Chester Courant* and the
Chester Chronicle vying in glowing description—'the

The local rejoicings.   marriage party passed through the clubs,
etc., which were ranged on each side, the
bands playing, the populace cheering, and many of the
poor weeping at beholding their generous benefactresses
leaving the scenes where they had so frequently stretched
out the hand of benevolence in relieving the widow and
fatherless.' After the wedding breakfast, Mr. and Mrs.
Gladstone went for the honeymoon to Norton Priory, the
Cheshire seat of Sir Richard Brooke, while Lord and Lady
Lyttelton proceeded in their travelling carriage to Hagley;
but their going did not end the festivities. There was a
dinner at the Glynne Arms, at which toasts to the happy
couples were enthusiastically drunk; every Hawarden
hostelry was opened wide for enjoyment; dancing was indulged in by the villagers until the night fell; and a display
of fireworks brought the day to a close. 'Never did a
wedding day pass off with greater *éclat*,' observed the
Gazette; and the recollection of it was made the sweeter
to the villagers by the fact that each bride, a few days
before the marriage, had given £100 to supply the neces-
sitous in their neighbourhood with clothing, while the

residents in the district subscribed about £120 for the poor in celebration of the event. And a more classical remembrance was embalmed a score of years later, when Lyttelton and Mr. Gladstone together published a volume of translations, and its dedication was in the words, 'Ex voto communi in memoriam duplicum nuptiarum, viii. kal., Aug. MDCCCXXXIX.'

Doyle, who was one of Mr. Gladstone's two groomsmen, has recorded that 'the occasion was a very interesting one, from the high character of the two bridegrooms, and the warmth of affection felt for the two charming young ladies by all their friends and neighbours in every rank of life. There was a depth and genuineness of sympathy diffused around, which, as the French say, spoke for itself without any words. Some verses of mine referring to this common sentiment . . . were welcomed at the time *Doyle's verses on* by the two families very kindly and plea- *the bride.* santly.'[1] These verses were addressed 'To Two Sister Brides, who were married on the same day;' and of them the following five stanzas were given to Mrs. Gladstone :—

> High hopes are thine, oh ! eldest flower,
>   Great duties to be greatly done ;
> To soothe, in many a toil-worn hour,
>   The noble heart which thou hast won.

> Covet not then the rest of those,
>   Who sleep through life unknown to fame ;
> Fate grants not passionless repose
>   To her, who weds a glorious name.

> He presses on through calm and storm
>   Unshaken, let what will betide ;
> *Thou* hast an office to perform,
>   To be his answering spirit bride.

[1] Doyle's ' Reminiscences,' pp. 279, 280.

> The path appointed for his feet,
>   Through desert wilds, and rocks may go,
> Where the eye looks in vain to greet
>   The gales, that from the waters blow.
>
> Be thou a balmy breeze to him,
>   A fountain singing at his side ;
> A star, whose light is never dim,
>   A pillar, to uphold and guide.[1]

In days long after, Doyle a little regretted his hearty praise of the politician-bridegroom ;[2] but second thoughts in poetry are not always the best.

A year later the first child of this union was born, and there is significance in the fact that the godfathers of

June 3, 1840. Mr. Gladstone's eldest son born. William Henry Gladstone (afterwards member for Chester, Whitby, and East Worcestershire, and who died in 1891) were Hope and Manning.   Of the close friendship existing between Mr. Gladstone and Hope, much has already been said : that between the former and Manning had been established even earlier.   They had been at Eton together, but it was at Oxford that, under the same private tutor and

Manning a godfather. in many ways brought into contact, their friendship began.[3]   In 1842, when Manning, then Archdeacon of Chichester, published his treatise upon ' The Unity of the Church,' it was to Mr. Gladstone that the work was ' affectionately inscribed ;' and this was one of the marks of a close and intimate connection which, with some necessary suspension after the future Cardinal-Archbishop of Westminster had joined the Roman Catholic

[1] Doyle's ' Miscellaneous Verses' (Edition of 1840), pp. 123, 124.
[2] Doyle's ' Reminiscences,' p. 280.
[3] A. W. Hutton's ' Cardinal Manning,' 1st edition, p. 148 *n*.

communion, was overcast only once, and that by the publication in 1874 of Mr. Gladstone's pamphlet on the Vatican Decrees.[1]

In the same year as Mr. Gladstone's eldest son was born, his brother-in-law, Lyttelton, though only twenty-three, was nominated for the position of High Steward of Cambridge University. His Churchmanship was the main ground for supporting him, but his Conservatism was of too mild a type to please the more extreme members of the party, who put forward Lyndhurst. The former was denounced as a 'Baby Lord,' a 'Lad Lieutenant,' an 'unfledged School-boy,' and a 'Petticoat Pet';   Lord Lyttelton. and, though heartily aided by the younger clergy, he was defeated—a defeat which was celebrated, rather than commiserated, by Lord John Manners (in the next year Mr. Gladstone's colleague for Newark, and many years later seventh Duke of Rutland, but then only known as the poet of the 'Young England' school), in a sonnet which apostrophised Lyttelton as 'Young heir of gentle glory!'[2] From a purely party point of view, this result was justified for the Tories by Lyttelton's subsequent development, as he became a Peelite and ultimately a Liberal—'moderate, from his balanced mind, but never lukewarm,' as Mr. Gladstone observed after his brother-in-law's death.[3]   They had

---

[1] Letter of Archbishop Manning to the *New York Herald*, dated Nov. 10, 1874.

[2] Lord John Manners' 'England's Trust, and other Poems,' p. 90.

[3] Biographical sketch in the *Guardian*, April 26, 1876. Lyttelton's opinion of Mr. Gladstone was expressed in an address at the opening of a Working Men's Industrial Exhibition at Birmingham in 1865. He had noted that Newman, in the 'Apologia,' had said that the contemplation of the vast material progress of the age was to him a simple bewilderment, and he set against this the spectacle of Mr. Gladstone, 'that great statesman, with whom you will not wonder that it is a

been associated, it may be noted, in the spring of this same
year, in what must have proved a specially interesting
function to both, for they were the examiners at Eton in the
April for the Newcastle scholarship, founded by the member

for Newark's political patron.   Lyttelton

himself had been the Newcastle medallist
ten years before ; and *John Bull* could well
observe that ' the presence of such superior examiners very
naturally added additional interest to the examinations.'
The prize was awarded to a youth named Seymour, but Mr.
Gladstone had keen pleasure in giving the medal to a
younger brother of his lost friend, Arthur Hallam ; while
not less noteworthy were some of the other names in the
list of twelve who, in the opinion of the examiners, had
distinguished themselves by their scholar-like attainments.
It was a list that included John Fielder Mackarness, afterwards for a time chaplain to Lyttelton, and nominated
Bishop of Oxford in Mr. Gladstone's first Administration ;
and Henry James Coleridge, younger brother of the
Coleridge who was later to be Solicitor and Attorney-
General, and Lord Chief Justice of the Common Pleas
and of England ; while the names of Farrer, Milman, and
Thring suggest associations of mark in politics, theology,
and finance.

Mr. Gladstone's interest in all matters affecting education
was further shown, not only by his efforts, commencing in
1840, and yet to be described, to establish Trinity College,
Glenalmond, but by his acceptance, in 1838, of a membership of the Council of King's College, London, a

main pride of my life to be so closely connected,' working with a cheerful and a pure conscience to the stimulation and facilitation of the pro-
ducts of labour among us, to the increase of our material wealth : Lord
Lyttelton's ' Ephemera,' 2nd series, p. 221.

distinctively Church of England institution ; and in this position he was able two years later, in company with Inglis, to render warm assistance to the election of Maurice as Professor of Divinity.[1] In another thirteen years, when Maurice was dismissed by the Council be- Mr. Gladstone and cause of certain theological views he had King's College. developed, Mr. Gladstone, though not agreeing with these, gave his old college friend much help, in his determination to see fair play, and unsuccessfully moved an amendment in his favour at the critical meeting;[2] while, curiously enough, he once more stepped forward, and with like lack of success, to act the part of a mediator in a somewhat similar dispute over the dismissal of Dr. Momerie from the Professorship of Logic and Metaphysics in 1889.[3]

What may also from certain points of view be regarded as an educational service which Mr. Gladstone rendered to the public apart from politics in his earlier period, was the hearty support he gave to the efforts, led by Serjeant Talfourd, to place the law of copyright upon a satisfactory basis. In 1814, after various tinkerings with the statutes bearing upon this subject, the legislature had fixed the term of copyright at twenty-eight years for the author and his assigns and for the author's life if he longer survived. But this period was obviously not of sufficient duration to secure to writers the best fruit of their The Copyright labour; just at the period of Queen Victoria's Question. accession the hardships especially involved to the family of the not-long-dead Scott and the possible hardships to that of the still-living Southey, were plainly before the world ; and Talfourd, then representing Reading, introduced in the

[1] ‘ Life of F. D. Maurice,’ vol. i., p. 283.

[2] Letter of Mr. Gladstone to Lyttelton, Oct. 29, 1853 : *Ibid.*, vol. ii., pp. 194-6 ; and see ‘ Life of S. Wilberforce,’ vol. ii., pp. 215, 216.

[3] *Contemporary Review* for April, 1891, pp. 573-8.

session of 1838 a Bill on the subject. He had written to
Wordsworth on March 21st that 'the booksellers threaten
me with a very strong opposition—and the doctrinaire
party are inclined to support them ;—so that we must
muster all our strength': and the poet despatched without
delay a letter to Mr. Gladstone, reminding him that the
second reading of the Bill stood for April 11th, incidentally
describing the booksellers as 'rapacious creatures,' and inviting his correspondent to Rydal Mount.

Mr. Gladstone, replying on March 26th,
the day he received the note, said : 'I am
firm and staunch in support of Talfourd's Bill, and I confidently hope we shall be able to carry him through. It
may not be able to save our literature permanently, but its
tendency is that way, and this should be enough. A ground
not less strong I certainly recognise in the anomaly now existing, and the extreme disadvantage at which literary
property stands, as compared with other and meaner kinds.'
And he added the interesting fact : 'This morning I had
the pleasure of seeing Mr. Southey for the
first time at Miss Fenwick's, which I owe
to Taylor; I have not yet forgotten the obligation he imposed on me by making me known to yourself.' [1]

*Mr. Gladstone in-
vited by Wordsworth
to assist Talfourd.*

*His first meeting
with Southey*

It is incumbent at this point to turn aside and to note the
friendship between the veteran poet and the rising politician.
If the memory is to be trusted of one who told Charles
Wordsworth he was present on the occasion and most distinctly remembered the circumstances, the earliest connection between Mr. Gladstone and the poet was singular.
Towards the end of 1832, according to this
anecdote, John Gladstone was dining at the
house of a Liverpool merchant, named Boiton, and in the

and Wordsworth.

[1] Knight's 'Wordsworth,' vol. iii., pp. 329, 330.

company was Charles Wordsworth's uncle, the poet. 'After dinner, my uncle took occasion to congratulate Mr. John Gladstone on the remarkable success of his son William at Oxford, and added an expression of hope and anticipation that he would be equally successful in the House of Commons ; to which the father replied, "Yes, sir, I thank you; my son has certainly distinguished himself greatly at the University, and I trust he will continue to do so when he enters public life ; for there is no doubt he is a young man of very great *ability*, but," he added, "he has no *stability*."[1]   Whatever of truth there may be in a story which, from the circumstances of the moment of which it is told, lacks likelihood, it is certain, from various references in the *Eton Miscellany*, that Mr. Gladstone was interested, though not over-impressed, even in boyhood, in Wordsworth and 'the Lake School ;' while ' Wordsworth used to come to me when I lived as a young man in the Albany,' he wrote many years later, 'and my recollections of him are very pleasing.   His simplicity, kindness, and freedom from the worldly type, mark their general character;'[2] and Doyle has recorded that it was at his friend's breakfasts in the Albany that he was first presented to Wordsworth : 'the great poet sat in state, surrounded by young and enthusiastic admirers.   His conversation was very like the " Excursion " turned into vigorous prose.'[3] Breakfasts were more popular then than now as a means for promoting an interchange of ideas, but Mr. Mr. Gladstone's Gladstone throughout life retained his taste breakfasts. for giving them.   Wilberforce more than once noted them ;[4] Mr. Sidney Cooper, the veteran animal painter, enjoyed

[1] Charles Wordsworth's ' Chapter of Autobiography,' p. 53.

[2] Knight's 'Wordsworth,' p. 355.

[3] Doyle's ' Reminiscences,' p. 164.

[4] *E.g.*, ' Life of S. Wilberforce,' vol. iii., pp. 16, 22.

them;[1] and, when Mr. Gladstone was Prime Minister for the first time, Dickens, only about a month before he died, breakfasted with him in Downing Street.[2]

Before passing from the friendship between Mr. Gladstone and Wordsworth, it is pleasant to note that, in the summer of 1842, the former used his good offices to secure the other a retiring allowance. The poet was Stamp Distributor for Cumberland, and he desired that the office should be transferred to his son, who for some time had acted as his deputy. He had seen Mr. Gladstone on the subject during a visit to London, and, on his return to Rydal, he wrote detailing his wish : 'As I have reached my seventy-third year, there is not much time to lose if I am thought worthy of being benefited. . . . I leave it to your judgment how to proceed, being fully assured that nothing will be done by you without the most delicate well-weighed consideration of person and circumstances'; and, in a subsequent communication, he gave 'a strong reason why time should not be lost in reminding Sir Robert Peel of me.' Peel next forwarded to Wordsworth a letter which looked like a promise, but still nothing tangible was done; and, after waiting for over two months, the latter once more communicated with Mr. Gladstone. 'If I should not succeed in obtaining what you have so kindly endeavoured to assist in procuring for me, I must be content; and should the pension come it would be welcome, both as a mark of public approbation, and preventing for the future the necessity of my looking more nearly to my expenditure than I have been accustomed to do. At all events I shall ever retain a grateful and most pleasing remembrance of

He assists Wordsworth to obtain a pension.

[1] Thomas Sidney Cooper's 'Recollections,' vol. ii., pp. 149, 153, 231.
[2] John Forster's 'Life of Charles Dickens,' vol. i., p. 82; vol. ii., p. 508.

your exertions to serve me upon this occasion ; nor can I
fail to be much gratified by the recollection of Sir R. Peel's
favourable opinion of my claims.'   Written on October
13th, this letter must have reached Mr. Gladstone by the
15th, on which day, it is significant to note, Peel forwarded
to Wordsworth an intimation that he had been granted a
Civil List pension of £300. Two days later, Wordsworth
told Mr. Gladstone this, adding : ' I will not run the risk
of offending you by a renewal of thanks for your good
offices in bringing this about, but will content myself with
breathing sincere and fervent good wishes for your welfare.'
And the story is thus completed by the poet's biographer :
' From the foregoing correspondence it is partly seen that
it was to Mr. Gladstone that Wordsworth owed his pension.
A paper of " Memoranda on Mr. Wordsworth's circumstances," by Mr. Gladstone, of date October 11th and 12th,
1842, makes it clear that it was to his kindness, and his influence, that the official recognition of the claim which the
aged poet had to this money grant was entirely due.' [1]

Throughout the long struggle for an improved law of
copyright, when year after year the measure was defeated,
Mr. Gladstone remained one of its steadiest supporters,
though more by vote than by speech.   In May, 1839, for
instance, he helped Talfourd through a tiring series of
divisions forced upon them by the obstructive opponents of
the Bill, and acted as a teller in two of them ; and when in
the next year, and in accordance with an intimation he had
given to Wordsworth, Talfourd published the three speeches
he had delivered in its favour, the work Talfourd dedicates
was dedicated ' To William Ewart Glad- his speeches to Mr.
stone, Esquire, M.P., Student of Christ Gladstone.
Church,' in the following flattering terms: ' The permission

Knight's ' Wordsworth,' vol. iii., pp. 426-30.

which you gave when, last year, I proposed the compilation of this little volume, to inscribe it to you, is one of the chief reasons of the renewal of my wish to publish it. I cannot decline the opportunity of recording that the exertions of those to whom the charge of the Copyright Bill has fallen, have been aided by the advice, and cheered by the kindness, of one whose genius naturally sympathises with the efforts of those who write for posterity ; who, unchanged by the excitements and successes of parliamentary life, cherishes academical associations with reverent ardor ; and who, amidst the cares and the struggles of party, pursues truth with as patient labour, and as single an aim, as the heroic student of other times.' [1]

The compliment, coming as it did from a determined political opponent, was a high one ; but another, curiously enough, was only a month later to be paid from the opposite camp.   Thomas Tegg, the anti-copyright bookseller—Carlyle's 'extraneous person' in the famous petition presented to the Commons in favour of the Copyright Bill in 1839—in a letter to Russell in February, 1840, asked : ' Who introduces this Bill ? ' and, with obvious reference to Inglis, Mahon, and Mr. Gladstone, proceeded : ' A country gentleman ?   A scion of nobility ?   A young first-class Oxonian ? '   And he replied : ' No : a practised barrister ;

Thomas Tegg's reference to Mr. Gladstone.

a man who knows that when he can make a case he will not trust to a speech, and that when he has no case he has no chance but that of misleading the jury by his eloquence.' But Mr. Gladstone was to receive yet another compliment upon his

Doyle's ' Plea ' to him.

exertions, and this time from an old friend, himself an author ; for Doyle, in ' The Poetaster's Plea,' which he described as ' a Familiar

[1] The dedication is dated ' Monmouth, 16th Jan., 1840.'

Epistle ' to the member for Newark, thus addressed him :

> One of a long-oppressed insulted crew,
> At length, dear Gladstone, I appeal to you ;
> I do not mean the warrior of the State,
> Clothed in bright armour at the temple's gate,
> Set in the front of battle, to uphold
> The truth that streams in glory from of old ;
> To praise thy bearing in that arduous fight,
> Proud friends, and unresentful foes unite ;
> And the hushed spirits of the future see
> Even now, a lord of humankind in thee.[1]

It need only further be noted here that, although at the commencement of the first session of 1841 Mr. Gladstone once more 'backed' the Copyright Bill, in company with Talfourd, Inglis, and Mahon, it was left to the Tory Parliament, chosen later in the same year, and to Mahon, to carry to a successful issue the work which Talfourd, who had not sought re-election, had begun.   The term of copyright was extended to forty-two years from the date of publication or seven years after the author's death, whichever term proved the longer ; but, as long after the victory as the summer of 1887, Mr. Gladstone, in forwarding to Wordsworth's biographer the letters he had received from the poet, added the remark : 'As to copyright, looking to all the interests involved, I now think the method of Talfourd and the present law faulty, and capable of being replaced by one better for all parties.' This memorandum is dated June 13th, 1887, and four days later was appended another : ' I was an eager supporter of Serjeant Talfourd, but have long since altered my view, and am of opinion that a more free

Mr. Gladstone's latest views on copyright.

---

[1] Doyle's ' Miscellaneous Verses ' (edition of 1840), p. 25.

system of copyright than the present one is possible, and would be more advantageous to the authors, the trade, and the public.' [1]

Educational endeavour in the case of Mr. Gladstone customarily proceeded side-by-side with religious effort. It has been noted that in 1829, and while at Oxford, he had become a subscriber to the Society for the Promotion of Christian Knowledge; and in his earlier parliamentary years he was connected with the Church Pastoral Aid Society, of which, with Sandon, Sir Andrew Agnew, and John Hardy, he was in 1836 one of the vice-presidents. Upon the question of the lay agency to be employed and the association to employ it, Mr. Gladstone parted company, however, with that organisation, and assisted to found the Additional Curates' Society. The original body had decided to assist, as it might be able, in the supply to destitute places of lay agents, whether candidates for holy orders or others, or whether partially or wholly to be maintained, such agents to act under the direction of the incumbent and to be removable at his pleasure ; and it was this decision which drove Mr. Gladstone forth. [2] Details are wanting of the earliest days of the Additional Curates' Society, but it is known that Mr. Gladstone was an ordinary member of the committee from its first foundation in 1837 to 1860, when he was elected a vice-president; and that during the commencing portion of his connection with that body, and while his political engagements allowed, no member was more regular in his attendance, or more willing to undertake work upon sub-committees. And it was not only in

Leaves the Church Pastoral Aid Society,

and assists to found the Additional Curates' Society.

[1] Knight's 'Wordsworth,' vol. iii., p. 356.
[2] Hodder's 'Shaftesbury,' vol. i., p. 211.

regard to the spread of religion in this country that he was concerned, for his first parliamentary effort in 1837 was to secure a return of copies of all despatches or instructions addressed to the governors or ecclesiastical functionaries in the Australian colonies after April 1st, 1835 (just the date at which he had left office), relating to the enlargement of the means of religious teaching and public worship.[1]

In regard to the Colonies, indeed, Mr. Gladstone displayed in various directions a philanthropic as well as an educational and a religious interest. It was a time when the ideas of our public men concerning the manner in which to deal with the nation's possessions over sea were in a state of flux, though still dominated with the idea that it was to Downing Street that the Colonies ought ever to look, and for 'Mr. Mother Country' that they ought always to work. In the earlier of Mr. Gladstone's days in the House of Commons, the mistake had begun to be perceived of forming settlements where there were no settlers; and on June 8th, 1836, a select committee was nominated to inquire into the different modes in which land had been and was being disposed of in the Australian Colonies, the Cape of Good Hope, and the West Indies, with a *1836. Mr. Gladstone on a Colonisation Committee.* view to ascertain the one that would be most beneficial both to the Colonies and the Mother Country. Mr. Gladstone was placed upon this body, and he generally coincided with his successor at the Colonial Office (Sir George Grey) in the recommendations, they opposing together one which was carried by a single vote, suggesting that the net proceeds of the land sales in Colonies, the climate of which was not unfavourable to the European frame, should be employed as an emigration fund, each Colony being

[1] February 10, 1837 : ' Mirror of Parliament' (1837), p. 126.

furnished with emigrant labour in exact proportion to its own land sales.   But they agreed with the idea that a plan of systematic emigration, upon a scale sufficiently large to meet all exigencies, should be set on foot, and with the concluding declaration, 'that in this, as in all their other recommendations, the Committee have looked with quite as lively an anxiety to the welfare of the Colonies, as to that of the Mother Country :—that, in all matters connected with emigration, they conceive the interests of the two to be inseparable ;—the one thing wanting in the Colonies, being precisely that free, or hired, labour, a superabundant supply of which is occasioning great local suffering in other parts of the Empire ;—while the transfer of this labour to the Colonies, by enabling them to turn to the best account the advantages of soil, climate, and great natural fertility, which they possess already,—cannot fail to open new channels of industry and commerce, both to them and to the Mother Country, and thus to enhance, incalculably, the prosperity of the United Empire.' [1]

One of the principal witnesses before this Committee was a certain Edward Gibbon Wakefield, a man who had had an astonishing career, for having at the age of thirty furnished one of the romances of the century by abducting a young lady of property, whom he married at Gretna Green, and having been sentenced to three years' imprisonment for the exploit, he turned his attention to colonial affairs with striking results.   His first great venture was a South Australian Association, which was to dispose of land in small parcels, and employ the proceeds in importing immigrants.   He was next the managing director of the New Zealand Company, which, like others of his projects, occupied the attention of Parliament in general and Mr.

[1] 'Parliamentary Papers,' 1836, vol. xi., pp. 499-765.

Gladstone in particular. In the session of 1838, the representative of Newark opposed a Bill introduced by a private member for empowering Wakefield's association to colonise New Zealand for its own profit, holding that whatever was done in regard to that country should be effected under the strictest

1838.
Opposes a Private Member's Bill for colonising New Zealand.

and most direct responsibility, by instruments under the immediate control of the Executive and of Parliament, and not by any intermediate body removed from their superintendence and control. He defended the Church Missionary Society from a charge of having countenanced undue acquisitions of land; but added that the unvarying and melancholy story of colonisation was that, wherever settlers from a people in an advanced stage of civilisation came into contact with the aborigines of a barbarous country, the result was always prejudicial to both parties and most dishonourable to the superior.[1] The measure was thrown out by a large majority, but though the next year the Government itself undertook to colonise New Zealand, the process was a slow one; and Mr. Gladstone was appointed on July 9th, 1840, on a select committee concerning the whole question. This body chose as its chairman Lord Eliot (then Tory member for East Cornwall, afterwards Chief Secretary for Ireland in Peel's second Administration, and third Earl of St. Germans); but, when it had taken much evidence, it declined even to consider Eliot's draft report in favour of

1840.
On another Colonisation Committee.

the Home Government assuming the whole responsibility of the Colony, which Mr. Gladstone approved, and contented itself with presenting the evidence to the House. Among the witnesses had been Wakefield, who meantime had accompanied Durham upon his famous but temporarily

[1] June 20, 1838: 'Hansard,' 3rd series, vol. xliii., ff. 873, 874.

abortive mission to Canada as his private secretary, and who, upon his return, had resumed work upon his former concern until circumstances constrained him to secede, and to join with Lyttelton and other High Churchmen in 1847 in

Lyttelton   successfully founding Canterbury as a Church of England colony.[1]   Wakefield had much complained, in his evidence before the second committee, of the interference of the Church Missionary Society with his endeavours to colonise New Zealand by company ; but Mr. Gladstone may have forgiven him this because his brother-in-law, Sir Stephen Glynne, was an active member of the

and Glynne and   New Zealand Church Society, which had
New Zealand.   been formed in this same spring, 'for the purpose of procuring for the colonists of New Zealand, in the very earliest period of the colonisation, all the advantages which are derived from the presence of a body of clergy acting together under the government of a bishop, and instructing the people in the pure faith of the Gospel, according to the doctrines and discipline of our Apostolical Church.'[2]

In this latter connection it is to be noted that a year later, and within some weeks of accepting his first important

Selwyn, its first   office, Mr. Gladstone had further cause to
Bishop.   be reminded of New Zealand, for his dearest Eton friend, George Selwyn, had been appointed its first bishop, and at a moment when the Colonial Episcopate was

[1] Nearly thirty years later, when Lyttelton visited New Zealand, he noted that at Wellington there was 'the plain tombstone of the renowned Gibbon Wakefield : a name almost like a spell to those interested in colonisation, that of New Zealand in particular, that of Canterbury most intimately of all :' Lyttelton's 'Ephemera,' 2nd series, p. 292.   A full account of the circumstances attending the formation of the settlement is in *ibid.*, 1st series, pp. 120-64.

[2] ' Parliamentary Papers,' 1840, vol. vii., pp. 447-665.

a subject for doubtful speculation by the many, and even for jest by a few. Sydney Smith, indeed, observed to Wilberforce of this appointment, that it would make quite a revolution in the dinners of New Zealand : '*Tête d'Evêque* will be the most *recherché* dish, and your man will add, "And there is *cold clergyman* on the side-table?"'[1] But it was matter of serious thought to Mr. Gladstone, who, in the spring of the same year, had spoken at a meeting, presided over by Archbishop Howley of Canterbury, which led to the establishment of the Colonial Bishoprics Fund by the united Episcopate on the following June 1st, the member for Newark being appointed one of its treasurers, in company with Sir John Taylor Coleridge and Archdeacon Hale, a position he continued to hold through life.[2] Four months later, Selwyn was consecrated, and his last Sunday at Eton was solemnly celebrated. Wilberforce preached in Windsor Parish Church in the morning, and Selwyn himself in the evening ; and among those who specially gathered at Eton for the occasion, were Mr. Gladstone, and Hope; Sir John Taylor Coleridge and Sir John Patteson,[3] both judges ; John Duke (afterwards Lord) Coleridge and (Sir) Henry Cotton, each to be raised to the judicial bench; Durnford, later Bishop of Chichester, and Chapman, subsequently Bishop of Colombo.[4] And Wilberforce declared it to have been 'a most *spirituel* gathering.'

April 27, 1841. Mr. Gladstone and the Colonial Bishoprics Fund.

[1] 'Life of Samuel Wilberforce,' vol. i., p. 203.

[2] Mr. Gladstone spoke at the jubilee meeting of the fund on May 29, 1891, under the presidency of Archbishop Benson.

[3] Patteson's son, who appears to have been present on this occasion, and who for some time laboured under Selwyn in New Zealand, became in 1861 first Bishop of Melanesia.

[4] Tucker's 'Selwyn,' pp. 78, 79.

The presence of Hope, indeed, was a reminder that early in the intimate friendship between Mr. Gladstone and himself, a point had been discussed between them which further sought to link the member for Newark with philanthropic effort in the colonies. Hope wrote to him on February 10th, 1837, inviting his aid for the Children's Friend Society, which was endeavouring to reclaim destitute and vicious children, by apprenticing them in healthy British colonies, and mainly Canada and the Cape ; and he asked whether a Bill, which was proposed relative to the distribution of waste lands in the colonies, was likely to furnish a favourable opportunity for putting forward the claims of these apprentices. Mr. Gladstone replied at once from the House of Commons in the negative as regarded the Bill, but added : 'Your project appears to me, as considered upon its own merits, to be well worthy of the attention of the Government.' Eight months later, in subscribing ten pounds, he said : 'I shall be glad to co-operate with you as far as my ability goes. The people at the Cape have made some use of me in Parliament, and I might be of use to your clergyman by introductions.' But, although Hope entertained the enthusiastic idea that the Society would be 'the means of breeding up a healthy and religious population in our colonies under the superintendence of the Church,' the undertaking ended in disappointment.[1]

Hope, Mr. Gladstone, and the Children's Friend Society.

'The people at the Cape,' Mr. Gladstone had said in this letter of October 16th, 1837, 'have made some use of me in Parliament ;' and in this he was doubtless referring to his questionings on their behalf on the Aborigines' Committee in the previous year, as already related ; but they were to make further use of him, and on an important point which

[1] Hope-Scott's 'Memoirs,' vol i., pp. 112-6.

had lasting results for both the rising statesman and the young colony. In the summer of 1838, he called attention to a petition he had himself presented from the inhabitants of Albany, a frontier post at the Cape, who complained that faith had not been kept with them by the Home Government, which had promised them protection and support, but had left them to suffer loss from a Mr. Gladstone and barbarous enemy. In itself, this looked a   Cape grievances. somewhat small affair, but special significance can be attached to it now, for such grievances as those of which Mr. Gladstone was then the exponent were the origin of the movement which led to the Boer 'trek' across the Vaal, and the foundation of that Transvaal State which is at this day the South African Republic. The member for Newark related how the feuds and contests between the settlers and the natives, which were of frequent occurrence, had generated such a feeling of insecurity that many of the colonists, and particularly the Boers, had been caused to emigrate. The Boers, in fact, disheartened by their misfortunes, had withdrawn into the desert, and placed themselves beyond the pale of society; and it was thus that Mr. Gladstone summarised a crisis which, being neglected by Downing Street in 1838, was forty years later to develop serious troubles for this country. The 'Great Trek' had been proceeding for some time; in the year Mr. Gladstone spoke, hundreds of Boers were slain in conflicts with His warning on the Dingaan, King of the Zulus; and it was Transvaal ignored. only by desperate exertions and abounding courage that the Transvaal State was founded. The member for Newark told the Commons how the representations of the colonists had been neglected and their interests sacrificed by the Home Government; and he moved an address for a commission to investigate the whole affair on the spot, and to

2 B

suggest the best means for preventing a recurrence of the
'trek.' But his warnings fell on deaf ears; in a thin House,
and with Praed as his co-teller, he was beaten by nine
votes;[1] the fine generalship of Andries Pretorius gave the
first check to Dingaan before the year was over; and the
Transvaal State, thus ignored in its beginnings, was to grow
into a thorn in England's side and—such was the irony of
fate—to the special disadvantage of the statesman who
first desired to remove the grievances of its founders. Yet
all was not forgetfulness, for at a Provincial Meeting of the
Afrikander Bond at Capetown in March, 1894, it was unanimously resolved (upon the motion of one who had been
well-known as an anti-British spokesman in former days,
and by a gathering largely composed of Dutch-descended
farmers) to express regret at Mr. Gladstone's final resignation of the British Premiership, and to place upon record
their faithful appreciation of the services he had rendered
to South Africa.

It may have been because of Mr. Gladstone's obvious
interest in the earlier colonising experiments that it long was
asserted and believed in Australia that he had joined in
1839 with a certain Neil Black and two others to secure a
squatter's run in the Port Phillip District of New South
Wales, which has now become the Western District of
Victoria. A touch of verisimilitude was sought to be given
to the story by the added statement that the manager of
the estate had at first considerable trouble with the blacks,
Alleged connection but that nothing could induce him to
with Australia. retire from the magnificent ground he had
secured; and that from 1846 to 1868, when the partnership

[1] 41·32: July 10, 1838: Hansard, 3rd series, vol. xliv., ff. 114-7.
Acland, Gaskell, Glynne, and Milnes, among his closest friends, were
absent from the division.

was dissolved, 'splendid dividends' were paid.   But, despite the fact that the story happens to have no foundation as far as Mr. Gladstone is concerned (though he had a cousin interested in the beginnings of Victoria about the period referred to),[1] it has been seen how in regard to the great work of colonisation, no less than upon every variety of subject, upon topics far removed from the notice of the average young politician, and upon some which necessitated the expenditure of much time and toil, he was in these years actively engaged.

[1] James Francis Hogan's 'Robert Lowe, Viscount Sherbrooke,' pp. 69-71.

XVI.—Continued Parliamentary Success.

FIVE days before he met Mr. Gladstone in social converse for the first time, Macaulay wrote to Lord Lansdowne, the Nestor of the Whig party—who, as Lord Henry Petty, had been Chancellor of the Exchequer in ' The Ministry of All the Talents' early in the century—' I think that, in the present unprecedented and inexplicable scarcity of Parliamentary talent among the young men of England, a little of that talent may be of as much service as far greater powers in times more fertile of eloquence.'[1]   In that winter of 1838, Macaulay was still outside the House of Commons, as he had been for years; and, therefore, he may be excused for not having intuitively perceived that two of the greatest parliamentarians of the century, Gladstone and Disraeli, were then sitting not far removed from each other on the Conservative benches.   The latter, by the very force of the genius he had exercised in other fields than politics, Mr. Gladstone as a worker. was obviously marked out for distinction: Mr. Gladstone was winning fame not only for his eloquence but for a dogged determination to work in well-nigh every field of human energy, which impresses and almost dazzles the observer even now.

This capacity for seemingly limitless toil was recognised by his contemporaries almost as soon as he entered the House of Commons.   It has been seen how his first session did not pass without his being placed upon a select committee;

[1] Trevelyan's ' Macaulay,' p. 364.

while, in his second, in addition to sitting with O'Connell upon that one which earliest brought them into close conversational contact, and that other which dealt with National Education, he was nominated in His labours upon the course of a single evening upon two Select Committees. more, the one to inquire into the circumstances of Ross's Arctic Expedition, with a view to ascertain whether any reward was due for the services rendered, and which recommended that those services should be fittingly acknowledged ;[1] and the other to investigate the origin and present state of a lottery that was being carried on at Glasgow, and which reported in favour of the system being ended.[2] The same determination to put him to the arduous, as well as the ornamental, work of Parliament was evidenced in succeeding sessions ; and the fruit of his labours upon the more important committees—those which considered the questions of education, apprenticeship, and the aborigines—has been seen.

But it was not merely for hard work in the legislative chamber and the committee-room that Mr. Gladstone was known ; record exists in various forms of His personal the personal impression he created upon his characteristics. contemporaries. His eloquence and his ardent political spirit naturally attracted admiration, but his amiability gained more. Arthur Stanley, when only a lad, had found William Gladstone at eighteen to be so very good-natured as to win much liking ; and Milnes had noted, about a year later, that the future Premier was the man who 'took him most' at Oxford. Three years afterwards, the testimony of the Conservative ladies of Newark was given to his estimable character and excellency of heart ; and, if that be set

[1] 'Parliamentary Papers,' 1834, vol. xviii., pp. 43-79.
[2] *Ibid.*, pp. 87-236.

aside as prompted by the ebullient enthusiasm of election-

His amiability time, or if the opinion of the *Nottingham Journal* as to his 'amiable character,' when in the first Peel Administration, be disregarded as the pre-judiced prepossession of a partisan, the private statement of Aberdeen at that period—'he appears to be so amiable that personally I am sure I shall like him '—with the similar opinion formed by Sir James Stephen while he was at the Colonial Office, cannot be thus dismissed. Subsequent evi-dence remains the same, for in 1839 Bunsen asked his wife to read the young statesman's 'beautiful letter;'[1] and a little later he wrote that he never spoke English half as easily as when seeing Mr. Gladstone and hearing him talk.[2] Just at the same time Macaulay told the editor of the *Edinburgh Review* that he had found Mr. Gladstone both

and cleverness. clever and amiable; while Mahon, in a letter to Murray, the publisher, described him as amiable and excellent. Newman, it is true (who, when 'The State in its Relations with the Church' was finding scarcely a defender, talked of 'poor Gladstone' but did not trouble to read his book), wrote of him after the publication of 'Church Principles Considered in their Results,' that 'somehow there is great earnestness, but a want of amiableness about him.'[3] But upon such a point the judgment of Aberdeen and Stephen, Macaulay and Mahon will be considered by those who have studied Newman's private but published letters to be the more sound.

In such estimates, an almost incalculable factor depends upon the point of view. One, for instance, who met him

---

[1] Bunsen's 'Memoir,' vol. i., p. 500.

Ibid., p. 510.

[3] Anna Mozley's ' Letters, etc., of Newman,' vol. ii., p. 322.

while travelling on the Rhine in the autumn of 1838, and in company with Sir Stephen Glynne and his two sisters, described his manner as having been marked not only by a certain courtesy and elegance, but by the degree of reserve one was accustomed in those days to look for in an Englishman of the upper class.[1]   But a recorder of impressions by hearsay a long time afterwards gives a different idea of this reserve.   From 1830 to 1840, it is said, Mr. Gladstone was a frequent visitor to and pamphlet-buyer at Hatchard's publishing-house in Piccadilly, and ' he is reported to have been taciturn and unapproachable in manner, handing in a list of pamphlets on a slip of paper, and even then demanding ten per cent. or threatening to go elsewhere.   There is no record of his ever having occupied a chair, or even condescended to refer to any subject except the list of pamphlets with which he came ready armed.'[2]   This may be true, though the fact that ' there is no record of his ever having occupied a chair' scarcely proves that he never sat down ; and it is not necessary to go far to find reasons for a rising politician not being anxious to cultivate garrulous acquaintances in an old-time book-shop.

His reserve.

The fact is that, although the name of this publishing house appeared with that of John Murray upon the title-page of one of Mr. Gladstone's earliest works, Hatchard's was Evangelical in connection, and the member for Newark was closely associated with the Tractarian party.   This, no less than his markedly severe temperament, laid him open during all the earlier part of his career to taunt concerning

---

[1] 'Gossip of the Century,' by the author of ' Flemish Interiors,' vol. i., pp. 207, 208.

[2] A. L. Humphreys' 'Piccadilly Bookmen, Memorials of the House of Hatchard,' p. 67.

his theological tendencies.   Even Cobden could not refrain
at a meeting of the Anti-Corn Law League in London, in
1843, from picturing the then President of the Board of

His religious cast.   Trade as 'calling up a solemn, earnest,
pious expression'; while, a dozen years
afterwards, Disraeli sneered in debate at his 'sanctimonious
rhetoric,' and Lytton at his 'Christian spirit that moved
them all.'   But his style lent itself to such taunts, for
Malmesbury has left upon record how, when dining in Mr.
Gladstone's company in the winter of 1844, he was 'disappointed at his appearance, which is that of a Roman
Catholic ecclesiastic, but '—and the addition was made as
if the fact were a revelation—' he is very agreeable.'[1]   As
to the agreeableness, indeed, there can be no doubt, for a
far shrewder observer, and one much better able to judge,
testified to it only a few years later.   At the Royal Academy
banquet of 1850, Disraeli, as he explained to a near relative,
was taken out of the wits, with whom he had been the previous year, and placed among the statesmen.   He sat within
two of Peel and between Mr. Gladstone and Sidney Herbert,
and the political circumstances of the time rendered the
position a delicate one.   But although, as Disraeli observed,
the Academicians seemed to have made somewhat of a
blunder, all   went   off   very   well,   'Gladstone   being
particularly agreeable.'[2]   The net impression, indeed,
gleaned from comparison of all the contemporary
evidence, is that with his intimates Mr. Gladstone was
amiable, with acquaintances accessible, and with strangers
aloof.

Not only his churchmanship but his scholarship will
account for this attitude.   In the one remembered passage

---

[1] Malmesbury's 'Memoirs,' p. 114.

[2] 'Lord Beaconsfield's Letters,' p. 231.

of Lytton's 'New Timon,' published in 1846, and descrip-
tive of Stanley, is a reference to Mr. Glad- His scholarship.
stone, which indicates that it was largely as
student that he was at this period regarded, for of

> The brilliant chief, irregularly great,
> Frank, haughty, rash—the Rupert of Debate !

it was said

> First in the class, and keenest in the ring,
> He saps like Gladstone, and he fights like Spring ! [1]

Mr. Gladstone, indeed, was enveloped in Etonianism as in
a garment, for he appeared to be inspired with the expectation of his old schoolfellows that he was to achieve great
things. While waiting for the accomplish- Eton's expectations
ment, the Etonians of that period were of him.
never tired of singing the praises of Fox and Grenville,
Canning and Grey. The half-dozen addresses delivered at
the annual visits of William IV. have come down to us;
and there is not one that does not ring the changes upon
these names. Mr. Gladstone was still at Oxford when an
Etonian was declaiming the belief in halting rhyme that the
school

> Another age another Fox shall give,
> Grenvilles and Greys in distant days shall live,
> And Canning's wit and eloquence revive ;

while George Smythe, afterwards one of Disraeli's companions in the 'Young England' movement, expressed the
fervent hope :—

[1] The Eton equivalent for study in the first half of the last line will
probably be to the general reader a less recondite allusion now than
the reference to the once famous pugilist, Tom Spring.

May glory's flame some Wellington inspire,
Another Gray invoke the Theban lyre ;
Some Grenville wise—some Canning yet be known
To charm the Senate—and uphold the Throne.

This last aspiration was uttered in 1836, and very soon it must have been felt by all old Etonians that it was being fulfilled in the person of Mr. Gladstone. It has been noted how so keen an observer as James Grant had failed to mention the member for Newark, even incidentally, in his 'Random Recollections of the House of Commons from the Year 1830 to the close of 1835'; but the time soon arrived for this omission to be repaired with effect, for in 1838 he wrote, in a similar work, an elaborate account of the coming man. Mr. Gladstone, said Grant, ' is one of the rising young men on the Tory side of the House. His party expect great things from him ; and certainly, when it is remembered that his age is only thirty-five,[1] the success of the parliamentary efforts he has already made justifies their expectations. He is well informed on most of the subjects which usually occupy the attention of the legislature ; and he is happy in turning his information to a good account. He is ready on all occasions, which he deems fitting ones, with a speech in favour of the policy advocated by the party with whom he acts. His extemporaneous resources are ample. Few men in the House can improvisate better. It does not appear to cost him an effort to speak. He is a man of very considerable talent, but has nothing approaching to genius. His abilities are much more the result of an excellent education, and of mature study, than of any

James Grant's description of Mr. Gladstone in 1838.

[1] It was not then twenty-nine, but Grant was liable to err in details, as, for instance, in a subsequent remark, ' Mr. Gladstone, I should here observe, is an extensive West India planter.'

prodigality on the part of Nature in the distribution of her mental gifts. I have no idea that he will ever acquire the reputation of a great statesman. His views are not sufficiently profound or enlarged for that ; his celebrity in the House of Commons will chiefly depend on his readiness and dexterity as a debater, in conjunction with the excellence of his elocution, and the gracefulness of his manner when speaking. His style is polished, but has no appearance of the effect of previous preparation. He displays considerable acuteness in replying to an opponent :· he is quick in his perception of anything vulnerable in the speech to which he replies, and happy in laying the weak point bare to the gaze of the House. He now and then indulges in sarcasm, which is, in most cases, very felicitous. He is plausible even when most in error. When it suits himself or his party, he can apply himself with the strictest closeness to the real point at issue ; when to evade that point is deemed most politic, no man can wander from it more widely.'

From analysis, Grant passed to description. ' Mr. Gladstone's appearance and manners are much in his favour. He is a fine-looking man. He is about the usual height, and of good figure. His countenance is mild and pleasant, and has a highly intellectual expression. His eyes are clear and quick. His eyebrows are dark and rather prominent. There is not a dandy in the House but envies what Truefitt would call, his " fine head of jet-black hair." It is always carefully parted from the crown downwards to his brow, where it is tastefully shaded. His features are small and regular, and his complexion must be a very unworthy witness, if he does not possess an abundant stock of health. Mr. Gladstone's gesture is varied, but not violent. When he rises, he generally puts both his hands behind his back, and having there suffered them to embrace each other for a short time, he unclasps them, and allows them to drop on either side.   They are not permitted to remain long in that locality, before you see them again closed together, and hanging down before him.   Their reunion is not suffered to last for any length of time.   Again a separation takes place, and now the right hand is seen moving up and down before him.   Having thus exercised it a little, he thrusts it into the pocket of his coat, and then orders the left hand to follow its example.   Having granted them a momentary repose there, they are again put into gentle motion ; and in a few seconds they are seen reposing *vis-à-vis* on his breast.   He moves his face and body from one direction to another, not forgetting to bestow a liberal share of his attention on his own party.   He is always listened to with much attention by the House, and appears to be highly respected by men of all parties.' [1]

At the time this description was written, the first Parliament of Victoria was in session, and Mr. Gladstone was markedly seen to be coming more and more to the front. The House of Commons at the immediately preceding general election had received a recruit who was destined to be his rival in political fame ; and Mr. Gladstone was present at the memorable scene of Disraeli's maiden speech when, hooted down by an undiscriminating knot of Radical members, the future Tory leader prophesied that the time would come when they would hear him.   Before 1837 was ended, and on the motion for the Christmas adjournment,

Dec. 22, 1837.   the member for Newark took part in a dis-
Speaks on Canada. cursive debate upon affairs in Canada, a theme to which he had previously addressed himself, and which remained of special interest just then.   His submission was that, if Canada were really oppressed, he would

---

[1] ' The British Senate in 1838,' vol. ii., pp. 88-92.

say, ' Let no consideration of shame and pride, let no reliance on the superior power and resources of this empire
hinder you from retracing your steps, rescinding your resolutions, and rendering full indemnification to this people ' ;
but he denied the existence of the alleged oppression,
attributing the insecurity of person and property to the
machinations of popular agitators, and urged that there
should be not only firmness but a conciliatory spirit in
their proceedings, with the grant of nothing that would
weaken the connection between Canada and the Mother
Country.[1] The same question was the first to occupy him
in Parliament in the new year, for when   Jan. 22, 1838.
Grote, then representing the City of London, Canada once more.
moved that Roebuck should be heard at the bar of the
House as the agent of the Assembly of Lower Canada
against the Canada Bill introduced by the Ministry, it was
Mr. Gladstone who extricated the Commons from a difficulty by suggesting that Roebuck should be heard, but not
as agent. Russell at first demurred to the emendation ;
but Stanley emphatically supported what he declared to be
Mr. Gladstone's well-judged and opportune suggestion ;
and the feeling in the House was so palpably in favour of
the idea that, although Charles Buller sneered at ' the ingenious and valuable precedent ' thus to be set, it was
adopted without a division.[2] Roebuck accordingly delivered his address, and on the next night Mr. Gladstone
made a long speech in reply. In this he argued that there
was nothing, in sober reason, which deserved to be called a
grievance in Canada. If there were, he would proceed immediately to redress it, caring nothing whether rebellion
was rearing its head in triumph, instead of sinking into

[1] ' Hansard,' 3rd series, vol. xxxix., ff. 1452-56.
[2] *Ibid.*, vol. xl., ff. 257-65.

extinction, or whether the British arms were covered with
that dishonour which some members had wished, instead
of carrying defeat into the ranks of rebellion, for that ought
to work no change in the wish to conciliate hostile feelings
and heal the wounds of civil discord.[1]

The speech is noteworthy for reasons outside its sentiments, for it was the first of Mr. Gladstone's efforts to
extract open praise from Peel and favourable criticism from
Disraeli.   The Chancellor of the Exchequer (Spring Rice),
who followed Mr. Gladstone, began by observing that it
was impossible to complain of any part of the argument
without bearing testimony to the ability of the address;[2]
His speech praised and Peel, who came next in the discussion,
by Peel and Disraeli. went to unusual length of compliment by
describing Mr. Gladstone's as a very able speech.[3] 'Gladstone spoke very well,' wrote Disraeli to his sister the next
day,[4] 'though with the unavoidable want of interest which
accompanies elaborate speeches which you know are to lead
to no result, *i.e.*, no division.   His speech, however, called
up a Minister, and then Peel.'

Another compliment from the Chancellor of the Exchequer was to be accorded to Mr. Gladstone a few weeks
later, when the member for Newark had
March 7. spoken in a debate upon a Radical motion
Another Canada speech.
of Sir William Molesworth concerning
Colonial administration, in which Canada once more largely
figured.   There was always a great satisfaction in rising
after Mr. Gladstone, now said Spring Rice, because,

[1] *Ibid.*, ff. 419-40.
[2] *Ibid.*, f. 440.
[3] *Ibid.*, f. 456.
[4] In 'Lord Beaconsfield's Letters,' p. 130, this letter is dated
'February, 1838,' but from the context it is obviously one of Jan. 24.

however widely he differed in opinion from the Government, not a word escaped from his lips calculated to give pain or to infuse into the debate any needless asperity. But there is more even than this high praise from a leading Minister to a young opponent to be noted in connection with this debate. Mr. Gladstone had taunted Howick, then Secretary for War, with having four years before denounced Aberdeen, when Colonial Secretary, as an enemy to the human race. Howick specially replied on the point to Mr. Gladstone by name, and added that he now considered Aberdeen to have manifested a spirit of liberality which reflected upon him the very highest degree of credit, whereupon Peel rose and said, 'I heartily rejoice that I gave to the noble lord the opportunity of explaining.'[1] The inference is obvious that Mr. Gladstone was on this occasion the chosen mouthpiece of his leader, who, keenly distrusting his theological views, was learning to more and more confide in him as a politician.

Meanwhile, the apprenticeship system was once again being forced to the front in Parliament. The Select Committee of 1837, which had had to wind up its work with some abruptness because of the dissolution, had recommended that a similar body should be appointed by the new Parliament;[2] but events moved too fast for this to be necessary. Buxton had lost his seat at the general election, but the abolitionists found other worthy champions ready to carry on the work. The narratives of continued cruelty to the apprentices, which reached this country in an ever increasing degree, so roused public opinion that petitions, signed by hundreds of thousands, poured in upon

The last of the Apprenticeship Difficulty.

---

[1] 'Hansard,' 3rd series, vol. xl., ff. 626-45.

[2] 'Parliamentary Papers,' 1837, vol. vii., p. 749.

Parliament, asking for the abolition of the whole system on August 1st, 1838, the date previously fixed for its complete extinction having been August 1st, 1840. Brougham in the Lords and Sir George Strickland in the Commons, brought forward motions to this end; and, when the latter submitted his proposal, the Ministry met the demand with a Bill for the better treatment of the apprentices.

Writing to Wordsworth on March 26th, Mr. Gladstone observed: 'At present I am looking forward to a busy week in the House of Commons, particularly on account of the question of the Negro apprenticeship;'[1] and four days later, and on the second night of the debate upon Strickland's motion, after Russell, Howick, and O'Connell had addressed the House, Mr. Gladstone spoke. Pease, the seconder of the proposal, had especially emphasised the cruel punishments awarded to the negroes in British Guiana, and the West India proprietors had been by no means spared throughout the discussion. It was late when the member for Newark rose, and those assembled were eager for the division, but he soon held them fast with a speech of unusual power. He was the first in the whole debate to fully take the part of the planters, with whom he frankly claimed to be connected; and he denied, not merely in general terms but with almost embarrassing wealth of detail, the charges against them. 'I am aware,' he exclaimed, 'that I must speak under prepossessions, though I have striven with all my might against them; and I desire that no jot or tittle of weight may be given to my professions or assertions;—by the facts I will stand or fall. And oh, Sir, with what depth of desire have I longed for this day! Sore, and wearied, and irritated, perhaps, with the grossly

March 30.
Mr. Gladstone defends the planters.

[1] Knight's 'Wordsworth,' vol. iii., p. 330.

exaggerated misrepresentations and with the utter calumnies that have been in active circulation, without the means of reply, how do I rejoice to meet them in free discussion before the face of the British Parliament.' And, after he had minutely examined the allegations against the planters, and attempted to show them to be virtually baseless, he concluded with an energetic appeal to the justice of Parliament for those on whose behalf he spoke.[1] 'The ablest speech he ever made in the House, and by far the ablest on the same side of the question,' was the verdict of James Grant,[2] who heard it from the reporters' gallery; while Charles Greville recorded that 'Gladstone made a first-rate speech in defence of the planters, so Fazakerley told me; he converted or determined many adverse or doubtful votes:'[3] and Fazakerley's may have been one of these, for this Whig member for Peterborough was in the same lobby as Mr. Gladstone. The division showed 215 for Strickland's motion and 269 against; but it was in no sense a party fight, Russell and Peel being with the member for Newark in the majority, while Disraeli, with Stephen Glynne, was on the other side.

When Mr. Gladstone sat down — 'amidst loud and general cheering,' as the *Times* recorded — Strickland merely observed, 'I think that I shall best discharge my duty by not offering one word in reply;' and the division was immediately taken. The *Times* the following morning declared that Mr. Gladstone's was 'a long and able speech of much detail, very fairly se- The speech is much lected, and very clearly arranged. . . . praised, This speech, which was both candid and accurate,

[1] 'Hansard,' 3rd series, vol. xlii., ff. 223-57.
[2] 'The British Senate in 1838,' vol. ii., p. 90.
[3] Greville's 'Victoria Journals,' vol. i., p. 86.

2 C

produced considerable effect, and brought the debate to
a satisfactory close.' Even the *Morning Chronicle*, the
Whig organ, sang its praises—a striking testimony to its
effect in those days of violent partisanship. 'However we
may differ from Mr. Gladstone,' it wrote, 'we are bound
to do justice to the great ability he displayed'; but it proceeded to criticise the matter of the address as merely that
of an advocate: and that Mr. Gladstone was on the unpopular side in the line he took may be considered proved
by the fact that the then Tory *Times* returned to the question in its next issue with the remarks, 'Mr. Gladstone's
eloquent and able speech was calculated to weaken, not
remove, many persuasions amounting to prejudices, with
regard to the extent of those misdeeds and criminal abuses
of the Abolition Act which have constituted the chief
materials of the agitation raised by Lord Brougham and
his accomplices of Exeter-hall. Still there is much matter
of obloquy, from which neither Sir G. Grey nor Mr. Gladstone has succeeded in exonerating the West India proprietors.'

The speech, as delivered by 'W. E. Gladstone, Student
of Christ Church, and M.P. for Newark,' was issued in
pamphlet form, with preface and appendix, this being the
first work of his put into print. 'In acceding to the request
which has been made to me from various and opposite
quarters to publish the following speech, or perhaps I
should rather say statement, in a form as accurate as possible, I find it necessary,' he wrote, 'to prefix one or two
remarks. The lateness of the hour at which
and is published. it was delivered, the promiscuous and dis-
cursive nature of the allegations which it was intended to
meet, and the number and variety of topics properly
belonging to the subject, made it necessary to study

compression. . . . I am sensible that the statement must appear, to those who know how moving are some of the facts in this case, to be hard and unfeeling. It was not for brevity's sake alone that I avoided, where I could, expressions of feeling which the conduct of several parties might have elicited; but rather because I was, in the first place, sincerely anxious to avoid introducing into the case any new elements of bitterness, and, in the second, unwilling to make professions which circumstances would have rendered fairly open to suspicion. I am, however, not the less sensible that I speak and act, with reference to the negroes of the West Indies, under a solemn responsibility; and that if those who term themselves the negro's friends are indeed his only or his best friends, the West Indians, collectively and as individuals, are deeply guilty of injustice and ingratitude.'

As an oratorical effort, the speech was a triumph; as a contribution to practical politics it was of none effect. The day for a defence of any form of colonial slavery had gone, and the result of the debate was a barren victory for both Ministers and planters. The abolitionists, nerved to further exertions, pressed their demand again and again and in division after division; and before the session ended, even the colonial assemblies themselves had taken the step which the Commons had declined to adopt, and all remnant of slavery in our empire passed away with the midnight chime which ushered in the First of August, 1838.

Almost exactly twelve months before that memorable date in the chronicle of human freedom, Mr. Gladstone, speaking on the Newark hustings, had congratulated his constituents upon the settlement of the slavery question, which, when he first appeared among them, had been all

engrossing, and in which his own feelings had been concerned and their rectitude challenged. Disclaiming the
idea that he had ever favoured the system, he submitted
that much remained to be done, as both the physical and
the moral condition of the negro required
The end of slavery.
improvement; and he added the deepest
conviction of a solemn duty and an important obligation to
advance the welfare of the black population. These were
not idle words, for the promise to take pride and delight in the task was speedily afterwards put to the test.
In the spring of 1839, Buxton was busily engaged in the
work of forming a Society for the Extinction of the Slave
Trade and the Civilisation of Africa, and in this he had the
aid of Mr. Gladstone. The two men, despite the apparent
antagonism which had marked their course upon the question of colonial slavery, were at heart one in the desire to
raise the condition of the negro. Buxton
Mr. Gladstone and
Buxton.
had been the first to compliment the member for Newark's earliest important speech; he had with
interest watched the younger man's brief tenure of the
Colonial Under-Secretaryship; he had found how keen an
attention and how constant an attendance Mr. Gladstone
had given to the various select committees, which had
inquired into the education of the slave and the condition
of the aborigine; and he of all men was likely to be least
surprised at the action the other now took. Many a
year later, when Buxton's grandson held the Under-
Secretaryship for the Colonies, in the fourth Administration
of Mr. Gladstone himself, and a question of the treatment
of the aborigine was under the consideration of the House
of Commons, the Premier claimed that the very name of
Buxton was a guarantee to the country of the part the
grandson was likely to take in such a matter. 'I recollect

very well,' he added, 'the great ability, the high character, and the great public services of his distinguished grand-father, and I rejoice to think that that name is still associated with tempers, principles, and dispositions which, I believe, that grandfather himself, if he could arise among us, would not be inclined to disown.'[1]

At a private gathering, preliminary to the formal estab-lishment of the Society for the Extinction of the Slave Trade and the Civilisation of Africa, Mr. Gladstone was present, and with him were Inglis, Acland, and Ashley: in fact, as Buxton wrote: 'It was a glorious meeting, quite an epitome of the state: Whig, Tory, and Radical; Dis-senter, Low Church, High Church, tip-top High Church, or Oxfordism, all united.'[2] It was determined to form two associations, distinct in method but having the common object of putting an end to the slave trade and slavery; and, while one was to be exclusively philanthropic, the other had a commercial side. The Whig Government was approached, and it agreed to send a frigate and two steamers to explore the Niger, and, if possible, set on foot commercial relations with the tribes on its banks. But delays took place; and, although one fruit of the establish-ment of the African Colonisation Society was the holding of a great meeting in Exeter Hall on June 1st, 1840, over which Prince Albert presided—that being his first function of the kind in England—and at which Mr. Gladstone was present and Peel spoke, the Niger Expedition was a complete and heart-breaking failure,[3] to be recalled

They join to help the negro.

[1] Nov. 9, 1893: 'The Parliamentary Debates,' 4th series, vol. xviii., f. 598.

[2] C. Buxton's 'Life of Sir Thomas Fowell Buxton,' 2nd edit., pp. 462, 464.

[3] *Ibid.*, p. 564.

now only for the further interesting circumstance in connection with it that William Edward Forster, Buxton's nephew,
and afterwards Minister for Education in Mr. Gladstone's
first Government, offered to join it but was dissuaded.[1] But
all this time Mr. Gladstone was assisting Buxton; and, referring in September of the year last-named to the battle
which had then commenced to rage around the importation
of slave-grown sugar, and to the attitude of 'the West
Indians,' the abolitionist leader wrote: 'Gladstone, Lord
Seaford, and John Irving have served the cause; and there
ends, pretty nearly, the catalogue of West Indian proprietors,
who have so much as lifted up a finger for us.'[2]

Slavery and Mr. Gladstone had not much further connection, though it formed an incidental portion of the great
debate of 1841 on the sugar duties, which ended in the
defeat, and virtually in the destruction, of the Melbourne
Administration. Seven years before, and during a discussion upon the annual renewal of those duties, proposed
by the Cabinet of Grey, Mr. Gladstone, 'appearing but for
a very few moments in the new capacity of
a West Indian,' had besought the House to
pause before it adopted any measures that
might tend to press further upon the already depressed
West Indian proprietors; and he had narrated, to strengthen
his appeal and in order to show the excited state of the
negroes, how, within the previous few days, accounts of the
most alarming character had reached him from a colony
with which he was closely connected, for on an estate of
his father the slaves had risen and beaten a number of
whites, cut the throat of the manager's horse, and refused

*Mr. Gladstone and
the sugar duties
in 1834,*

---

[1] *Ibid.*, p. 464: T. Wemyss Reid's 'Life of William Edward
Forster,' vol. i., pp. 122-6.
[2] 'Life of T. F. Buxton,' p. 531.

to work, though subsequently induced to return to their labour.[1]   Sugar, indeed, was of much concern to the Gladstone family for many years to come : it was a question upon which John Gladstone was a frequent correspondent of the newspapers in 'the forties,' and it almost caused the resignation of the member for Newark from the Cabinet of Peel : but previously, when in 1840 the Melbourne Government introduced one of the many Bills on the subject, Mr. Gladstone urged that the interests of the negro must not be overlooked in the matter[2]   *in 1840,* —which exposed him to an angry retort from Hawes, and to the taunt from Ewart, son of his father's friend, that some sensibilities on the subject of slavery were only of recent growth, and conveniently matured in accordance with their own interest and with the maintenance of monopoly.[3]

More important loomed the question in the next year, when the Whigs proposed to reduce the duty on foreign sugars, and the Opposition met this with a motion by Sandon, declaring that such a course would assist slavery and the slave trade.   The battle   *and in 1841.* raged for eight nights.   Arrayed against the Ministerial plan were such strange colleagues as the various West Indian Associations and the British and Foreign Anti-Slavery Society, and the debate reflected the incongruousness of the alliance. On the second evening, following Labouchere (whose post as Master of the Mint he was soon to hold), Mr. Gladstone submitted that the Ministerial plan would favour slave-grown sugar, for it was upon that article that the slave trade depended for its existence.   'Is it not enough for us to know,' he asked, ' that, at this moment, the slave trade is a

[1] Feb. 28, 1834 : ' Mirror of Parliament' (1834), p. 414.
[2] June 25, 1840 : *Ibid.* (1840), pp. 4027-29.
[3] *Ibid.*, pp. 4029, 4030.

monster which is consuming day by day, and every day, the
lives of a thousand of our fellow-creatures : that while war,
pestilence, and famine slay their thousands, the slave trade,
from year to year with unceasing operation, slays its tens
of thousands?' And he taunted Macaulay, as a son

May 10, 1841.
He taunts
Macaulay, of Zachary Macaulay, a fellow-struggler with
Wilberforce, with being in the Cabinet that
proposed such resolutions. 'I can only
speak from tradition of the struggle for the abolition of
slavery,' he said; 'but, if I have not been misinformed,
there was engaged in it a man who was the unseen ally
of Mr. Wilberforce, and the pillar of his strength ; a man of
profound benevolence, of acute understanding, of indefatigable industry, and of that self-denying temper which is content to work in secret, and to seek for its reward beyond the
grave;'[1] and it was Zachary Macaulay whom he thus
described.

This was the last speech of the night; and Macaulay,
who was absent at the moment, took the earliest opportunity

and Macaulay
replies. of replying, for he rose the next evening before even the member who had moved the
adjournment. Although keenly smarting under the taunt,
he so much appreciated the praise of his father that he
averred he would still call his assailant 'my honourable
friend'; and he strenuously denied having abandoned any
principle.[2] Sir George Grey, who by this time had become
Chancellor of the Duchy of Lancaster, struck at Mr. Gladstone with more determination. He sneered at the failure
to propose some principle upon which the conscience of the

---

[1] *Ibid.* (1841, 1st session), pp. 1592-97 : 'Hansard,' 3rd series, vol.
lviii., ff. 160-80. Curiously enough, the compliment to Zachary Macaulay is omitted from the former report.

[2] 'Mirror of Parliament' (1841, 1st session), p. 1612.

State should be guided; and he unkindly recalled that the member for Newark spoke no longer in the character of a West Indian, the greater part of the interest in sugar he or his connection possessed having been transferred to the East Indies.[1] Howick, Grey's kinsman, who was now again out of office, was even more outspoken with revived memories of Vreed-en-Hoop; and Gisborne, the Whig member for Carlow, declared that Zachary Macaulay would have rejected Mr. Gladstone's eulogium with scorn and disgust, if he could only know that the object was to give point and venom to a stigma upon his son.[2] Sidney Herbert, speaking from Mr. Gladstone's side, retorted that these attacks were a just tribute, unwittingly paid, to the pungency of the remarks and the force of the reasoning of one whose character and principles stood too high for either to be endangered;[3] but Vernon Smith countered this by recalling the treatment of John Gladstone's hill coolies,[4] and Hume recommended the member for Newark to extend a little of his sympathy towards the industrious and oppressed classes at home.[5] Mr. Gladstone, meanwhile, sought a speedy chance to answer Howick, as already described;[6] and though Francis Baring, the Chancellor of the Exchequer, recognising that there had been enough of the personal element in the controversy, later replied to the member for Newark's arguments,[7] Sheil, on the very last night of the debate, bitterly taunted Mr. Gladstone concerning

---

[1] *Ibid.*, pp. 1636-8. As an 'East Indian,' Mr. Gladstone had been placed upon the East India Produce Committee in the previous year : 'Parliamentary Papers,' 1840, vol. viii.

[2] 'Mirror of Parliament' (1841, 1st session), pp. 1650, 1651, 1658.

[3] *Ibid.*, p. 1658.   [4] *Ibid.*, p. 1661.   [5] *Ibid.*, p. 1702.

[6] *Ante*, p. 181.

[7] 'Mirror of Parliament' (1841, 1st session), p. 1746.

his old connection with the West India interest.[1]   But this was almost the end of Mr. Gladstone's participation in discussion upon slavery.   He wrote various despatches concerning it when Secretary for the Colonies five years later; he sat in 1848 and 1849 upon a select committee to consider the best means which Great Britain could adopt for providing for the final extinction of the slave trade; but virtually for him slavery, as a problem of current politics, was no more.

Mr. Gladstone's progress in Parliament and in the estimation of its leading members has been shown in more than one episode before narrated, and it was commencing, indeed, to be displayed with increasing frequency, for even Russell, early in 1838, was moved to compliment him upon his sense of what was courteous between private individuals and due between public men.[2]   Part of this growing ad-

Mr. Gladstone's miration was due to his pluck, for he never
political pluck. hesitated to take the unpopular side when convinced he was in the right.   Against the opinions of Peel and Stanley, and the votes of such tried friends as Mahon and Praed and Sandon, he opposed in this same year the provision of religious instruction for English prisoners not belonging to the Established Church, contending that the pecuniary support of the State ought to be confined to one particular denomination.[3]   And he showed equal courage only a few days later by indignantly replying to an attack Morpeth had made upon the Oxford Movement, and especially upon the once famous ' Froude's Remains.' He denounced as a mere vulgar calumny the assertion that Roman Catholic doctrines were inculcated in his old

[1] *Ibid.*, p. 1790.
[2] Feb. 27, 1838 : ' Hansard,' 3rd series, vol. xli., ff. 204, 205.
[3] July 20 : *Ibid.*, vol. xliv., ff. 493-6.

University; and he pointed to Newman's preface to the work as expressly guarding that divine from being supposed to entertain the opinions of the author.[1] Newman, in a letter of three days afterwards to James Mozley, noted that 'Gladstone has defended me,'[2] but without a word to indicate appreciation of or thanks for the pluck such a defence needed.

As has been seen, the publication of 'Church and State' and the education controversy, with the intervening tour in Italy, occupied Mr. Gladstone during the succeeding autumn, winter, and spring; and, now that his position as a politician was assured, he resolved to abandon all thought of the law. Accordingly, as the records of Lincoln's Inn attest, 'At a Council held the 15th day of April, 1839, Upon the Petition of William Ewart Gladstone, Esq., a Fellow of this Society, praying *April, 1839. Withdraws from Lincoln's Inn.* that his name may be taken off the Books having given up his intention of being Called to the Bar, It is Ordered accordingly.' Only about a month later, a chance for a moment seemed to offer that Mr. Gladstone would attain the Ministerial position which upon all hands it was admitted his position in Parliament entitled him to expect. The Whig Government had proposed to suspend the constitution of Jamaica for five years, because of disobedience to instructions from home, in somewhat the same fashion as had precipitated the crisis the previous year in Lower Canada; and Mr. Gladstone more than once took part in the resulting debates. On the night that Laboubchere, as Under-Secretary for the Colonies, asked for leave to bring in the necessary *April 9. Mr. Gladstone and the Jamaica Bill.* Bill, the member for Newark expressed very serious doubts

[1] July 30: *Ibid.*, ff. 817-9.
[2] Anna Mozley's 'Letters, etc., of Newman,' vol. ii., p. 255.

as to the propriety of its passing [1]—doubts which he
amplified a month later in a speech declaring that the

May 6.
Again speaks
upon it.

measure could tend only to bring the
sovereign power of parliamentary legislation
into general discredit, and shake the confidence of our colonial fellow-subjects throughout the whole
circle of our possessions. [2]   On this latter night, and owing
to Radical defections, Russell's motion to resolve the House
into committee was carried by only five votes, and the
Ministry at once resigned. [3] Wellington was sent for by
the Queen, but, upon his advice, Peel was charged with the
formation of a Cabinet, an endeavour that broke down only

Melbourne resigns.

because her majesty refused at his bidding
to change the ladies of her bed-chamber;
and the Tories had to wait for more than another two years
to gain the offices for which they had so long and strenuously struggled.   Mr. Gladstone afterwards held that 'possibly it was suspicion, the most obstinate among the be-

Mr. Gladstone
and the
'Bed-chamber crisis.'

setting sins of politicians, even in men of
upright nature, which interfered on the side
of rigour,' [4] which, in that case, was the side
of Peel.   But for the time this kept him out of office; and
that he would have received distinguished preferment if a
Tory Administration had been formed, is sufficiently indicated by the fact that he was invited to join the members

---

[1] 'Mirror of Parliament' (1839), pp. 1639, 1640.

[2] *Ibid.*, pp. 2354-62.

[3] Mr. Gladstone spoke once more on the subject that session, when
the reconstituted Melbourne Ministry introduced another measure on
the subject, but he added little, except what he himself admitted to be
'a hasty and erroneous reference,' to his previous remarks: June 10,
Ibid., pp. 2825-9.

[4] 'Gleanings,' vol. i., p. 39.

of the front Opposition bench at Peel's first parliamentary dinner in the ensuing session.[1]

Though the law had failed to attract, and politics could not yet claim him as all its own, the Church retained its hold upon Mr. Gladstone, and that not only in England but in Scotland. 'Aye, man,' had observed to him an old Edinburgh bookseller, as, when quite a youth, he asked at the shop for Booth's 'Reign of Grace,' 'but ye're a young chiel to be askin' after a book like that;' but Scotland, resembling England at the period of his advance in public life, was seething with religious discussion, in which he could not fail to have part. He had a special interest, indeed, in the controversy which led to the disruption of the Scottish Kirk, for, in the spring of 1839, the Presbytery of Edinburgh objected to an offer by John Gladstone to build and endow a church in his native Leith, because he wished to retain the patronage for himself and his family, 'declaring thereby,' commented so generally fair an observer as Lord Cockburn in his diary, 'that they would rather have the people kept ignorant than made religious through that abominable thing;'[2] but the objection was afterwards waived, and the church, with manse and schools attached, was erected and endowed. Whether for the English or the Scottish Establishment, whether for Episcopalian or Presbyterian, John Gladstone continued to justify to the end his old character of 'a builder of churches,' for in 1841 he likewise erected and endowed St. Thomas, Toxteth Park, Liverpool,

1839.
John Gladstone and the Scottish Kirk.

[1] This was given on Feb. 8, 1840, but Mr. Gladstone was not at the more general Tory assembly of some sixty guests who (including his friends Herbert, Lincoln, and Milnes) dined under Peel's chairmanship at the Carlton two days later to celebrate the marriage of the Queen.

[2] 'Memorials of Henry Cockburn,' 1831-54, vol. i., p. 227.

with schools attached,[1] and five years later St. Andrew's Chapel, close to his own residence at Fasque.

The member for Newark's interest in religious affairs in Scotland was specially proved by the share he took in founding Trinity College, Glenalmond. This institution, which was designed for the education of the clergy and wealthier members of the Scottish Episcopal Church, had
1840. its inception in the summer of 1840; and
Mr. Gladstone and although the credit for its original idea has
Trinity College, Glenalmond. been given to both Mr. Gladstone and Hope, the probabilities are in favour of the former, though each was most active in its promotion. Much correspondence passed between the two regarding it; an episcopal synod in Edinburgh warmly thanked them for their pains; they were empowered by the Scottish bishops to form a committee in London to forward the work; and, while Hope visited Italy in the autumn for the benefit of his health, Mr. Gladstone, who had the assistance of Dean Ramsay, remained the chief prosecutor of the scheme. John Gladstone displayed almost as keen an interest in the plan. 'He could not understand or tolerate,' said his youngest son, in later describing this period, 'those who, perceiving an object to be good, did not at once and actively pursue it;' and when the institution was nearly complete, with Charles Wordsworth as its first Warden, it was the father who laid the foundation-stone of the chapel. But the result in the end was disappointment to Wordsworth, and possibly to Mr. Gladstone himself; while, before the college had thoroughly settled into working order, Hope joined the Church of Rome.[2]

[1] *British Magazine*, July, 1841, p. 116.
[2] Hope-Scott's 'Memoirs,' vol. i., pp. 206-13, 274-82; vol. ii., pp. 278-81.

Just when the Glenalmond scheme was being projected, Mr. Gladstone was associated with Hope in another matter affecting religion. The former was deeply interested in the Ecclesiastical Duties and Revenues Bill, introduced by the Whig Government for the purpose of dealing with cathedrals, and, on the measure being sought to be moved into committee, he made a long speech against it, though the position he took had not, as he admitted, the full support of his own side.[1] This address (which was full of ecclesiastical learning, and which was published in pamphlet form) was included with that on the same night by his friend, Thomas Acland, and two made a month later by Knight-Bruce and Hope (as counsel against the measure, heard at the bar of the House of Lords) for special analysis and commendation in the *British Critic* for the following January. It was an unusually strong number, for in it Newman, as is understood, dealt with Milman's ' History of Christianity'; Roundell Palmer wrote upon the education of the intellect in English public schools ; Frederic Rogers criticised William Sewell's ' Christian Morals'; and Thomas Mozley attempted to demolish the works of Channing. The reviewer of the Cathedral Bill speeches singled out for special praise ' the most earnest resistance' made by Philip Pusey, Acland, and Mr. Gladstone, who had stood ' foremost in their high and manly opposition to the whole measure.' Enthusiastic, indeed, was the praise Mr. Gladstone received. ' Of the condensed reasoning of his most masterly speech, one can by extracts give a very imperfect sample': he spoke 'as a man in whom the blind, paltry, short-lived, selfish policy of these days has no share': and 'in concluding, he lashed with a deserved severity of rebuke the temper of the times which has

Marginal note: June 29. Mr. Gladstone and the Cathedrals Bill.

[1] ' Mirror of Parliament' (1840), pp. 4122-33.

rendered possible the conceiving and defending of such a measure.' [1]

Even with these labours in the cause of the Church, Mr. Gladstone was not satisfied ; and in the autumn, though so greatly occupied with the Glenalmond scheme, he gave proof that he was equally willing to continue at work for religious education in England. In the middle of September —and at a moment when a rumour was current that, in the event of a dissolution, he intended offering himself for his native Liverpool—he paid a visit to New-ark ; but it was only a flying one, for, although he went to two churches, attended a concert, and called on the members of his committee, he felt constrained to decline an invitation of the local Tories to a dinner in his honour, because of having promised to speak at a meet-ing in support of the Chester Diocesan Board of Education, held the same week at Liverpool. Received with very marked and lengthened applause, he emphatically declared that children must either be instructed by those who have a sense of the truth of Christianity, or must be abandoned to practical infidel-ity ; and he submitted that a Christian country which was not penetrated and pervaded by religious education could have no stable advantage.

In regard to ecclesiastical affairs, indeed, Mr. Gladstone through all this earlier portion of his career remained the follower and even the henchman of Inglis, and no oppor-tunity was lost for displaying his zeal. His attitude towards the various attempts to abolish the civil disabilities then imposed upon the Jews

Sept. 12.
Visits Newark.

Sept. 18.
Speaks at Liverpool on religious educa-tion.

Mr. Gladstone and Jewish disabilities.

[1] *British Critic*, No. lvii., pp. 114-50. Mr. Gladstone opposed the Cathedrals Bill to the end, speaking on July 20 against the third reading : ' Mirror of Parliament ' (1840), pp. 4705, 4706.

affords a striking instance in point. As Secretary of the
Union, he while at Oxford opposed a motion for their
removal : in his earliest session at Westminster he voted at
every stage against a measure to the same end : and at the
commencement of the first Victorian Parliament, he went
into the majority lobby against an instruction to committee
on the Municipal Officers' Declaration Bill, designed to extend to Jews the relief afforded to persons of other religious
denominations. When, at the beginning of the session of
1841, Divett, the Whig member for Exeter,   1841.
sought to introduce a Jews' Declaration Bill, His action upon
to enable Jews to hold office in corporations   them.
on the same terms as 'Quakers, Moravians, and Separatists'
(David Salomons, who was so often to be in the front of
the fight until it was won, being unable to take the position
of alderman of the City of London to which he had been
elected), Inglis opposed it, on the ground that Jews were of
a different nation to ourselves. Mr. Gladstone held the
same course, but upon the contention that the measure really
involved the whole question of whether Jews were competent to sit in Parliament, and legislate for a Christian
country. 'I have no desire to inflict any hardship on individuals,' he exclaimed ; 'but I am sure there is a universal sentiment in this country that it would not be a safe
general principle to admit into the Legislature persons of a
peculiar character, whose religious belief is incompatible
with the duties they would have to perform.'[1]   He repeated his objections at some length on the third reading,
of which he moved the rejection,[2] and in a speech which
Macaulay immediately described as most unfair, though
delivered by one whom the essayist went on to mention as

[1] Feb. 9, 1841 : 'Mirror of Parliament' (1841, 1st session), p. 194.
[2] March 31 : *Ibid.*, pp. 1121-4.

2 D

'so great an ornament of the House of Commons.'[1] The third reading was carried by an overwhelming majority, including a few Tories; and, though the Lords threw it out, the measure was adopted some years later, and at a time when Mr. Gladstone, newly elected for Oxford University, went against the wishes of the majority of his constituents, and supported a far wider plan of Jewish relief than that which he now opposed.

'Of association with what was termed ultra-Toryism, in general politics, I had never dreamed,' has written Mr. Gladstone concerning the period when he was in the Cabinet of Peel; but the same cannot with exactness be said of his attitude throughout the earlier time when he was the faithful, though not the slavish, supporter of the Conservative chief. It has been seen how upon Church matters he took his own line, though it might be to his detriment;

His attitude in general politics. and during the prolonged and tedious discussions upon the question of privilege involved in the dispute between the House of Commons and the Courts of Law regarding the published reports of debates, the member for Newark declined to follow his leader, and, in company with only one occupant of the front Opposition bench [2] but of many independent Tories, voted against the Commons' claim. Negro apprenticeship had been his leading theme for speech in 1838; national education had furnished his chief topic in 1839; while in 1840, not only did the Cathedrals Bill give opportunity for a strik-

1840. The China question. ing address, but the burning questions of China and Canada brought him even further to the front. A long series of blunders and

---

[1] *Ibid.*, pp. 1124-6.

[2] Herries: see Edward Herries' 'Memoir of J. C. Herries,' vol. ii., p. 178.

misunderstandings with the Celestial Empire, because of English smuggling of opium, had resulted in a condition of affairs at Canton which closely resembled war. It was accordingly resolved by the House of Commons in the spring of 1840 to appoint a select committee to inquire into the grievances complained of in a petition of merchants interested in China, by reason of the surrender of opium to the British superintendent there; and Mr. Gladstone was nominated upon it, in company with Palmerston and Peel, Herbert and Inglis, Charles Buller and Horsman. Much evidence was taken and Mr. Gladstone's questions were many, but the result of the investigation was negative.[1]

April.
Mr. Gladstone on a China committee.

A positive outcome of the member for Newark's interest in the matter was that an incautious utterance in debate concerning it brought upon him such an amount of obloquy as he had not previously experienced, but of which he was to taste much more. In April, Graham, acting on behalf of the Opposition, moved a resolution declaring that the interruption in commercial and friendly intercourse between the two countries was mainly to be attributed to the want of foresight and precaution on the part of Ministers. Macaulay replied in a brilliant speech; and on the second night of the debate, immediately following Charles Buller, Mr. Gladstone, who had been industriously taking notes, entered the lists. It is not necessary at this date to go into the details of the supposed iniquities of the Chinese Commissioner Lin or the difficulties of Captain Elliot, the British representative at Canton; but Mr. Gladstone's contribution to the discussion was concerned with more than these, for it contained an unsparing denunciation of the traffic in opium and the war it had

April 8.
His speech.

[1] ' Parliamentary Papers ' (1840), vol. vii., pp. 1-221.

occasioned, and a glowing eulogium upon the British flag.

Macaulay had referred to a letter from Elliot, describing the enthusiasm which greeted his hoisting of the national banner over a threatened factory at Canton, 'because he knew that no Englishman could look upon that flag, even in that far extremity of the world, without remembering the glories, and confiding in the power, of his country.' Mr. Gladstone His eulogium upon endorsed the sentiment. 'We all know,' he the British flag. exclaimed, 'the animating effects which have been produced by the flag in the minds of British subjects on many a critical occasion, in many a hard-fought field. But, how comes it to pass that the sight of that flag always raises the spirit of Englishmen? It is because it has always been associated with the cause of justice, with the protection of the oppressed, with respect for national rights, with honourable commercial enterprise ; but now, under the auspices of the noble lord [Palmerston, then Foreign Secretary], that flag is hoisted for the purpose of protecting an infamous contraband traffic ; and if it were never to be hoisted except as it is now hoisted on the coast of China, we should recoil from its sight with horror, and should never again feel our hearts thrill, as they now do, with emotion, when it floats proudly and magnificently in the breeze.'

This outburst was the more remarkable as an example not merely of eloquence but of self-possession, since it followed upon a slip which only a few moments before Mr. Gladstone had made, and which gave him temporarily into the hands of his opponents. Macaulay, adopting an accusation which the Whigs as a body professed to believe, had said that the Chinese at Macao poisoned the water the British residents had to drink. The member for Newark replied that the natives feared that the intention of these residents was to resume the opium smuggling which was being endeavoured to be put down. 'The Chinese,' he said, 'had no means of expelling them by an armament; they could only expel them by refusing a supply of provisions; and, of course, they poisoned the wells.' As the words fell from his lips, a roar of cheers, which were not of approval, went up from the Whig benches, and was repeated several times with considerable warmth and indignation. 'I am ready to meet those cheers,' Mr. Gladstone proceeded, 'I understand what they mean. I may do the Chinese injustice by saying they poisoned the wells. All I mean to say is that it has been alleged that they had poisoned their wells.' The Whigs having received the explanation with derisive shouts, the speaker resumed: 'They had given you full notice, and wished to drive you from their coast. They had a right to drive you from their coast if you persisted in carrying on this infamous and atrocious traffic.' It was now the turn of the Tories to applaud; and Mr. Gladstone concluded this portion of his remarks by saying: 'You allowed your agent to aid and abet those who were concerned in carrying on that trade; and I do not know how it can be urged as a crime against the Chinese that they refused provisions to those who refused obedience to their laws whilst residing within their territories.'[1]

He had thus avoided repeating his reference to the wells, but his opponents were not as ready to let the matter drop. Ward, the member for Sheffield, who followed him, commenced, it is true, with a half compliment, but immediately proceeded, amid loud cheers from the Whigs, to denounce Mr. Gladstone as having justified the blockade of the English factories, the seizure of the innocent and guilty together, and the poisoning of the

Marginal note: 'Poisoning the wells.'

Marginal note: Mr. Gladstone bitterly attacked.

[1] 'Mirror of Parliament' (1840), pp. 2452-61.

wells. Mr. Gladstone interjected the remark, 'I justified
only the allegation'; but Ward enlarged upon the theme.
'The honourable member justifies the poisoning of the
wells on the whole line of the Chinese coast, in order to deprive of fresh water English women and children.' And
such attacks did not cease even with the sitting. On the
third and closing night of the discussion, Dr. Lushington,
the Whig representative of the Tower Hamlets, took up the
parable, and said of Mr. Gladstone's contribution, as one of
the most eloquent of the debate, 'It was a memorable
speech! I can never forget it, nor will, I believe, the
people of this country. It was a most able speech—and I
have the greatest admiration for the honourable gentleman's
talents—but it contained doctrines which I heard with a
horror that I cannot describe. . . . I respect him; I know
him to be a powerful champion in every cause he thinks to
be right; but I own I shall never cease to reprobate the
argument which he used last night, or to avow my abhorrence of the doctrines he endeavoured to maintain.'[1]
Hobhouse, as a Minister, joined in the condemnation,
declining to believe that the unfortunate remark was a slip
of the tongue, for it appeared to him to have been as deliberately spoken as anything ever said in the House;[2]
and Peel felt it necessary to come to the rescue. The
Conservative leader entirely deprecated the advantage that
had been taken of an expression used in the heat of debate,
'an advantage which, from the joyfulness with which it was
seized, proved to me how happy honourable members

He is defended by   opposite are to have any adventitious aid,
       Peel,   even from the casual expression of a man
whose character and uniform demeanour ought to have
taught them that they were putting a construction on his

---

[1] *Ibid.*, pp. 2491-4.   [2] *Ibid.*, pp. 2504, 2505.

expressions which he never meant to convey.' Peel went
on to cast doubt upon the whole poisoning-of-wells
story;[1] but Palmerston, who followed, declared that this
was only a part of an ingenious defence of   and assailed by
Mr. Gladstone's words—words which he had   Palmerston.
heard with deep regret and pain—and that the member for
Newark's mistake lay in the sentiment and not in the fact.
Mr. Gladstone intervened to deny Palmerston's assumption
that he had implied approbation of well-poisoning; and the
Foreign Secretary repudiated the intention of any offensive
imputation, avowing his willingness to believe that his
young opponent was the last man in the House who, upon
reflection, would stand up in his place to defend a doctrine
so monstrous, but adding regret that he had not admitted
having hastily and inconsiderately used the now famous
remark.[2]   And the last word spoken in the Commons on
the matter was by Graham, who, in winding up, told Palmerston that, while commenting with so much severity upon
the unguarded expression of Mr. Gladstone, he might have
remembered that his own friends had not been remarkable
for their measured language.[3]

The *Times*, in summarising its impressions of the whole
debate, averred that the speeches of Mr. Gladstone and
Sandon were eloquent and striking manifestations ' by
those exemplary representatives of the virtues which most
adorn the British character,' for ' the dreadful consequences
of an extensive trade in opium are as indisputable as Mr.
Gladstone's exhibition of its criminal and hateful spirit was
appalling.' The *Morning Herald* declared   The Press join the
Mr. Gladstone's utterance to have been one   controversy.
of great power, and the reply of Ward to have been merely
glib; but one may doubt the absolute soundness of a

[1] *Ibid.*, p. 2524.   [2] *Ibid.*, p. 2529.   [3] *Ibid.*, p. 2543.

judgment which characterised the speech of Palmerston as 'feeble beyond description, yet as a specimen of easy impudence in style and manner it was absolutely a curiosity.' To the *Standard*, Mr. Gladstone's appeared a speech of both power and beauty; and on the following day it bitterly assailed Palmerston for his reference to the 'poisoning the wells' remark. 'Being rebuked for the falsehood,' it exclaimed, 'he sneaks out of it in the style of mingled pettifogging and cringing. . . . This may be *triumphant* in a Whig, but we should blush at such an exhibition as exceedingly sneaking and discreditable in a Conservative.' This outburst had been provoked by an article in the *Morning Chronicle*, for, in its summary of the debate, the leading Whig organ had observed, 'Mr. Gladstone will not soon forget the lecture he received from Lord Palmerston on the subject of poisoning: we will answer for it the honourable gentleman will be shy about poison as long as he lives;' and in its editorial article it had trampled on the member for Newark at some length. 'Mr. Gladstone,' it said, 'bravely throws down his gauntlet on behalf of the morality of poison; if poison be good against opium and smuggling, why not also against Chartism and Whiggism and Corn-láw agitation?' It did not believe that the speaker meant to carry out the principle unflinchingly, but he had 'pleaded for poison as if it were a weapon which God and nature had put into the hands of the Chinese against British traders. It is well for him that there is no Chatham in the House of Commons: he must have been unsainted for ever. . . Who knows but that, through the Oriental world, to poison a well may soon be designated the Gladstonian operation?' The next day, the Whig journal resumed the attack; and, having ironically averred that Mr. Gladstone's had been the only straightforward speech in the debate, since that gentleman had maintained that throughout the whole course of the proceedings the Chinese had been perfectly in the right, and the British entirely in the wrong, it wrote, ' Mr. Gladstone, since the publication of his work on Church and State, seems to be considered even by his own party as privileged to utter what paradoxes he pleases. Of his speech it is sufficient to observe, that it would have been better adapted for the meridian of Pekin than of London ; and that the defence of the right of the "enlightened and civilised " Chinese to poison their wells, might be rewarded in the celestial empire with a two-eyed peacock's feather, but in "barbarian " England is likely to excite nothing but feelings of indignation and contempt.'

Unaffrighted by this storm, Mr. Gladstone in the summer returned to the attack upon the expedition, which was then on its way to China. Feeling that the greatest moral responsibility is incurred by those who commence a war, he could not in *July 27. Again speaks on China,* his conscience allow the vote for the expedition to pass unchallenged; and, once more denouncing the opium traffic, he declared that the war had been entered upon without full justification.[1] Hobhouse expressed himself at a loss to know what earthly use the member for Newark proposed to obtain by his speech ; taunted him with the bareness of the Tory benches, ' star after star having faded, one by one having retired from the scene' ; told him that his lenient view of the Chinese was utterly opposed to that held by Wellington ; and added the belief that he had not with him the sympathies of twenty men, in or out of Parliament.[2] George Palmer, the Tory member for South Essex, thanked Mr. Gladstone for thus enabling him to disavow the course the Government

[1] *Ibid.*, pp. 4974-9.
[2] *Ibid.*, pp. 4979-82.

had taken, and which, in his opinion, was a disgrace to the
and is once more
attacked. country; but Sir Charles Grey, the Whig
representative of Tynemouth, and a retired
Indian judge, censured him for having attempted to throw
upon the Ministry the whole blame of the struggle.   Sandon
defended Mr. Gladstone, but Palmerston agreed with Hobhouse in declared inability to discover his object, and denounced him in bitter terms as having attempted to poison
the public mind.[1]   Peel (who had not heard Mr. Gladstone's speech, and who had formed so erroneous an idea of
its contents that his young follower had to publicly correct
his version) considered Palmerston to have been too harsh,
but he evidently wished an inconvenient discussion to
close;[2] and, after a little further talk, the vote was allowed
to pass without challenge.

How the efforts of Mr. Gladstone on the China question
were estimated and appreciated by one of his friends,
and that one as clear-sighted and experienced as Bunsen,
is shown in what the latter wrote him from Berne,
Bunsen praises him. early in August.   'Let me now thank you,'
the Prussian Minister said, 'in the name of
all Christians, and of all well-wishers to the glory and welfare of England, for your indefatigable efforts to rescue your
dear country from the eternal reproach of the opium question.   You can scarcely be aware what good you have done,
in enabling the friends of England abroad to maintain their
ground against her numerous enemies, all Romanists,
Atheists, Jacobins, of all colours and nations, Montalembert
and his friends at the head, throwing that question in our
face, as proving the humbug and hypocrisy of all pretended
Christian profession and works of the English nation, as
abolition of slavery, Bible and Missionary Societies, &c.   I

[1] *Ibid.*, pp. 4985-8.　　　　　[2] *Ibid.*, pp. 4988, 4989.

have thanked God, that Sandon and all to whom my heart and soul are attached in England, followed the same course with you.' [1]   And, in point of fact, no more scathing condemnations of the opium traffic have ever been uttered than in those speeches of 1840.

Mr. Gladstone, indeed, was as far removed from the ordinary members of his party on this question as he was upon that of Canada, which also and once more was under discussion in this same year.   At the end of May, when the House of Commons was going into committee upon the Canada Government Bill (which, introduced by Russell as Colonial Secretary, proposed the union of the two provinces, over which Poulett Thomson was now Governor-General), Mr. Gladstone, in separating from such Tories as wished to reject the measure, considered himself called upon to explain the reasons by which he was actuated 'in following the line which I have chalked out for myself.'   Nothing daunted by the cries of 'divide' which met him as he rose, he attributed a great portion of the existing difficulties to the much-disputed report of Lord Durham ; and he repeated his doctrine

May 29.
His attitude on the
Canada question.

as to the retention of the colonies, submitting that nothing could be more ridiculous or mistaken than to suppose that the United Kingdom had anything to gain by maintaining a union with her colonial possessions in opposition to the deliberate and permanent conviction of the colonists themselves.[2]   Buller and Howick generally approved the speech, while Russell showed himself much pleased with it, for it was more entirely in accordance with the Ministerial plans than even Peel had proved himself to be;[3] and, when the Bill went into committee, Mr. Gladstone joined with

---

[1] Bunsen's ' Memoir,' vol. i., pp. 582, 583.

[2] 'Mirror of Parliament' (1840), pp. 3410-14.   [3] *Ibid.*, p. 3422.

Russell to defeat a Radical amendment for striking out a property qualification for members of the Assembly.[1]

According to the Whig *Chronicle*, Mr. Gladstone's speech gave evidence throughout of great grasp of mind and ability of the first order; his language, it declared, was that of a true British statesman, who, in the war of party, never forgets the best interests of his country; and it ecstatically concluded its praise with the exclamation, 'What a contrast between this enlightened gentleman and the bigoted Bishop of Exeter and his narrow-minded brethren in the House of Lords!' The fact, of course, was that (as the *Globe*, another Whig journal, phrased it) Mr. Gladstone had brought the olive-branch to the hands of the Government; and this would account for the *Morning Herald* almost and the *Times* absolutely ignoring the speech as a theme for criticism. But the *Newark Times*, a newly-established Tory paper in his own constituency, was emphatic in eulogium: 'We would especially impress upon our Canadian brethren the deepest consideration of the whole and every point of Mr. Gladstone's address. It is the reasoning of a true philosopher no less than a statesman, it is the warning voice of a friend no less than of a christian, it is replete with the affectionate counsels of a brother and the solicitude of a parent, forecasting for the future welfare of offspring in their entrance into life. . . In truth, it deserves to be written in letters of gold, and hung up over every Canadian hearth.'

The Press upon it.

In the next month, on the second reading of a Ministerial Bill to settle the question of the clergy reserves in Upper Canada, which had for years convulsed the province, Mr. Gladstone, while disliking the measure, felt he could not vote against it;[2] and he was

June 15. Canada again.

[1] *Ibid.*, p. 3428.   [2] *Ibid.*, pp. 3765-9.

accordingly with the Whigs in the majority, though Inglis told for the minority, and Glynne in the one House and Lyttelton in the other opposed the Bill.   But with this action, and an ineffectual suggestion in committee a month later, Mr. Gladstone's immediate concern with Canada ceased ; and, save for the address on the sugar duties in 1841, before described, his principal parliamentary speeches during his earlier period were ended also.

XVII.—ONCE MORE A MINISTER.

By the time 'the Forties' had opened, Mr. Gladstone was
so distinctly a figure in the political world that not merely
what he said but how he said it furnished material for more
than one pen to depict.   James Grant's description of him
as he was in 1838 has been given; but one from another
hand, published two years later, equally deserves quotation,
as reading with singularity now.   The *Britannia*, a weekly
Conservative organ, and in a sense a rival of *John Bull*, was
issuing at that period, under the suggestive heading, 'The
Anatomy of Parliament,' a series of sketches of the leading
politicians of the day, and Mr. Gladstone's turn came in
the winter of 1840.   Of the House of Commons generally,
it was said that 'the kind of speaker who, above all, earns
the respect and regard of the assembly, is he who approaches
his subject with a reverential earnestness, and develops, by
the simplicity of his diction, and the warm sincerity of his
manner, that he recognises in addressing them, a more
stern duty and a higher aim than that of merely talking
down to their interests, or appealing to their prejudices and
passions.'   Mr. Gladstone was declared to be such a man.
'Great expectations were formed of him as a parliamentary
speaker from his known abilities, and he did not disappoint
the good wishes of his admirers and friends.   He at once
stamped himself as a man of a very high
order of intellect, and also as having entered
Parliament the sworn champion of principles
from which no consideration would induce him to swerve.

A Conservative de-
scription of Mr.
Gladstone in 1840.

Strange to say, in a House composed, for the most part, of men of all degrees of flexibility of conscience, men like this are the most respected. It would not be possible, I think, to find throughout the House of Commons, a man who would not join spontaneously in expressing admiration of such men as Mr. Gladstone.'

But 'Lorgnette,' as the writer signed himself, proceeded to a singular criticism. 'It must not be supposed that Mr. Gladstone is at all a brilliant speaker ; on the contrary, his powers as an orator—physical powers, that is to say—are of a rather insignificant kind. Nevertheless, he always insensibly enchains the attention of the House when he speaks. The charm of his style consists in the earnestness and sincerity of his manner, his evident conviction of the importance of the truths which he is uttering, and, above all, the mild gentlemanly humility with which he offers the result of his deep and secluded thinking to the world. . . . But Mr. Gladstone's voice is unfortunately weak. The tone is not bad, being very mild and musical ; but it sounds like a good voice heard a great way off, or through a partition. It is better adapted for persuasion, quiet argument, or for the expression of that subdued earnestness which results from deep religious feeling, than for discharging the more usual and more stormy functions of a public speaker. It is such a voice as might have been bred in a cloister, passive amid the working of inward inspiration, repressed and pent up by pious forms. Indeed, Mr. Gladstone's whole appearance, and the general tone of his mind, is that of a student—a student of the old times, such as we read of and wish to be, but never are, because the world will still distract us. Gentle he is and absorbed, silent and reserved, without being unamiable—a passive being in all but the intense and abstracted working of the intellect burning in the bright eye, whose steady though unaffected gaze fascinates you like that of a basilisk. You know that it is but the external symptom of a mind absorbed in contemplation, yet you cannot but believe that its gaze is directed to you, for it seems to read your very soul.'

After compliments to the high ground he took in his speeches, especially upon church questions, and the ejaculation, 'Were there more Mr. Gladstones there might be fewer dissenters,' the writer proceeded to personal description. 'He is altogether a man of no ordinary kind; his mind is cast in no common mould. Had he physical powers commensurate with his intellectual endowments, he would become a first-rate public man, for he has those essential qualities of greatness—strength of mind and sincerity of purpose. His countenance is, as has been said, intellectual, but not what would be called handsome. His complexion is pale, with a slight tinge of the olive, and his dark hair sets off both that and the brilliancy of his intellectual eye. He wears his hair cut close to his head, and, like the late Earl of Durham, has no whiskers. His person is not advantageous, and he has the short, stealthy, stooping gait of a man accustomed to and absorbed in studious pursuits. Nevertheless, no one could pass him without at once noticing that he was a man of great mental acquirements. He is looked upon as a very rising man in the House, but he does not appear to be ambitious—at least not to be actuated by that more common kind of ambition which aims at dignities and worldly honours.' [1]

This description is the more interesting because, at the

[1] The *Britannia*, Nov. 7, 1840. The same number contained a bitter versified attack upon Lyttelton as candidate for the Cambridge High Stewardship, describing him *inter alia* as 'a thing of the Court.'

very period it was being circulated, the Newark Tories were subscribing to procure for the ornament of the local Conservative News-Room and Reading Society portraits of Mr. Gladstone and Frederic Thesiger (afterwards the Lord Chelmsford who had to complain that Disraeli dismissed him from the Chancellorship with less notice than is accustomed to be given to a chambermaid). Thesiger, though then sitting for Woodstock, was at the moment highly popular at Newark, where he had stood at a bye-election of the previous January, caused by the promotion of Wilde to be Solicitor-General. The Serjeant, when threatened with opposition, paid in his address a special compliment to Mr. Gladstone, observing, ' the high talents of my amiable Coadjutor so justly estimated by all parties secure you from any disparaging comparison so far as he is concerned.' But the unmollified Tories brought out an-   The Newark Elec-
other lawyer in the person of Thesiger ; and   tion of
' An Old Voter for Wilde ' indignantly in-   January, 1840.
quired on a handbill why the new law-officer should no longer be considered independent because he had joined the Government. ' Did the Reds ask you to reject Mr. Gladstone, when he was chosen to sojourn three months under Peel's administration ?   Did they, like honest men, come forth and say we cannot now present Mr. Gladstone ; he being no longer a man worthy of our confidence ? Oh, no ! the case was far different.   Know all men ; he was infallible ! from the fact of his being a *Tory.*' Mr. Gladstone put in no appearance, either by person or pen, during the contest—though Lincoln stood by Thesiger's side on the hustings—which may account for the fact that, after Wilde had snatched victory out of the fire by a majority of only nine, the old President of the Red Club (T. S. Godfrey) declared at a parting dinner, and amid enthusiastic

2 E

applause, that Thesiger was the best Conservative candidate
who had ever been seen in Newark.

Such resentment at Mr. Gladstone's absence as there may
have been, however, speedily disappeared. He had always
kept himself in touch with his constituents, and he seldom
went among them without strengthening his popularity.
In those early days he had an excellent singing voice, and
once when at a dinner at Newark he pleased himself and
delighted his friends by taking part in the old glee, ' Could
a man be secure.'   His musical as much as his clerical
tastes, indeed, led him in the spring of 1839 to present an
organ to Christ Church, which had just been erected and
endowed by voluntary subscription in the
borough.   At a local Conservative ball a
year later, and just after the Wilde-Thesiger
contest, one of the banners displayed was that given to him
long before by the ladies of the town ; in the early autumn
of 1840, he paid a flying visit to his friends there ; and in
the October, at a supper of the Conservative News-Room
and Reading Society, ' our distinguished representative ' was
toasted as a man of whom every Red elector was justly
proud, one of the speakers exclaiming that ' when an
O'Connell, a Melbourne, and a Russell usurped the place
of a Wellington, a Peel, and a Gladstone, it was indeed a
matter for surprise.'

Mr. Gladstone's relations with Newark.

A little later, the *Newark Times* was able to announce
that ' our talented townsman, Mr. Cubley,' was about to
execute the two portraits ; and that gentleman, who survived to see Mr. Gladstone four times Prime Minister,
travelled to London to execute the task. ' Those who remember the right honourable gentleman during his early
career at Newark,' says the historian of that town, ' describe
him as being a fine, healthful-looking man. His figure was

somewhat slim ; his face was plump, with scarce a line upon
it ; his cheeks possessed the ruddy glow of   His portrait
health ; his hair was dark and plentiful ;   subscribed for.
his eyes were large and expressive ; and his countenance
was animated with an ever-varying expression.'[1]   Mr.
Gladstone gave the artist sittings at his then residence in
Carlton House Terrace ; but Mr. Cubley's remembrance is
that his task was executed under somewhat difficult circumstances, for he never obtained five minutes' uninterrupted
work : ' he was most kind in giving me all the time he could,
but he was constantly being called upon ; in fact, I believe
almost every bishop in England visited him during those
sittings.'

In the following February, and just after ' our admirable
representative' had given £50 towards a subscription for
the relief of the Newark poor, the portraits were formally
presented to the Society at a meeting of the
subscribers, and the speeches were most   February 22, 1841.
encomiastic.   One even contrasted ' the fine   The portrait
                                                    presented.
intellectual countenance' of Mr. Gladstone with ' the
malignant expression' of Wilde ; and the orator added that
all Englishmen had a prejudice in favour of those whose
faces bore the stamp of truth and honesty, and he hoped
that such a man as the one before them would shortly be at
the head of the Government—a sentiment which was received with loud cheering.   Mr. Gladstone was not there to
speak for himself, but his agent was ; and, after it had been
declared that the family of their representative was much
pleased with the portrait, and the artist had been most
warmly thanked, ' this interesting meeting,' said the local
chronicler, ' concluded by three times three cheers for Mr.
Gladstone and Mr. Thesiger, and nine times nine for the

---

[1] Brown's ' Newark,' p. 289

Queen.' It was said at the time that the editor of a publication, entitled 'The Portraits of Eminent Conservatives and Statesmen,' had asked permission to engrave both pictures for the series ; but, although portraits of Thesiger and Mr. Gladstone appeared in this work (in the latter case not until after he had become President of the Board of Trade in 1843), they were not those of Mr. Cubley, but were respectively painted by artists named Holmes and Severn. The Cubley pictures stayed on the walls where they were originally hung until the dissolution of the Society, when they passed into the possession of Alderman Branston, a Newark justice of the peace, in whose hall they remain, though in the time to come the National Portrait Gallery will not be complete without them.[1]

Only four months after the presentation, Mr. Gladstone was able to put the political affection of his Newark friends to an electoral test, and with the most gratifying success. Having lost at the commencement of the Parliament the company of his eldest brother, Thomas, who had been His brothers and Parliament. defeated upon seeking to sit again for Leicester, Mr. Gladstone had the satisfaction, just as its last session commenced, of seeing another brother, Neilson, win a seat from the Whigs at Walsall ; and, though it was as ' a decided Conservative' that he stood, he boasted that he did not come before the electors as the advocate of the landed interest, as all his family were connected with trade. During the session, as has been described, the member for Newark made one great speech, and that upon so essentially a trading question as the sugar duties ; but a vote which he gave might have had for him

[1] Hearty thanks are due to Mr. Cubley, the artist, and to Alderman Branston, the owner, for their permission to reproduce the Gladstone portrait, and to Mr. Cornelius Brown for his friendly aid in the matter.

THE RIGHT HON. W. E. GLADSTONE, M.

1843

awkward consequences. It has been seen how he generally supported the principle of the new Poor Law, passed by the Whigs in 1834; and when, early in 1841, Russell introduced a Bill for continuing its operation, though Disraeli moved its rejection, and despite His attitude on the the fact that popular prejudice against the Poor Law. workhouses (which by some were called ' Bastilles ') was at its height, Mr. Gladstone went into the majority lobby for the second reading. This gave umbrage to some of his staunchest Newark supporters ; and, at the meeting in February concerning his portrait, his agent read a letter from him, explaining that, whatever might be said of his opinions on the subject, at least they were not those of one who went ' the whole hog.' He had voted for the second reading, and should support it going into committee, but partly because he wished to see some mitigations introduced into the general administration of the system. Broadly speaking, he was a firm friend to the ordinary use of the workhouse test for able-bodied labourers ; while, with respect to the aged and infirm poor, he was an advocate for their being comfortably maintained in their own homes in all cases when it could be done with advantage, and, if in the workhouse, without any separation of husband and wife. Upon another point, that of illegitimacy, he anticipated the more humane ideas of later days, and his own arguments upon the Divorce Bill of sixteen years later, by declaring, ' I wish to see the burden and penalty equitably divided between the guilty parties, and not laid solely upon the woman.'

Mr. Gladstone took no part in the great debate upon Sir Robert Peel's motion of want of confidence in the Melbourne Ministry, which was carried by a The dissolution majority of one, and which necessitated a dis- of 1841. solution in June ; but he at once issued an address to the

electors of Newark, soliciting a renewal of the trust which
for three successive Parliaments they had placed in his
hands ; and in this he said :

'There are two questions among those at present agitated,
which will naturally excite a peculiar interest among you ;
those namely relating to the Poor Law and

June 8.
His address to the
Newark electors.
to the Corn Law. With regard to the
former, I rejoice that the late House of
Commons has sanctioned some proposals intended to prevent severity in the administration of relief, and has
rejected others which tended unduly to enlarge the powers
of the central authority. It would be my desire, as a
Member of the new Parliament, to contribute to such an
adjustment of the law, as while securing *support for the
destitute, the liberal treatment of the aged, sick, and the widowed
Poor*, and the reasonable discretion of the local administrators
of the law, should likewise effectually preclude the recurrence
of former abuses, and should *encourage the industry*, and *promote the comforts*, of the independent labourer.

'With respect to the Corn Law, I wish for a just balance
of the great interests of the Country : I regard the protection of native agriculture as an object of the first economical
and national importance, and I am of opinion that such
protection should be given, for the sake both of the pro-
ducer and the consumer, by means of a graduated scale of
duties upon Foreign Grain.

'It has been my study to represent with fidelity those
principles of attachment to the Queen, and to the Constitution in Church and State, which I believe to prevail among
yourselves ; and I am persuaded that your Votes at the approaching Election, will indicate and affirm the censure so
recently passed upon the existing Ministers by a House of
Commons which was summoned under their auspices, and

which, after long endurance, has declared that their continuance in Office is at variance with the spirit of the Constitution.'[1]

The *Newark Times* was enthusiastic in praise of this document: 'We refer our readers with pleasure to the manly and straightforward address of our present excellent and high-minded representative, Mr. Gladstone. We need say no more upon this subject than that the address is the honest appeal of an upright mind, relying upon past exertions as an undeniable recommendation to future favours, and not descending to any of the canting and humbugging professions which sometimes characterise election addresses.'

Wilde, warned by the narrow majority of eighteen months before, left Newark to seek and find a surer seat at Worcester; Thesiger felt himself comfortably settled at Woodstock; but, while the Whigs were without a candidate, the Tories secured a colleague for Mr. Gladstone in Lord John Manners. The newcomer was the poet of the 'Young England' party, a Tory section with the members of which Mr. Gladstone was never in sympathy, though the expression of his wish, when he stood on the Newark hustings for the first time, for a return to the manly and God-fearing principles of centuries before, was in marked anticipation of one of its aims. Over three years previously, Milnes had written to a

The contest.

[1] This address was dated from 13 Carlton House Terrace, Mr. Gladstone's first true London home. On leaving Oxford, he had established himself in the Albany, where his brother Thomas also had rooms; but early in 1837 he let his chambers, nominally for a twelvemonth, and went to live with his father at 6 Carlton Gardens. There he spent the first months of his married life, but he then moved to 13 Carlton House Terrace, in which, and No. 11 hard by, he dwelt for some 35 years.

friend, ' I go on with small " young Englands" on Sunday evenings, which unfortunately exclude the more severe members—Acland, Gladstone, etc. ; ' [1] and two years after

Mr. Gladstone and ' Young England.' the present contest, the senior member for Newark severely censured the tactics of the ' Young England' leaders, who included Disraeli and George Smythe. But even then he excepted from condemnation the philanthropic efforts of Lord John Manners ; [2] and, in the contest of 1841, they worked closely together. The canvass commenced on June 17th, and the candidates, who were accompanied by a procession with banners, were attacked by a crowd, with the result of a general disturbance. Their card bore the inscription, ' Mr.

Mr. Gladstone, co-candidate with Lord John Manners. W. E. Gladstone and Lord John Manners respectfully solicit your vote and interest ; ' and of the new-comer, the Whig *Notting-ham Mercury* observed that he was ' a mere youth, and as much fit to be an M.P. as he is to be an Archbishop.'

But that was soon shown to be far from the opinion of the electors generally ; and on the 19th, the day they had finished their canvass, Mr. Gladstone and Lord John Manners felt able to issue a joint address, declaring the certainty of their being returned by a very large majority, and adding that ' should an Opposition be raised, it can have no other effect than to exhibit the numerical weakness of the antagonists of those Political Principles to which we are attached : the Principles, namely, which pledge us to defend the Altar and the Throne, as the best guarantees of the Rights and Liberties of the People.' At the very last moment, Thomas Benjamin Hobhouse (who had repre-sented Rochester in the defunct House, and who later sat

[1] Reid's ' Houghton,' vol. i., p. 218.
[2] *Ibid.*, p. 313.

in a single Parliament for Lincoln) offered himself as their opponent; but there was very little interest in an election the result of which was a foregone conclusion. Of one of the speeches delivered by Mr. Gladstone during the campaign, the *Times* had been moved to declare that 'his allusions to the Poor Law Amendment Act brought tears into the eyes of both old and young, and his happy method of cutting up the Baring budget was met by the repeated and long-continued cheering of his hearers'; while its summary of the hustings speech on the 28th did not lack colour: 'Mr. Gladstone invited the most rigid scrutiny of his speeches and votes in Parliament, and was prepared to defend every word he had spoken and every vote he had given. He then, in a powerful strain of caustic irony, exposed the tergiversation and jobbing of the Whig Ministry, and defied their supporter *His hustings speech.* and nominee, Mr. Hobhouse, to explain away the numerous and damning cases of imbecility and apostacy from their own professed principles which were recorded against them.' But, during this latter address, Mr. Gladstone was so much interrupted that he was not fully reported by even the local Tory organ, the *Newark Times*, though it endeavoured to compensate for the omission by saying, 'What little we could hear of Mr. Gladstone's speech, appeared to us to be the master-piece of the day. We perceived Mr. Hobhouse tremble and shake as if the judgment day had arrived, when all the evil deeds of the Ministry were to be brought to light.' And, although the show of hands was given in favour of the Whig as against the second Conservative, *Once more returned.* Mr. Gladstone polled 633 votes, Lord John Manners 630, and Hobhouse 394, a substantial victory with which the Tories were hugely pleased.

Mr. Gladstone was the only member of his family who

was fortunate at this general election which almost swept the Whigs away, for, on the day before the Newark contest, Defeat of his brothers. Thomas was beaten at Peterborough; while, on the day itself, Neilson lost his four months' seat at Walsall. But consolation was soon to come. The overwhelming defeat of the Whigs in the constituencies did not prevent the Melbourne Administration from facing the new Parliament; but, on the morning of August 28th, it was thrown in the House of Commons on the Address by a The Whig Ministry majority of 91, and it at once quitted power. resigns. Two days later, Peel received the Queen's commands to form a Ministry; and among those whom he summoned to an interview on the following morning was Mr. Gladstone, who, at the moment, was commencing to be involved in another theological controversy, this one touching the establishment of that Jerusalem Bishopric which was to drive Newman over to Rome. The offer made by the incoming Premier was far from satisfactory to his young lieutenant, who, having hoped to get the Chief Secretaryship for Ireland, which was given to Lord Eliot, was tendered the Vice-Presidency of the Board of Trade. He was thus disappointed in an early ambition to redress the grievances of Ireland, and to undertake the settlement of the Irish diffi- Mr. Gladstone culty upon drastic lines; and, placed in a appointed to office, subordinate position under so ineffective a chief as Ripon,[1] he returned with some depression to his home.[2] Peel, whose antipathy to Mr. Gladstone's clerical

[1] 'I remember,' said Mr. Gladstone to one of his latest colleagues in 1894, 'when I was appointed to Lord Ripon's department, I felt appalled at the mysteries and difficulties which, I assumed, pertained to it. "Oh," they said to me, "in a month Ripon will have shown you everything." But at the end of the month I found I knew more about the business even than Lord Ripon:' *Daily News*, April 6, 1894.

[2] Statement of Mrs. Gladstone in *United Ireland*, October, 1886.

views may have specially decided him not to send the member for Newark to the Irish Office, gilded the pill by making him a Privy Councillor; and on and sworn of the Privy Council. September 3rd, Mr. Gladstone, in company with Eliot and his old friend Lincoln, was sworn of the Council before the Queen at Claremont, on the day upon which the new Ministers received the seals.[1]   Six days later, Peel went even further, for Mr. Gladstone was then in addition appointed 'Master and Worker of Her Majesty's Mint,'[2] a post for which Herries had been nominated in the newspapers; but even that could scarcely have smoothed away his disappointment, for Labouchere, his predecessor at the Mint, was in the Cabinet and he was not.

As regards his desire to be actively connected with Ireland as early as 1841, it is to be noted that gleams of Mr. Gladstone's opinions concerning the way in which that country had been governed are to be found at various periods of his opening public life.   In his work on Church and State, while ardently defending the Irish Mr. Gladstone and Irish misgovernment. Established Church, he had said, 'We have to consider and digest the fact, that the maintenance of this church for near three centuries in Ireland has been contemporaneous with a system of partial and abusive government, varying in degree of culpability, but rarely until of later years, when we have been forced to look at the subject and to feel it, to be exempted, in common fairness, from the reproach of gross inattention (to say the least) to the interests of a noble but neglected people.'[3]   Even more emphatic is another contemporary

[1] 'Bulletins for 1841,' p. 574.   [2] *Ibid.*, p. 588.
[3] 3rd edition, chap. ii., sec. 80 : 4th edition, chap. vi., sec. 12, the only alteration in the latter being to strengthen the passage by inserting the word 'very' before 'least.'

testimony, for, speaking at Canterbury just before the new
Parliament met, George Smythe, of 'Young England' fame,
(and, as later events proved, no warm friend of Mr. Gladstone,) observed : ' Most assuredly he would allow no
monopoly of kindly feeling towards Ireland to the Whigs.
He had heard the wrongs of that country as touchingly described by Mr. Gladstone as by Lord John Russell.' [1]   And
it is to be noted that Smythe had been returned for Canterbury at a bye-election early in the previous February, and
that the first speech he could have heard from Mr. Gladstone
was that of March 31st, on the third reading of the Jews'
Declaration Bill, in the course of which the member for
Newark made pointed reference to the manner in which
Ireland had been misgoverned. [2]

'Gladstone's appointment to the Board of Trade,' wrote
Milnes to Guizot, then Prime Minister of France, four days
after the Peel Administration had received the seals, ' is not
very distinguished in itself, but at the present moment when
the Corn Law fills up so large a place in public and party
interests, it has acquired a great importance,
and will give him great and frequent means

*Milnes on Mr. Glad-
stone's appointment.*

of displaying his fine abilities.' [3]   Guizot was naturally interested in the intelligence, for in August of the previous
year, when French Ambassador in London, he had entertained Mr. Gladstone at a dinner, where

*Mr. Gladstone and
John Mill,*

John Stuart Mill, who had much desired
the opportunity, was introduced to the member for Newark. [4]   And it is interesting in this connection to recall that when Guizot's greatest rival,

Guizot,

Thiers, was in England in the spring of 1852, compelled

[1] *Canterbury Journal*, Aug. 5, 1841.
[2] ' Mirror of Parliament ' (1841, 1st session), p. 1123.
[3] Reid's ' Houghton,' vol. i., pp. 270, 271.
[4] Caroline Fox's ' Memories of Old Friends,' vol. ii., p. 315.

to leave France because of the lesser Napoleon's *coup d'état*, and a dinner was given him, among the guests at which were Mr. Gladstone, Henry Hallam, Lytton, Sidney Herbert, Cardwell, and Abraham Hayward, the last-named held the opinion that while Thiers, in a varied and animated conversation, had the *Thiers,* advantage of language and choice of subject, the general impression was that Mr. Gladstone was, if anything, the better talker of the two.[1]

But these were not the only men of distinction on the Continent with whom the member for Newark was closely acquainted in his earlier period, for Hope's visit to Italy in the autumn of 1840, undertaken in company with Frederic Rogers, had been rendered the more agreeable by an intro- duction which Mr. Gladstone gave him to Manzoni. The founder of the Romantic *Manzoni,* School in Italian literature—who, born four years before the fall of the Bastille, lived to see Mr. Gladstone five years Prime Minister—had long then been known as the author of ' I Promessi Sposi,' which Scott averred to be the finest novel ever penned ; and although he was generally unwilling to receive strangers, especially Englishmen, the member for Newark had met him during a long previous visit to Italy. ' I wrote in bad Italian a letter of introduction to Manzoni,' Mr. Gladstone has said : ' I wish I could recover that letter, on account of the person, and the person to whom it was written.' After an interview, Hope recorded in his diary that ' he touched slightly on the Fathers, and when I told him of W. E. G.'s love for St. Augustine, he expressed his satisfaction at the agreement of taste between himself and him. G. seems to have made a strong impres- sion on him ; he speaks often of him.' And, writing to Mr.

[1] Abraham Hayward's ' Eminent Statesmen : Thiers,' p. 67.

Gladstone, Hope said : ' I am much beholden to you for
your introduction to Manzoni. He has treated me with
the utmost kindness, continually referring to you, and
speaking of you with much and real cordiality.' [1]   Nearly
five years later, and just after Mr. Gladstone had resigned
from the Peel Cabinet on the question of Maynooth,
Manzoni is to be found telling Hope that he had given
himself the satisfaction of writing to the member for
Newark ; [2] and Hope very shortly afterwards returned the
and Döllinger.   advantage which had been afforded him
by according his friend an introduction at
Münich to Döllinger. [3]   Mr. Gladstone's range of acquaintances in the world of intellect, both at home and abroad,
about that period was ever-increasing; and his social re-
lationships were broadened by his becoming in 1840 a
member of Grillions Club.   This is a dining club, founded
in 1813 and still existing, where members of both parties
meet and eat in peace, though a careful watch is kept
upon their drink, the chairman's duty being to enter upon
the minutes the numbers present at the dinners and the
amount of wine taken.   Eliot and Thomas Acland had
been elected members two years previously, as had been
Morpeth and Mahon some time before; and Mr. Gladstone
was accompanied into the club in 1840 by such close

[1] Hope-Scott's ' Memoirs,' vol. i., pp. 236, 244 ; vol. ii., pp. 278,
279.

[2] *Ibid.*, vol. ii., p. 53.

[3] *Ibid.*, p. 69; but Mr. Gladstone, in a communication to the
Speaker of January 18, 1890, stated, concerning this incident, ' I called
without an introduction upon Professor Döllinger;' while, in his
article on ' Heresy and Schism ' in the *Nineteenth Century*, for August,
1894 (p. 163), he said that the purpose of his visit to Munich, which
was purely domestic, ' required' him to call upon the great German
theologian.

friends as Lyttelton and Charles Canning, Lincoln and Herbert, as well as by Leveson, who, as Lord Granville, was to prove so faithful an ally; but Milnes, the future Poet Laureate of the club, who was destined to celebrate in verse a Gladstonian dinner-adventure at Grillions, was not to be chosen for several years.

It is thus upon the threshold of what was to prove so great a Ministerial career that we leave Mr. Gladstone ; and, although not even the most prescient could then foresee how he was to mould the coming half-century, and himself be moulded by it in return, it was recognised of all that a foremost position was certain to be his. The developments of later days are accustomed to be held to account for the long delayed fruition of his hopes ; but, even Mr. Gladstone's in those earlier years which have now been hopes examined, reasons suggested themselves why with the hopes should have been mingled fears. He had been bred to public life as Fox and Pitt and Peel had been. No charge of political adventurership was ever levelled at him, as it had been at Canning, as it was to be at Disraeli. There was not even the taunt that he could not get commerce—as Peel was said not to be able to get cotton—out of his blood. He would, in fact, have been the spoiled child of Toryism but for his Tractarianism ; this repelled the and drawbacks. more robust spirits who would otherwise have gladly hailed him as leader ; and strange indeed it is to think that, save for his clericalism, he might always have been Conservative. As it was, his Toryism was checked before it crystallised, and his mind retained its suppleness to the last.

The average politician must assuredly have thought that

speedily to outgrow his family environment which made for Protection, as he had done that which tolerated, if it did not foster, slavery. For John Gladstone, though he had been a steady supporter, both in and out of Parliament, of Huskisson's Free Trade proposals—a support for which the statesman heartily thanked him [1]—was inexorably opposed

John Gladstone and Protection.
to the repeal of the Corn Laws,[2] which he regarded with even more scorn and deeper foreboding of woes to come than the establishment of Penny Postage itself.

How and with what striking results Mr. Gladstone burst the bonds of early associations, and, as John Bright once said of him, turned ever like the sunflower towards the light, belongs to that portion of his public life which has yet to be fully traced. It will then be seen how applicable to his policy is the phrase he himself has used concerning eloquence, for he has taken up from those around him

Mr. Gladstone's statesmanship.
in vapour what he has returned to them in flood. To him, indeed, belongs not the idea but the execution, for among statesmen he is of the constructive, not of the creative, type. He is not the pioneer, hewing a path through a trackless forest, but the settler who makes it habitable; not the man who prophesies the promised land, but he who discovers for his fellows its milk and honey.

Though this is to regard Mr. Gladstone as from the close, and not the beginning, of his career, it is difficult to dissociate the man from what he has done. Were

[1] 'Biographical Memoir of William Huskisson,' pp. 120, 121.

[2] He published in 1839 a pamphlet containing his views, a second edition of which was issued in 1841, this being supplementary to a pamphlet, under his old signature, 'Mercator,' condemning a proposal to repeal the Corn Laws, and printed in 1833.

this a complete chronicle of his public life, his admirers would be entitled to ask, upon a survey His conscience and of all the facts, whether any one in our his career. political history has sacrificed so much and so often upon the altar of conscience. Even those who study only his earlier years will vainly seek for another who, at the opening, and therefore the most perilous, portion of his public progress, took, in the cause he thought right, so many risks by arousing the susceptibilities and offending the prejudices of his countrymen. The caution of such a course may be doubted : the courage cannot be denied. And, when the time comes to form a full and fair estimate of what Mr. Gladstone has done, much of the judgment will assuredly be based upon those opening years, full of noble aim and purity of purpose, and marked by a vigilant readiness to brave all for the truth, which have now in detail been described.

THE END.

INDEX.

452

Printed by Cowan & Co., Limited, Perth.